Following SWEET DREAMS HOME

By
Rebecca Thein

You may also enjoy

Rise Above the Truth

Copyright 2008 Rebecca Thein

Blossoming *Act*

Copyright 2014 Rebecca Thein

Not A Planned *Affair*

Copyright 2019 Rebecca Thein

Cover design by KRDesigns at www.kristineraymond.com
Clip Art Hat by D0r0thy at Deposit Photos.
Clip Art Divider by 27kornmongkol at Deposit Photos
Formatted by BB eBooks

Hardcover Edition

DEDICATION

This novel is dedicated to my sister-in-law Tina. She was my muse for this story.

I would not be where I am today without my Grandmother Mary's unconditional love and support. She baked something sweet every day to share with those she loved.

My daughter Christina asked me if I could describe every detail of the houses. So, for you, my sweet girl, I did.

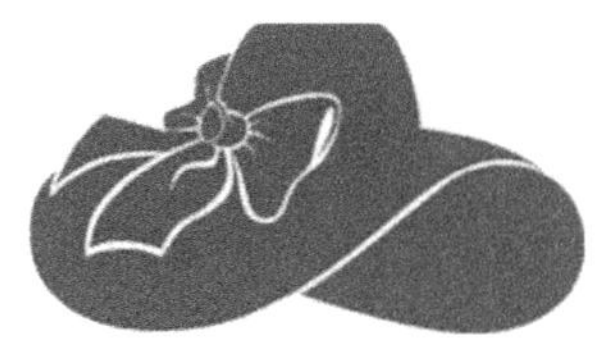

ACKNOWLEDGMENTS

I have so many people to thank, so I will start with everyone who keeps encouraging me to continue telling my stories.

I want to express my gratitude and adoration to my husband and my three children. Your love and support mean everything to me.

A big hug to my mother, who is my sounding board in every endeavor I undertake. She has always been guiding me through my life with her love.

Thank you to the beta readers for reading this story and for giving me your feedback. I have some extraordinary people in my life that keep me grounded.

Hugs to Becky, Joan, and Janet for your honest feedback and for always being there for me whenever I need you.

A very special thank you to my editor, Amy Magee, for all her hard work. Without whom, this story would still be a dream. She saw my vision for the story and helped me bring it to fruition.

A heartfelt Thank You to Kristine Raymond for creating the new, updated cover for my book. Kristine is not only a great author but also an incredible cover designer. I am blessed to have her as a dear friend who I cherish.

Finally, a warm thank you to all who purchased a copy of my novel. I hope you enjoy reading about Candice as much as I enjoyed telling her story.

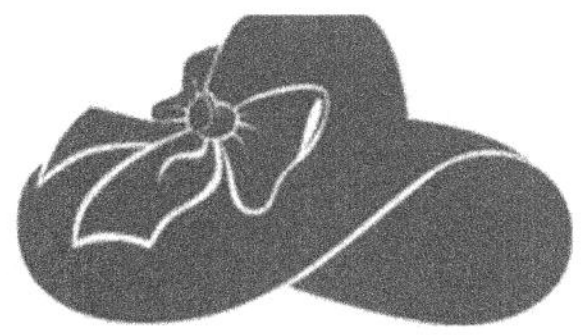

CONTENTS

One

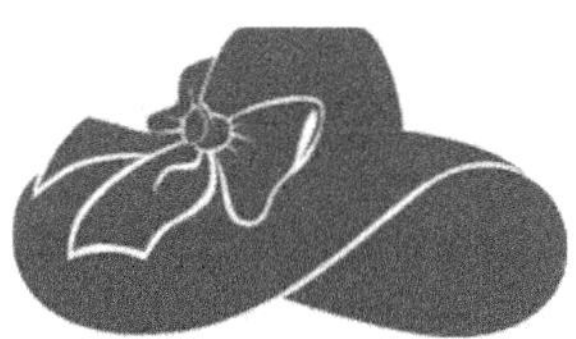

The bells on the door jingled as Candice entered the antique store. "Good morning," a smiling elderly woman sang out as she leisurely walked toward the counter. She reminded Candice of her first-grade teacher, her gray hair neatly wrapped in a bun on top of her head, resembling a cinnamon roll minus the sugar glaze. She wore a fifties-inspired navy blue dress with a crisp white starched lace collar, an ensemble that matched her blue and white oxford shoes. Balanced above her left ear was a #2 canary yellow pencil that added a touch of casualness to her pristine appearance.

"Hello, just thought I'd look around," Candice responded, needing a little retail therapy.

"Well, if I can be of any assistance, just holler." The woman smiled and proceeded to open a large box on the counter.

Candice made her way up and down the aisles looking for anything to make her feel better. She stopped abruptly when she spotted a perfect little bistro table with two chairs. The table was dark mahogany with drop-leaf sides and would be ideal up against the wall in her tiny kitchen. The chairs matched the beautiful mahogany with white accent paint contrasting the dark wood. She quickly made her way to the exquisite piece and sat in one of the two wooden chairs. She leaned forward to look closer at the wood grain while carefully crossing her legs.

"Beautiful dinette. Just arrived yesterday," the elderly woman informed her warmly without looking up from the ornate hat she had just lifted from the box.

"Yes, it is." Candice's eyes quickly shifted and focused on the hat. "How much for that hat?"

"Dear, this hat needs to be cleaned and repaired." The woman carried the hat as she stepped out from behind the counter. She gently placed it on

Candice's head. "Go take a look in the mirror. It accentuates your beautiful features and compliments your blue eyes. Not to mention it goes perfectly with the dress you are wearing," the woman spoke softly, pointing to an armoire with an uncommonly large mirror.

Candice gazed at her reflection. "Oh, my," she remarked, mesmerized by the elaborate black velvet hat. A large bow was on one side, surrounded by enough feathers to make a peacock jealous. "How much for this hat as it is?"

"I can sell it to you for $75.00. It's from the early 1900s," the woman replied, smiling.

"I'll take it. Now, how much for that table and chairs?" Candice turned, making her way back to the bistro set.

"I'd be willing to part with that for $1000.00," the woman offered. "It's sturdy construction. They don't make things like that anymore. You know, with all the particleboard and veneers these days. That table there, it's a durable piece of furniture."

"I'll take that too. Can I pick it up tomorrow?"

"Of course. And we deliver free of charge for furniture purchases within ten miles."

"Oh, that would be great." Candice pulled out her checkbook. "Now, how much do I owe you?"

The elderly woman opened a receipt book as ancient as the antiquities in her store and started filling in pertinent information. "I found this receipt book while going through my father's things," the woman remarked tenderly. "Now, is there anything else I can help you with, dear?"

"Well, actually, yes. Around the corner, there was an interesting piece that was painted like a rainbow? What exactly is that used for?"

"You must be referring to the credenza. That particular style would have been used to store papers, or maybe you could repurpose it and put silverware in it. My grandson found it in an old barn. I'm pretty sure it's solid oak under all that paint, so once it's stripped of its many coats of color and refinished, it will be a stunning piece of furniture."

"How much are you asking for it?" Candice inquired.

"I can sell that for $1700 if you want to refinish it yourself. However, if you prefer we refinish it, the price would be around $3800."

"I'd like that as well. I will refinish it myself, as I need something to keep me busy. I'm going to have a lot of time on my hands," Candice said, placing her purse on the counter so she could fill out the check.

"I look forward to seeing you again," the shop owner said, handing her the receipt. "I'll have my grandson deliver your dinette set and credenza tomorrow around four?"

"Sounds great." Candice positioned the hat on her head with a slight tilt.

"Nice meeting you," she said, exiting with a wave.

Candice stood tall, balancing her huge hat on her head, and began strolling down the street in her high heels, obviously designed for looks and not comfort. A strong breeze started blowing, and Candice reached up, attempting to keep her hat in place, but she was not quick enough. The hat took flight and continued swirling down the street like a ballerina, twirling around. Trotting in five-inch stilettos, she did her best to keep up with the traveling hat. Each time she got close, another gust of air carried it further. The wind finally died, allowing the hat to gently settle on the sidewalk. Candice quickly reached for it, but then the wind lifted the hat and tossed it onto a porch stoop. Out of breath and cursing her broken heel, Candice climbed the steps and bent over to retrieve her new hat. As she reached for the hat, she noticed a large mound of mail scattered on the floor just inside the glass-paneled door. Cupping her hands on the side of her eyes, she pressed her face against the door, trying to get a better look inside. It was very dark. All she could see were cobwebs and shadows. *Interesting.-I wonder what's going on with this building?* There was rarely a vacant building in the heart of Noe Valley, a trendy neighborhood in San Francisco.

Candice turned to head back down the steps, holding the hat tightly in her left hand to avoid any more impromptu exercise. *No wonder I've never noticed anyone wearing a hat on a blustery day.* She limped down the stairs with the hat in hand and a broken heel.

"What a day this is turning out to be," Candice sighed.

When she reached the bottom of the stairs, her cell phone began to chirp. "Hello."

"What's going on?" It was her best friend Jazzlene, whose voice sounded noticeably concerned.

"Well, I just bought some antique furniture. Now I'm going to head for home, I guess." Candice turned around to regard the vacant building again.

"Candi, I just called your office to see if you wanted to meet me for lunch, and I got a message saying you were no longer an employee."

"Oh, boy, they don't miss a beat. I got my pink slip this morning. And yes, it was actually pink," Candice said, trying to toss some humor into the situation.

"What? But I thought everything was okay. Didn't they say they'd move you to another department?"

"Well, what can I tell ya? They really made big cuts this time. My job as a meeting manager, planning all the conferences and community events, just isn't in the budget."

"But you are the most organized and ambitious person I know. No one else can run in five directions and coordinate like you can."

"What can I say? I loved my job, but there has to be something else I can do besides planning meetings with clients to help promote business and morale."

Candice tried to keep her tone positive. She did not want to drown in the emotional undertow grabbing at her.

"You can help me at the studio. I'm always in need of a good assistant." Jazzlene moved the phone to her other ear.

"Of course. I'd be happy to help you while I figure out what to do. I should also explore some business ideas. I do party planning and pass my clients to you for their photography needs. We'd work great together."

"Why don't I stop by your house tonight, and we can brainstorm. I'm sure we can come up with something creative." The enthusiasm in Jazzlene's voice soothed Candice's bruised spirit.

"Yes, I would like that. And then, we can have a glass of wine and a good movie to finish the night."

"How 'bout I pick up Chinese food on my way to your house?"

"That would be great. I'll see you around seven."

Candice's focus returned to the unoccupied dwelling before her. She noticed two words scrawled on the large window. She dropped the cell phone into her purse and briskly climbed the stairs again. There, in small lettering, were the words *For Sale,* followed by a phone number. Candice dug out her pen and the receipt from the antique store and scribbled down the number.

Wanting to soak in the grand scale of the neglected house, she walked across the street to view its entirety. The architecture was incredible. She examined the facade, absorbing the ambiance of the old Victorian. San Francisco is known for magnificent historical buildings throughout the city.

A white van pulled to the curb, blocking Candice's view of the house. The driver got out. "Good morning," the cheery man said as he opened the sliding door on the side.

"Hello," Candice responded, stepping aside, not taking her eyes off the house.

The driver reached up to steady each passenger as they stepped out of the van onto the sidewalk one by one.

"My name is Tom. Tom Morgan. How are you?" the first passenger asked, acknowledging Candice's presence. He maneuvered his white cane, trying to get his bearings.

Candice stepped forward and took his hand. "Well, good morning Tom. I'm Candice," she replied, tenderly rubbing his hand. "Nice to meet you."

"Tom, Tom Morgan," he announced loudly. "You have soft hands." He felt every finger.

"Thank you." Candice realized that each person that exited the van was disabled. Tom was obviously blind. A petite girl staring up at the clouds suddenly became very animated when she made eye contact with Candice. She smiled and attempted to say something, but every word she spoke was inaudible.

"Marni is trying to say hello," the driver informed Candice.

"Well, hello, Marni. Nice meeting you." Candice reached out, and Marni latched onto her hand, squeezing it tightly. The strength that this tiny girl exhibited shocked Candice.

"Did you come to visit us?" a round-faced boy asked, excited at the prospect of a guest.

As Candice turned to face him, Marni held her grip on Candice's hand, refusing to let go. "Well, no. I was actually just admiring that building across the street."

"We live here. This is our home. I'm Hector," the round-faced boy said with pride. "Those are my flowers. They smell really good. You want one?"

"Maybe next time. I don't have any free hands right now. I need to carry this big hat because the wind blows it off my head."

Hector looked down at Candice's feet, "Hey, your shoe's broken!"

"Yes. While chasing this hat down the street, the heel broke right off."

"You need to be careful. If you trip and fall, you'll get hurt." Concern appeared in Hector's eyes.

"Well, Miss, I need to get these three in the house for their lunch now," the driver said, putting Tom's hand on his shoulder to help guide him.

"Bye, Candice," Tom said, following his sighted leader.

"I hope to see all of you again soon." Sincere warmth came through Candice's voice.

Marni waved frantically, flapping her hand wildly in the air, turning around briefly to get her last peek at Candice as she stepped across the threshold of the front entrance.

Candice stood there a few moments longer, unable to take her eyes off the deserted house that was in need of repair. Lively colors flooded her mind as she let her imagination soar. The house became a soft shade of pink that appeared almost white, accented by dark plum trim. Above the door was a stained-glass art piece of purples, blues, and greens, welcoming each guest upon arrival. Bordering the pathway were petunias in every shade of purple that encouraged each passerby to stroll through the entrance. A blossoming dark pink crape myrtle shaded a park bench underneath its colorful foliage. The house beckoned to each person that approached it. At least, that is what Candice envisioned the house would look like in its heyday. She finally took her cell phone out of her purse and snapped a picture of the formerly stately house.

Once again, Candice was hobbling down the street, wondering where life would take her. She had no doubt it would be a struggle, but she was a strong woman with many aspirations. Her job loss was just an obstacle she would tear down to forge her path.

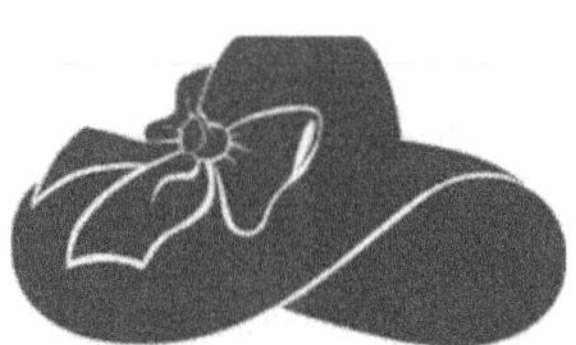

Candice entered her condo, walking straight to the trashcan. In flew the shoes that had seen better days. She was frustrated and cold, which required chamomile tea to calm her nerves. After filling a stainless-steel teapot with water, she retreated to her living room and waited for the water to boil.

Flopping down on the soft sofa, Candice lifted her feet onto the ottoman with a sigh. As she struggled to get comfortable, she contemplated her future. *Where am I going to find a job?* The tension in her neck grew, so she moved her head in circles to release the tightness. Then, leaning her head back, she spotted a spider crawling across the ceiling. *Well, now I will have time to give this place the thorough cleaning it needs.*

Stretching her arms above her head, she yawned as the spider descended along his silver thread. "You little bugger," Candice commented, glancing for something she could use to catch the spider. She carefully trapped him under a glass, making sure not to snag his delicate legs. "Here ya go. Be free little fella," she declared, releasing the spider onto her balcony and watching him scurry for cover.

The teapot gave a high-pitched squeal to alert Candice that her water was ready. While the tea steeped in her cup, she opened the kitchen cupboard, looking for something stronger than tea to wash her blues away. *Hmm, not many choices. Scotch...this must be dad's.* She grabbed the bottle and poured a little into her tea, tasting it tentatively. *Ew, Nasty.* She ran to the sink and spit the concoction out. *I must have something else here.* Continuing her search, she removed a large glass pitcher, trying to peer into the back of the cupboard. *Oh, there is something.* Reaching deep into the cabinet, she found a half-empty, or maybe it was a half-full bottle of Crème De Menthe. *Much better.* She twisted open the top and sampled the liqueur. *It has a medicinal taste, the perfect prescription to end my day.*

Back on the couch with the bottle in one hand and a petite cordial glass in the other, she felt despondent. Slowly pouring the syrupy liquid into the tiny glass, she watched it gradually fill as if it was the most exciting thing she had ever witnessed. *Is this what my days are going to be like? Watching an emerald liquid fill my world.* Candice took a small sip, resting the sweet liqueur on her tongue and letting it awaken each taste bud. *Not bad*. She took another sip.

Grabbing her blanket from the back of her couch, she curled up into a ball and turned on the television. Flip. Flip. Flip. She went through the stations like a true channel surfer. *Nothing worth watching. The public station will certainly have something.* She started to watch the program and quickly realized it was about the economic downturn and job loss in the great USA. “I’m quite aware of that. Now tell me where to find a job,” she ordered the commentator sternly. Flip. Flip. She finally settled on a station dedicated to old television shows. Within twenty minutes of beginning a mindless sitcom, Candice dozed off into a restless sleep.

The sun was starting to set. Candice looked skyward at the mountain peak and realized that this would be the most challenging part of her climb. Carefully, she placed her right foot on a rock and steadied herself before pushing off with her left foot, propelling herself upward. It was a slow process, but she was determined to reach the top before dark. Cautiously, she inched up the steep slope, briefly resting to contemplate her next move. She lifted her tired leg and positioned it onto a small rock on the side of the mountain. The rock shifted suddenly and sent her plummeting toward the ground. Her body jumped with a twitch, alerting her to the danger, and her eyes flew open just before she hit the ground.

Oh, thank God, it was only a dream. Feeling a little shaken, she sat up and looked at the clock. Squinting, she focused on the time. *6:32 p.m. Jazz will be here soon.*

Still struggling with the day’s news, she poured herself another drink. *Maybe some music will soothe my soul.* Riffling through her enormous CD collection, she found just the mood-altering music she needed. Seventies disco, it could make anyone feel better. Cranking up the volume, she started dancing around. She took several more sips of her Crème De Menthe and finally felt the booze kicking in. She spun around like a disco diva, singing, “One more drink to get this party started.” Candice waved her arms in the air while pointing toward the ceiling. Five songs later, sweat was rolling down her face. She danced into the kitchen for a towel to wipe her forehead. *Maybe I should get a little more exercise, now that I will have all the time in the world.*

Jazzlene could hear the deep bass beat of the music as she approached Candice's condo. She knocked loudly, but Candice did not answer the door. Sighing, she retrieved the spare key from her purse and let herself in. "Hey!" she yelled, but Candice still did not respond. Then, Jazzlene saw Candice dancing in the kitchen and smiled. This was a perfect moment; Jazzlene set down the food, grabbed the camera hanging around her neck, and started snapping pictures. Then she switched the camera to the video setting, allowing it to capture the wild dance solo. Finally, she slowly went to the stereo and turned down the music.

"Whatcha do that for? I was just getting started." Candice turned around, chasséing over to Jazzlene.

"I brought dinner, wine, and movies." Jazzlene tossed the movies on the couch and proceeded to the kitchen. "Where'd ya put that big serving spoon?"

"Try the dishwasher," Candice answered as she spun around, making herself dizzy.

"How much of that green monster did you drink, anyway?"

"Just enough to feel warm and fuzzy." Candice shimmied her way to the kitchen. "Here, let me pour you a glass."

"I think I'll stick to wine. That stuff is just too sweet." Jazzlene grabbed plates and started serving the food. "Here's your favorite. Egg roll with sweet and sour sauce." She handed the plate to Candice.

"Oh, this smells so good." Candice took a bite. "Hey, this is not from our usual place, is it?"

"No, I didn't have time to go across town. I got it from a new place I read about in the newspaper. It got great reviews."

"I think we found a new favorite restaurant," Candice said, licking her fingers with a grin.

"The place was full of people. I had to wait thirty minutes. And they say people aren't spending their money," Jazzlene mockingly said before taking her first bite. "Oh my, this is so worth the five-star review it got. Looks like you're right. We just found a new place to frequent. That is when you get back on your feet."

"Yeah, but who knows when that will be? Good thing I'm a penny pincher. It certainly will pay off. However, today I went a little overboard. I bought a three-piece dinette set that I'm thinking of putting in the kitchen, over there in that corner," Candice told her, pointing to an empty space, "and I also bought this very unusual thing called a credenza. I need to strip the paint off and stain it before it looks stunning. I'm not sure what got into me. I shouldn't be spending money."

"Maybe you could cancel the order and wait until you find a new job. That said, I already told you I could use some help. I have so many events coming up. Tomorrow I have a wedding, then Sunday a Quinceañera. With the warm weather approaching, I'm getting swamped. I need someone to answer phones, do the paperwork, schedule my appointments, plan photo shoots, and work on my website. You know, the stuff I hate to do."

"I'm always here for you. I think I'll be able to keep my new furniture since I have a temporary job, courtesy of my best friend. Hey, what happened with that cute guy working for you? He seemed pretty efficient."

"He went back to school. Seems he got wise and decided he needed an education after all."

"That's too bad. He was always so pleasant when I called you. I'll do my best to fill his shoes for a while, so I'll be at your studio Monday morning, ready to work on whatever you've got."

"I realize this is temporary, but I appreciate that someone I trust will make sure everything runs smoothly. And maybe when you find another job, you can help me hire a good assistant that won't leave after I have the person trained."

"Sure, I'm great at reading people." Candice picked up the movies Jazzlene had brought with her. "How 'bout we go for a comedy. I'm not feeling this mushy movie." She opened the case to retrieve the disc without waiting for Jazzlene's response.

"I'm gonna freshen up my wine. Do you want more?" Jazzlene asked, picking up her glass.

"Nah, I think I had enough for one night. I'm such a lightweight," she replied, turning the stereo off in favor of the DVD player. She placed the movie into the player. "Gosh, how many trailers do they need before the movie starts?" Candice asked with a mocked annoyance, hitting the fast-forward button.

"I never watch the trailers. They always show only the best scenes in the movie. Just tell me who's in the movie. That's all I need to know." Jazzlene poured more wine into her glass.

"Oh, Jazz, look at the hat I bought today," Candice mentioned, pressing the pause button as she walked to the bookshelf where the hat was resting atop a large vase.

"That is...uh...interesting?" Jazzlene commented, trying to visualize Candice in the hat.

"It's adorable." Candice lifted the hat from its makeshift display and placed it on her head. "Now, come on, it's darling." She did her best model pose, tilting her head slightly to the left while jutting out her hip.

"It certainly is different," Jazzlene said dryly. "Where would you ever wear a hat like that?"

"Well, I wore it walking down the street today. Come to think of it, people were kinda looking at me funny. On the other hand, maybe it was the fact the hat blew off my head, and went tumbling down the street like a child doing somersaults. There I was, running after it in my dress and heels. I just couldn't catch it. Finally, it came to rest on the porch of an old Victorian house." Candice reached for her purse to grab her cell phone.

"How far did you have to chase the darn thing?"

"Only a couple of blocks, but far enough to break the heel off one of my shoes." She chuckled. "Anyway, look at this picture. Now tell me that's not the coolest house you've ever seen."

"Wow, it sure needs a lot of work. I wouldn't say it's cool. Maybe spooky would be a better way to describe it."

"Come on, Jazz, you know it was beautiful once. I bet it could be beautiful again with a little love."

"Well, maybe the people can't afford to repair it. Old Victorians can cost a fortune to bring up to city building codes. So, the people living in it probably survive on a fixed income."

"No, it looks vacant, and it said *For Sale* on the window."

"Why are you so interested in that run-down place?" Jazzlene did not see the same charm in the house that Candice did.

"Because, well, I don't really know. I'm just curious to see the inside of the house. Aren't you? We could go together."

"Sure, I'll go with you. I'll snap some pictures if there is anything that looks interesting."

"I'm having my furniture delivered tomorrow at four. So maybe I can set something up for the morning or possibly Sunday," Candice said, placing the big hat onto a tall vase.

"I can go first thing in the morning, but I have that wedding in the afternoon. Sunday is out because I have a Quinceañera. It's an all-day event. Why don't you try calling now?" Jazzlene suggested, knowing Candice had sobered up a bit after eating.

"Yeah, why not?" Candice dialed the number she had written on the back of her receipt. An answering machine picked up, and then a voice apologized for not being available. At the beep, Candice left a message inquiring about the house and requesting a return call.

"Okay, hopefully, we'll hear back soon." Candice sat next to Jazzlene on the couch and hit the play button on the remote.

"Well, let's plan to meet tomorrow morning around nine and go for a walk. I will need some energy to make it through this busy weekend." Jazzlene proposed as the movie's main menu appeared.

The two women settled in on the couch for what Candice hoped would be a good laugh as she pressed play.

Three

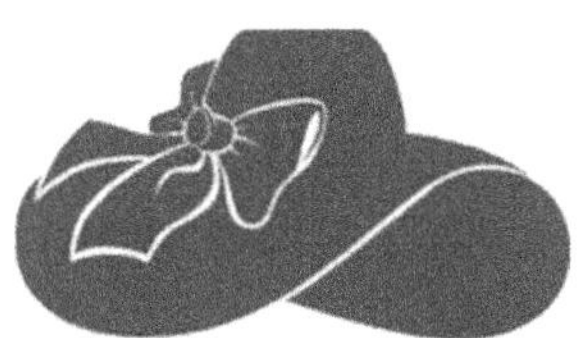

The alarm clock beeped loudly, jostling Candice from a deep sleep in an annoying manner. She rolled over and groped for a button to stop the jarring noise. Candice maintained a routine of waking up at the same time every day, including weekends. This morning, she did not want to leave bed and face a day of uncertainty. She placed her arm over her eyes to shield them from the sun and drifted blissfully back to sleep.

"Candi, wake up." Jazzlene was lightly nudging her.

"What are you doing here?" Candice asked sleepily.

"I called you three times, and you didn't answer. Remember last night? We made plans to meet at nine to go for a walk. I got worried when you never returned my call. So here I am, and relieved to see you're okay."

"Oh yeah, sorry. I guess I'm just not thinking too clearly. What time is it anyway?"

"It's a little after ten. We can still do a short walk and then I have to go home to prepare for that wedding. I'm shooting this afternoon."

Candice pushed the blankets aside and slowly sat up. "Just give me a minute to throw some water on my face."

The phone started to ring. "It's not me. I'm already here," joked Jazzlene with her familiar soft chuckle.

"Hello," Candice said, clearing her throat, "Yes, I can meet you there in half an hour."

Jazzlene looked quizzically at Candice, wondering who was on the phone. Candice held up her index finger and mouthed the words *hold on* to Jazzlene with a sparkle of excitement in her eyes. "Okay, sounds good. See you then." Candice placed the phone back in its cradle.

"What's going on?" Jazzlene asked, realizing their morning walk was about to be canceled.

"We're meeting the real estate agent I told you about at that house. You still want to see it with me, right?"

"Sure, but really, what's the point? You're not going to buy a house."

"Come on, just humor me. Don't you ever come across an *Open House* and want to go inside out of curiosity? You know, just to see the asking price and then dream of owning it someday?"

"Only when I'm with you. Otherwise, why torture myself with something I can't afford?"

"Well, I just *have* to see the inside of this house. I'm sure you'll understand when you see it in person. It's so welcoming." Candice grabbed her keys, and the two women walked out the door.

Jazzlene never wanted to miss a photo opportunity. Therefore, she always kept her camera slung around her neck for quick access, and today was no different.

They had little time to make the appointment, and the next bus was not due for another twenty minutes. So, Candice hailed the first cab she saw. "24th and Noe, please."

The driver fiddled, trying to reset the taximeter, and then started to accelerate so rapidly that Candice grabbed the door handle and held on for dear life. She turned to Jazzlene with wide eyes and grimaced. The driver weaved through traffic as though a pregnant woman was about to give birth in his cab. The only thing missing was a loud siren. When he finally reached their destination, he abruptly screeched to a halt, causing the girls to lunge forward. Candice handed him his fare and thought twice about tipping him but threw in a few extra dollars anyway.

"Next time we take the bus, even if we're going to be late," Jazzlene informed Candice, trying to sound calm. "Where's the house?" she asked, looking from one house to the next.

"Right there." Candice pointed across the street.

"Oh, it's set back from the street. I didn't see it. That large tree is totally obstructing the view."

"Come on." Candice led the way.

Jazzlene stood in front of the house, just staring. Finally, she spoke, "This is the house you're in love with?"

"Yes, isn't it beautiful? Can't you just imagine the people that once lived here?"

Before Jazzlene could respond, the realtor arrived, walking up to greet them. "Hello, ladies, I'm Trevor," he said, extending his hand. Trevor was dressed in blue jeans and a nice polo shirt, not the outfit Candice expected a realtor to wear when showing a house to potential buyers.

"Hi, I'm Candice. This is Jazzlene, my friend." Candice returned the handshake.

"Nice you were able to meet us this morning," Jazzlene said, trying to sound like they were not wasting his time.

"How did you hear about this property?" he questioned Candice, peering at her curiously.

"Well, I noticed the *For Sale* written on the window there." She pointed to the window where she had seen the writing, but there was no visible sign of it. It had been merely wiped clean. Candice took a double take of the window and shook her head.

"Oh, I thought maybe you heard from the woman selling the house," Trevor commented, turning to look at the window. But, unlike Candice, he knew he had removed the For Sale paint months earlier. "Let's head inside. I'll show you around and give you a little history about the house."

On the first level was the porch where the hat had landed the day before. They all walked up the steps and stood before the glass door Candice had peeked into just after recovering her hat. Her heart started to race when she heard the door squeak as Trevor pushed it open. "I'll need to put a little grease on those hinges." He brushed away the cobwebs, which now clung to his fingers like cotton candy.

Candice stepped inside and deeply inhaled, enjoying the aroma of the lemon oil. Trevor followed the women through the door. He knelt and picked up the mail resting on the foyer's granite-tiled floor.

Trevor noticed Candice looking down at the foyer floor. "That granite was shipped over from Italy. It is original to the house and is in excellent condition. This is the commercial unit of this building." Trevor stopped just before walking through an archway. "Look up at the stunning plaster detail. The family would have hired the best tradesman to do the work."

He continued under the archway and headed into a large room. "We have now entered the open area. When the original owners built this house, they designed it so they could open a neighborhood grocery store below their living space. The last tenant to occupy the unit used it as a tearoom." Trevor walked through the open dining room toward the back of the house. "Adjacent to this room is the kitchen. Originally, it was the deli counter for the grocery store. Now you'll find it is equipped and ready for preparing the tea, soup, and sandwiches." Trevor walked through a narrow doorway into the kitchen as the women followed closely behind. "This kitchen has a gas range and a large prep counter. The site is zoned commercial. Therefore, the first floor has been used for various businesses over the years, but I must say, the tearoom was a neighborhood favorite."

"So, if I understand correctly, this first floor can still be used to house a business?" Candice asked, considering the possibilities.

"Yes, that is correct. When this house was built, the top two floors were the family's residence, and the bottom level was their business. Pretty convenient to wake up and walk downstairs to work."

"It would be nice not having to worry about the cost of public transportation also," Candice stated, letting her mind drift once again to the full potential of the building.

"The family, or should I say, the woman who now owns this house, closed it about five years ago after her husband passed away. He had inherited the house about forty years ago when his parents died. The couple already owned a home, so they converted the top two floors into separate apartments and left this bottom unit as a commercial rental space. She is finding it very difficult to manage the upkeep of the property while maintaining her own home, as she is getting up in age. So she feels it is time to sell, although it is breaking her heart." Trevor's eyebrows furrowed together when he spoke about the old woman. He appeared to have a genuine concern for her.

"Aren't there any family members who want it?" Candice asked, having difficulty believing no one in the family was interested in the house.

"She only has one son, and he has his hands full. To be honest, I think this house may hold too many sad memories for her son. He lived here with his wife when she passed away thirty years ago. He used the second floor as his family home. It happens to be the larger of the two apartments. He managed the first-floor and the third-floor rental units. At the time of his wife's death, he had two small children to raise, so he moved into his parents' large home at the urging of his mother. Plus, her offer to help with the children while he worked seemed logical at the time."

"How sad," Candice softly said.

"Well, I think everyone in the family is doing well now. That was a long time ago, and as you know, time heals wounds. They just want to move on and release the past." Trevor quickly changed the topic. "So anyway, this door off the kitchen leads to the backyard and to the basement where the laundry facilities are located. The yard is the common space on this property, shared by the tenants. It's really quite charming when the weeds are tended to. It has that English garden feel, with wildflowers growing freely around the yard. Oh, and this door here opens to the powder room or half bath, as it would be called today." Trevor opened the door to reveal a small restroom with a toilet and sink.

"Some color might liven up this bathroom," Candice commented, peeking into the room. The all-white décor reminded her of a snow flurry where everywhere you looked, all you saw was stark whiteness. A whiteness that made the whole world seemingly devoid of color yet somehow still beautiful.

"Each unit has separate gas, electric, and water meters, as well as its own garbage bins. When this house was constructed, as I told you earlier, it was designed specifically for the family that built it. So, when they converted it into three separate units, they added the extra meters so each unit could be a stand-alone property. That ensured that each tenant would be responsible for the utilities they used. We can move on to see the first apartment if you'd like. It's on the second floor."

"Do you mind if I take a few pictures?" Jazzlene asked.

"Be my guest." Trevor stepped out of the camera's view as Jazzlene began snapping away.

"Okay, that should do for now." Jazzlene let her camera dangle from her neck.

"Before we head upstairs, do you have any questions?" Trevor inquired, looking from one woman to the other.

"No, I can't think of anything," Candice answered, following Trevor as he returned to the front of the building.

"Well then, let's head up to the second floor." Trevor motioned, leading them out the front door. He turned to lock the door to the tearoom. "When the weather is warm, this patio makes a nice outdoor seating area for the customers." Trevor pointed to a brick inlaid street-level patio.

"I can picture myself sitting here drinking a nice hot cup of Earl Grey." Candice nodded as she calculated how many tables would fit in the patio area.

The three of them climbed the stairs that led to the second and third floors, stopping on the landing to take in the view. Candice moved to the middle of a quaint porch that was just big enough to put two chairs and a small table.

Trevor paused in front of two large doors. "This porch is meant to be shared by both apartments. Sitting out here on a warm summer day would be very nice. That is, of course, when that tree is properly pruned. It's quite overgrown at the moment." Trevor tried to find the correct key on the large key ring. "I think I found the right one." He put it into the lock. "Ladies, after you," he stated, holding the door open for the women.

Candice gasped excitedly, "Is this all original?" She went to the fireplace enthusiastically and ran her hand gently across the mantle.

"Yes, that is the original mantel. You'll notice the hearth and filler panels are the same granite you saw on the floors downstairs. When the owners converted the house, they tried to keep as much of the original architecture as possible. But, of course, they did need to upgrade to meet city building codes, like rewiring. The house had the knob and tube wiring that had become a fire hazard. They also decided to change all the plumbing to copper and remove the old lead paint. However, the stunning hardwood floors, doors, windows, and crown molding are all original. Even in the kitchen, they managed to salvage some pieces. Like the cabinets, those are just too beautiful to replace. I will say the bathrooms did get quite an update."

"Is this a working fireplace? I've always wanted a fireplace." Candice remarked, enthralled by the intricately carved details that beautifully framed the firebox.

"Yes, it works. It was actually modified to gas a while back. More economical and eco-friendly, or so I'm told. I'd love to show you how nice it is, but the gas is turned off."

"That's okay. I just like knowing it works." Candice walked over to the bay window facing the porch area. "This window would make a nice reading nook."

"It does get a lot of sunlight, perfect for reading," Trevor agreed.

"How many bedrooms does this unit have?" Jazzlene asked, looking up to admire the detail in the crown molding. She was beginning to see the beauty Candice had seen all along.

"This apartment has three bedrooms and one luxurious bathroom. They essentially combined two small bathrooms to make one spacious bathroom. The crown molding you are looking at runs throughout the house."

"You can tell they took very good care of this home," Jazzlene commented as she grew more enamored with the house.

"Yes, they certainly did take pride in this house. I've seen many houses as a real estate agent and can honestly say this one is a hidden jewel," Trevor divulged with confidence as he also admired the room. "Shall we make our way into the dining room?" Trevor motioned the women to follow him.

The dining room was larger than Candice had expected. It had two built-in corner hutches for displaying china. Rich brown wainscoting covered the lower third of all four walls. "Again, you will notice the corner cabinets and wainscoting are original features of this home." Trevor opened the hutch doors to show that the interior boasted quality craftsmanship. The hinges were brass, and the dark green patina enhanced the elegance of the cabinets. "Now, as we continue, I think you'll find this kitchen to be spectacular." Candice let out another gasp. "I take it you like what you see?" Trevor smiled at Candice.

"I'm so...uh, I guess I'm surprised by how charming this house is. The house looks run down from the outside, so I expected the inside to be in a similar condition. I thought the house would cost a pretty penny and take tons of man-hours to restore. But wow, I could move right in." She turned to Jazzlene and gave her a look that said *I told you so*. Candice knew the house would be beautiful once restored, but she never expected it to be completely move-in ready.

Jazzlene smiled and reached for her camera. "I think this kitchen's essence needs to be forever captured on film." She started taking pictures from every angle.

"As you can see, the oven is cast iron. And you might be surprised to learn it is not original to the house." Candice walked over to it as Trevor continued to tell her about the piece. "It is an antique stove that has been converted to meet current guidelines. Don't you just love how today anything that is old can be upgraded to meet today's energy standards?"

"It is so beautiful. And look at those cute legs. I've never seen anything this adorable. Today the ranges are just boring boxes with no character. This stove is full of personality. And the polished brass is sparkling like it's brand new," Candice expressed before turning her attention to the refrigerator.

"That fridge is also an old vintage appliance that has been restored. Doesn't it feel like it's been in this house forever?" Trevor asked, beaming with pride as though it had been his addition.

"Yes, it really does. If this is a dream, then please don't wake me." Candice laughed.

"There is no dishwasher. I appreciate that most homeowners today really want one included. But it just wouldn't fit the look of this kitchen." Trevor tried to convince them.

"You're right. It wouldn't fit the feel of this kitchen. And anyway, a little hand washing never hurt anyone," Candice agreed.

"Now, if you love this kitchen, wait until you see the bathroom. Remember, the woman who owns this place wanted her son to be happy living here, so she redid this entire floor for him and his family." Trevor led them down the hall and opened the door, revealing an exquisite bathroom. The first thing Candice noticed was the old-fashioned pull-chain toilet.

"Is this original to the house?" she questioned.

"Yes, and it is in great working order after all these years. I'd show you how it works, but as you know, the utilities are turned off," Trevor replied with regret.

Candice stepped over to the vanity. "This marble reminds me of a vanilla fudge swirl ice cream bowl with hot caramel drizzled on top."

"It is a gorgeous piece of marble. The variegation of color in the swirls is interesting. And the cabinet is actually an old dresser altered to fit the plumbing. And I'd like you to notice the shower enclosure has the same marble as the vanity sink," Trevor conveyed.

"The marble in this bathroom is similar in color to the granite floors," Jazzlene noted, admiring the sheer elegance of the bathroom.

"I was told they tried to keep the entire house in the same color palette so everything would be cohesive throughout the three levels."

Looking down at the floor, Candice admired the creamy café mocha ceramic tile with complimentary dark chocolate grout. Although the floors' stunning appearance could easily steal the show, the marble was still the star of the room for Candice.

"The pattern of the tile is known as *Opus Ramano.* I just love its varied sizes," Trevor said.

"I have to agree." Candice turned her attention to the walls.

The walls had an interesting swirling, textured pattern that mimicked the swirls found in the marble, but because it was painted all one color, it did not detract from the marble's beauty.

Candice ran her hand over the texture on the wall.

Trevor explained, "The texture was done by a master in hand troweling. He was the best in his trade because I'd never seen this pattern before, and it turned out very subtle. It could have competed with the marble, but using flat base paint in a muted color does not command your attention like the marble does."

"You really know a lot about this house. I love all the details you are able to give us," Candice commented, loving Trevor's informative descriptions.

"May I?" Candice asked before removing her shoes to step into the tub.

"Yes, of course." Trevor smiled upon seeing how delighted Candice was. "That claw foot tub is original to the house and has been reglazed. However, the shower is more of a modern feature, as this house never had a shower originally, only tubs. Likewise, the faucets are reproduction pieces, again chosen to maintain the house's integrity."

"I can't believe no one in the family wants this place."

"Well, as I said, it holds some very sad memories for the family." Trevor looked toward the hallway. "How 'bout I show you the bedrooms now?" He lent a hand to help Candice step out of the tub.

"If we go through this door, it will lead us to what is considered the master suite," Trevor said, turning the doorknob.

"Oh, now that's smart. The same idea as a Jack and Jill bathroom," Jazzlene said, admiring the convenience of having two entrances for the room.

"You just lock that hallway door when you need adult time." Trevor blushed.

All three bedrooms had wallpaper and small closets. "Now the wallpaper is a vintage reproduction, the design based on what was originally in the house. A company specializing in reproducing wallpaper created this by copying the original paper. You just have to have enough to serve as a template." Trevor pulled the drapes back so they could see the stunning wallpaper in the sunlight.

"Wow, not a detail missed." Candice put her reading glasses on for a clear view of the wallpaper.

"Now, what do you think of this unit?" Trevor turned, facing both women.

"As I said earlier, this home has exceeded my expectations. It's truly," Candice paused, trying to think of the right words to describe her feelings, "extraordinary. I just love it." Her voice grew excited with passion.

"I agree with Candice. I didn't expect much from seeing the outside, but gosh, once we entered the units, it just took my breath away." Jazzlene smiled sincerely when she looked at Candice.

"Well, I suppose you'd like to see what's behind door number three? Let's go have a look."

Trevor unlocked the door to the second apartment. Once they crossed the threshold, they had to walk up a flight of stairs to reach the landing for the third-floor unit.

"This entire floor was once a grand master suite. The family's children would have had the bedrooms on the lower floor," Trevor explained as they entered the apartment's front room. It was similar to the lower unit, but everything appeared scaled down, and the layout was slightly different.

"As you'll notice, this apartment uses the footprint of lower units as far as the location of the various rooms, such as the kitchen and bathroom. That made it cheaper and easier to install the plumbing and gas for the kitchen. The other difference is the open concept that gives it a larger feel."

"Yes, it does have a nice open feel, but it takes away from the Victorian charm with the open concept." Candice sighed with slight disappointment.

"I would have to agree, but it made better use of the space considering a renter's needs." Trevor knew this apartment would appeal to the younger generation. "Now, as we step into the living room and dining area, you'll notice the beautiful fireplace that has also been converted to gas, just like the one downstairs. Both of these rooms were the original master's sleeping quarters." Trevor stood quietly before speaking again, "Follow me through the dining room to the adorable kitchenette. Of course, these are not original furnishings, but the owner did manage to obtain most of the cabinets and fixtures from a reclamation store. Therefore, they are from old Victorians and are authentic to the era of this house. Once again, the owner found antique refurbished appliances. You will notice they are smaller than the appliance downstairs and fit perfectly in this kitchen. I think the owners maintained the charm of this apartment by putting in the extra effort to find old furnishing."

"This is very cozy and cute," Jazzlene complimented, snapping more pictures.

"Shall we move onto the bathrooms?" Trevor asked, turning toward the hallway. The women followed without hesitation.

Trevor continued his historical account, "They downsized the original master bath to make room for the smaller of the two bedrooms, and the contractor was able to re-use everything from the bathroom. You'll notice the marble on the wall surrounding the tub is the same marble you saw in the first apartment. And I'd like to point out that this bathroom has no separate shower. There wasn't enough room to have a tub and shower. So, this clawfoot tub does double duty."

"I actually love the curtain bar that encircles the tub. The way it hangs from the ceiling is unique. Was that custom-made?" Jazzlene inquired, taking a picture of it.

"If I remember correctly, that was commissioned by a local metal artist some thirty years ago," Trevor said, tilting his head as he recalled the information.

"Well, it sure fits the era of the house. And I love how it is suspended from the ceiling," Jazzlene commented, zooming in to snap one last picture.

"Shall we move onto the larger bedroom?" Trevor suggested, leading them out the door and over to the next room. "Now, this bedroom is located where there was once a library for the master of the house. He did all his bookkeeping for the grocery store in the library."

"I like that they left the built-in bookshelf in the room. It gives this room some charm," Candice stated, admiring the finial at the top. "You know, that decoration resembles a *key*." She noticed, pointing to the finial.

"Yes, it does," Trevor agreed, eyeing the finial.

Trevor stood still a moment before speaking. "Let's see the backyard now. The door in the kitchen leads to the yard," Trevor noted, making his way back to the kitchen. He opened the door that led onto a large deck. "Let's take a walk out there." Trevor held the door for the women as they stepped out onto the deck. "Now, you will notice the top and second floors have these rather large decks. The commercial unit can use the grass area, but the backyard has no dedicated space because it has a patio in the front. You would use these stairs to get to the yard and basement, where the laundry facilities are." They descended the two flights of stairs, heading toward the basement.

"This backyard is larger than one would expect for San Francisco," Candice acknowledged cheerfully when they reached the yard.

"It's big enough for a swing set and small vegetable garden," Trevor suggested.

"Oh yes, perfect for an herb garden. I grow a few herbs on my balcony now and use them in my cooking," Candice added as her vision for the house grew clearer and grander.

Trevor jiggled the key, trying to get the basement door unlocked. "I think this will need to be replaced," he commented once the door finally popped open. "That is one old lock." Trevor reached inside the door and grabbed a flashlight hanging on the wall. "Since there is no power, we'll have to see the basement with my trusty flashlight. Watch your step."

It grew darker as they moved down the stairs. Then, finally, a sliver of light peeked through the small window, struggling to brighten the room.

"This basement is large enough to store the extra items tenants may have, like holiday decorations. Some modern upgrades were needed," Trevor stated, pointing to three separate outlets installed for the washers and dryers. "Each electrical outlet is marked with a number, indicating the unit to which the electricity goes. In the center of the room, you'll notice this large table that can be used for folding clothes. There's even this drying rack."

"That's wonderful. No need to use the Laundromat." Candice's eyes were finally adjusting to the darkness of the basement. She could see the laundry area come into view.

"Over here is a larger space for garden tools, shelves for storage, and a wash bin." Trevor turned the flashlight to illuminate the area, revealing a few garden tools on the shelf.

"Well, that pretty much does it for the tour of this house." Trevor sounded a little disappointed that the viewing was over. "Neither one of you has asked what the price of this home is."

"I would have to say, after seeing the inside, it must be close to two million," Candice's voice cracked as she spoke those words.

"I have to agree with her," Jazzlene concurred.

"That's pretty close. She's asking $1,895,000. But I'm sure she'd be willing to work out a deal to please both buyer and seller."

"I have a lot of things to consider. What do you think the apartments would rent for?" Candice asked with curiosity.

"Well, I think with the economy and how prices keep going up, you will get top dollar for the units. I will research the current comps and rental prices to ensure they have not changed since the last time I reviewed them. In today's real estate climate, you must constantly check to review what the market is doing."

"Trevor, let me think it over. I'll get back to you in a few days."

"Sounds good," he replied, handing Candice his business card. "If you are serious, I'm positive the lady that owns the property would love to meet you. She's pretty sentimental about this house and won't sell it to just anyone. She must feel that the new owners will love and care for it. That's why it's not on the MLS and is represented exclusively through me. She only allows me to show it and won't consider speaking to other agents."

"Well, thank you so much for taking the time out of your day to show it to us." Candice shook Trevor's hand.

Trevor locked the house's front door, then turned and watched the women walk down the steps.

Jazzlene broke the silence. "Well, I will say that house was incredible. I apologize for not seeing it through your eyes earlier."

"Yes. For once, I'm speechless. Thanks for going with me. It's the kind of place you must see for yourself. I could never put into words how wonderful it is. Can you believe those appliances? They've got to be worth a fortune."

"I know. I'm glad I saw it too. I'm pretty sure I got some nice, artistic photos of the place. I'll develop them later this week."

"Thanks. I can't wait to see them." Then, the two women parted ways so Jazzlene could get home and ready for the wedding shoot.

As Candice rode the bus home, she daydreamed about the lovely old house and what it would feel like to own it. *I would need new furniture to go with the style of the house.* She could not imagine filling it with the modern furniture she had acquired when she moved into her condo. *Oh, stop already,* she scolded herself.

Four

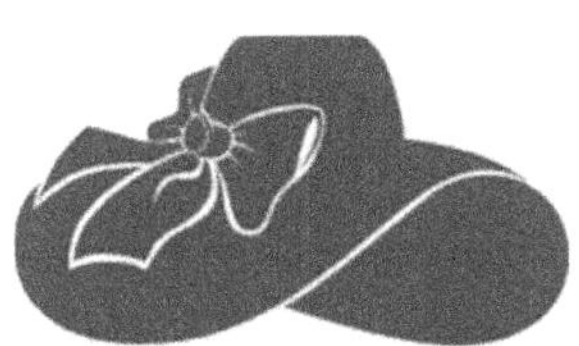

It was four o'clock that afternoon when the intercom buzzed loudly, signaling that someone was at the lobby door. "Hello," Candice greeted cheerfully.

"We have a furniture delivery for Candice Smythe," a deep male voice responded.

"That's me. Come on up." Candice pressed the button to release the lock on the building's main door. She opened her front door and entered the hallway, anxiously glancing at the elevator. A minute later, the elevator dinged, its doors opening as it stopped on her floor. "Over here," she called out, waving at the men.

One of the men was on the tall side, with shiny black hair, soft cocoa-colored eyes, and a day's worth of beard growth shadowing his jaw. He appeared to be in his mid-thirties and very physically fit. Candice could see his bicep muscles flexing as he carried the credenza through the door. The other man was slightly shorter and appeared much younger, possibly in his early twenties. He was wearing his baseball cap backward, with baggy jeans hanging low on his hips, revealing plaid boxers. As the men walked toward Candice, she thought she saw something familiar in the taller man. It was something about his eyes.

"Where would you like us to put this colorful credenza?" the taller man inquired in a sonorous voice.

"Out here on the balcony," Candice replied, sliding the glass door open.

"That is not a good idea. The moisture will warp the wood," the taller man responded, setting the heavy credenza inside.

"Really? Even if I put a plastic cover over it?"

"Yeah, I still wouldn't leave it outside. What are you planning to do with this piece?"

"Well, I thought I'd refinish it. The sales lady at the store said I'd probably find some nice wood under all this paint."

"Oh, you were talking to my grandmother," the man warmly replied. "I'm Shane, by the way, and this is Josh." Josh just nodded without saying anything.

"That's right. I guess it was your grandmother. She said this credenza just arrived at the store."

"I found it not too long ago in a barn. I have a business that deals with clearing out what some people refer to as *garbage.* But often, there are salvageable items. Sometimes there's a treasure like this credenza. I'm pretty sure it's oak. I also do all the refurbishing of items for my grandmother. So, have you ever done any furniture refinishing?" Shane asked, hoping his expertise might be of use.

"No, but all I need is some sandpaper and elbow grease, right?"

"Well, that won't remove all the paint. What you need is a good chemical stripper. It will loosen the paint, making it easy to scrape it right off. While you're working, you'll need good ventilation, so using the patio would work as long as you bring the credenza in at night." Shane's passion for furniture restoration came through in his detailed explanation.

"I guess you can just put it over there against the wall for now," Candice suggested, pointing to the other side of the room. Now that she realized how much work it would take, she had no idea if she wanted to tackle the credenza's beautification.

"I'd be happy to come over and show you how to refinish this to its former glory," Shane offered.

"That would be great. I obviously have no idea what to do." Candice chuckled, a little embarrassed.

Shane grabbed his cell phone. "Give me your number, and I'll call you to set up a day to come by." He punched in Candice's number as she recited it.

"So, you were saying your business is clearing out houses and properties? That's gotta be fun. Kinda like a treasure hunt every time."

"You wouldn't believe some of the interesting things I stumble upon. Once, I even found a 14-carat gold tennis bracelet in the basement dirt. Sometimes, when I take down walls, relics will be hidden between the plaster and studs."

"I used to play in the dirt as a child. I'd bury something and pretend I found a treasure when I dug it back up." Candice smiled, fondly remembering her great childhood adventures.

"Yeah, it's cool. I have a reclamation store where I put things like old barn wood, sinks, and lighting fixtures. Anything reusable can be found in my salvage store. I give my grandmother the furniture and knickknacks to sell at her antique store. She loves staying busy and helping her customers. It's what keeps her young."

"I've heard people who stay active live longer," Candice replied, recalling the elderly woman's youthful spirit.

"My grandfather used to say, 'The day I quit working is the day I'm dead, and he died within a few months of retirement." Shane's eyes were saddened at the mention of his grandfather. "So, I plan on staying busy every day."

"Well, I would love to go with you sometime on one of your treasure hunts. There's just something about old buildings I love. I guess it's the character and charm. Each house has a story to tell. As you can see, I really have quite the imagination."

"Well, I'm going to Napa tomorrow to scout my next job. If you'd like to go, I'd enjoy the company."

"Sure, I have nothing planned for tomorrow."

Josh cleared his throat and interrupted quietly, "Shane, we are double parked out there."

"Right, we'll be back with your table and chairs."

"I'll come down and hold the door. Then you won't have to be buzzed back in." Candice grabbed her keys and followed the men. She watched Shane run his hand through his hair, trying to get a curl out of his eye.

Shane carried the bistro table over his head while Josh grabbed both chairs.

"I can carry a chair for you," Candice offered.

"Nah, I got it, but thanks," Josh replied. He was a person of few words.

Candice ran ahead of the men and pushed the *up* button for the elevator. The three of them stood there looking up as they watched the floor numbers light up on each floor the elevator passed.

"This has to be the slowest elevator in San Francisco," Candice commented, knowing that the table had to be heavy.

"It's not bad. At least you have an elevator. But, unfortunately, sometimes we have to walk the furniture up the stairs. That can be a real challenge," Shane said as he shifted his weight.

"I never thought of that. What if the piece is too big to make the turns in a stairwell?"

"I always measure before I attempt the stairs. If the piece is too big for the stairs, I will see if we can hoist it up to a balcony and through sliding doors. If not, then I will offer a refund. My grandmother doesn't always remember to ask if there is a cargo elevator when selling huge pieces. I try to find a creative solution to get the furniture into a customer's home, like removing door jams, but sometimes the furniture simply doesn't fit no matter what I do."

"Gosh, I didn't think of that either when I bought the credenza. I bought it without considering whether it would fit in the elevator."

"It was a tight fit, but we stood it up on its side, and then there was plenty of room for us to fit."

The elevator finally stopped, and the door slowly opened. Candice held the *open door* button so it would not shut until they were in the hallway.

"This is a great building," Shane stated.

"Yeah, it was an old warehouse. I love the view from my living room. That's really what sold me on the place. Plus, it has covered parking. Although I don't own a car. I figured having parking was great for resale."

"Smart move. Parking is so important in San Francisco. The first place I owned didn't have parking, and my friends hated to drive out and visit because they would have to circle the block twenty times waiting for a spot to open."

Josh did not say anything during the entire elevator ride. Instead, he just listened and watched Shane, who appeared smitten with Candice.

They reached the condo and placed the bistro table and chairs in the empty corner of Candice's tiny kitchen. "Oh, that's so cute there," Candice remarked, delighted with her purchase.

"It does look like it was custom-made for this kitchen," Shane agreed, taking a step back to get a broader view.

"Well, thank you so much for delivering it so quickly." Candice reached for her purse to give the men a tip.

"No need for that." Shane held his hand up, refusing the money.

"Um, well, maybe I can treat you to breakfast tomorrow before we head out to Napa."

"Breakfast sounds good, but I prefer to treat you. There's a great little place in Sausalito. I'll pick you up around eight."

"I look forward to it." Candice's heart began beating a little faster.

"Oh, I almost forgot to tell you; my grandmother said she put something in the top drawer of the credenza for you. She thought you might like it."

"That is so sweet," Candice said, wondering what it could be.

Candice watched as the men walked out her front door. Then she ran to her window to wait for Shane to exit the building. She wanted just one last glance at this rugged man. She decided it was definitely true; this condo had a great view.

Once the truck drove off, Candice stood before her new credenza. She wondered if she should just paint it white or put effort into restoring it. The thought of working with harsh chemicals was not appealing. Although having Shane show her how to refinish it would make the job worthwhile.

She reached for the top drawer and pulled it open. Inside, she found an old recipe book. Handwritten on the cover it read, *Grandma Pela's Secret Recipes.* Several loose recipes fell into the drawer when Candice picked up the book. She opened the book, and the first recipe was *Grandma Pela's Secret Truffles.* Followed by *Grandma Pela's Over the Moon Yellow Cake.* She turned to the next page, *Grandma Pela's Hard Cherry Candy.* There had to be well over one hundred recipes, probably more. *Grandma Pela sure liked treats,* Candice thought as she picked up the loose recipes to put them back into the book.

A yellowed newspaper was folded and resting in the drawer. Candice read the year 1946, then the headline, which jumped out in bold letters: **Grandma Pela Does It Again**. Apparently, her Fluffy Mountain cake sold for a whopping two dollars, and the proceeds were going to a charity that helped children.

Then Candice noticed a note written on beautiful stationery. She picked it up and read:

> *Ms. Smythe,*
>
> *I found this recipe book inside this credenza. I was going to sell it separately, but I thought that would be wrong. The book belongs with this wonderful piece of furniture. Let me know how the recipes turn out, should you decide to make any of them.*
>
> *Regards, Beatrice.*

Candice tried to push the drawer closed, but it refused to budge. She removed the drawer and looked to see what the problem was. She found an old apron with a bib top and hand-embroidered orange flowers decorating the skirt. She shook out the apron to ensure no bugs had decided to make their home in the folds. Then she slipped the bib over her head and tied it around her waist. She looked back into the space behind the drawer, where she saw more recipes, old measuring spoons, some sort of ancient kitchen utensil that resembled a small cheese grater, and several photos of an old woman. *Could this be Grandma Pela?* Candice wondered. She placed everything on top of the credenza and gently replaced the drawer.

Candice gathered the loose recipes from under the drawer and the book and sat on her couch. Many recipes had exotic-sounding ingredients that she was unfamiliar with, so she turned on her laptop and started searching. Shortly into her quest for knowledge, she decided to see if there was anything about this woman, Grandma Pela.

It did not take long before the search engine returned a tribute that read:

Valeria Pela, better known as Grandma Pela, was a woman who dedicated her life to providing food and shelter to the needy. It was not uncommon to hear about another weary homeless person that was given a place to rest in her home. She had a special connection to orphaned children and volunteered at the orphanage, rocking the newborn babies for hours.

Many neighborhood residents suspected that Grandma Pela was once an orphan too, but there is no confirmation on this speculation.

She was known in her community as a loving and caring woman who could brighten everyone's day with her warm smile and kind words. She loved to bake and deliver treats to hospitals and nursing homes for over seventy-five years. She won many awards for her baked goods and always had at least one entry in every contest in the area.

Her humanitarian efforts fed her soul and kept her young. She celebrated her 103rd birthday by making her final cake. The angels called her home two days later, on September 3rd. There are no known children or relatives, but she will always be fondly remembered as Grandma Pela by her community.

Under the article about Grandma Pela, Candice saw an obituary:

Valeria Pela (1910-2013)

Obituary

There will be a celebration of life for Valeria Pela at **Love for All** nursing home this Friday from 11:00 a.m. to 2:00 p.m. Everyone is welcome to share in this memorial and convey how Grandma Pela touched your life.

Wow, I guess there really is something to this idea of keeping busy. Candice printed the tribute and obituary about Grandma Pela and put them with the recipes.

Just for fun, I will try to make one of Grandma Pela's treats. Next to Candice's phone were a pen and notepad. She jotted down the ingredients for the recipe that looked the simplest: *Kumquat Lemon Drizzle Cookie.* So out the door and off to the market, Candice went with her reusable grocery bags.

"Excuse me," Candice politely said, holding her grocery list. The man turned, happy to take a break from stacking apples. "Do you have any kumquats?"

"Sure, they're right over here." He walked toward some small orange fruits.

"Oh, these are so cute. Thank you for your help."

"No problem. Anything else on that list you need?"

"Nope, this was the last thing I needed." Candice started filling a plastic bag with the five kumquats the recipe called for. She passed the whole-wheat pastry flour and grabbed a bag as she made her way to the checkout. *I think that should do it for now.*

Once she arrived back home, she started the process of baking.

Step One: Preheat oven to 350°. Candice set the oven control to the instructed temperature. *Where did I put those measuring cups?* She opened each drawer, but the measuring cups were not there. When Candice had a job, she rarely had the energy to cook. She often put in twelve-hour days and spent much of her weekends at work. She stood there looking at her cabinets as if the cups just might call out, 'Yoo-hoo, over here.' She bent down and reached in to grab a large mixing bowl. *There they are.* She thought, looking inside the mixing bowl. *Jazzlene must have stuck them there.* She found her grandmother's sifter and decided she would give the flour a thrice sifting for good measure. Longing to use her grandmother's old sifter, she told herself it couldn't hurt to sift the flour even if the recipe didn't call for it.

Step-by-step, Candice followed the recipe to a tee. The kumquats were challenging to peel before she realized she had misread the recipe. She was supposed to cut them into small pieces with the rind intact.

The dough for the cookies was mixed and ready to place on the cookie sheet. She rolled small balls of dough and flattened them with a spatula. While they were baking, she thought she would start on the drizzle. It called for lemon zest. The only grater she had was a cheese grater, which would not work. This meant another trip to the store, but now she had to wait for the cookies to finish baking. She sat down to look at the other items from the credenza. She picked up the old small grater. *Oh, this must be a rind grater.* She washed it and then started to grate the lemon rind. An hour passed, and the cookies were cool enough to drizzle the lemon on top. Now all she needed was a cup of tea.

Okay, the moment of truth. She took a bite of the cookie and let out a moan loud enough for the neighbors to hear as the cookie melted in her mouth. Candice picked up her phone and dialed Jazzlene. She knew Jazzlene was working, so she left her a message.

"Hey, you have to taste these cookies I made. They're amazing. I'd say better than sex. Well, that's a slight exaggeration. But, I will say, you won't be able to eat just one."

Candice went to her desk and found a box of plastic sheet protectors. She gently placed each recipe into a protective holder. Then she saw a binder currently holding her work rules and emptied the contents into her desk drawer. One by one, she put the recipes into the binder. The first one, of course, was the *Kumquat Lemon Drizzle Cookie.* On a sticky note, she wrote: Melt in your mouth delicious. Green tea goes well with this cookie. She stuck the note into the plastic protector with the recipe. Next, Candice started reviewing the other recipes. She would have to try another one of Grandma Pela's recipes to see if it was as good as the first.

Eight o'clock and her phone rang. She looked to see who it was. "I see you got my message," Candice said.

"I'm on my way home now, but I can stop by if you want. Or can the cookies keep until tomorrow?"

"Yes, it can wait, but I really want you to try one of these cookies while they're fresh. I'm not sure if they'll be as good tomorrow."

"Okay, I'll be there in a few. But then I have to get home. I'm exhausted."

Candice put on the water to boil for the tea. She wanted Jazzlene to experience the cookies with tea as she had earlier.

Jazzlene let herself into the condo with the spare key. "Okay, where are these *better than sex* cookies? Lord knows I need one after the wedding today. And since when do you bake?"

"Just try one and tell me what you think." Candice held the plate up, showing off neatly displayed cookies.

First, Jazzlene smelled the cookie. "Very fragrant. I believe I smell a hint of lemon." Then she took a bite that made her taste buds dance. "Oh, my!" She took another bite. "These just melt in your mouth. When did you learn to bake like this? And where did you get that cute apron?"

Candice forgot she still had on the vintage apron. "Well, see my old but *new-to-me* credenza?" She pointed to her brightly painted piece.

Jazzlene turned to see this infusion of color that was actually the credenza. "Yes, quite pretty. I can see the potential."

"Well, there was a recipe book in there, given to me by the lady that owns the antique store. And trapped under the drawer was this apron, some old photos, and this grater. The recipe book has over a hundred of Grandma Pela's secret recipes. I was curious, so I did an internet search and found an old newspaper article from 1946 and Grandma Pela's obit, which I printed out." Candice handed the binder to Jazzlene. "I thought I would try a recipe that looked simple. And voilà, here you have *Kumquat Lemon Drizzle Cookies.* Amazing, right?"

"I'll say. May I have another?" Jazzlene asked but did not wait for Candice to answer. Instead, she just reached for the plate and snatched a cookie.

"My day actually started off even better. Let me tell you about the man that delivered this credenza. Well, there were two, but one doesn't count. He was too young. The other guy, Shane, he looked to be in his mid-thirties. Beautiful brown eyes that just light up his face. Anyway, he looks like he takes good care of himself, rock-hard arms. He invited me...oh wait, I think I invited myself to go look at some property in Napa with him tomorrow."

"What? You're going to look at land now?"

"No, he owns a reclamation business. He empties out houses and clears out debris. He's going to look at a potential job, size up what is valuable, and what will go to the dumps. So I thought it would be fun to tag along sometime."

"Hmm, you really invited yourself?" Jazzlene looked surprised. It was out of Candice's character to be so forward.

"Sorta. I just said it sounded fun, and I'd love to tag along. He said I could go with him tomorrow. Who am I to turn down a gorgeous man?"

"Take your camera. You may get some great pictures," Jazzlene advised, an eyebrow raised.

"Good idea."

"Well, I guess I'd better head home. Tomorrow is going to be a long day. I'll call you when I get home after the Quinceañera and see how your date went. I mean treasure hunting."

Candice turned out her light that night and lay in bed, trying to *will* herself to sleep. She wanted to be bright-eyed and bushy-tailed in the morning, but in all her excitement, sleep did not come quickly.

Five

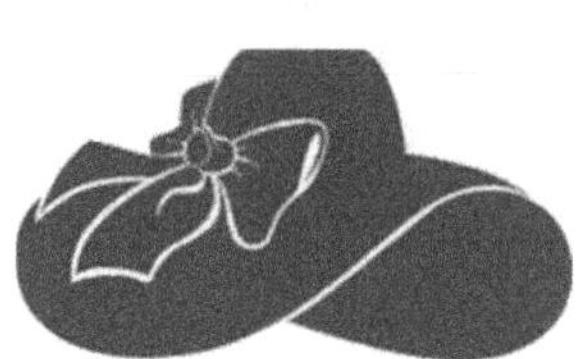

Your chariot awaits," Shane said, opening the truck door and helping Candice stepped up into the cab.

Chivalry is so uncommon these days, Candice thought, smiling at Shane. "Thank you." She could smell the faint musky fragrance of his cologne as it lingered in her nose.

"What's your preference in music?" he asked, handing her a CD holder.

"Gosh, I'll listen to just about anything. Well, maybe not opera for a car ride," she answered, flipping through the assortment of music. "You have just about every type of music imaginable."

"Well, I like variety. But it also depends on my mood that day."

"Yeah, I agree. The other night, I pulled out my seventies disco music and danced around my condo. The upbeat tempo always puts me in a good mood."

"I often wondered what it would have been like to grow up in the seventies. You know, with those shiny polyester shirts that never wrinkled. And what about those platform shoes the girls wore? They looked pretty precarious. What a balancing act that had to be. But everything old is new now. I've seen so many women wearing platforms lately."

"I've tried to wear those shoes. My mother let me borrow a pair she had tucked away in her closet. They did take some getting used to, and at first, I felt like I was walking on stilts."

Candice grabbed Journey's Greatest Hits CD and popped it into the player. "This should take us back in time," Candice told him as the first note started to play.

Shane started tapping his thumb on the steering wheel as they crossed the Golden Gate Bridge.

Candice gazed out her window at the water below and noticed hundreds of boats sprinkled on the bay like seashells scattered along a shoreline. "Being on the bridge in such a high truck, you get a great view of the bay."

"Looks like a perfect day to be out on the water," Shane commented after briefly scanning the scene below.

"The only time I've been on the bay was going on an Alcatraz tour, which was just a short ferry ride."

"I have a friend with a sailboat, so I've been out a few times. Once, it was way too windy and very choppy. I would not recommend that without taking a Dramamine." Candice turned to look at Shane's expression. "I'm just saying it was not a pleasant experience."

"I would imagine not," Candice sounded sympathetic, "but the cool sea spray had to invigorate you."

"Yes, it is refreshing. Hey, maybe you'd like to go sometime."

"That sounds like fun. I'd love to."

Suddenly Shane hit his brakes, veering to the right as his squealing tires sent up wisps of smoke. He barely missed the car in front of him. The traffic had come to an abrupt halt.

"Sorry," Shane apologized as he removed his arm that he stretched across Candice in a vain attempt to keep her from flying forward.

Candice tried to look between the cars to see what was going on. "I don't see anything ahead that would indicate an accident. Oh, wait. Here comes a bunch of people running towards us." Panic started to seep into Candice's voice.

"Scoot over here, and you can see what's happening." Shane leaned back so Candice could see through the steering wheel. Her long hair brushed across his arm, sending a spark through his body.

"Oh, we have to help. Put on your emergency flashers!" Candice shrieked, jumping out of the truck.

Shane turned the engine off, grabbed his keys and a blanket from behind the seat, and ran to catch up to Candice. She managed to maneuver through the crowd of people gathering outside their cars. Quickly, she approached the cause of the traffic jam and cautiously knelt down.

"It's okay," she softly said, reaching out and gently placing her hand on the fawn's head. The fawn appeared to have collapsed from exhaustion and was panting heavily, gazing up at her. Shane came up behind Candice and swaddled the little deer in the blanket.

"Where's its mother?" Candice asked, scanning the bridge for any evidence of a panicked Doe.

"I'm not sure, but we must get this little guy to safety." Shane cradled the fawn as if it were the world's most natural thing. They slowly returned to the truck as Shane kept the fawn wrapped securely in his arms. He placed the fawn in Candice's lap once she was in the truck's cab. Everyone got back in their cars. Finally, the traffic began to crawl.

"What are we going to do?" Candice asked in a whisper.

"Once we get off the bridge, I'll see if I can find a wildlife rescue on my cell and call them. No way we'll leave this little fella on the side of the road. He's way too young to fend for himself."

Candice coddled the fawn, trying to reassure it. "I think he understands that we're trying to help. He's not shaking anymore."

"Well, animals can sense danger even at a young age. But I bet all he feels right now is the safety of your arms." Shane put his blinker on to exit the freeway. As they circled down the off-ramp, they spotted a lifeless doe on the side of the road. Most likely, it was the little fawn's mother. "Oh, that's sad," Shane mumbled, continuing down the road until he saw a parking lot.

The little fawn began to squirm when the movement of the truck came to a stop. Candice rubbed his forehead, trying to soothe him. The last thing she wanted was for the fawn to become agitated and try to escape.

Scrolling through a list of wildlife rescues, Shane located one in Marin. "I'll just call them and see what we should do."

Candice kept stroking the fawn while she listened to Shane talk on the phone.

"Okay, so they said to bring him in, and they'll make sure he is well taken care of," Shane informed Candice as he entered the address into his GPS system. "Just a little detour, and then we'll be able to have breakfast."

"Shane, I'm sorry I just jumped out of the truck, but I had to make sure the fawn was not hurt."

"No need to apologize. With that mob chasing him, no wonder he was running for his life. I'm just thankful that you were able to calm him. That made it easy for me to wrap him in the blanket and get him off the road."

"He sure is cute. I've never been this close to a deer before. How old do you think he is?"

"Probably under four months by the number of spots he has, but that's just a guess."

Candice gently started rocking. The fawn slowly closed its eyes. "Well, look at that; he fell asleep. I bet he was so worn out when we finally got to him."

"You're probably right. He'll be in good hands once we get him to the rescue facility."

The tires created dust clouds as the truck pulled into a gravel parking lot. The fawn lifted his head, sensing the change in the road, but remained calm.

A rescue volunteer approached the passenger side door and slowly opened it, trying not to frighten the fawn.

Softly Candice whispered, "He seems to be pretty calm now."

"I'm sure he's very tired and scared. And you've given him some sense of security," Shane said, opening his door.

"Why don't you carry him inside," the volunteer requested. "That way, he'll feel safe until we have him in a secure enclosure."

Shane and Candice followed the woman through the makeshift lobby. "We have an area in here where it will be warm. I've already put some food in a bottle so he can eat. I'll let him settle in before I examine him and ensure he's not injured."

Candice looked around and saw several areas for caring for injured or orphaned wildlife. "This is a great place. What a fulfilling job. You must love coming to work."

"Most days, yes, especially when I can save a life. Like right now, this makes me feel good knowing this little guy will have a chance at survival."

The fawn wiggled as Candice set him on the ground. He looked up at her with huge eyes as if to thank her.

"He'll be fine. Why don't you leave me your email address, and I'll update you on his progress? You can even visit our website as we regularly post updates on our patients and guests."

"Oh, I would love that." Candice jotted down her email address.

"Here's a brochure on all the services we offer here. We have excellent educational programs, as well as volunteer opportunities. Our website is full of great information."

Candice looked down as the fawn nudged her leg with his nose.

"Would you like to feed him?" the volunteer asked, handing the bottle to Candice.

"Yes, I would like that." Candice turned toward Shane, seeking his approval.

"Sounds good to me," he said in a reassuring tone.

A very tall man in blue scrubs walked in. "Hi, I'm Dr. Harris. I'll oversee this little guy's care." He extended his hand to Shane and then to Candice. "From this quick visual, he looks to be in great shape. But we'll have to keep him for a while, as he's still too small to survive independently."

Candice no sooner got down onto the floor, and the fawn quickly found the nipple on the bottle. Shane pulled out his cell phone and took a few pictures. "What an interesting start to this day," he commented, shaking his head in disbelief and putting the phone back in his pocket.

"I'll say." Candice stood up, giving the empty bottle to the volunteer. "Thank you for letting me feed him."

"My pleasure. It's a wonderful thing you two did for him. You both have a great afternoon."

"On the road again," Shane sang, entering the freeway again. Candice chuckled at his attempt to sing a little country. "I say we skip Sausalito since we'd have to backtrack and head straight to Napa. Instead, we can stop by a little place off route 37 and get a bite to eat," he suggested.

"That sounds great. I'm sorry it took so long, but I would have felt so bad leaving him."

"No problem. We're not on a tight schedule. Anyway, saving a life is well worth a little detour."

Candice looked over at Shane and saw warmth in his smile. Despite his hard-bodied appearance, he could not hide his softer side. Shane glanced over at Candice, and their eyes met, captivating her until he turned and broke the spell, fixing his eyes back on the road.

Shane continued cruising Highway 101, focusing on the road ahead. When he looked into Candice's eyes earlier, a jolt of desire ran through his body. All he could do now was focus on driving and not allowing his mind to run wild.

"This may not be the quickest way to Napa, but I do enjoy the scenery," Shane mentioned after a few moments of awkward silence.

"I must agree. It's turning into a lovely day," Candice responded, rolling her window down to let the breeze fill the truck. "Don't you just love the fresh air?"

"Yes, especially after it rains. I love the smell of damp earth. It reminds me of camping when I was in the boy scouts," Shane said, veering onto route 37.

"Oh, you were in the scouts? I was a girl scout, but stopped when I entered junior high school."

"Yep, we had the best Scoutmaster. Unfortunately, he passed away, and the troop was never the same. Plus, by high school, I found other interests."

"I can relate." Candice could only imagine what interested Shane as a teen-ager.

Candice noticed a billboard, *Clara's Sweet Jams,* with a large red arrow; underneath the arrow, it read, *Straight Ahead.*

"Not much further," Shane announced, following the red arrows off the freeway onto a one-lane road.

As far as the eye could see, were rows and rows of grape vines. "It's amazing how straight the rows of grapes are. Can you imagine the years of dedication it took to establish these vines so they could produce the grapes needed for wine?" Candice's question was more of a statement.

"It certainly is a labor of love. Or maybe just the love of fine wine." Shane started to slow down and pulled to the side of the road.

"Why are we stopping here?" Candice asked, looking at the vast field of stately vines.

Shane hopped out of the truck and made his way around to the passenger door. He opened the door and helped Candice as she jumped from the cab.

"I want to get a picture of you in front of the vineyard." He pulled his cell phone out of his back pocket.

Candice tried to look natural, but every pose felt forced. Then, she heard a noise in the field and quickly turned to look. Only then did she hear the distinct sound of the camera click.

"Perfect," Shane declared, reviewing the photo. "Look." He turned the camera so Candice could see the picture.

The tiny screen revealed a woman enamored by the beauty surrounding her. The sun highlighted her candid face, giving her an ethereal glow. "You'll have to email me that photo so I will always be reminded of this day."

They returned to the truck and continued approximately a mile down the road. Another sign: *100 feet to Clara's Sweet Jams.* Candice could see a little building up ahead. It was so small it reminded her of a little girl's playhouse.

There were a few parking spaces right in front of the building. "Well, here we are." Shane turned off the truck.

"This is darling. How did you ever find this place?"

"Well, I was hired to work for the family that owns this vineyard. They wanted to tear down their old barn and build a larger one. So anyway, they offered me some toast with jam one morning when I arrived. The best damn jam I've ever had. I asked what brand it was because I needed to buy some. That's when I was told that their granddaughter made it. They have several fruit trees on the property, and she makes the jam every year. Guess you could call it her passion. Like the winemaking is to her grandparents. I mentioned she should sell the jam on the roadside."

"And she took your advice?"

"When they walked me to the barn that they wanted to be removed, we passed this cute playhouse. I was told it was built for their granddaughter when she was young. I suggested they could move it by the roadside and sell the jams out of it. Of course, it was too small, but they replicated it on a larger scale. It's quite deceiving. It looks tiny from the outside. If we walk over here, you will see that it goes back pretty far. You just can't see it from this angle."

"So, the granddaughter loved your idea and started selling her jam?"

"Yep, kinda like a lemonade stand."

They entered the quaint little house, causing the bell above the door to jingle. Candice could smell something baking. She looked around and saw jars and jars of jam neatly arranged on the rustic shelves. The preserves were lined up as precisely as the rows of grapes outside. Each row was a different color. First, she saw apricot, followed by apple, grape, orange, peach, plum, and strawberry. Candice noticed several small tables had been set for a tea party.

"Well, look what the cat dragged in," a cheery voice said as the girl approached.

Shane gave the girl a hug. "Sandy, this is Candice."

Candice looked puzzled. "But the name says Clara's Sweet Jams."

"Clara's my grandmother. She taught me how to make jam when I was little. Thought I'd pay homage to her since these are her recipes.

"How sweet," Candice replied, and then realized the pun she had just made and chuckled to herself.

Shane motioned Candice to a small table by the tiny window, which looked out at the vineyards.

"My grandfather built a porch on the back if you prefer to sit out there. It's a beautiful day for outside dining."

"Yes, that would be nice," Shane agreed.

"Right this way." Sandy led them out to a beautiful patio. "I'll give you two a few minutes to review what we have today. But just to let you know, the scones are fresh out of the oven."

"Would you like to try the scones?" Shane questioned Candice.

"Yes, is that what I smelled baking when we walked in?"

"I think you're smelling the cinnamon rolls. They're baking now."

"Shane, let's get the scones. I've never had them before."

"Two scones." Shane smiled at Sandy, placing their order.

"Would you like coffee or tea with those scones?"

"I'll have black coffee. How 'bout you, Candice?"

"A cup of Earl Gray, if you have it."

"Be right back with your drinks." Sandy skipped away, appearing still quite childlike.

"How old is she?"

"If I'm not mistaken, she just turned eighteen. Should be graduating high school soon."

"Wow, to be so young and so driven. This is really a cute little place."

"It's only open on the weekends."

Sandy quickly returned with piping hot coffee, the steam rising and making little swirls. "Here ya go. Just like you like it, hot and black. The tea will be ready in a minute," she stated, placing the coffee cup in front of Shane and darting off toward the kitchen.

"What do you think she'll do after she graduates?"

"Not sure. But I'm guessing something to do with food. She loves this little place."

"Well, she is quite the businesswoman."

Sandy returned with a small plate of scones and an assortment of jams in cute little bowls. She set them in the middle of the table. "Be right back with your tea."

Candice picked up a scone and split it open. Then she scooped up some strawberry jam, putting a dollop on the pastry.

"Here ya go." Sandy poured the tea into Candice's cup and left the teapot on the table. "This is lavender sugar and raw sugar cubes." Sandy pointed to the little bowls holding the sugars.

"Thank you." Candice took a bite of her scone, her eyes lighting up. "Wow." She was speechless after that.

"I see you like them?" Shane blew on his coffee before taking a sip.

"Oh, my god...yes. I must buy a few jars of this jam." The fruity flavors stimulated Candice's taste buds, encouraging bite after bite.

Candice walked out with a satisfied grin, twenty jars of jam, and a few cinnamon rolls.

"What are you going to do with all that jam?" Shane asked.

"Well, I was thinking of giving them as gifts. Thank you so much for taking me to Clara's. Just think, if we didn't stop for that fawn, we would never have stopped at that hidden gem."

"Well, I wouldn't say never, but you're right; Clara's was not the plan for today. But it worked out great," Shane responded, starting his truck.

"Recalculating," the GPS informed them in a robotic voice.

They both laughed as *Ms. GPS* had recalculated several times on this trip, trying to keep them on course.

They were cruising along California State Route 37 when the GPS politely announced, "½ mile to your exit." Shane put on his blinker and started to merge into the slow lane. "Exit right." Shane did as he was instructed, exiting the freeway. "One mile to your next exit."

"According to the GPS, we're almost there," Shane said, looking at the on-screen map.

"Turn left ¼ mile," Ms. GPS directed.

Shane entered the property through dilapidated rod iron gates with a *No Trespassing* sign dangling. He continued along a dirt road. About ½ mile down the path, the vegetation started to envelop the way, closing in on the truck.

"It doesn't look like anyone has been down this road in years." Candice observed looking around as tree branches slapped against the truck.

"From what I was told, this land was owned by the same family for generations. Old man Keller was the last known surviving member of the family. He lived here until his death five years ago at age ninety. He was a bit of a recluse.

"Anyway, according to records, he had no heirs and no will when he passed away. So it was in probate for years until low and behold, the courts found a woman who was, at one time, Mrs. Keller.

"Evidently, he just disappeared when he found out she was pregnant. She had no idea where he went and never knew about this property. Finally, after years of him missing, the courts declared him dead. I was told his widow met him when he was a long-haul trucker passing through Tennessee. Apparently, there was quite an age difference, something like thirty years. The courts located her through the old missing person report she filed years ago."

"Wow, so what is she doing with this land?" Candice questioned.

"Well, this is where it gets interesting. Since Mr. Keller vanished when he found out his wife was pregnant, she feels her daughter should have the land. So, she gave it to their daughter. The daughter apparently wants to build a house and move her family here. At least, that is what the daughter told me over the phone. She wanted me to come out and remove anything salvageable. She said she was trying to be eco-friendly and recycle."

A large tree branch slapped against the windshield, and Candice turned her attention away from Shane to the window and the surrounding vegetation. Slowly, the truck emerged out of the dark forest into a clearing.

"This looks like it might have been a horse corral." Shane speculated, stopping the truck and turning off the engine.

"Feels like we're in the middle of nowhere." Candice looked at the immense clearing bordered by trees.

Shane reached behind his seat and grabbed some gloves. "Here, you might need these," he offered, handing her some leather gloves.

They both stepped out of the truck and stood there surveying the land. "There's supposed to be a barn or shed somewhere around here."

"That would make sense if this was a horse corral. Probably some stables too." Candice shielded her eyes from the sun. She looked around for a likely spot for a barn.

"Guess we'll be taking a hike through the woods." Shane went to the back of his truck and opened his toolbox. He reached in and pulled out a large sickle knife. "This should help us cut through the thick brush. They said it was overgrown, so I came prepared. Always a boy scout."

Candice eyed the knife. She was out in the middle of nowhere with a man she did not know, holding a threatening sickle that could cut her into tiny pieces. She pulled her cell phone out of her pants pocket and quickly texted Jazzlene, informing her of their approximate location. *Better safe than sorry.*

"I think if we go this way, we should come to the barn." Shane started hacking at the dead grapevines to clear them a path.

"Lions, tigers, and bears, oh my," Candice sang as they crept further into the brush.

"I may be wrong, but I thought the barn would be around here. It seemed the least overgrown, so I figured it would have been the original path." Shane parted some bushes, peering through only to see more brush.

"Well, maybe the barn collapsed, and that's why we aren't finding it."

"Look." Shane pointed straight ahead.

In the distance, Candice could see what appeared to be a weather vane.

"Could that be the top of the barn?"

"I think so," Shane responded as excitement spurred him into hacking at the vines more quickly. Candice made sure she stood several feet behind Shane. One wrong move on his part, and she could lose a limb. "Come on." He grabbed her hand and led her through the last of the grapevines.

They both stood there like two statues. Before them was the biggest barn Shane had ever seen. And it was in much better condition than he thought possible. "You know, this would make a great house. I saw a barn converted into a house on *This Old House*. It was quite unique and impressive what they did with the barn."

"What a great idea. Lord knows it's big enough."

Shane took some pictures with his cell phone. "You never know. I might be able to sell the entire barn instead of just scrapping the wood."

"Do you think someone would buy an old barn and then resurrect it?"

"Yes, for the right price. I just need to mark the boards and make a diagram to put them back together. It would be like building one of those prefab log cabins."

"Boy, you think of everything." Candice smiled, realizing that Shane had the same love of old buildings that she did.

"It's my job to be creative. Sometimes I'll take the old wood I retrieve and make a beautiful coffee table or maybe a headboard. It's something I really enjoy doing."

The two of them walked closer to the barn. Candice observed how Shane was analyzing every inch of the front façade of the barn. He continued to walk around all four sides of the enormous structure.

"Well, it looks sturdy enough to enter." He pulled the large door, and it creaked open. "Let me go in first and make sure it's safe." He grabbed his flashlight from his tool belt.

Candice stood outside, waiting for Shane to say it was safe to enter. She kicked up dirt with her foot, anticipating what the inside would be like. Finally, Candice could not stand the wait any longer. Therefore, she stepped inside the barn. "Shane, where are you?"

He held the flashlight in the air. "Over here."

She followed the beam of light like a lighthouse beacon.

"Here." He handed her a small flashlight. "I have one for you."

"You really are prepared." She turned her flashlight on and started to explore the barn.

"I'm going to climb onto that hayloft, but don't follow me until I tell you it's safe."

"Okay," Candice agreed, choosing not to tell him she feared heights and would not be following him up anyway.

Shane opened the little shutter that covered a small window.

"What a view," he gasped.

"What do you see?"

"Come on up and see for yourself."

"That's okay. You can just tell me."

"I can't. You have to see it with your own eyes." Shane started heading down the ladder. "It's perfectly safe up there. This barn was built to withstand an earthquake and most likely did."

Shane took Candice's hand. "Come on."

She took a deep breath and put her right foot on the first rung.

"Go on, I'm right behind you," he stated, coaxing her up the ladder.

Candice stood frozen. "I don't think I can." Her legs began to shake.

"I'm right here, see?" Shane put his arm on Candice's back for support.

Carefully, she put her foot on the next rung and slowly climbed to the top. The minute she felt the hard surface of the hayloft floor, she sensed relief. "Now I suspect getting down from here will be more of a challenge than climbing up," she alleged with trepidation.

"Well, I'll help you. Now go have a look out that window."

Candice crawled to the window and pulled herself up, grabbing the windowsill. What she saw quickly stifled her panic about being twenty feet in the air. Off in the distance was a house, not just any house, but a mansion. "Did you know there was a house here?" Candice asked.

"No. I'm not sure if the daughter even knows. We have to go explore it."

"Just one problem. How will I get down from here?"

Shane chuckled. "Same way you got up."

Candice took a deep breath, lay on the floor, and scooted herself to the edge of the hayloft. "Let me go first so I can help you," Shane offered, climbing over the side of the loft. "Okay, just put your right foot over the side, and I'll help guide it to the rung."

Candice did as he instructed; before she knew it, she stood on solid ground with wobbly legs.

"Now, if I'm right, we head in this direction and will come across the house."

"How far away do you think it is?"

"It looked like about ¼ of a mile or so," Shane replied, hacking away at the vegetation again.

"Shane, how are you going to do this job? There are no roads leading to the barn or even that house."

"I'll bring a backhoe and make a path. If I can find the original roads, it will make the job easier."

"I was wondering. If the old man was a recluse without any known family, who do you think, found him when he died?"

"Well, I'm not really sure. I would imagine a neighbor. He did live here for years, so maybe he had people that did welfare checks on him."

"Oh, that would make sense," Candice concurred, stepping over a large tree root.

Shane continued moving through the thick brush as he chopped a pathway. "I don't think it's much further."

Candice followed closely behind Shane, maybe too close. He abruptly stopped, and she bumped right into him, hitting her nose on his shoulder. "I'm so sorry," she apologized, rubbing her nose.

"You okay?" he questioned, seeing her eyes tear up.

"Yeah, fine," Candice replied, trying to hide her embarrassment.

Shane was just happy that she was following so close behind him. He had her within touching distance. "Look up," he told her, pointing toward the top of a tree.

Candice tilted her head and gazed up at the top of the tree. "I don't see anything."

"Look on the trunk of the tree. Right there." Shane pointed again, guiding her eyes down.

"Oh, now I see it."

Attached to the tree was a weathered birdhouse, and peeking out through the small hole was a baby bird. "How cute is that?" Candice asked, watching the baby bird poking its head in and out, happily chirping.

"Very cute. We must be getting close to the house." Shane gave another swift chop at the brush and pushed the branches aside. "There it is!"

Candice stood silently, reveling in the grand estate. The house was much more substantial up close than it appeared from the barn. They could only see the tower and four chimneys from the barn window. Standing in front of it now revealed three distinct levels. Each was slightly different from the one below it.

The first floor had incredible wood detailing around the boarded windows. The magnificent front door stood adorned with brass doorknobs that accentuated the beautiful hand-carved detail.

The second-floor windows were also covered by plywood, but a slight arch above the wood indicated that Palladian windows would be underneath.

The third story had much smaller windows, as the plywood covering them appeared to be around three feet by four feet. The cornice at the top of the third floor was dressed with corbels. This gave the house its stately appearance. A square tower with several windows was at the top, nestled between the four chimneys. It could be the attic space or possibly a lookout.

"Wow, it's beautiful. Or at least you can tell it was beautiful at one time." Candice's voice was soft as she stood still and mesmerized.

"Let's go explore." Shane grabbed Candice's hand and pulled her toward the house.

She looked down at their hands connected and felt the warmth of his skin. *For a man that works with his hands, they were surprisingly soft.*

"Watch your step," Shane warned, still holding her hand.

They climbed carefully up the decaying steps to the porch that seemed to be more stable. The eaves had protected the wood on the porch, but the roof was barely there anymore. Patches of sunlight were visible through the overhang. Shane laid the sickle down and released Candice's hand. He reached up to jiggle the doorknob.

"I was hoping it would be unlocked."

There was no way to get a peek inside since every window remained protected by plywood. The ornately decorated colonnade wrap-around porch would lead them toward the back of the house.

"Let's go check out the back. Maybe there's a back door we can shimmy open," Candice suggested. She thought this might be considered breaking and entering, but she yearned to see the inside.

The two of them walked around the side of the house, where they observed more boarded-up windows. Finally, they reached the back of the house with beautiful details mimicking the front. A big sheet of plywood covered the back door.

"You know, I think I can remove this plywood." Shane grabbed a Phillips head screwdriver and started the tedious task of removing the screws. "Wow, I think that was overkill," he commented after removing screw number fifty.

Carefully, he rested the sheet of plywood against the house. They were both surprised to find that the back door was missing entirely.

"Well, that explains why they boarded this doorway and not the front door. Let's check this place out." Shane grabbed his flashlight from his tool belt and eagerly entered the house.

Candice did not hesitate to follow him inside. She stayed by his side until her eyes adjusted to the darkness. The two of them were stunned by the massive kitchen they had just entered.

"Who would have thought a house this old would have a big kitchen?" Candice's statement sounded more like a question.

"Well, by the size of this house, the family probably had a staff that cooked. I bet they hosted big parties," Shane commented.

Passing through the kitchen, they entered an oversized dining room. Shane swept his flashlight around the room and spotted a long table that could comfortably fit twenty guests.

"It looks like the county left everything in this house when the old man died. They simply boarded it up."

Candice was almost too giddy for her own good. She loved exploring old houses and learning about their history. "Look, there are still old cigarette butts in the ashtray." In fact, the house smelled of smoke and lemon wax. "Can you smell the lemon?" Candice inhaled to get another whiff.

"Yes, I think that is probably what they used to polish all the wood here. I love using lemon oil after restoring an old wooden piece."

"The art alone has to be worth a fortune. I wonder how old these paintings are." Candice kept thinking aloud.

"I think I'll need to call Mr. Keller's daughter. I bet she has no idea what a wonderful piece of property this is. Although the house is a little weathered, repairing it wouldn't take much. She could fix it and sell it or turn it into a hotel. And the barn, that can be salvaged too. She could have horse stalls and let people board their horses here. The possibilities are endless. And let's face it, Napa is such a beautiful weekend getaway."

"You're right. This is like a diamond that just needs to be polished. She could do a lot with this property," Candice agreed.

"At least it's worth her flying out to look at the land and the buildings before she has them destroyed. I'd feel better about removing the contents of the house and taking what can be salvaged and re-used if she at least came and saw what is here. Who knows what family treasures she might find?"

"Maybe you could take some more pictures and email them to her. It would be a shame to tear down this beautiful house." Candice appreciated that Shane had the same infatuation for old houses that she did.

"Yes, that's a great idea, but all I have is my cell phone, and the flash isn't working. I guess I could run back to the truck and get the camera."

"Let's finish exploring, and then we'll go back together," Candice suggested.

Shane opened a pocket door, revealing a grand ballroom. It had a massive stone fireplace and an impressive crystal chandelier hanging in the center of the room.

"I think that chandelier originally used candles. I bet it was fitted for electricity later because I can see where the candles would have been secured."

"You're probably right. Can you imagine the music and the laughter that would have filled this room?" Candice's voice echoed through the empty space.

"Amazing. A band could play in that corner, leaving enough room to waltz around." He took Candice and twirled her, making their way over to the other side of the room, where a small door opened onto the foyer.

"Look at this beautiful floor." Shane shined the flashlight on the marble.

"I saw something very similar to this the other day in a house I looked at. It was a beautiful Victorian," Candice said, smiling at the memory.

They continued across the foyer and ended up in the living room. It was much smaller and cozier than the other, more significant rooms.

"I guess this would be where the man of the house would sit at night and have a brandy." Candice assumed, walking over to a chair with a small table beside it. She sat down in the Queen Anne chair. "You'd have a beautiful view out this window and could relax while watching the sunset."

Shane sat in the matching red velvet chair across from Candice. "This is very comfortable considering its age." Shane could see the fabric was wearing thin, especially on the armrest. "It almost looks like someone was constantly rubbing their fingers across this area. The other arm does not have the same wear." He thought about how people have nervous habits like Candice licking her lips before she spoke to him.

Shane stood, walked over to Candice, and offered his hand to help her. "Let's head upstairs."

The stairs were in front of the foyer, curving up and around the wall. The varnish on the treads had worn off from years of feet going up and down the steps.

"Here." Shane offered Candice the brighter flashlight. "Lead the way." He wanted to follow Candice up the dark stairwell. If the house had not been so dark, he would have had a really great view.

Once Candice reached the landing, she quickly scanned the hallway. "Which way should we go first?"

"Let's keep heading to the top and work our way down."

They started up the next flight of stairs. "Where do you suppose the old man slept? I mean, this is a lot of stairs for an elderly person to climb. I'm getting winded, and we haven't even reached the top." Candice questioned, inhaling deeply. *Lord, when did I get so out of shape?*

"I was wondering that myself. It is sad that he lived here, isolated from everyone. But I guess that's how he wanted it, or why would he have disappeared?"

Finally, they reached the third floor. Shane looked around for what would be the obvious entry point to the cupola. He opened one door that was a closet, followed by another door leading to the master suite. "Let's check out this room," he suggested.

Candice handed him the bright flashlight and followed him in. An unmade, king-size Victorian four-poster bed was centered between two windows. It had a canopy trimmed in red velvet draping down all four posts' sides. The red velvet headboard had exquisite diamond pattern tufting that added a touch of feminine charm to the otherwise masculine bed.

A beautiful bookcase lined the opposite wall, with an overstuffed chair with a matching ottoman in front. Next to the chair stood a tall pedestal lamp that would have made reading there convenient. On the adjacent wall was a custom-built floor-to-ceiling dresser. Off to the side, Candice spotted a sliding ladder necessary to reach the top drawers. She walked over and opened one of the lower drawers. Inside, she found clothes neatly folded and coordinated by color. Candice pulled out a beautiful silk scarf.

"It feels strange to be looking through this house. It's like we're invading his privacy." She folded the scarf and placed it back in the drawer.

"Yeah, feels like the house is trapped in time, and we've gone back to the 1920s." Shane opened another door. "Finally, here's the pathway to the cupola."

Candice quickly shut the dresser drawer and practically leaped across the room. "This is exciting. It's better than walking through an antique store." Shane did not miss the excitement in her voice.

Reaching the interior of the cupola, they had a 360° view. "Look, you can see the entire property from here. There's the barn, and if you look over here, you can see an area that looks like it once had a pool," Shane stated in his observation.

"Wow." Candice stood shoulder to shoulder with Shane, looking at what appeared to be an old pool. There was so much plant growth covering it that all you could see was the hint of a diving board. "I think you're right. That must be a pool."

"Let's head back to the truck and get that camera. I really need to take those pictures you suggested."

Returning to the truck was much quicker since Shane had already created a clear path.

"What a find this place is." You could hear the thrill in his voice. "I love old houses. Guess that's why I got into the business I did. And I hate seeing wonderful craftsmanship thrown away."

"Me too. I often walk by old Victorians in San Francisco just to look at them."

Shane grabbed the camera. They quickly made their way back to the house. He started taking photos of every room. The second floor remained unexplored, so they would save that for last. Shane snapped pictures from every window in the cupola so Mr. Keller's daughter could see the entire landscape.

"Usually, I think of a cupola as decorative. I have never seen a functioning one." Shane said.

"Really? Then we made another new discovery." Candice enjoyed the view.

After a quick stop on level three and more pictures of the master bedroom, they descended to the second floor. Shane opened a door, revealing nothing but an empty room. The same thing happened with the next bedroom. "Funny how these rooms are completely empty," Shane mentioned, opening a closet.

"Well, maybe he sold some furniture for cash. It had to be expensive to keep this place up." Candice assumed.

Candice made her way down a narrow hallway and opened the door. "Shane, come look at this." She shined her flashlight into the room, illuminating a nursery. All the furniture looked to be from the 1920s. A photo of a tiny baby in a christening outfit was hung on the wall. "I wonder if that was the baby this room belonged to."

Shane did not comment. He just continued to snap more pictures before closing the door. "Let's head back downstairs and out to the pool."

Once they made their way through more overgrowth, they arrived at the pool. Hidden by grapevines peeked out a cabaña. "That certainly doesn't fit the house. It looks so out of place." Candice remarked.

Shane took a sweeping look around the area and noticed an odd reflection in the woods. "Wait here. I'll be right back," he instructed, returning with the sickle he had left on the mansion's front porch.

"What did you see?" Candice questioned as she watched Shane chopping at the vines.

"I'm not sure."

Candice stepped in line with Shane, following him along the path he was creating. "This place just keeps getting better," he said as they finally reached the source of the reflection.

A darling cottage with a small porch appeared before them.

"This had to be a guest house or maybe the groundskeeper's home," Shane stated, surveying the house.

Hung from the eaves were several hanging pots, which now displayed dead plants.

Shane tried the doorknob. To his amazement, it was unlocked. "Ladies first," he said, holding the door for Candice.

Candice scanned the room that contained floor-to-ceiling boxes and furniture. "It looks like this was used for storage, maybe after the old man moved here."

They walked between the neatly stacked boxes and entered a kitchen. Shane grabbed his camera and took some pictures of the kitchen. Then, they continued to explore the house, locating three fully packed bedrooms and a bathroom.

"The woman who now owns this land could make a bed and breakfast. Or a resort spa out of the main house and use this as her home. The possibilities of this property keeps getting better," Shane said, snapping more pictures.

"That would be perfect, and she could rent the ballroom for weddings and parties. But, really? What are the chances of ever coming into an inheritance like this?" Candice questioned.

"I really must email her. I'll give her names of people that can help her transform this place into a bed and breakfast type inn."

"I bet all these boxes are stuff that was removed from the larger house. Remember all those completely empty bedrooms?" Candice recalled.

"You're probably right. Well, I think I'm done taking pictures here. Let's head back to the main house so I can screw that plywood back over the doorway. Then we'll head back to the barn. I'd like to take some pictures of that, too."

A short while later, Shane took his last picture of the barn and closed the big, creaky door. "Guess we can head home now. I did not expect to find anything on this property but a barn. But, boy, what a surprise."

"That was thrilling going through the mansion, but it also felt like we were intruding in Mr. Keller's home."

"Yeah, I felt the same way, but I am glad we got inside to take the pictures for his daughter. I'll send these photos and tell Mr. Keller's daughter about the property's potential. Hopefully, she won't tear it down, or maybe she can sell the big house, and someone can move it to a new location. It would be so sad if she entirely destroyed it. I may have to return here for the salvage job, but I sure hope not. This is one job I wouldn't mind losing."

"I predict she will decide to keep and repair the big house. Like you said, it's a great place with so much history and character."

"If I need to return, I'll let you know. Maybe we could get to that restaurant in Sausalito after all." Shane helped Candice step into the truck, closed the door after her, and headed south.

"Shane," Candice turned to look at him, "thanks for bringing me. This was a great day. I think I've done more today than in the past month."

"You're welcome. I enjoyed your company. Maybe if you're free next weekend, I can stop by your place and show you how to strip the credenza."

"What day would work best for you?" Candice had an open calendar.

"How 'bout Saturday?"

"Sure, what time?"

"Is noon too early?"

"That would be perfect." Candice was excited to know she would see Shane again. She licked her lips, leaned over, and grabbed her purse to retrieve lip gloss. Her lips seemed overly dry today.

Shane pulled up along the curb outside of Candice's condominium. "Well, thank you for the fun afternoon." He got out of the truck and went around, opening her door.

"I really enjoyed today. Do you think you can email the photos of the house? I'd love to show them to my friend."

"Sure, I'll upload them when I get home." He hugged Candice and waited until she was safely inside her building before driving off.

Six

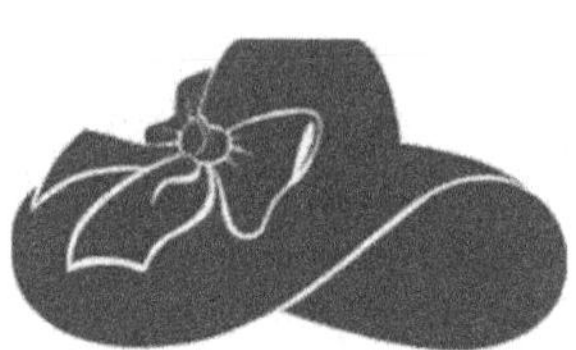

Candice grabbed her purse, sweater, and keys before heading out of her condo to start her first day working for Jazzlene. She stood at the bus stop, shrouded in the morning fog, watching the Monday morning bustle.

The bus dropped Candice off right in front of Jazzlene's studio. She knew Jazzlene would not be arriving until nine. That gave Candice a half hour to settle in. After letting herself in with the key Jazzlene had provided, she hung her sweater on the coat rack next to the door and placed her purse inside the reception desk drawer. Next, she powered up the computer before heading for the break area.

The room was cozy with a tiny refrigerator just big enough to hold a few bottles of wine and possibly three or four cans of coke. The sink was so small that the coffee pot had to be wedged under the faucet to fill it. Candice angled the carafe under the spout and filled it with tap water.

There was no stovetop in the area, only a small plug-in electric burner upon which the stainless-steel teakettle rested. Candice looked through the cabinets, trying to locate the coffee filters and coffee. Stacked neatly were box upon box of an assortment of teas. Several bottles of wine lined the shelf, and long stem wine glasses stood next to them. She saw cute teacups and a few coffee mugs on the higher shelf but no coffee or filters. She opened the small refrigerator, wondering if Jazzlene was trying to keep the coffee fresh, but all she found in the fridge was cheese and more wine.

Surely, she has coffee. Candice reached down and opened a cabinet that was under a small drawer. *Oh, there it is.* She grabbed the bag and then noticed the coffee filters. *She really should keep this expensive coffee in an airtight container.* Candice recognized the coffee from one of their favorite coffee shops in the

Haight Ashbury neighborhood.

The lovely smell of coffee brewing energized Candice before she even took her first sip.

Candice turned on the CD player and set the volume low. The music was soothing. She knew that was what Jazzlene would listen to when inside the darkroom developing her photos.

The computer booted up just as Candice sat down. She logged into her email account.

Oh, an email from Shane. She quickly opened it and started to read it.

Subject: Photos

Candice, thank you for going with me yesterday. I had so much fun exploring the property with you. I emailed Mr. Keller's daughter, and with any luck, she will get back to me soon. I'll keep you posted. On another note, I know I'm going to help you refinish that credenza Saturday, but I was wondering if you'd like to go out Friday for dinner and maybe catch a movie afterward? I'm not sure what's playing, but we can find something we both would enjoy. Hope to hear from you soon. Oh, and here's the link to my online photo album.

Shane

Candice clicked on the link, quickly directing her to Shane's album. She flipped through the photos, examining each detail of the house and grounds. It was just as unique as she remembered, and the pictures captured the house's appeal. She hoped that Mr. Keller's daughter would also see the beauty in the property. The last photo in the album was the one Shane took of her in front of the grapevines. Candice smiled at the memory.

Subject: Perfect

Morning Shane,
The pictures are wonderful. I think Mr. Keller's daughter will see the beauty in the property and take your advice. Thank you for sending me the link. Also, Friday sounds great. What time? I could meet you somewhere after work. I get off at five.

Looking forward to it,
Candice

Candice scrolled through the rest of her emails, finding nothing of importance. So she got up and went to get a hot cup of coffee, returning to her desk just as Jazzlene strolled through the door.

"Good morning. How was your day yesterday? I was so busy. I didn't get a chance to call you last night."

"It was amazing. You'll never believe the day I had. But before I explain, look at these pictures." Candice opened the photo album.

"Where is this?"

"Somewhere in Napa. I'm not sure exactly. It was a surprise to Shane. He thought we were just going to look at a barn. But what we found was a huge house hidden in the dense overgrowth. We had to remove a piece of plywood covering a doorway to get inside the house."

"And how was your non-date?" Jazzlene teased.

"Shane's such a gentleman. He opened my car door, pulled out my chair, and get this, he held my hand."

"Really? Candice, you should stop with the handholding. Who knows what that could lead to?" Jazzlene cracked up.

"Now that you mention it, it does sound corny. Like when we were in sixth grade and a boy held our hand. But it was more like a protective hold so I wouldn't lose my balance on these old uneven stairs. Anyway, it was sweet." Candice smiled at the memory.

"You're so silly. Give me a man that can knock my socks off."

Candice laughed. "Has it been a while since your socks were knocked off? You seem a little hot and bothered."

"Well, I can say not as long as you. How long since you've dated anyone?"

"I had a job that required a lot of my time. But now, it seems I have time to enjoy myself. But, you know me, my career came first."

"Well, I really want to know how you feel about this guy?"

"He's nice," Candice blushed. "Very attractive and a body that... well...would knock your socks off."

"Tell me more."

"What's to tell, oh, except he asked me to dinner Friday. So that's a good start. We'll see what happens."

Candice glanced down at the computer and noticed another email from Shane.

Subject: Dinner

Hi, give me your work address. I'll pick you up there at five if that works for you.

Awaiting your response,
Shane

"Well, I should let you get back to work. Or should I say, emailing your admirer? Oh, and by the way, the coffee smells like heaven. Thanks for making it. It's just what I need." Jazzlene headed into the break area to grab a cup of Joe.

RE: Dinner

How 'bout I meet you at my place at around 6:30 on Friday?

Candice

The phone started to ring. "Jazz Photography. How may I help you?" Candice answered, trying to sound sweet and professional. A few keystrokes later, Candice had added the Kline's to Jazzlene's busy calendar.

"Candice, would you mind downloading these photos for me? I'm heading into the darkroom, so you won't see me for a while."

"Sure, I'll man the fort and print out your schedule for the week. You have a full calendar this month."

"That is exactly why I need you. I can't do everything. My head's spinning with all the jobs I've committed to."

"You do realize I'm always here to help when I can."

"I hate that you got *laid off*, but I'm so happy you're here. I was losing my mind trying to find good help." Jazzlene placed her drained coffee cup on the counter and headed into her darkroom.

Candice started to work on organizing all of Jazzlene's finished projects. She needed to find some time in Jazz's calendar to schedule customer reviews of their proofs. *Why does she do this to herself? We may have to work late for several evenings just to accommodate everyone.*

Looking at the computer screen, Candice realized she would have to be the one to meet the clients and show them their proofs. There was just no way Jazzlene had any spare time this month if she wanted to work *and* sleep.

Standing outside the darkroom, Candice knocked softly.

"Yeah?" Jazzlene responded.

"I was wondering if you'd like me to review the proofs with your clients? That way, you won't have to stay late every night for the next month."

"That would be great, but make sure they know I won't be personally available. If they insist on me handling it, I'll be happy to stay late."

"Okay, I'll see what I can do." Candice made her way back to her desk.

Flipping through the portfolios of the new proofs, she saw the passion in the portraits. Candice knew Jazzlene was talented, but most, if not all of the photos were breathtaking. The way Jazzlene captured the endearing warmth in the eyes of a new husband. The snapshots were more than just memorializing a special day. The pictures looked right into the soul of people. She continued flipping through the albums in awe of her best friend's talent.

The phone began to ring. Candice sat back down at her desk and cheerfully answered. "Yes, we do have your proofs. I was just getting ready to call you. Sure, if you'd like to come in this afternoon, I could show them to you. My name is

Candice. Jazzlene is not available today." Candice wrote Simmons in the two o'clock time slot on the calendar. "I look forward to seeing you."

Candice opened her email again, for no reason except to see if Shane had responded to her email. *Boy, I need to get a grip. I'll be seeing him Friday.* And that's when she noticed a new email from the Marin Wildlife Rescue in her box.

Subject: Little Fawn

Just thought you would like to see the latest picture of the baby you brought in. He is doing great. Thanks to you for stepping in and helping him.

Sincerely,
Marin Wildlife Rescue

Oh, how cute. Candice quickly forwarded the email to Shane.

RE: Little Fawn

Shane, I got this today from the Wildlife Rescue. Thought you might enjoy seeing the picture. Look how relaxed he looks.

Thanks for helping me with him.

Candice

She looked at the clock and saw that it was almost noon. *Boy, this day is flying by.*

RE: RE: Little Fawn

You're welcome. That is so cute. He does look comfortable. What are you doing right now? Want to meet up for lunch?

Shane

Subject: Lunch

Yes, that would be nice. Where do you want to meet? There's a great deli next to the studio.

Candice

The phone began to ring. "Jazz Photography, how may I help you?" Candice greeted.

"Well, for starters, you can give me the address to the studio, so I can come pick you up," the very authoritative voice said.

Candice knew it was Shane, and her heart jumped. "Umm...ok, where are you?"

"I'm exiting the freeway. So tell me where I'm going, and I'll be right there."

After taking a breath, Candice gave him the directions. *Could this day get any better?*

"Hey Jazz, it's almost noon. Shane is picking me up to take me to lunch." Candice tried to sound calm, but her voice was barely audible.

"Did you just say Shane is coming to get you? The hot sexy guy you're pining for?" Jazzlene inquired excitedly, already knowing the answer.

"Yep, one and the same." Candice playfully giggled.

"When you leave, flip the sign on the door that says *Be Back Soon* and adjust it to the time you think you'll be back."

"I'll definitely be back before two because I have to show the Simmons' their proofs."

"Okay, have fun," Jazzlene said through the door.

Candice set the answering machine to pick up the calls while she was out. Then she grabbed her purse and made a quick run to the restroom. She reapplied her lipstick and ran a brush through her hair. Now she felt ready.

Coming back around the corner, she saw Shane sitting on the couch in the reception area, looking in her direction. "Your friend is a great photographer. I was admiring the photos on the wall."

"She really has an eye, and she's very successful. She always planned to be a fashion designer, but she really enjoyed photo shoots and took some photography classes. You must follow your passion when you find your passion."

"Where is she now?" Shane asked, looking around.

"In the darkroom. She won't be out for quite a while."

Shane stood up and held his hand out to Candice. "Shall we?"

Candice did not hesitate to take Shane's hand. It felt warm and soft, sending a current to her heart and butterflies to her stomach. This time she knew he held her hand to establish a physical connection, not just to steady her on some rickety old stairs. The ice that had formed around her heart was melting fast, despite her best efforts to keep it frozen.

"So, would you like to walk to the deli, or should I take you to a cute little café?"

"Oh, the café sounds nice. I just need to be back by two."

"Café, it is."

They had only walked a few more steps when Shane stopped in front of a 1970 Rally Sport Camaro and unlocked the door. Candice's eyes grew large. "You like?" he asked, raising his eyebrows.

"My dad has one of these. He used to let me shift the gears when I was little."

"I'm pretty fond of her. It took me a few years to restore. I wanted all original parts, which meant many hours spent in wrecking yards."

"Well, I'm sure you felt right at home," she teased. "There is always a way to reuse something. It's a shame how wasteful people are now."

"I agree." Shane opened the car door. Candice brushed against him as she passed, stepping off the sidewalk and into the car.

As the car purred to life, she thought of the warm memories of being a little girl sitting next to her father in his car.

"So, does your father still have his Camaro?"

"Yes. It's garaged, though, and he rarely takes it out on the road."

"I'd love to see it someday."

"I think I can arrange that."

"Where does your dad live?"

"San Jose. He's a financial advisor, so he likes working in the heart of Silicon Valley. He says that's where the money is. Plus, he prefers the warmer weather. Mom lives in Burlingame with her second husband in a cute bungalow."

"It must be nice that they live so close."

"Yeah, it is. Although my parents aren't supposedly together, they secretly meet every year around their anniversary. I figured it out when I realized they both took a vacation at the exact same time every year. It's strange on so many levels. So I just try to stay out of their business."

"Well, you're probably right. It's best to let them handle it. Who knows what goes on behind closed doors?"

"Yeah, I love them both, so I try to copy the three monkeys. I close my eyes, plug my ears, and keep my mouth shut."

"Your friend Jazz...now, that's an interesting name."

"Actually, her name is Jazzlene. Her dad is a professional jazz musician. He plays all sorts of wind instruments. Her mother's name is Charlene, so they took his love of jazz and blended it with her mom's name."

"It's a unique name."

"Yeah, it fits her."

Shane found parking on the street, pulled into the space, and turned the car off. "We can dine outside if you like."

"It's a beautiful day. Outside would be nice."

He pulled her chair out before sitting down himself. Candice smiled. "Thank you."

The waitress arrived with two glasses of water with lemon slices floating on the top. "Is there anything I can get you to drink besides water?"

"I'll have the strawberry lemonade," Candice replied.

"And for you, sir?" the waitress asked, smiling.

"I'll have the same."

"I'll be back with your drinks." She turned and left.

"My turn to ask questions," Candice began, looking into his eyes.

"Ask away." Shane leaned forward and gave Candice his full attention.

"Where were you raised? In the south?"

Shane laughed. "No, San Francisco. Why? Do I sound like I'm from the south?"

"No, but you have the manners of a boy raised in the south. Opening the car door. Pulling my chair out. A girl could get used to that."

"Isn't that what every man should do for a lady?" he politely asked.

"I guess so. But in my experience, as limited as it is, very few men actually do that."

Shane's expression was one of shock. "My grandma raised me to treat a lady with respect."

"Well, she did a good job."

"I'm always a gentleman...most of the time." He gave Candice a mischievous smile.

Her mind was wandering to places she could not afford to go. And thankfully, the waitress arrived just in time to take their order, allowing Candice's mind to focus on something other than Shane and his lustful stare.

"Do you have any siblings?" Candice tried to concentrate on something other than Shane's eyes.

"A sister, she's a few years younger than me. And you?"

"Not exactly, just a stepbrother. In fact, Jazzlene is in an on-again-off-again relationship with him. Right now, they're off. He just can't seem to settle down, even though he says he loves her. I try to stay out of that relationship, too. I love them both and don't want to choose sides. They'll work it out if it's meant to be."

"You're right. It's never wise to interfere. I take it you are not with anyone, or you wouldn't have agreed to meet me."

The question made Candice oddly uncomfortable. She looked away briefly, and then she turned to Shane. "I'm not sure if you really want to hear about my past. But to answer your question directly, I'm definitely single now."

Shane smiled and then took a sip of his drink. "Don't we all have a past?"

"Yeah, but isn't that where it should stay, a faded memory?"

The food arrived just as the conversation was getting to a topic Candice did not want to discuss. Candice looked at her meal and pushed it around with her fork. Finally, she said, "Okay, I'll tell you the basics, but you must tell me something about yourself first."

Shane looked deep into her eyes. "I'm divorced, lost my house in the settlement, and ended up moving in with my grandmother. It was either that or give up the business that I love."

"Oh, any children?" Candice could deal with divorce, but raising someone else's children did not appeal to her.

"No. My ex didn't want kids."

"And you? How do you feel about children?" Her voice sounded a little too relieved.

"I suppose with the right person, it would work, but when I married her, I knew it wasn't in her plans."

"How long have you been divorced?"

"A little over five years. It took me that long to get my finances back in order. Okay, now that I told you something I don't like talking about, it's your turn to share."

"In a nutshell, I was engaged to my college sweetheart. My career was going well, and things were on the right track. One day I went home for lunch and found him in my bed with not one but two women. Needless to say, minus the gory details, I kicked him to the curb and never looked back. I always suspected he was cheating. I just never had the evidence. I still have trust issues. I mean, when you give your heart to someone, you hope they will hold it dear and not break it."

"How long ago did this happen?"

"Coming up on a year. To be honest, I'm glad it happened when it did. We were two weeks away from getting married, so it was actually a blessing in disguise."

"I agree. Divorce is certainly not something I ever want to experience again."

The waitress dropped off the check. "Let's get you back to work. Then I have to make a delivery to Berkeley." Shane stood up and pulled out Candice's chair.

"Thank you for inviting me to lunch. That was a very quaint place. I'll have to remember it."

"You're welcome," Shane replied, shutting the car door.

Winding through the back streets of San Francisco, they arrived at the studio quicker than she wanted. Candice was enjoying her time with Shane and did not want it to end. Shane parked along the curb and gave Candice a hug before she made her way inside.

He watched as she flipped the closed sign to *open,* relishing in the sincerity of her hug. She looked out the window and waved as he slid into his car. Then, after a toot of his horn, he drove away.

"So, how did lunch go?" Jazzlene asked, coming out from the darkroom.

"Jazz, I don't think I should be seeing him." Worry was evident in Candice's eyes.

"Why? What's wrong?"

"Nothing. He's perfect, and I'm falling hard. I can't do this again. I'm just getting on with my life and becoming my own woman without a man."

"Don't you think you may be rushing things in your head? I mean, it's only dating. You deserve to go out and have some fun."

"I agree, but after Brent...well, you know...it just hurt so much."

"Brent was an ass. He didn't deserve a woman like you. So, move on, and don't let him ruin your chance for happiness. I mean, really, you're still letting him control your life."

"You're right, but what I'm starting to feel for Shane is way too intense. I just met him, so how can I feel this way?"

Just then, the door opened, and in walked a happy couple.

"We'll talk over drinks later," Jazzlene suggested, grabbing her purse. "I have an appointment across town. I should be back by four."

"May I help you?" Candice walked over and greeted the couple.

"We would love to look at some portfolios. We hear that Jazzlene is the best, and that's what we want for our wedding." The girl looked over at her fiancé with adoring eyes.

"Well, please sit while I get the wedding portfolio."

The two snuggled on the loveseat reviewing Jazzlene's incredible artistry.

"I'll be at my desk if you have any questions." Candice let them cuddle and dream about their special day.

The door opened again. It was her two o'clock appointment. "Hello, you must be the Simmons." Candice assumed, standing up to greet them. She grabbed their proofs and sat them at a large table so they could spread them out.

"Excuse me?" The girl on the loveseat spoke up, waving to get Candice's attention.

Candice bounced between both couples, trying to answer all their questions and ensuring they made the right decisions. She was enjoying the busy afternoon. It made her feel great to be helping Jazzlene, and it also kept her mind off Shane. Once she had satisfied both couples, she could finally sit down at her desk and add the young couple's name to Jazzlene's calendar. They wanted an engagement announcement photo that they could put in the newspaper. That would be a quick session for Jazzlene. She would be able to do it in the studio.

Looking at her computer screen, she saw another email from Shane.

Subject: Lunch

Thank you for a wonderful afternoon. See you Friday.

Shane

RE: Lunch

Yes, it really was a beautiful day to sit outside and enjoy the afternoon with you. Friday seems a long way off. I'll just keep myself busy at work.

Candice

Jazzlene walked through the door, exuding excitement. "I got a huge account to do a photo shoot of the city for a travel magazine. They said they may want to use me for some other locations."

"How exciting."

"The best part is, I'll be getting paid to travel, and I may need you to come along."

"Oh? Can we talk about that when you have more details? I'm not sure if I want to go traipsing off right now."

"Okay, but it would be fun."

"Everything is fun with you." Candice smiled. "We'll cross that bridge later. Okay?"

"Sure. Let's have that drink so you can fill me in on this Shane character."

Candice stepped into her apartment and quickly made her way into the kitchen. She grabbed a recipe for Grandma Pela's Amazing Creamy Truffles on her fridge. Before she knew it, she pulled out bowls and measuring cups from her cabinets.

A therapeutic sense of calm came over her when she made one of Grandma Pela's recipes. She stirred and warmed the chocolate, precisely following the recipe. Then, rolling each truffle into bite-size balls, she popped one warm treat into her mouth before she arranged them on a serving plate. She enjoyed the second truffle, allowing it to melt slowly, savoring the rich chocolate. *God, these are heavenly.* She covered them after snatching up one last truffle.

Seven

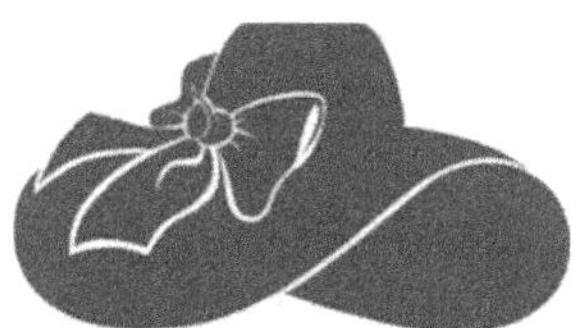

Candice's face was the last image in Shane's mind as he drifted off to sleep and the first thing he fantasized about before opening his eyes in the morning. It would be a long day if she kept consuming his mind.

Shane grabbed his cell phone from his pocket for the third time that morning and scrolled through his contact list until he found her number. He stood there looking at the screen, staring at the picture of Candice by the grapevines. All he wanted was to hear her voice and get his day off to a good start. After gazing at her picture for a few more seconds, he put his cell phone back in his pocket. His obsession with her scared him, but he could not help himself. He felt deep in his core; there was something extraordinary about Candice.

He took one last bite of his toast before heading out the front door to work.

"Sorry I'm late," Candice called as she walked in the door, scanning the office for Jazzlene. She walked into the storeroom and found Jazzlene stacking some boxes. "You have to try one of these." Candice removed the lid of the container housing the truffles.

Jazzlene reached inside, never able to resist chocolate in any form. "Wow, those just melt in your mouth, and oh...wow, that was an unexpected kick. What's in them?" she asked, licking her fingers.

"A pinch of cayenne pepper." Candice popped a truffle into her mouth, enjoying the smooth, creamy texture.

"May I?" Jazzlene reached for another truffle. "Is this another one of Grandma Pela's recipes?"

"Yes. They're amazing, right?"

"I can honestly say I don't think I've ever had a better truffle." Jazzlene stacked another box as she chewed.

"Well, I'll put them in the break area. They'll certainly give you the boost of energy you need." Candice headed out of the storeroom just as the phone began to ring. "Jazz Photography, how may I help you?"

"Hi, you busy?" Candice heard a familiar voice, and it sent her heart fluttering.

"Not yet. I just walked in a few minutes ago."

"I won't keep you, but I was wondering if I could stop by your place this evening and pick up the credenza?"

"Why?"

"Well, I figure we can work on it at the shop. That will give us more space than your balcony, and we won't have to keep bringing it in at night. Plus, I have all the tools and solutions at the shop."

"Oh sure, I'll be home around six. Will that work?"

"Perfect, I'll see you around six then. Have a great day." Shane's cheery voice put a smile on her face.

"You, too. See ya tonight." Candice hung the phone up and continued to smile as Jazzlene came out of the stockroom.

"Well, I bet I can guess who that was by your huge grin."

"Is it that obvious?"

"Oh, you know you can't hide anything from me. And it seems he can't stop thinking about you either."

"He just wants to pick up the credenza tonight so we can work on it at his shop."

"Really? Are you sure it isn't an excuse just to see you again?" Jazzlene questioned.

Before Candice could answer, the phone rang again. "Jazz Photography. How may I help you?" She turned on her computer. Her day had officially begun.

It was finally five o'clock and time for Candice to lock up the studio and head home. She stood outside the darkroom. "Hey Jazz, I'm leaving. I'm gonna lock up on my way out."

"Okay, see ya tomorrow," Jazz responded loudly.

Candice stopped by the grocery store on her way home. She still needed a few ingredients to make the next Grandma Pela treat. This time she chose to tackle peanut brittle. She arrived home by five-fifty. *That's cutting it close*, she thought, knowing how punctual Shane was. She had just finished emptying the grocery bags when her buzzer sounded.

"Come on up." She released the lock and went to open her front door.

Shane and Josh exited the elevator and walked quickly down the corridor. Shane felt an intense longing to see Candice as he excitedly approached the condo. He noticed she left the door ajar but knocked anyway.

"Come in." Candice was at the refrigerator when she turned to greet the men. She was trying to act nonchalant, but her insides were doing somersaults. "Can I get either of you a drink, beer, water, juice?" She held up her glass.

"No, but thanks," Shane answered. Josh just shook his head.

"Hey, try these," Candice offered, holding a cute floral plate with the remaining truffles.

Shane took one, and Candice turned to Josh, offering him one.

"Did you make these?" Shane's eyes grew wide. Candice knew the cayenne pepper had just made its presence known. "Oh, now that was interesting."

"Yes, it's another one of Grandma Pela's recipes."

Josh finally uttered his first word since arriving. "Wow." One word said it all.

Candice smiled. "Tonight, I'm making peanut brittle. I had to buy a candy thermometer and some ingredients. We'll see how it turns out."

"I predict it will be as good as the other sweets you've been making."

"I can't argue with that. They've all been so sinfully pleasing. I'll let you try the brittle tomorrow. You can stop by Jazz's if you're in the neighborhood and try a piece while it's fresh," Candice suggested, giving him a reason to stop by.

"I think I have a job in your neck of the woods tomorrow." Although that was a little white lie, he would make the trip regardless.

"Great. Then I'll see ya tomorrow. And if the brittle is a flop, maybe we can just grab lunch."

"Sounds good. Okay, Josh, let's get this credenza loaded so you can officially be off the clock." The men picked up the credenza, and Candice followed them down to the lobby, waving goodbye.

Josh jumped into the truck and turned to Shane. "You got it bad for her, man," he chuckled, shaking his head.

Shane just smiled.

Alone once more, Candice got out all the utensils and ingredients and started on the peanut brittle. It was much easier than she expected, and once it reached the optimal temperature, she turned the flame off. Then, carefully, she poured the molten sugar onto a cookie sheet to cool.

She put on her pajamas and crawled into bed, hoping to read a chapter of her new book. That did not happen. After reading a few pages, she dozed off, the book resting gently on her down comforter.

Candice arrived at the studio bright and early. She had a lot of updating required on Jazzlene's website and wanted at least an hour to work on it before the studio opened. New photos needed to be uploaded, and outdated content had to be removed. She also wanted to make it a little more user-friendly. She noticed many links did not work, so those would need correcting. She turned on the computer and proceeded to the break room, placing the peanut brittle on the counter. *Another Grandma Pela's winner,* she thought before breaking off a chunk, unable to resist the temptation.

She made some headway on the website when Jazzlene came through the front door. "Morning. How did your visit with Shane go last night?"

"He just picked up the credenza and left. But even those few minutes made my night."

"I bet they did."

"And he's stopping by to try the peanut brittle I made last night. Go try a piece. It's in the break room."

"I must admit, I'm not going to be able to let you look for another job if you keep spoiling me with these treats every morning."

"Well, good, because I need this job to help finance my new cooking hobby."

"And we're going to have to consider lunchtime walks so we can keep enjoying them."

The phone rang, and both women started their workday.

Friday had arrived. Candice was primping for her date with Shane. Like clockwork, he arrived right on time. Six thirty, and her buzzer chimed.

"Come on up," she told him, releasing the door lock. Taking one last glance in the mirror and a little fluff to her hair, she felt ready for her date. Her legs were shaved, lotion smoothed over the curves of her body, sexy bra, and matching panties. Yeah, she was ready. She smiled at herself before leaving the bathroom.

Candice waited for Shane to knock on the door, trying in vain to remain calm. Her insides warmed, anticipating what the night might have in store. This was an *official* dinner date, followed by a movie. She remembered what could happen in a dark theater.

Shane approached Candice's door, reaching for his breath spray and giving a little squirt. *You can never be too careful,* he thought, putting the freshener back into his pocket. He gave a hardy knock and stood back, waiting for a beautiful woman to open the door. He was not disappointed. Candice wore a skintight sweater and jeans that accentuated every curve of her body and left very little to his imagination. Her blond hair was loose and flowing down her back. Shane loved how her hair had a carefree look.

"You look beautiful," he complimented, drawing in her essence.

"You said casual, so I figured this would be okay," she said, grabbing her purse.

Shane reached for her hand as they walked to the elevator. He recalled the first time he held her hand in Napa and how it had sent sparks of lust to his loins, just as it did now.

"Oh, you brought the Camaro," Candice said excitedly.

"I wasn't sure what you would be wearing, and getting in the truck in a dress would be a challenge."

Shane started the engine, and the car hummed to life. "So, did you check what was playing at the theater?" he asked, pulling away from the curb.

"Several movies look good. We can pick one when we get to the theater."

"Sounds like a plan," Shane replied, turning into a parking space near the restaurant. "How lucky is that? A spot right in front on a Friday night." Even Shane could not believe his luck. He hopped out of the car and quickly went to the passenger side, where he opened the door for Candice. Shane put his hand out for Candice. She really was starting to get used to this courteousness.

"Thank you." Candice smiled.

They walked to the restaurant, where Shane once again held the door for Candice and for the patrons exiting the restaurant.

"Candice?" a deep male voice called out from the bar.

Candice spun around, "Steve!" She walked over and gave him a hug. "How have you been?"

"I'm great. Just moved back to the city about a month ago. And you? How's life been treating you?"

Shane approached and took Candice's hand. She turned quickly, making eye contact with him. "Shane, this is Steve. Steve, Shane." After the awkward introduction, Candice could tell Shane was sizing up the other man.

Steve reached forward to shake Shane's hand.

"So, where are you working?" Steve asked, not seeming concerned by the fact Candice was on a date.

"Right now, I'm helping Jazz. You should stop by." She grabbed a business card from her purse and handed it to Steve. "She has her own studio now."

Steve examined the card and then placed it in his wallet. "Maybe I will." He smiled his sheepish grin that Candice knew so well.

"I'd be happy to clear her calendar Monday if you can make it at around noon," Candice offered, making a mental note of what she would have to shuffle around to make this meeting happen.

"Sure. I can take my lunch at noon."

"Great. This is going to be such a wonderful surprise for her." Candice noted, aware that she was putting her matchmaking skills to work.

"Shane, party of two," the hostess called.

"That's us. I'll see you Monday, and we'll catch up," Candice said, releasing Shane's hand and giving Steve another hug. She stood back briefly, looking at him with a smile.

The hostess led them to a private corner and placed the menus before them. "Your waiter will be Tim. Enjoy your meal." With a grin, she turned and walked back to the front of the restaurant, seeming to put an extra sway in her hips.

"Wow, I haven't seen Steve since high school. That was a pleasant surprise."

Shane wanted to ask questions but did not want to appear jealous or insecure, even though his pride had taken a hit. Candice was evidently fond of Steve by the warmth in her eyes.

"I can't believe how different he looks. The long ponytail he sported in school is completely hacked off. He was tall and skinny as a teenager, but I can't say that anymore. Jazz is going to be so shocked when she sees him."

"So, you all went to high school together?" Shane tried to sound indifferent.

"Yeah, we hung around in the same crowd. Steve had the biggest crush on Jazz, but she was dating one of the football players. She was so into jocks back then. Poor Steve didn't stand a chance, not for lack of trying. I can't wait to see her face when he walks into her studio on Monday."

The waiter arrived to take their drink order. "Can I get you something to drink?'

"I think we'll have the house wine," Shane responded, looking at Candice for her approval. She nodded her silent agreement.

The wine could not have arrived soon enough. Shane took a big swig, trying to settle his nerves. *Okay, not a threat,* he assured himself.

Candice glowed when she smiled at Shane. She knew exactly how uncomfortable he was meeting someone from her past, especially not knowing their history.

"Did you notice how Steve's eyes lit up when I mentioned Jazz?" She was hoping that statement would put Shane at ease.

"Yeah, he did seem happy when you handed him the business card."

Tim arrived. "Ready to order?"

Shane looked at Candice. "Know what you want?"

"Yes. I'll have the minestrone soup with the cheese bread," Candice replied.

"And for you, sir?" Tim turned his attention to Shane.

"I'll have the minestrone soup to start and then the parmesan chicken with rice."

"Anything else I can get you? Appetizer or water, perhaps?"

"No, I think we're good," Shane responded.

Tim left after refilling their wine glasses.

"You're not eating much," Shane commented.

"Well, I want to save room for dessert and, of course, popcorn." She smiled.

"I'll give you a bite of my chicken. It's the best I've ever had. You'll wish you ordered it."

"Guess that means we'll have to come back so I can." Candice's heart quivered at the thought of another date with Shane.

After their meal, Shane and Candice shared a piece of Tiramisu. "My god, this is so creamy." Candice moaned, letting the flavors mingle in her mouth before taking another bite. "I think I saw a Tiramisu recipe in that stack of Grandma Pela's recipes."

"I guess you should think about making some of those recipes and going to a farmer's market to give samples. Then, see what others say because you might be onto something great."

"I have thought about doing something with them. I'm unsure what, but I like the idea of the farmer's market. I've learned a lot from my experience in planning functions and working with the caterers. You know, a few weeks back I saw the cutest place where I could open a little café. It was a perfect location and was previously a tea room."

"That would be great." Shane was all about pursuing a dream. He had done that with the reclamation business. He loved saving the beautiful wood from being taken to a landfill. It was just such a waste of precious resources.

"It would be cute. I can see it now. I'd get great pieces of furniture and old dishes. I could have all the furniture for sale. You know, so I'm constantly rotating and revamping. And then, every time someone comes in, it's a little different. And I bet Jazz would let me put up some of her photography to sell."

"Seems like you've been considering this before I mentioned it."

"My mind has been swirling with all kinds of business ideas. I love Jazz, but I have to pursue something more stable. I could get a job at a hotel in hospitality, but I'd really rather work for myself. Jazz is so much happier now that she opened her own studio."

Tim showed up with the bill. "Is there anything else I can get you?"

"I think we're done." Shane took the last bite of the Tiramisu.

"You two have a nice evening," Tim said, moving on to the next table.

"So, shall we go catch that movie?" Shane stood and walked over to pull Candice's chair out.

The theater was within walking distance of the restaurant. "It's a beautiful night. Let's just walk to the theater." Shane put his arm around Candice's shoulder as they strolled, pulling her closer to him.

Stepping inside the cinema, they went to the ticket counter, where they reviewed the list of movies and times. "Well, looks like we can either see that horror movie or a risqué comedy." Shane was not sure either was appropriate for a first date.

"I'd say the comedy unless you want me to jump into your lap and bury my face in your chest."

"The horror movie it is," Shane laughed. He could think of nothing better than having Candice crawl onto his lap.

"Candice!" a voice called.

Candice turned to see the familiar face of Mrs. Gallager and her daughter Alexa.

"I thought that was you," she said, quickly approaching.

"Hi," Candice responded, returning the hug Mrs. Gallager tightened around her.

"How have you been, dear?" she asked, eyeing Shane.

"I've been great." Candice stepped back slightly.

Shane turned away from Mrs. Gallager to address Candice softly. "I'll go buy the tickets."

"Oh, okay." She was not happy when he left her alone with Mrs. Gallager.

"I can't wait to tell Brent who I ran into. The men are having their Friday night poker game. So, Alexa and I are having girl time." It seemed that Mrs. Gallager wanted to see if the mere mention of Brent would change the expression on Candice's face.

"Oh, yes, I forgot about Friday night poker," Candice said.

Shane returned with the tickets, so Candice grabbed the opportunity to withdraw from the uncomfortable conversation. "Well, we should get going so we can find a seat. Nice seeing you." Candice gave hugs to both women and grabbed Shane's hand for security. Or maybe just to let Mrs. Gallager know she had moved on.

"You sure are popular tonight," Shane stated, squeezing her hand.

"Well, that's the last person I wanted to see. That was Brent, my ex's mother and sister. Talk about awkward."

"If I'd known that, I would have planted a kiss on you that would tell them in no uncertain terms you moved on."

Candice secretly wished he had. "So, which movie are we seeing?"

"I went for the comedy, although I almost bought tickets to the horror movie. It was a very enticing idea, you sitting on my lap." Shane opened the door to the dimly lit theater and spotted two seats way up at the top. They had to climb over several pairs of legs but managed to get recliners centered on the screen.

The air conditioner blew above their heads, so Candice put her hands between her thighs to keep them warm. Shane noticed and lifted the armrest between the chairs.

"Come here," he whispered in her ear. She scooted as close as she could get, and he covered her with his jacket, then pulled her into him, warming her with his body heat.

She felt so secure in his arms and rested her head on his shoulder. Shane smelled her gardenia-scented hair and started running his fingers through it. Every ounce of Candice's willpower was being tested because all she wanted to do was grab and kiss him.

This was the first date she had been on in over a year because, quite honestly, no one had really sparked her interest. Or maybe it was because she had not gotten over the pain Brent had caused her. With Shane, she felt relaxed and comfortable. She rested her hand on his thigh, feeling him twitch when she squeezed slightly. His muscles tightened, and she knew she was having an arousing effect on him. Knowing she was not the only one feeling a strong attraction felt nice.

The house lights went dark as the movie began. Candice snuggled a little closer to Shane and comfortably settled against him. Having her body touching his did more than just warm him. It stirred deep feelings that had been buried since his wife left him.

"Well, that was much funnier than I expected," Candice commented as they left the theater.

"It was pretty damn funny. I don't think I've laughed like that in, well, I can't even remember."

The two of them headed to the car at a leisurely pace. Shane did not want the evening to end. He had such a great time he decided to take the long route to Candice's home and tried to hit every red light he could.

"Shane, turn here and park in the garage. Punch this code: nine, five, six, two." He did, and the gate slowly slid aside, allowing him access to the underground garage. "That's mine." Candice directed, pointing to an empty spot. "Come on up. I'll make us a drink." Candice did not care if she was presumptuous, but there was no way she was letting him go home yet. The night was still young.

"Never thought you'd ask." Shane winked at her, followed by a boyish grin.

Candice kicked off her shoes by the front door, and Shane did the same. She walked over to her CD collection and pulled out some mood music. She placed it in the player and set it to a low volume. "Okay, so I'm having chamomile tea. I'm still trying to warm up from that icebox of a movie theater. What would you like? I can make you bourbon and coke or something else."

"I'll have tea. Who is this we're listening to? I like it."

"Sam Salter," she responded, grabbing the teapot. She turned to the sink and began filling the pot with water. Shane came up behind her, encircling her in a hug.

"I'm pretty sure I can warm you up, too."

She set the teapot down on the counter before turning around. "I bet you can." She draped her arms around his neck and looked up into his eyes. There was something mischievous behind his chocolate eyes.

He lifted her up and sat her on the counter. Now they were eye to eye. The intensity of his stare sent a rush of excitement through her body. If she were still standing, her legs would have buckled underneath her.

Shane moved forward, pushing her legs apart as he stepped between them. Candice did what felt natural and wrapped her legs around his waist, pulling him closer. He had longed to kiss her since the day they met. Slowly, he inched his lips towards hers, nuzzling her nose and stalling until she could wait no longer. Then, forcefully, she grabbed and pulled him to her lips, kissing him as if she were famished. She pulled away momentarily to catch her breath and licked her lips. The taste of him lingering there. Everything told her to slow down, but she wanted to consume him. Feel his tongue sliding across hers. Shane plunged his tongue into her mouth, and she returned the kiss with the same intensity.

Candice ran her fingers through his dark hair, feeling the soft silky texture. He let out a guttural moan when she ran her tongue down his neck. She had hit his sweet spot, which made her even more aroused. Shane grabbed her head with both hands to look at her face.

Candice smiled. "You taste so good," she said, leaning into him again and melting their lips together.

Shane lifted her off the counter with her legs still trapping his waist and carried her down the hallway.

"Turn left," she purred softly into his ear.

Once he reached the bed, Shane gently laid her down, and she finally released her legs. He gave her a questioning look as he reached for her top. Candice arched slightly up to him as he pulled the shirt over her head and tossed it onto the nightstand. Her delicate lace bra emphasized the curves of her breasts.

"Your turn," she said, grasping at his shirt and swiftly removing it. Her eyes rested on his chest, admiring the beautiful tattoo above his heart. She traced the tattoo with her fingers, running lightly over the letters that spelled *Mom*. "This is beautiful." She understood Mom tattoos usually held significant memories. He lifted her hand and kissed the fingertips that had caressed his tattoo. Then he reached for her other hand and held her arms above her head as he straddled her. He examined her with awestruck wonder.

"My god, you're gorgeous." He leaned forward and gently kissed her lips. Then, Shane stood up, pulling her up with him in one swift move. Shane found the zipper on her pants and did not hesitate to pull it down. Candice quickly shimmied out of them, revealing the lace panties that matched her bra. The beauty of her porcelain skin wrapped in lace and adorned with a sparkling belly button ring drove Shane wild.

He felt his heart speed up as Candice grabbed his waistband. She unbuttoned his pants and then unzipped them. Sliding her hands inside his jeans, she eased them down his legs, ensuring his boxers were not left behind.

Shane was not used to this take-charge type of woman and enjoyed letting her have her way with him. It was the first time he had ever been with a woman who knew exactly what she wanted and was unafraid to go for it.

"Are you sure this is what you want?" Candice answered Shane's question with a smile. His next question was something they should have discussed earlier. Shane did not think the evening would go in this direction so quickly. He had fantasized about it but thought it was better to take things slow. Seemed as if slow was not an option anymore. "Birth control? I didn't bring anything."

Candice swallowed, allowing herself to contemplate her answer. "No need to worry. I'm on the pill. I was tested after I found Brent cheating. I'm clean. I haven't been with anyone since." The mood shifted as she made eye contact with Shane. She could see his face darken at the mention of Brent. She pointed to her nightstand. "There are condoms in there, but I can't tell you how old they are."

"Well, that makes two of us. I'm clean, too." He opened the nightstand drawer and grabbed a foil packet anyway. Shane held it in his hand and then reconsidered. He needed to feel Candice without a barrier between their bodies. Candice removed the foil packet from his hand.

"I'm good without this if you are," she said, holding it up.

"We don't need it," Shane responded, and Candice tossed it back in the drawer.

Shane embraced her and then quickly unhooked her bra. He slid the straps down her arms, allowing his fingers to skim across her skin. He could barely slow himself, desire building to the exploding point. He wanted to taste every inch of her body with his tongue, so he started with her neck, working his way to her lips. He lingered there before moving his tongue to her breasts and gently circling her right nipple, making her body tremble. She grabbed his head and held it in place, not allowing him to move on until she could no longer take his tongue's caress.

Candice knelt in front of Shane, running her hands up his thighs. She looked up at him before closing her eyes.

"Well, what do we have here?" a sarcastic voice came from the doorway.

Candice's eyes flew open as Shane lunged at the intruder. He was so swift that the man was pinned against the wall before Candice could get off her knees.

"What the fuck are you doing, Brent?" Candice spat in his face.

"Mom said you were getting cozy with some guy. I had to see who you were fu—" Candice slapped him hard before he could finish.

"Give me the key and get the hell out of here before I call the police," Candice ordered.

Shane released him, but not before reemphasizing her command. "She told you to leave. Do I need to escort you to the door?"

Brent tossed the keys on the bed and stared at Candice. "Honey, let's talk about this."

"Brent, leave," Candice stood there stark naked as he stared at her. "Take a good look because this is the last time you'll see me naked."

Brent watched her walk to get her robe. "Hell, Candice, so I made a mistake. We can make this work."

"Are you delusional? God, you don't get it. I'm done with you. The only thing I feel for you now is...well, nothing." It hurt to say the words, but they were valid. She had purged Brent out of her system long before she met Shane.

Candice tossed Shane his jeans, but he did not put them on. Brent stood there, not budging. "Well, we'll see. I don't believe you, Candice. I'm not done with you. I'm not letting anyone else have you."

Candice reached for the phone. "I'm not going to say it again. Leave, or I'll call 911."

Shane grabbed Brent again, twisting his arm behind his back before helping him find the front door. "The lady said leave." Shane threw him into the hall.

"I'm so sorry," Candice apologized as she sat on the couch. "He must have made a spare copy of my keys. I took them back when we broke up."

"I'll change your locks tomorrow," Shane advised, sitting beside her and pulling her into his arms.

"Yeah, that's a good idea. Who knows if he has another key? He's such an ass when he drinks."

"Has he ever hurt you?" Shane was trying to assess if he should take Brent's threat seriously or if it was fueled primarily by alcohol.

"No, he's never laid a hand on me. But he beat the crap out of a guy at a bar once for asking me to dance."

Shane did not want to judge Candice. He made his own mistakes, but he had to ask. "Why did you stay with him?"

"Who knows? Love, I guess. I'm not sure what I saw in him. Maybe security." Shane understood how love made you do things that go against who you are. He had agreed not to have children with the woman he was in love with, and then she left.

"Let me make you that tea," Shane offered, standing up.

"No, that's okay. Maybe you should leave. I'll see you tomorrow." Candice just wanted to curl up into a ball and cry.

"I won't be able to sleep. I'll worry that he might come back. I can sleep on the couch if you like." Their intimate moment had passed for the night. That much he knew.

Candice looked at Shane, who was still shaking with anger. "Okay." She walked to the front door and turned the deadbolt. "I don't think he has the deadbolt key. I don't remember ever giving it to him."

Shane stood up, still naked as a jaybird, and walked into the bedroom. He picked his boxers up off the floor and put them on. Candice followed him into the room. "You don't have to sleep on the couch, though. That's just silly," she said, pulling the bedding down. She untied her robe and crawled into bed. "Come keep me warm. I need your arms around me. Oh, and take those boxers off. I like what's underneath them."

The last thing Candice would allow is for Brent to ruin her evening with Shane.

Shane slid in next to Candice and engulfed her with his body. She could feel him hard against her. "Shall we finish what we started?" she asked, climbing on top of him. Brent was not going to control her any longer.

"Yes," he responded, taking control and flipping her over. She let out a soft moan. Skin touching skin, two bodies became one with pure rapture.

Eight

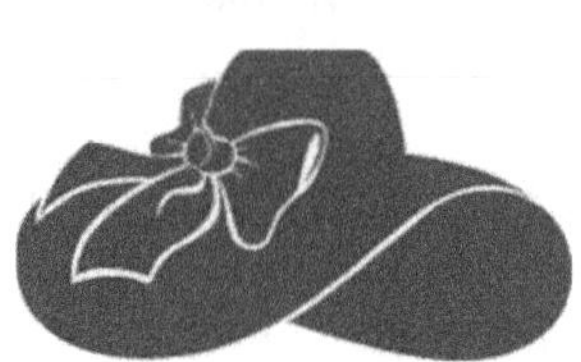

Candice woke up and could feel Shane's arms still holding her tightly. When he promised to protect her, he was not kidding. She rolled over slowly to face him and watch him as he slept.

"Morning, beautiful." He smiled.

"Morning. Did you sleep okay?" Candice realized her full-sized bed was small for a man over six feet tall.

"Yes, it was quite cozy." He kissed her forehead. If the truth is known, he did not sleep much at all. He had his senses on alert, listening for any further intrusion by Brent.

"I'll go make us some eggs." Candice was starving from the night of uninhibited lovemaking.

"If you have cereal, I'll have that."

"Sure, but making eggs will be no problem," Candice said, leaving the bedroom. Shane pulled on his boxers and followed her into the kitchen.

"May I?" He spotted a plate covered in saran wrap.

"Oh, I forgot about those. I made them a few days ago. Another creation from those recipes your grandmother gave me."

Shane took a bite and then looked at Candice. "These are really good, even if they are a day or two old."

"Amazing, right? I had to order one of the ingredients online. None of the stores carried açai berries, just the juice." She grabbed a cookie. "I'd never even heard of them until I went to make the cookies. The recipe said cranberries could be substituted, but I wanted to stick to the authentic ingredients."

"I think you are on to something with your idea for opening a little sweets café."

Candice reached for a cookie and took a nibble. "Well, it's a scary thought. What if it doesn't work? I will have to sell this condo to afford the place I think is perfect. And, well, I could lose everything. It's just so risky."

"Tell you what. Maybe I can go with you and check out the location you saw and give you my opinion. Then, I can check what you need to get a license and permit. I have some friends that are in the construction business, too. If it needs some updating, I can call them for estimates."

"Okay. I'll call the realtor and maybe set up something next week."

Candice pulled the cereal down. "You sure you want this for breakfast?"

"Yes, that will tide me over." Shane reached for a bowl. "Are you having some?"

"Sure." Although, what Candice really wanted was more Shane. Cereal would have to do.

Candice placed the empty bowls in the dishwasher. "I'm gonna take a quick shower." She turned around and made eye contact with Shane, lifting an eyebrow. "Care to join me?"

With the look of a kid granted permission to eat dessert before dinner, he stripped as he followed her to the bathroom.

He lathered his hands and soaped every inch of her body, massaging her tight neck muscles. The way she moved her head back and forth, he knew she was enjoying his hands working her sore muscles.

Candice took the shampoo from the shelf and poured a little onto her hands. "Kneel down," she boldly instructed. She did not have to ask twice. He quickly knelt, facing her belly button ring. Shane tried to control his breathing, but his deep exhales caressed her skin, sending a spike of arousal through her body. She leisurely worked the shampoo into a lather as she gently massaged his scalp.

"That feels wonderful," he said, reaching between her legs.

"Just returning the favor," she replied breathlessly as he ignited her desire, sending her over the edge.

After a final rinse, Shane stepped out of the shower and grabbed the closest towel he could find. Then, he turned and started to dry Candice before drying himself.

"I was thinking earlier. Maybe we can swing by my grandmother's and let her taste those cookies. I'm sure she'll gladly let people sample them at the store if she likes them. Get some feedback and create a buzz before the café opens."

"Oh, good marketing plan. But really, Shane, this is no more than a dream."

"You never know. It's always good to keep your options open. I never thought I'd own a green business, either. But I do, and I love it. You have to follow your passion and do what you enjoy."

"Well, I guess I'm just scared. I do need to eat. I shouldn't pour every penny

I've saved into a dream."

"We'll come up with a business plan. Then you'll know exactly what is needed to get it off the ground," Shane sounded so confident.

"You sound like you've got this all worked out."

"I just know what it took me to get my business started. What I had to implement to ensure it would be a success. And, of course, you have Jazzlene, who can also share her expertise. I'm sure she was scared, too."

Shane carried the plate of cookies while Candice locked up the condo.

Pulling up in front of a beautiful Edwardian house, Candice was speechless.

"My grandmother's home," Shane said nonchalantly.

"Wow, it's so gorgeous. So you grew up playing in this house?"

"Yeah, and let me tell you, it was fun. There were so many great hiding places. When my cousins would come for a visit, we would play hide and seek for hours. Mainly because it took that long to find everyone." Shane got out of the car and walked around to open the door for Candice. She looked toward the front door and saw Shane's grandmother stepping onto the porch.

"Good morning," Beatrice called out, waving.

Shane rested his hand on Candice's lower back, guiding her to the house. "Candice, this is my grandmother, Beatrice. Grandma, you remember Candice?"

"Yes, of course." She reached for Candice's hands to give them a squeeze. "How are you doing, dear?"

"Great, thank you. And I must tell you, those recipes in the credenza were fantastic. I brought some cookies for you to try." Candice held up the plate of cookies.

"They look lovely. Let me make tea to have with them."

"That would be nice," Candice happily replied, following Shane's grandmother inside. "Your home is beautiful."

"It's a little too big for just me, but it was perfect when the kids were little."

"I love how you decorated it." Candice looked around, noticing the beautiful wallpaper that appeared original to the house. The draperies were dark crimson velvet, with fabric pooled on the floor. The wing-back chairs still looked pristine, with very little wear. It was clear that the living room was too formal for everyday use.

"Most of the furniture has been handed down through the family. Many pieces Shane found, and I simply could not bring myself to sell them. I appreciate the intricate detailing and the love that went into each piece in my home. My husband refurbished many of them back to their original state. So many people paint over beautiful wood, such a shame." Beatrice shook her head.

"I can understand why you'd want them restored. I'm excited to strip the paint and see the wood grain underneath my credenza," Candice said enthusiastically.

"It should turn out beautifully."

Shane interrupted, "Why don't you two have a seat, and I'll go make the tea."

"That would be nice." Shane's grandmother sat and patted the couch, encouraging Candice to join her. Candice sat, imagining that it was reserved for dignitaries back in the day.

"I'll be right back," he said, leaning over and kissing his grandmother's cheek.

Shane disappeared into the kitchen. "I don't know what I would do without that boy," she declared proudly after watching him leave the room.

"I'm pretty fond of him, too. He's such a gentleman." Candice smiled, knowing his grandmother had a lot to do with his manners, especially how he treated women. Although what he did last night, he had definitely learned on his own.

"He was a sweet little boy, and now he's such a caring man."

Candice could hear Shane's footsteps approach on the hardwood floor. "Should be ready in a minute. Grandma, where did you put the tea service?"

"Look in the pantry, on the top shelf. I think it's stored in there."

Shane gave Candice a smile before turning and heading back into the kitchen.

"So, what do you two have planned for today?"

"We're heading over to his shop to work on the credenza. Shane's going to teach me how to strip off the paint and restore it."

"I don't doubt it will be gorgeous when you're done. Shane does know a thing or two about refinishing fine pieces of furniture. His grandfather taught him everything he knows about the process of restoring an antique piece without removing any of the aged character."

Shane walked into the parlor with a tray carrying the tea service. He set it down and began to pour his grandmother a cup. "Thank you, dear," she said as she reached for it.

Candice uncovered the cookies and held out the plate, offering a cookie to Beatrice. "Okay, give me your honest opinion," Candice requested, watching for any telltale signs of enjoyment.

Shane's grandmother took a delicate bite and seemed to be concentrating intently on the sweetness in her mouth. Finally, a smile broke out on her face. "Well, this may be the best cookie I've ever tasted."

Candice sat quietly while waiting for her to take another bite.

"So, grandma, could you place them on the counter in your store and get some customer feedback?"

"I can and I will. I would love to take them to my church and let the members try them after Sunday mass."

Shane turned to Candice. "I told you she would love them. I really think you have to do something with those recipes."

"Yes, I agree with Shane. These are too good to keep to yourself." Beatrice took her last bite of the cookie and then a sip of tea.

"Shane thinks I should open a little sweets café."

"Oh? The food business is tough." Beatrice turned, looking toward Shane.

He grabbed a cookie from the plate. "Yes, it is, but I think Candice can't lose with these great recipes. Once word gets out around town, everyone will stop by to try a treat."

"True, but maybe she should start at the Farmer's Market," Beatrice offered her opinion.

"Yes, that was one of our thoughts. It would be a great way to build a customer base before opening a café," Shane responded.

Candice sat silently, listening to the two of them talk business. They outlined what Candice would need to do to start a profitable business. She was mesmerized at how they honed in on the minor details.

"Well, I suppose I can have your uncle look at the business plan you two create. He's had his restaurant for forty years. I'm positive he can give you great advice and insight into the food business."

Candice cleared her throat. Shane and his grandmother both turned to look at her. "Um...I love the enthusiasm, but I really need to think about this. It's just a silly dream."

"Dear, no dream is silly. If we don't follow our dreams, then, in the end, we will always have regrets." Beatrice patted her leg for reassurance.

"She's right," Shane agreed. "If my grandmother hadn't pushed me, I would never have found the courage to open my business. You just need a good team around you, cheering you on and helping you when you are unsure of which direction to go."

"There's nothing better than the pride in knowing you had an idea you followed through on. It is absolutely worth the risk. At eighty-three, I still love going into my antique store every morning. Seeing the faces of my customers when they find exactly what they were looking for. It always delights me to know I filled a void for them."

"Well, I will give it some serious thought," Candice responded, entirely surprised by the overwhelming support and encouragement these two gave her.

"Write down everything that comes to your mind, all your questions, and the ideas you might want to implement," Beatrice instructed. "If you wake up in the middle of the night with an idea, write it down. Just keep jotting down all your thoughts. Some will be great, while others you may decide to toss, but don't overlook anything."

"While you two hash over some ideas, I'm going to run and change." Unbeknownst to his grandma, Shane was in yesterday's clothes and wanted to freshen up.

Beatrice retrieved a pad of paper and a pen. "Let's write some things down."

Candice started jotting down some of their collaborative ideas.

Shane finally returned to the room. "Well, grandma, we need to head to the shop to start working on the credenza. I'll just take the dishes into the kitchen for you. Then we'll be on our way."

"Candice dear, when can I expect the first batch of treats? I would love to get the word out to my customers. Maybe Shane can send out a mass email for me. Unfortunately, I'm not good with the computer."

"You have an email-based customer list?" Candice was surprised.

"Well, yes, thanks to Shane. I know how to send an email out, but he has some fancy program he uses to make it look professional."

"Grandma, you want to send out a mass email?"

"That would be a great way to draw people to the store and get their comments. I have very loyal customers, as you know."

"That you do," Shane responded with a smile.

Candice stood there, stunned by how these two were still planning and working out details. "So, dear." Beatrice turned to Candice. "How does next Saturday sound?"

"That will work. I could make several different treats for sampling."

"What a splendid idea." On the surface, Beatrice seemed to be more excited than Candice was.

"Okay, grandma, we need to get going," Shane leaned over and kissed her cheek.

Beatrice and Candice both stood up and embraced in a warm hug.

"You two have fun today," Beatrice said, waving as they entered the car.

"If your grandmother only knew how much fun we already had today." Candice giggled, resting her hand on Shane's leg.

Shane pulled into the parking lot of his reclamation warehouse. "This is huge." Candice sounded shocked.

"I started in a little warehouse down the street but quickly outgrew it. So if you can't find what you're looking for here, it probably doesn't exist," Shane proudly responded. "Come on, I'll show you around before we start working on the credenza."

As they entered the warehouse, Candice spotted Josh helping a customer. He noticed Candice too and nodded his head in acknowledgment.

"Josh is in charge most weekends," Shane said, nodding back at Josh.

Shane took Candice on a tour of the warehouse. Everything was in neat, organized rows with headings at the top of the aisle to help locate particular items. He did not miss one detail in the layout of the store.

While making their way toward the back of the warehouse, Shane stopped to introduce Candice to several other employees working the floor.

"Everyone looks so young," Candice observed.

"I try to hire people just out of high school. Most of the employees work part-time, so they can still attend college. I can usually work around their school schedule. It's so important for them to get an education."

Passing the office, Shane noticed Stacy examining the computer screen. He leaned his head into the room. "Stacy, this is Candice."

Stacy peeked over the top of the computer screen. "Hi." She stood up and approached Shane. "I need your approval on this estimate." She handed Shane a detailed work estimate.

Stacy was a petite blond with pouty lips and long, dark lashes that she fluttered in Shane's direction. She had to be around twenty, maybe younger. Candice wondered if Shane even noticed her flirtation.

Shane examined the proposal and signed it. He handed it back to her, and Candice noticed she brushed his hand against hers, seemingly trying to get his attention. Shane reached for Candice's hand and gave it a squeeze. He was keenly aware of Stacy's overt flirting, and holding Candice's hand sent a nonverbal message to both women.

Candice smiled at Stacy. "Nice to meet you," she said as Shane led her toward two big doors on the far back wall.

Josh walked by with the customer he was helping. "Josh, I will be in the shop working on the credenza." Shane's trust in Josh was evident in the responsibility he gave him to handle the business.

Josh nodded in response and continued to address the customer.

"How long has Josh worked for you?" Candice asked. As they moved away, she heard Josh explain the different door styles to the customer. He was very competent and confident when he spoke.

"Three years. I hired him right out of high school. He's a quick learner and a very conscientious employee. I can't remember the last time he took a day off."

"You're lucky to find such dedicated people to work for you."

"I have to agree with that. I have some great employees. Josh is by far one of the best. He attends San Francisco State, so he only works on the weekends. And, of course, I call on him to help me with deliveries for my grandmother. So, having him supervise on the weekends gives me more freedom to have a personal life."

"Tell me, what is up with Stacy? I noticed she has a little crush on you." Candice needed to know how he felt.

"Stacy flirts with everyone. She's harmless. I think if you're a male, she will try to charm you. She has a boyfriend, but I don't think the relationship is solid.

I try to stay out of my employee's personal business, but occasionally I can't help but overhear her on the phone."

Candice felt more at ease understanding the situation. It sounded like Stacy had insecurities and was probably looking for positive validation from the men around her. "Sounds like she's just trying to feel good about herself but going about it in the wrong way."

"You're right. She really is a sweet girl and a hard worker. I think if she ever dumps her boyfriend, she'll realize how special she is," Shane said, trying not to be too analytical.

"Yeah, we both understand how a bad relationship can strip you away from yourself." Candice thought about Brent's appearance last night. There was a time when he had so much control over Candice that she would have fallen right back into his arms, thinking that his outlandish behavior was a gesture of love. This past year of growth helped her to understand herself. She knew she was worth much more than he had to offer her. She would settle for nothing less than the best.

Shane could tell Candice was deep in thought. He could not stop thinking about his disappointing relationship with his ex-wife. Did he really want to get that deeply involved with anyone again? The answer was *no,* but he could not stop the runaway train that was his heart.

They walked out the metal door into the back lot. "The shop is over here." He motioned to his right.

Candice could see a gigantic metal structure with one sizeable paneled garage door. Shane unlocked it and rolled it up. She gazed inside, seeing all the furniture. Most were in need of some type of repair. She saw her credenza resting on a big sheet of plastic. Shane had prepared the area so they would be ready to work on the psychedelic piece.

"Let's suit you up." Shane reached for a pair of overalls. "Here." He handed the dark blue jumpsuit to her.

Candice looked at it and laughed. "Don't you think this is a little too big for me?" she asked, stepping into it and zipping up the front. The sleeves covered her hands. The legs were so long they bunched around her ankles. She sat down so she could roll them up.

Shane smiled. "Sorry, that's the only size I have." He knelt to help roll up the pant legs and sleeves for her.

Candice stood up, posing for him as he stepped into another set of overalls that fit him like a glove.

"Okay, this is so not fair. I feel like I'm in a potato sack, and you look like a race car driver."

"Here." Shane handed her a pair of blue latex gloves. Candice held them up to her hand.

"Really?" She put her hand inside one glove and flapped it around until the glove flew off, sailing through the air. "Don't you have any smaller ones?"

Shane caught the glove mid-flight. "Nope. Gotta make these work." He handed her back the glove. Candice went with the program and put them on.

"And the final accessory to your already glamorous outfit." Shane held up a respirator and safety goggles. Candice raised her eyebrows. "You must," he said, "it's for your safety.

"I had no idea what this would entail when I bought the credenza." Candice held her arms straight out like a scarecrow. "Not my best look."

"You look cute. I like a woman that can get down and dirty," Shane said in a muffled voice after putting on his respirator.

Shane reached down and opened a can of paint stripper. "So, the first thing we'll do is brush this onto the credenza." He handed her a paintbrush. "Once we have it covered, we'll have to wait for the chemical to do its job."

Candice spread the chemical in even strokes. She could see the paint bubbling up immediately. "I didn't expect this to work so fast," she commented, spreading more chemicals onto the credenza.

Once the entire credenza was coated in paint stripper, Shane grabbed two chairs and set them outside in the sun. "Now we wait," he said, removing her respirator and then his. "You want something to drink? I have bottled water or coke."

"Sure, water sounds good." Candice felt a little parched.

Shane returned, handing her an ice-cold bottle of water. "So," he sat down and opened his bottle, "I really didn't want to bring this up, but I'm a little concerned."

"About?" Candice gave him her full attention.

"After last night, well—" How would he say this without sounding jealous? "I was wondering. You said Brent never hurt you, but do you think he could? I think what he did was a little scary, for lack of a better word."

"I don't want to believe he'd ever hurt me. He hasn't in the past, but his eyes last night..." she paused, gathering her thoughts. "There was something different in them. I'm just not sure anymore. I told you he beat the crap out of that guy for asking me to dance, but I didn't tell you the guy had to have his face reconstructed by a plastic surgeon."

Shane stared at Candice with intensity and confusion. "And you stayed with him anyway, knowing he could inflict so much damage on someone without good reason?"

"I'm not proud of that fact, but there was a good side to him that helped me block out the cruelty I witnessed. Honestly, in some primitive part of my brain, I thought he was protecting me. I know, it sounds ridiculous when I hear myself say it now." She did not like the way Shane turned away while hearing her confession.

Shane was deep in thought, running scenarios before he looked back into Candice's eyes. "I realize love is blind. I get it." Shane stopped talking and looked down at the ground. He was struggling with what to say next.

Candice reached over and took his hand to help snap him back to her. "Look, what happened last night was unacceptable. I was so embarrassed I put you in the middle of it."

"How did you put me in the middle?"

"Well, I knew that when Mrs. Gallager saw me with you, she'd run home and tell Brent. I expected Brent to call, and I guess I should not have been so forward, inviting you in for a drink. I should have left you out of it."

"I still don't understand how it's your fault. Did you know he still had a key?" Shane remembered her saying Brent must have made a spare copy of the key.

"No. As far as I knew, I took back the only key I ever gave him. Obviously, I was wrong. It's my fault because I should have been smart enough to anticipate what Brent would do and keep you out of this mess."

"How? You didn't do anything wrong. We went out, had a great time, and one thing led to another. I don't believe either of us expected to—hell, I wasn't even prepared. It's not like I just hop in bed with every woman I go out with." He reached over and took her hand. Why had he even opened this can of worms?

"Anyway, I'm concerned for your safety, Shane. I don't want his rage to come out again. Last night I think he was too drunk to do any harm, but I don't trust him.

"You don't need to worry about me. I can handle myself. One thing you don't know about me is I'm a fourth-degree black belt in Taekwondo." Shane rarely shared that fact with anyone, but he wanted to put Candice's mind at ease.

"Ah, so that is why you were so quick in subduing him." Now Candice understood his immediate response to the threat.

"I guess." He smiled, pulling her closer to him. "So, for my piece of mind, can you let me know if he shows up at your place again?'

"Yeah, but I'm pretty sure he got the message."

"I don't think so. You do remember what he said when he left, right?"

"I think it was the alcohol talking," Candice responded.

"You know alcohol can be a truth serum. He meant every word he said last night. I saw it in his eyes. He's not done, and I'm going be there to protect you," Shane proclaimed.

"Thank you, but I'm going to be fine. He won't hurt me, but he may try to get to you." Candice was starting to feel panicky. How would she handle Brent and convince him to stay out of her life for good?

They finished their water and went in to check on the credenza. "It looks like we can remove the first layer of paint." Shane and Candice put their respirators back on.

He handed her a scraper. "So, once you scrape off the paint, put it in this bucket. Then I can dispose of it properly."

The two of them worked in silence. They were both trying to decide how to move forward in this new relationship without allowing their baggage to detour them.

"So, as you can see, we still have layers of paint left. We need to go through the process again." Candice nodded in agreement as they painted on the second coat of stripper.

Taking their chairs once again in the sun, there was an uncomfortable silence. Finally, Shane spoke, "After we remove the next coat of paint, we'll call it a day. I still need to go to the hardware store and buy you some new locks."

"Okay, that sounds good." Candice closed her eyes and inhaled the fresh air.

They finally finished removing that second coat of paint an hour later. "I think we're close. Next time we should have everything removed and can move to the next step." Shane tightly secured the lid to the chemical stripper and cleaned up the tools.

The car ride to the hardware store was short. They were in and out and back on the road in no time. Shane automatically pulled into the underground parking, but someone was in her space.

"Damn it," Candice said, irritated.

"It's okay. I'll park on the street."

"No, that's not why I'm upset. That's Brent's car. Shane, let me handle this and call you later."

Shane noticed Candice was shaking. "I don't think so. We'll go up together." There was no way Shane was letting her go confront Brent alone.

"It's only going to agitate him more. Seriously, I can deal with him. I want to keep you out of this."

"Afraid I can't do that. We're in this together." Shane was seeing red and not from jealousy. His only concern was safeguarding Candice. His intuition said she was in danger, and he always trusted his gut. "Let's get this over with," he said, grabbing the new locks.

After an anxious elevator ride, Candice stopped in the hall and turned to Shane. "I'm so sorry you have to deal with this." She put her key in the door lock and opened her front door.

There was Brent sitting on the couch, watching TV and eating a bowl of ice cream. "Hey, hope you two had fun," he said nonchalantly as he looked at them.

"Brent, what are you doing here? I told you last night we're done. It's over between us. Can't you get that through your head?"

"And I believe I told you that we're not. So no one is going to take what is mine." He took another bite of ice cream.

Shane picked up the remote and turned off the TV. "It's time for you to leave," he stated calmly.

"I believe I should be saying that to you." Brent placed the ice cream bowl on the coffee table and stood up.

"We can do this the easy way or the hard way. Your choice." Shane glared into Brent's eyes.

"Candice, tell this joker to leave," Brent ordered her.

"The only person that needs to leave is you, Brent," Candice firmly said.

"Nah, I don't think so." Brent suddenly raised his fist, but before he could make contact with Shane's face, Shane had him in a headlock.

"Now, you either head for that door, or you're gonna need your mother to come pick you up because you'll be in no shape to walk out of here."

"I think you better listen to him, Brent." Candice was shaking. She suspected Shane could do some damage if he wanted to.

"So, are you going to leave on your own? Or do you want Candice to call your mom?" Shane loosened up his grip on Brent. "Well?"

"Candice, what the hell? Why are you cheating on me?"

"Brent, you need help. I don't need to explain myself to you or anyone else. Now just leave before you get hurt." She turned away and walked to the door, holding it open.

Brent relaxed, and Shane let him go. "Do I need to escort you out, or do you think you can find the door?" Shane growled.

Brent turned and walked past Candice, stopping to give her one last look. His eyes told her he would be back.

"Bye, sweetheart," he said, closing the door behind him.

Candice let out a big sigh and plopped onto her couch. "You realize this isn't over, right?" she told Shane. "I saw it in his eyes. It was the same look he had when he beat that guy to a pulp."

Shane sat down next to Candice and wrapped his arms around her. He leaned over and kissed her forehead. "I'm afraid you're right."

"This is crazy. I've probably spoken to him three, maybe four times in the last year. Now he's like a madman. I don't get it."

"I don't have the answer either, but it's obvious he's not mentally stable right now."

"Maybe I should talk to his mom. I don't want to go the restraining order route, but I may have to. Not that it will do any good, but at least it's better than nothing."

"I agree, they don't help much, but sometimes it's your only option." Shane stood up and grabbed the locks. "Let me get those locks changed. At least then he won't be able to get in."

"Do you mind if I bake some cookies while you change the locks?" Candice asked. Lately, baking was the one thing that gave her peace when she felt stressed.

"That's a great idea." Shane was happy she had a diversion.

A moment later, Candice was clinking around the kitchen, preparing everything she needed.

"So, I want you to stay with me at my grandmother's tonight," Shane said as he removed the doorknob.

"I can't do that. I'll be fine here."

"Why can't you? Knowing that Brent has threatened you, she'll be very upset if I let you stay here."

"Because it would be disrespectful," Candice answered as if he should know that.

"Look, I live in the back part of her house. She doesn't care if I have anyone staying with me."

"Really? You've brought other women there, and she doesn't care?"

"Well, no. I've never brought anyone home. You'd be the first. Believe me, I know my grandmother. She'll be fine with it. I'll call her and explain what happened if that will make you feel better. I know I'll sleep better if you're not alone here."

"Okay. Call her first, and then I'll decide." Candice stirred the cookie batter.

Shane finished replacing the locks and gave them a test run.

"Looks good. I guess we should go make you some spare keys."

"Good idea. I have to give Jazz a set." Candice scooped up some cookie dough and placed it on the cookie sheet. "Do you think your grandmother will want to take these to church tomorrow? I doubled the recipe just in case."

"Yeah, I know she will." Shane took the raw dough off the spoon before Candice had a chance to release it onto the cookie sheet. "That was good." He smacked his lips.

"You know there are raw eggs in the dough, right?"

"Yeah, I've never been sick yet."

Candice braved a bite too. "Oh, that is good. I could leave out the egg, and we could eat raw cookie dough like two little kids."

Shane grabbed a beer from the fridge. Candice looked at him bewildered. "When did you buy those?"

"I didn't. I thought you did." Shane looked puzzled.

"Brent," they both said in unison.

"Well, gotta hand it to him; he has great taste in beer and women." Shane took a long drag on the beer and smiled at Candice.

The cookies were in the oven. The timer was set, so Candice curled up on the couch next to Shane.

"I think the credenza is going to be nice when we're through," Shane said, taking another drink.

"I agree. I'm excited to see how it will look once the stain enhances the wood grain. I think it really is going to look nice on that wall." Candice pointed to where it was initially placed in the condo.

Shane pulled his cell phone out of his pocket and dialed his grandmother.

"Yes, that's exactly what I told her. Okay, hold on." Shane turned to Candice. "She wants to talk to you." Candice's eyes widened. Shane shrugged his shoulders, handing her the phone.

"Well, yes. If you're sure, I won't be a bother or in your way. Okay, thank you so much." Candice ended the call.

"I told you she wouldn't want you staying here alone. Now go pack a bag while I watch the cookies."

Candice entered her bedroom to find a dozen red roses in a vase beside her bed. She stood there frozen for a few seconds. She finally broke her stance and walked to her closet to retrieve her overnight bag. She set it on her bed and opened it. Noticing something in the pocket, she pulled it out. Brent had given her a romantic card when they went away for the weekend. Candice held it and contemplated if she should read it but tossed it into the trash instead. Those words he wrote meant nothing anymore because they were not true. She was not his one and only. She was more like his, one of many.

Shane walked into the bedroom and noticed the flowers but said nothing. "So, I think the cookies are ready. Do you want me to start the next batch?"

"Yeah, can you loosen the ones on the cookie sheet? I'll be out in a minute." Candice turned and went into her bathroom, closing the door.

She stood looking at herself in the mirror, trying to stifle her emotions.

Shane retreated to the kitchen to give her the time she needed. Although he was unsure how to help her emotionally, he was confident in his ability to protect her from physical harm.

Candice came out of her room, bag packed and ready to go. She set it by the front door. Then she walked into the kitchen and picked up a cookie. "Perfect. Thank you." She stood beside Shane, watching him put more dough onto the cookie sheet.

"Looks like you're ready to go?"

"Yeah, just as soon as this last batch of cookies is done, we can head out." She let out a little sigh.

Shane wrapped his arms around her waist, hugged her, and continued to soothe her by rubbing her back. "It's gonna be okay. Tonight, we'll relax and cuddle while watching a movie." He did not know what else to say to reassure her.

"Yeah, I know. I just feel so violated. He just strolls into my home as if he owns the place when in fact, he never lived here. We always had our own apartments. Yet he used my home to hook up. It must have been the adrenaline rush he got off on. The more I think about it, the madder I get. At first, I felt bad for him, but now I'm just so pissed off."

The timer on the oven beeped, alerting Candice to check on the cookies. Ten minutes later, they were driving to his grandmother's house.

"Candice dear, I'm so glad you are staying with us. I want you to know you are welcome to stay as long as you need." Beatrice gave her a reassuring hug.

"Thank you. I hope it will only be for a day or two. Shane's afraid to let me stay there alone."

"As he should be until this situation is resolved. I don't want you to be alone, either. Safety in numbers, as they say."

"Oh, I also made these cookies for you to bring to church tomorrow."

"They smell delicious. I'm sure everyone will love them." Beatrice placed them on the kitchen counter. "I'll see you two later. I'm going to head into my sewing room and work on a quilt."

Shane took Candice's hand to lead her to the back of the house. "Here's the bathroom and my bedroom."

Candice followed Shane into his bedroom. He had an unmade king-size bed with a dark comforter and four large pillows. He pulled the bedding off and tossed it across the room toward the door. Then he opened his closet and walked inside, entirely out of view.

"Fresh sheets," he said, tossing them onto the bed.

Candice unfolded the fitted sheet and started hooking the corners to the mattress as Shane put fresh pillowcases on the pillows. After they finished making the bed, Candice sat down, removing her shoes.

"So today was both fun and terrifying," she finally said.

"I did enjoy most of the day," Shane commented with a hint of regret. He felt remorseful that he could not quickly end her tormenting ex-fiancé behavior.

Shane sat beside her and held her head between his hands while looking into her eyes. He leaned in and tenderly kissed her, laying her on the bed. She curled up next to him and let him wrap himself around her while he stroked her hair and soothed her soul. He knew right then that she needed stability and reassurance that she was safe. And he would make sure she felt every bit of his love, even if that meant spending all night just embracing her.

Nine

The sun danced through the window, beckoning Candice from her sleep. She rolled over to find Shane missing. His side of the bed was already cold. Squinting at the clock, she saw it was already mid-morning. She lay back down with no intention of leaving the comfortable bed.

Fifteen minutes later, barefoot and wearing Shane's t-shirt, Candice stood up and stretched. She found Shane's robe hanging behind the bathroom door, so she removed it and quickly wrapped it around her body, knotting the tie to secure it. It definitely was not as good as his arms holding her, but it would have to do until she found him. Heading down the hallway, she could smell the coffee welcoming the day.

"Good morning, dear," Beatrice said, looking up from the Sunday paper. "I trust you slept well."

"Yes, I did. Thank you." Candice looked around for Shane.

"There's fresh coffee made or orange juice in the refrigerator. Please help yourself to some toast or cereal. Shane left a note saying he had to run over to his warehouse and he would be back soon," Beatrice informed Candice.

"I'll just have coffee. I can't believe how long I slept." Candice found a coffee mug on the counter next to the coffee pot. She sat down at the table across from Beatrice.

Beatrice removed her glasses and regarded Candice with concern. "I'm not one to pry, but if you want to talk, I'm here to listen."

Candice smiled and then diverted her eyes. "What are all those?" She pointed to the neatly stacked colorful coverlets on the table.

"Those are baby quilts." Beatrice stood up and unfolded one small quilt. Then, taking a few steps back, she held it up so Candice could see the intricate block pattern in soft pastel colors.

"That's very pretty. What did you make them for?"

"The quilt guild I belong to donates these tiny quilts to hospitals and various charities. Knowing that a quilt made with love comforts a child makes me happy." Beatrice folded the blanket and then opened another quilt done in shades of blue.

"Truly a work of art," Candice complimented. "Maybe someday you can teach me how to quilt."

"I would love to." Beatrice smiled. "Possibly this evening, we can go through my fabric collection and pick out some material in colors you like."

"Well, I'm planning on going home today. I think everything will be fine. Brent should have calmed down by now."

Beatrice's smile faded. "Well, I understand you want to be in your own home, but I hope you'll stay here until we can take additional steps to keep you safe."

"Shane changed my locks, so Brent won't be able to get in." Candice tried to sound reassuring, but she was not too convincing.

"As I said before, you are welcome here for as long as you need. This house is big enough for an army."

"I can't thank you enough for opening your home to me," Candice stood to refill her coffee cup, "but I think I'll be safe at home."

"Well, if you want to return, my door is always open. Now it's time for me to go get ready for church. Hopefully, I'll see you this evening."

Candice sat at the table contemplating how to handle Brent. The one thing she knew for sure was that he would fail in scaring her out of her own home. She finished her coffee and returned to Shane's room.

Standing alone in Shane's bedroom and seeing his discarded clothes on the floor felt oddly comforting. She picked them up and carried them to the hamper. The bed was a rumpled mess, but that comforted her, knowing that Shane had held her in his strong arms all night. She started to make the bed when she heard a noise outside that made her jump. *I really need to get a grip.* She finished making the bed and headed for the bathroom.

The hot water from the shower cascaded down Candice's back. Leaning her head into the pulsing stream, she inhaled deeply, trying to purge the trepidation trapped in her mind. Not because she feared Brent but because she was concerned for Shane. She was falling fast and hard for him, which had never happened before. The intense feelings were scaring her because she knew that Shane already held her heart, and she gave it willingly, without hesitation. She was alarmingly aware of how emotionally attached she had become.

Candice stepped out of the shower and began drying herself off. She noticed a shower radio on the wall and turned it on. The song playing had a danceable beat, so she started to sway back and forth. It was going to be a good day, she thought, as the lyrics stated. Caught up in her own little karaoke moment, allowing the music to occupy her mind, relaxed her anxiety more than any alcoholic beverage could hope to do.

Candice turned to go to the bedroom and get dressed when a form materialized before her. Her heart jumped, as did her body.

"When did you get home?" Candice asked, wrapping her arms around Shane.

"Long enough to watch my own private show. I must confess...I really enjoyed it."

"Why didn't you wake me before you left?"

"I tried, but you just mumbled and rolled over. So I figured you needed the sleep. And I didn't expect to be gone as long as I was."

"I was surprised when your grandmother told me you went to the shop. Don't you have today off?"

"I do. However, the alarm company called around five this morning, so I had to head out and check the shop. Seems someone tried to jimmy the back door. Obviously, they didn't get far because they tripped the alarm, which scared them off."

"Oh?" Candice did not like what she was thinking. "You don't think it was Brent, do you? I mean, he doesn't know you, so he'd have no idea that was your business." Candice started anxiously biting her thumbnail.

"That thought crossed my mind," Shane responded, leaving out what the surveillance video captured. He didn't want to add to her anxiety.

"Maybe he followed us there yesterday." The notion made Candice shiver.

"I thought of that too, but I watched in my rearview mirror the entire trip. I didn't see any car that looked like the one parked in your spot at the condo."

"Well, I hope you're right, and it wasn't Brent." Candice stepped away from Shane to go grab her clothes.

"Don't get dressed yet." Shane gently pulled her back to him.

"I want to go home and take care of a few things. Anyway, don't you need to take your grandmother to church?"

"Yes, I'll drop her off and be right back. I thought we could go to lunch at The Cliff House and walk along the beach after. It's a beautiful day."

"Okay, that sounds nice. But how will your grandmother get home?"

"Her friend Lydia usually drives her home. They spend a little time after church socializing with the other parishioners." Shane gave Candice a kiss. "I'll be back in twenty minutes."

Candice could not help but analyze all the events that had happened since Friday night. With Shane gone, she grabbed her cell phone. She really needed to talk to Jazzlene. *Oops*—she had turned it off Friday at the theater and forgot to turn it back on. Forty-three missed calls and several text messages. Candice scrolled through her texts. Most were from Jazzlene, but then she spotted one that disturbed her.

Brent—You are mine. I know where you are.

Did Brent really know where she was? She started to panic. *Was that the noise she heard earlier?* Her brain could not comprehend the ramifications this would have. She was putting Shane and his grandmother in danger if Brent knew where she was staying. She got dressed, then paced back and forth waiting for Shane. It was taking him longer than twenty minutes, so she tried to reach Jazzlene, but it went straight to voicemail.

"Hey Jazz, it's me. I forgot to turn my phone back on after the movies. Anyway, I'm fine. See you tomorrow." Candice tossed the phone on Shane's bed.

Shane walked into his room and saw the look on Candice's face. Her eyes were apologetic. His heart dropped. "What's wrong?"

"I need to go home. I can't stay here any longer. I'm sorry. This just isn't going to work out."

"What are you talking about? Everything was fine when I left. What changed?"

"Earlier, before I got into the shower, I heard a noise outside. It made me jump, but I figured it was a cat knocking over a rake or something. Then I got this text." Candice picked up her cell phone, showing Shane the text message. "I think he's watching me."

Shane went to the window, looked outside, and noticed nothing unusual.

"I can't stay here. This is putting your grandmother and you in danger. I'm not sure what Brent is capable of anymore, and I won't chance having you two hurt."

"I understand your concerns, but I can't leave you alone at your place, and I can't leave my grandmother alone either. So we have to think this through."

"If I stay at my place, he will stay away from here. I think your grandmother will be safe if I leave."

"You may be right, but you won't be safe."

"It appears I'm no safer here than there. But at least at home, your grandmother will be removed from the scenario."

"Okay, so we'll stay at your place. But I'll drive you to and from work. I don't want you alone until we take care of this threat."

Candice nodded her head in agreement. "Maybe I can get my stepbrother to stay with me," Candice suggested.

"If there comes a time I can't be there with you, then you can ask him. But right now, I can and will be there for you," Shane said.

Candice stared at the floor. "I thought the worst thing he could do was get caught cheating, but boy, he's taken this to a whole new level."

"As you said the other day, he needs help."

"Yeah, I think I really should talk to his mom. Then, maybe his family will step in and find him the help he needs before someone gets hurt."

"You know what I want to do?" Shane lifted Candice's chin, forcing their eyes to meet. "I want to take you to lunch and spend the day on the beach."

"Thank you." Candice kissed his cheek. "Lunch sounds good." She stood up and hugged Shane. "You really know how to redirect my thoughts and calm the situation."

Shane, however, was anything but calm. He was strategizing how to defuse the further actions he feared Brent would take. One thing he knew he had to do was contact his friend Kevin. He did not like that he would have to reach out for help, but he felt he needed more information about Brent's past. Kevin was a police officer and Shane's best friend since childhood. If anyone could check into Brent's background discreetly, it was Kevin.

They arrived at *The Cliff House* just after noon. Shane put his name on the list to dine at Sutro's Restaurant. Unfortunately, it was busy, so they were in for a long wait if they wanted a window seat. Candice deserved nothing but the best. So, nothing else but a view of the ocean would do.

"Can we walk down to the Sutro Baths ruins after lunch?" Candice turned around to see the skeleton of the former indoor swimming pools.

"Yes, I haven't walked down there in years."

"I've never been down there. In fact, this is the first time I've been to *The Cliff House*."

"Really?" Shane was shocked. "You've lived in San Francisco and never enjoyed its history?"

"Funny how a person can live in one of the most famous cities in the world and not explore it."

"I guess we should make a list of sites we need to visit in San Francisco. That should give us plenty to do for a few years at least."

"Okay, well, one thing I'd like to see is Coit Tower. I've seen it from the outside, but I want to go up to the top," Candice suggested.

"I'd love to do that. I've never been inside, either. I hear the view is spectacular. So we'll add that to our *must-see* list."

"I just happen to have my trusty planner in my purse." Candice pulled out her notebook to jot down the sites they wanted to see around the city.

"Now, that was a meal to rave about. Thank you for suggesting this place,"

Candice said. She ate everything on her plate and was barely able to move.

"The food was great, but the view was even better." Shane smiled as he admired Candice.

Shane stood up and walked behind Candice, pulling her chair out. "Shall we go exploring?"

Candice reached for Shane's hand as they walked down the trail to the Sutro Baths.

"It's hard to imagine this was once the premier spot to swim," Candice commented as she climbed onto the rim of one of the old pools.

"I bet my grandmother has pictures. We should ask her."

"Yeah, I would love to see them if she does." Candice jumped down as gracefully as she could.

They continued to explore, entering a short tunnel that emptied onto a rock overlooking the ocean.

"This is so beautiful." Candice looked out to the horizon.

Shane stood behind her and enclosed his arms around her chest. He was a foot taller than her, so he had no trouble looking above her head at the waves rolling in.

"Don't you just love the sound of the waves crashing onto the rocks?" Candice closed her eyes and listened to the rhythm of the ocean.

Shane took several pictures of the ruins, ensuring Candice was in each snapshot. Then, after exploring for a while longer, they headed back up the trail toward Ocean Beach.

"One minute." Candice reached down and kicked her shoes off. "There's nothing better than walking on the beach in your bare feet."

The warm sand between her toes felt soft and soothing. Shane followed suit and removed his shoes. It had been several years since he walked along the beach. The last time was when he got married, and that memory was one he did not want to dwell on. Instead, he reached for Candice's hand as they strolled down to the surf.

"I'm going to roll my pants up and walk along the water's edge." Candice quickly rolled up each pant leg to her knee. The contrast between the warm sand and frigid water made her wince, but she was determined to walk in the healing ocean.

"You okay?" Shane could feel her tense.

"Yeah, I'll adjust." She kicked some water toward Shane with her foot. "Get your feet wet." She tugged on his arm, pulling him into the water with her. They walked silently, enjoying the cool, salty breeze that kept the sun from overheating their stroll.

"It looks like you're starting to get burned," Shane said, noticing the pinkness on Candice's face. "We should get out of the sun."

"You're right. You're a little red, too."

Once they were on the road, Shane broke the silence. "So, we can remove another coat of paint on the credenza. Or stop by my grandmother's and tell her what's happening. And I need to get some clothes for tomorrow since I'll be staying at your place."

"Let's just head to your grandmother's. I'm curious to hear what her friends said about the cookies. But maybe we should be vague on the Brent situation."

"Sounds good," Shane agreed, taking the scenic route through the city.

"Oh, just the person I wanted to see," Beatrice excitedly announced when they entered the foyer. "Your cookies were a hit. The women couldn't get enough of them."

"Wow, that is wonderful. So, you think next Saturday will go just as well?"

"I'm positive my customers at the store will want to know where I found them. Therefore, you need to get to work on that business plan. Hit while the iron is hot, or maybe I should say oven," Beatrice chuckled.

"Grandma, I'm staying at Candice's for a few days." Shane did not see any reason to alarm her by going into too much detail. He was confident Brent would not harm his grandmother. Brent only wanted Candice, so Beatrice was safe as long as Candice was not in her house.

"I probably won't see you until next Saturday. So, I'll bring all the treats to the antique store. Say around nine?" Candice asked Beatrice.

"That sounds marvelous. I open at ten, giving us time to set up." Beatrice was grinning from ear to ear. "I can't wait to hear all the compliments."

Candice gave Beatrice a hug when Shane was ready to leave. "Talk to you soon. And thank you for everything."

"Anytime, dear," Beatrice assured, returning the hug.

Candice turned the key in her door and prayed that Brent had not somehow found his way in again. She sighed in relief when she saw that her condo showed no signs of his presence.

"Babe." Candice turned toward Shane, making eye contact when he spoke, "It's going to be all right."

"I know, but I'm just not sure what he's capable of anymore." Candice laid her purse on the table and then pressed the power button on her computer.

She entered her bedroom to put her overnight bag away and saw the flowers. Picking up the vase, she carried it into the kitchen and discarded the vase and flowers into the large trash bin. It was a gesture that did not go unnoticed by Shane. In fact, it made him smile.

"Mind if I put the football game on?" Shane knew the game was halfway over but wanted to catch the score.

"Knock yourself out." Candice sat down in front of her computer. "Oh, I got an email from the *Wild Life Rescue*." She opened it up, and a picture of the fawn greeted her. "Come look at how cute this picture is. It says he's very healthy and doing well."

Shane had one eye on the TV, trying to catch the score as he walked over to look at the computer screen.

"Wow, he's grown quite a bit in such a short time."

"As soon as I'm making some money again, I think I'll start donating to the rescue," Candice vowed, scrolling through all the pictures of rescued animals.

"It certainly is a good cause." Shane agreed, turning back to the TV.

Candice scrolled through her other emails and abruptly stopped when she saw Brent's email. She did not want to open it but needed to know what he was doing to be prepared. So she clicked on the email, and attached was a photo of Beatrice's house—no message, just the picture. "Oh, shit."

Shane turned away from the football game and immediately viewed the picture. "All that means is what we already knew. He must have followed us there."

Candice took a deep breath, trying to keep tears of frustration from escaping. She felt so guilty for allowing Shane to become involved in this mess. "Well, he certainly is leaving enough evidence for me should I decide to obtain a restraining order. I'll have some solid documentation."

Shane needed to call Kevin but did not want Candice to know he was worried. He retreated to the bathroom to send Kevin a quick text.

"Well, I think I will do what soothes my nerves and bake one of Grandma Pela's recipes. Do you want the computer before I shut it down?" Candice asked when Shane returned.

"No, go ahead and turn it off." Shane made his way back to the couch. "Hey, can you grab me a beer?"

Candice looked in the fridge and reached for the beer Brent had left. She opened the beer and brought it to him. "Here ya go. Nice and cold, compliments of Brent."

"Thanks," he said, focused on the game. "Sit with me a minute." Shane wanted to feel her warmth next to him.

Candice slid off her shoes and curled up next to Shane. He rested his arm on her shoulder while she laid her head on his chest. Slowly, Shane rubbed his hand up and down her arm, softly stroking her skin. Candice closed her eyes, letting herself enjoy the caress of his hand while trying to release the stress of the weekend.

Shane heard Candice's breathing slow down and realized she had fallen asleep just where he wanted her, protected in his arms. He softly kissed the top of her head. *Damn,* he thought, *I'm completely in over my head.* His cell phone vibrated in his pocket. He did not want to disturb Candice, so he let it go to voicemail.

"Honey, I need to get up," Shane whispered. He had been sitting on the couch holding her for two hours, but nature called.

"Hmm," she responded.

"I'll be right back." Shane laid her head on a pillow.

Candice opened her eyes when she felt his warmth depart. "I see the game is over. How long have I been sleeping?"

"Two hours."

"Sorry, I guess the big meal, long walk, and stress did me in." She sat up and rubbed her eyes.

Shane did not mind. He watched football while holding a beautiful woman. What more could a man ask for?

Standing up, Candice spotted the recipe book on her dining room table. She flipped through it until she located a peanut butter and chocolate chip cookie recipe.

When Shane turned the kitchen corner and saw Candice removing ingredients from her cabinets, he knew he was in for another tasty treat. "What are you going to spoil me with this time?"

"I think this peanut butter chocolate chip recipe sounds delicious." She grabbed the coffee beans and espresso maker she had underneath the cabinet.

"Don't you think it's a little late to drink espresso?" Shane asked.

"It's for the recipe. It calls for two tablespoons of espresso."

"Interesting. There's always something unexpected in her recipes," Shane said while reading the ingredient list for the cookies.

"Exactly. That's what makes them so unique," Candice replied as she measured the flour.

"Can I help you with anything?"

"Yeah, grab me two eggs." Candice leveled off the flour and dumped it into her large mixing bowl. Step-by-step, she followed the recipe.

While Candice was baking, Shane looked at his cell phone to see who had called earlier. He had a voicemail from Kevin.

Shane dialed Kevin, hoping to reach him and set up a meeting.

"Hey, man. I got your text. What's going on?" Kevin asked, sounding concerned. He knew Shane would never contact him asking for information if it was not significant.

"Can you meet me for lunch tomorrow?" Shane asked, trying to sound casual.

"Sure, the usual place at noon?" Kevin and Shane had a favorite family-style diner they had frequented since high school.

"Yes, that would be great," Shane agreed.

"I'll check on that name and license plate you gave me and see what information I can find on the guy. You want to give me a clue as to what this is about?"

"We just need to go over the contract." Shane did not want Candice to know he was concerned enough to seek outside help handling the Brent situation.

"Is someone listening to this conversation?" Kevin queried, always in cop mode.

"Yes, that's right. Noon will work for me."

"Got it. You will fill me in tomorrow, right?"

"Yes. See you then."

Candice walked into the living room just as Shane ended his call.

"So, ten minutes until this latest creation is ready for the taste test."

"Well, they smell good, so I bet they'll taste great. But then, everything you've made has been delicious so far."

"Yes, the recipes really have been quite special. You know, I never thought I would enjoy baking so much. But there is just something so therapeutic about it. People meditate to clear their minds, but I'm finding that baking has that same effect on me. It just calms my nerves."

"I understand. I feel the same way about refinishing a piece of furniture. You can zone out and just be in the moment. Clears your mind and helps you figure things out."

"Yes, exactly," Candice concurred, sounding very relaxed.

When the oven's buzzer sounded, Candice got excited. "I can't wait to taste this batch."

"If they taste as good as they smell, we're in for another mouthwatering treat."

Candice poured two small glasses of milk to go with the cookies. Milk seemed more appropriate than tea. "Here." She handed a warm cookie to Shane. "Now, let's taste them at the same time." Each took a bite, and neither could contain their moans of delight.

"God, I hope the neighbors can't hear us." Candice laughed.

"These are beyond good. I don't even know how to describe them." Shane took another cookie. "You can't eat just one."

"I have to agree." Candice took a sip of her milk. "I think we need to stop at two cookies, or we'll be up all night from the caffeine."

"Well, that's okay. I think we can find something to do that will exhaust us." Shane gave her his *I want you now look,* and Candice was all too willing to oblige.

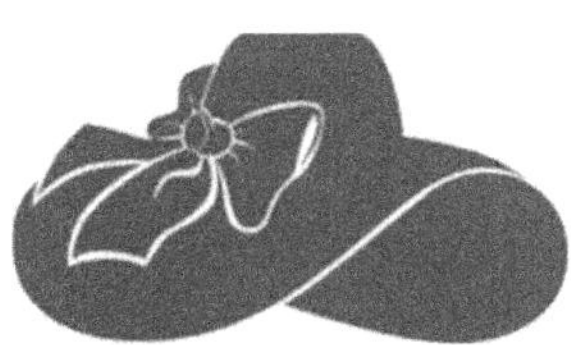

Shane left his car running while he walked Candice to the door of Jazzlene's studio.

"So, I'll pick you up at five." He leaned over and gave Candice a passionate kiss that would linger on her lips throughout the day.

"Okay. Monday's are busy, so if I need to work past five, I'll call you," Candice said as they parted.

Candice unlocked the door to the studio but left the closed sign facing the street. She liked to arrive early to get a few things done before it was time to deal with customers.

Once Shane knew she was safely inside, he drove off.

Candice began reviewing the entire week's calendar to see if she could take Friday off or possibly work a half-day. She would need at least a portion of Friday to prepare the pastries and cookies for Saturday's sampling with Beatrice.

"Mornin', how was your weekend?" Jazzlene asked.

"Hi," Candice responded, looking up from the computer screen. "I have some things we need to discuss."

"Should I be worried?" Jazz did not like the tone of Candice's voice or the worry on her face.

"Well, the first thing is you have a noon appointment, and the person will only see you."

"I guess I can stay out of the darkroom this morning. But, you know me, once I go in there, it's several hours before I come back out."

"Yeah, sometimes I think you like that darkroom a little too much."

"You might be right. It's very peaceful in there."

"The other thing is," Candice began, handing Jazzlene the spare keys to her condo. "Shane had to change my locks, so here are the new keys. One is to the door, the other the deadbolt."

Jazzlene held the keys while giving Candice a quizzical look. "So, you want to tell me what's going on?"

"Where do I begin?" Candice sighed, rewinding her thoughts to the beginning of her date on Friday.

Jazzlene sat on the desk, giving her full attention to Candice. Each sentence that came out of Candice's mouth weaved an alarming story, giving Jazzlene good reason to worry about Candice's safety.

"I can't believe this all happened in three days." Jazzlene stood and gave her friend a hug she needed.

"I know. I'm not sure what to do. I'm really not afraid for myself, even though I should be. I'm more worried about what he might try to do to Shane."

"Well, it sounds like Shane can take care of himself."

"You're not forgetting what that poor guy in the bar had to endure after Brent pulverized his face?"

"No, in fact, that's all I can visualize right now. I really never understood why you stayed with him after that."

"You and me both," Candice responded with regret heavy in her voice.

"So, let me get this straight. You have spent every waking minute with Shane since Friday?"

"Yup, he won't leave me alone. It's like Brent is actually pushing us together. Taking it slow with Shane is no longer an option."

Jazzlene raised her questioning eyebrows.

"What can I say? He has everything a woman could ask for, down to his boxer briefs."

"Oh? You didn't waste any time. What happened to my friend who said she would take her next relationship slow? Watch for those telltale signs that he's not the right guy for her?"

"Heck, I think I tossed that strategy right out the window the day I met Shane. There's a sense of family, honor, and pride in him. You should see how he is with his grandmother. It's so sweet, and she's such a remarkable and kind woman. I'm trying to find anything that would make me run for the hills, but I can't find one thing that raises a red flag."

"I guess it's time I meet this guy since it sounds like you two are getting serious. When did you say he was coming to pick you up?"

"Five."

"Well then, I will definitely make sure I'm here and not in the darkroom."

The phone began to ring, putting an abrupt end to the conversation. "We'll have to finish this later," Candice said, reaching for the phone.

"Good morning, Jazz Photography. How may I help you?"

"Hi babe, I had to call you. Mr. Keller's daughter Maggie just called me. She saw all the pictures I sent her and is flying here in two weeks to assess the property. She wants me to meet her there. She's open to hearin' my ideas for the property."

"That's wonderful. Maybe you can talk her into saving it."

"That's what I'm hoping for too. Anyway, I thought we could leave for Napa after work on Friday and spend two nights at one of those spa resorts."

"Really? If you want to be pampered, I can do that for you, and it won't cost you a dime."

"Well, don't you think it would be relaxing to lounge in a hot mineral spring together? Heck, I might even go as far as the mud bath."

"You in a mud bath? Now that I have to see."

"So, I'll book a room for two nights."

"Yes, it sounds like fun."

"I'll email you the details so you can mark it in your planner along with the other places on our *must-see* list."

"Sounds great. See ya after work." Candice hung the phone up.

Candice nervously glanced at the clock and then the door. It was 11:55, and Steve should be arriving any minute.

"What is wrong with you?" Jazzlene asked, noticing Candice's foot uncontrollably wiggling.

"Nothing," Candice answered innocently, just as the door opened.

She turned to Jazzlene to see her reaction when Steve walked in. For a moment, no one said a word. Candice watched the change in Jazzlene's expression when she recognized Steve.

"Are you my noon appointment?" she questioned in shock.

"Yes, but I'm really here to take you to lunch so we can catch up."

Jazzlene turned to Candice. "Can you mind the fort while I'm gone?"

"Of course," Candice said, happy to see Jazzlene so receptive to Steve's lunch offer.

"Let me grab my purse, and we can head out." Jazzlene turned, leaving Steve and Candice alone.

Candice winked at Steve. His smile said it all. He might have had to wait years for Jazzlene to come to her senses, but hopefully, it would be worth the long wait.

Just as they were heading out the door, Candice spoke up. "Hey Jazz, I've cleared your calendar for the day. So, feel free to take an extended lunch."

Jazzlene squinted and gave Candice the, *we need to talk when I get back* look.

Mission accomplished, Candice thought as she watched the two of them stroll down the street.

Shane sat down at the diner and ordered a cup of coffee. He was in a booth by the window people-watching as he sipped his coffee.

"Hey man, sorry I'm late," Kevin apologized as he took a seat.

"No problem, just glad you were able to make it."

Shirley, their waitress, filled Kevin's coffee cup, leaving enough room for cream. "The usual for you two?" she asked as a formality. Kevin always ordered a medium rare hamburger with extra Swiss cheese and no onions. While Shane preferred a well-done barbeque burger topped with onion rings.

"Yeah, sounds about right," Kevin said, pouring cream into his coffee. He stirred in the sugar before addressing Shane.

"So, why did you need me to research this Brent guy?"

"He's the ex-boyfriend of a woman I'm seeing."

"Yeah, but there's got to be more. What prompted you to call me?"

"He's been stalking her. Even let himself into her condo at a very inopportune moment."

"He had the keys?"

"Yes, but she said he must have made duplicates without her knowledge. And then the next day, when we arrived back at her place, he was sitting on her couch, waiting for her as if he lived there. Needless to say, she was pretty shaken up. So we ended up staying at my place."

"Okay, before you go any further, you took her to your place?"

"Yeah," Shane responded, knowing that would shock Kevin.

"Now that I understand how important this woman is to you let me tell you what I found out. He was charged with aggravated assault and battery two years ago. He had a damn good attorney because he was able to get the charges reduced. He did no prison time and is still on probation. There was nothing else on his record until yesterday when he was arrested for DUI and possession of narcotics. Cocaine, to be exact. He had an arraignment this morning and is sitting in county waiting for bail to be posted."

"Really? What do you think will happen?"

"Hard to say. If he hires the same attorney, he could get a fine and be released to drug rehab as part of his sentence. It's his first offense for DUI and drugs. The judge may see rehab as the best route since the jails are overcrowded."

"Should my friend file for a temporary restraining order? He's been at my grandmother's taking pictures, so he must have followed us there. And I can tell by the picture he sent her he was on the property. He did not take the picture from the sidewalk."

"Well, with everything else going on with him, it might be a good decision."

"Oh, and were you able to check on the case about the attempted break-in of my shop?"

"Yeah, I spoke with the detective on your case. I gave him the information you gave me. If the prints they found match him, he may also be looking at some trespassing charges."

"I think my surveillance footage got a pretty clear picture of him, and with the facial recognition program, your detective should have solid evidence if it was Brent."

Shirley came back and placed their meals in front of them. "Anything else I can get you boys?"

"Not now, but I think I'm gonna want dessert," Kevin answered.

"Then I'll check back when you're done." Shirley turned and moved to her another table.

Shane looked worried. "Okay, I'll have to talk to her tonight, but I know she's reluctant to file the restraining order."

"I'll keep my eyes and ears open. Check with the arresting officer when I see him."

"Thanks, man. I really appreciate your help."

"Anytime. You know I'm always here for you. Now fill me in on this woman you are fiercely protecting."

"What's to tell? I've gone out with her a few times."

"Really? Seems like more than that to me."

"You know I can't go down that road again. I lost everything in my divorce and well—" Shane trailed off and never finished his sentence.

"Shane, not everyone is a cold-hearted bitch like Aubrey."

"I can't explain what this woman is doing to me. It's like I can't get her out of my head. I sound like Brent, come to think of it."

Kevin smiled. "Oh, you're so in trouble with this one."

"I know. How the hell did this even happen? One minute I'm a happy bachelor enjoying life, and now I'm in deep shit."

"Why don't you try to just let what happens to happen. Stop overthinking it. I swear, Shane, there really are great women out there. Look at my wife."

"Well, you did find a great woman," Shane acknowledged.

"Why don't we get together at my place? Have a barbeque some Sunday soon. Stella would love to have you and your lady friend over. She was just commenting Sunday on how she missed seeing you."

"Sorry about that, but I had to change some door locks."

"We've been talking for a half hour, and you still haven't told me this woman's name."

"Candice Smythe."

Kevin almost spit out his coffee.

"What? Do you know her?" Shane lifted his eyebrows.

"Is she the same Candice that has a friend named Jazzlene?"

"Yeah, and?"

"She's been to my house several times. My wife is friends with Jazzlene and Candice. They went to high school together."

"What a small world." Shane shook his head in disbelief.

"Now I know why you're so torn. She has a body with curves in all the right places and a smile that draws you into her. But, like I said earlier, you are in so much trouble with this one. I don't think you'll be able to resist her, even if you put blinders on. You should see her with my kids. They adore her. She gets right down on the floor and plays with them."

"Okay, now you know my dilemma and why I can't stay away from her."

"And now, I also know I must help you to ensure she's safe. If I don't, Stella will tan my ass."

"So, have you met this Brent guy?"

"No, but I remember Stella being happy when they broke up. She said he was a real piece of work."

"She got that right."

Shane left lunch feeling better about where his relationship with Candice was heading, even though he often tried to deny his feelings for her. He was still apprehensive about Brent's threatening behavior, but with Kevin's help, he felt confident he could be one step ahead of him.

Jazzlene walked back into the studio with Steve. "I'm going to show Steve around."

"Hey, Steve, try one of those peanut butter cookies while you're in the break room. Let me know what you think," Candice requested, looking up from the computer screen.

"Jazz was telling me about the sweet treats you've been bringing in every morning." Steve took a bite of the cookie and reacted like everyone else who had tried one of Grandma Pela's treats. "Amazing."

"I told you. She's toying with the idea of opening a bakery café," Jazzlene informed him.

"Yeah, it's an idea, but I still need to think it through. First, I'd have to sell or rent out my condo," Candice informed them.

"Where's your condo located?" Steve inquired. "I'm looking for a place to rent, sorta living on a friend's couch right now."

"Tell you what," Candice said, jotting a note onto a scrap of paper. "Here's my address and phone number. Maybe you could stop by and see my place. I have no idea what I'm doing at this point. But if I decide to rent or sell the condo, you'll know beforehand if you might be interested."

"Jazz, you want to go with me to Candice's, maybe after work one day this week?" Steve sounded hopeful.

"Yes, I would love to."

Candice sat there listening to them as Jazzlene took Steve into the darkroom. *Oh boy, they may never come out the rest of the day,* Candice thought.

Before opening the file to work on Jazzlene's website, she decided to call the real estate agent. When Trevor answered, she became tongue-tied. She had been expecting his voicemail.

"Hi, this is Candice. I was wondering if you had time Sunday afternoon to let me go through the house in Noe Valley again?"

"Yes, what time are you thinking?"

"How 'bout around two?"

"That would work out perfectly. Shall I meet you there, or would you like me to pick you up and show you some other houses in the area?'

"No, I'll have a friend drive me. And right now, this is the only place I'm interested in viewing."

"Well then, I'll see you at two on Sunday."

Candice started working on removing outdated information from Jazzlene's website when Steve and Jazzlene emerged from the darkroom. They could not hide their attraction to one another. Candice suspected it might have gotten a little hot in that room.

"So, Steve is a computer programmer and does some web designing. He said he'll look at my website and see what he can do to make it more user-friendly and aesthetically pleasing."

"That would be so helpful. I'm stumbling around trying to come up with some ideas and getting nowhere." Candice was happy to know she would have some expert help.

"Are you working on the site now?" Steve asked.

"Right now, I'm just removing old content and bad links. Kinda cleaning up the site a bit."

"Can I have a look?" Steve walked over.

"Sure." Candice got up and gave Steve her seat.

Steve navigated through each page, checking out the continuity of the site.

"Well, I can change a few simple things, but I'd like to completely overhaul it. Make the site look as professional as your photos, Jazz. Once I get it redesigned, I will show you how to make changes like removing content and uploading new photographs."

"How much does it cost to redo the entire site?" Jazzlene knew this would not be cheap and was on a tight budget.

"Nothing. I want to do this for you."

"I can't have you do that for free. I know it will take many hours to build a new site."

"Tell you what. You agree to make me a few home-cooked meals while I work on the site. I'm sorta tired of eating fast food."

"Really? I can do that." Jazz agreed happily, aware this meant she would be spending more time with Steve.

"Give me the login information, and I'll do some work over the next week."

Jazzlene wrote down the information so Steve could access Jazzlene's site and start the new design. "This is exciting," she said, handing him the paper.

"Well, I really have to get back to work. I can take a long lunch but still have to put in my eight-plus hours." He gave Jazzlene a quick kiss and hug. "Nice seeing you again, Candice." He hugged her and whispered in her ear, "Thank you."

Candice whispered back, "You're welcome." Then she stood back smiling. "I'm so glad I ran into you the other night."

"Me too," Steve agreed, heading for the door. "I'll call you tonight, Jazz."

"Fill me in," Candice prompted once Steve was gone.

"Well, my, my, you are a sneaky one," Jazzlene smirked.

"Hey, what can I say? I ran into Steve Friday night, and he asked about you. I figured if I told you he was coming in, you'd make sure you were unavailable. It's time you moved on from my stepbrother and found someone that will appreciate you."

"I'd just like to say, well played, and thank you."

"I couldn't wait to see your reaction when Steve walked in."

"When did he get a body like Adonis? I mean, Steve was one of the nicest guys we hung around with, and he was good-looking, but wow, he's certainly filled out since high school."

"So true. He's the whole package. Sweet and smart with his beautiful physique," Candice commented.

"Yeah, like we would have said when we were twelve, he's dreamy." Jazzlene chuckled, batting her eyes.

"So, what went on in that darkroom?"

"I never kiss and tell." Jazzlene sheepishly grinned.

"Just tell me it was as good as I imagine."

“Probably better. Now I really must get to work. I have to go develop some pictures.” Jazzlene left for her darkroom.

“Have fun in there with your recent memories.”

“And you thought I liked my darkroom before.” Jazzlene closed the door to her darkroom and inhaled Steve’s cologne that lingered in the air.

Eleven

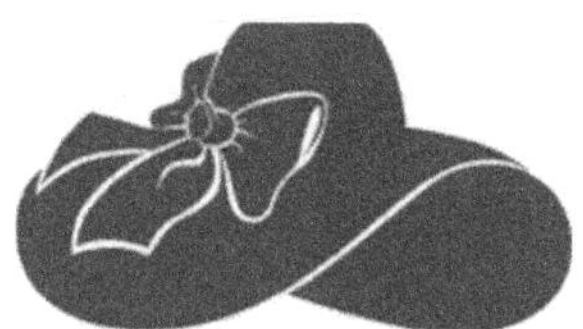

Five o'clock arrived, and Shane walked into Jazz's studio. He did not hesitate to approach Candice, pulling her in for a warm embrace. "I missed you." Sincerity and conviction laced his voice. Something had changed, and Candice could not imagine what had happened between the morning and now. There was a deeper level of lust in his expression. Could it be love?

"I missed you too, more than you'll ever know." Candice encircled her arms around his neck and looked deep into his eyes, mesmerizing him.

"I don't know what you are doing to me, but whatever it is, don't stop," he said before kissing her again.

Jazzlene walked out of the darkroom to find Candice kissing a tall, muscular man she could only assume was Shane.

"Hi," Jazzlene said, clearing her throat. "You must be Shane?" She presumed. *Who else would Candice be in a lip lock with?*

Candice and Shane broke apart. "Hi, and you have to be the one and only Jazzlene," Shane responded, smiling. Her beauty surprised him. Jazzlene had an exotic look that he did not expect. Her hair was midnight black, hanging straight down to her waist. She had a sun-kissed glow that made her green eyes stand out against the contrast of her dark skin. He could only imagine what kind of attention Candice, Jazzlene, and Stella received when they went out together. It would be like three angels entering the room.

Jazzlene stepped forward and gave Shane one of her tender hugs she reserved for close friends. "Well, it's about time I finally met the man that makes my friend so happy."

"Likewise. I've heard a lot about you. It's nice to meet you as well," Shane replied.

Jazz had difficulty staying focused on the conversation, but she blocked the vision of Shane's chiseled masculine features and replaced them with Steve. *Yep, that worked.*

"Well, guess we'll head out. See you in the morning," Candice said, grabbing her sweater from the back of her chair.

Candice felt a little tension as she entered her home. She quickly looked around for anything out of place, but nothing seemed out of the ordinary. Then she looked over at Shane and realized the tension emanated from him.

"Shane, what's wrong?"

"I want to talk to you about some information I learned today."

"Okay, I guess I'll sit down," Candice said, curling her legs underneath her as she sat on her couch. She gave Shane her undivided attention.

"Well, I didn't tell you this earlier because I didn't want you to worry." He paused.

"And?" She was starting to become concerned.

"I have a friend who is a cop. Anyway, I gave him Brent's license plate number and asked him to check on the specifics of Brent's record. He was able to tell me what we already knew about his assault and battery charge. However, yesterday the police pulled him over and arrested him for DUI and possession of a controlled substance. Apparently, they found cocaine on him. So as of earlier today, he was in jail waiting for bail to be posted."

"Oh, my God!" Candice looked torn. "I have to call his mother to make sure she knows she has to get him help."

"Well, if he's lucky, drug rehab will be part of his sentence."

"I hope so. As much as I want him out of my life, I hate to see him going down this road. Maybe I'll go talk to him."

Shane stared at her as though trying to read her mind.

Candice continued when she saw worry in Shane's eyes. "I mean, I did love him once, we had some good times, and I still care about him."

Shane knew this could open up the door for them to rekindle their broken relationship. "Well, I'd advise against it, but I won't try to stop you." Shane needed to trust Candice.

"So, is there anything else you found out?"

"No. That's all Kevin had so far."

"So far? What's that mean?"

"Well, I have surveillance video of the person that tried to break into my shop, and it looks exactly like Brent. So, I'm pretty sure that with the fingerprints the detective retrieved and the video they have of him, he'll be charged with vandalism, at the very least. And that picture he sent you of my grandmother's house, well, he had to have taken that on her property, so that could be considered trespassing."

"I don't even know what to say. I feel so bad for him. He's completely ruining his life." A tear slipped from Candice's eye, and she quickly wiped it away. "Why do people do this to themselves?"

Shane did not comment.

"I mean, he had it all. He has a loving family. Had a great job and could have had any woman he wanted."

Shane lifted his eyebrows. "Isn't that what broke you up? He *did* have any woman he wanted?"

"Yeah."

"Here's another bit of news you might find interesting. My friend, Kevin, turns out he knows you and Jazzlene."

"How?" Candice was now intrigued.

"Do you have a friend named Stella?" He watched as she registered what he had just asked.

"It's Stella's husband, Kevin?" Candice questioned, shocked.

"Yup, seems we run in the same circles."

"Then you're probably the guy she's been trying to introduce me to since I broke it off with Brent." Candice realized she knew more about Shane than he would probably like. She also knew all about his ex-wife and the turmoil she caused.

"That would be me, and Kevin did the same thing to me. He kept telling me about this friend of Stella's that was a knock-out." Candice blushed when he said that. "Well, I should have gotten my head out of my ass earlier and listened to him."

"You know, it probably wouldn't have worked then. We both needed time to move on from our pasts. When the expectation is too high, it is too much pressure." Candice conveyed.

"You're right. I like the way things seemed to fall into place."

"So, I guess this means we'll be spending time with Kevin and Stella?"

"I'd love that. I usually go to their house on Sundays and watch football with Kevin. They invited us this Sunday," Shane informed her.

"That would be great, but I made that appointment with the realtor to look at the house at two. Can we go after we meet the realtor?"

"Yeah, that will work. We'll see the house, and then go watch some football. I'll let Kevin know I'm bringing you Sunday."

Candice's cell phone started to ring. "Speak of the devil," Candice answered the call. "Hey, Stella." Shane listened to the one-sided conversation. "Yeah, I just found out. Who would have thunk it?" Shane smiled at her, and she winked back. "Well, we'll be at your place Sunday to watch football. Or should I say, to let the guys watch football? So maybe we can take the kids to the park." Candice laughed. "Yeah, I know guys and their football. Okay, we'll see you then." Candice ended her call.

"Sounds like we're on for Sunday. Has Stella tried any of your treats?"

"Yes, we're on for Sunday, and no, I haven't even told her yet. So I'll put some aside from the batches I make for your Grandmother's sampling."

"Now the burning question, how did the afternoon with Steve and Jazzlene go?" Shane inquired.

"I'd have to say better than expected. They spent an awfully long time in the darkroom. I haven't had a chance to sit down and talk to her, but her constant smile indicates they'll be seeing a lot of each other."

"Well, if they start dating, we should invite them to Sunday football. We could rotate where we gather, but I'm pretty sure Stella prefers her house because of the kids. She said it's easier that way. I can only imagine what carting around two children under the age of four would be like," Shane said, aware of the energy involved when you had to take care of someone, especially toddlers.

"Let's get back to Brent for a minute." Candice reintroduced the subject. Shane was hoping they had put that discussion to rest, but apparently not. "I'm going to hold off on applying for a temporary restraining order. I'm pretty sure he'll be under lock and key at his mom's."

"You're probably right. I agree, we'll see what comes of his charges and what the courts decide, but for now, I think he'll stay away."

"If I know his mother like I am sure I do, she'll secure him a room in a drug rehab facility."

"Kevin will also call and let me know if there is any new information. So, as soon as I know something, I'll let you know." It was killing Shane that Candice was so concerned about a man that betrayed her, but he also understood it was in her nature to care.

Candice scooted next to Shane, curling up against him. She wanted him to know that Brent may have her empathy, but he had her heart. She reached under his shirt and caressed his chest, enjoying his muscles tense with excitement as her hand gently glided over them. Shane let himself relish in her touch a minute longer, but that was all he could take. He needed skin to skin contact, so he removed his shirt and then reached for hers. Candice crawled onto his lap, straddling him, so he was now eye to breast. He wanted to bury his face between them, so he did.

Candice reached back and unhooked her bra, giving him total access to her voluptuous breasts. He looked up at her with a lustful smile.

"Shall we take this to the bedroom?" she asked, wanting to get cozy under her blankets.

Later that evening, they were tired and back to lounging on the couch. "Shane,

I've been working a little on the business plan. Let me show it to you and get some insight, see if I'm on the right track." Candice handed him her notebook.

He intently scrutinized her entries, making some notes of his own. "You know the part about tables and chairs? I like your idea to have each one different with nothing matching."

"Yeah, I thought that would be cute."

"Well, you've seen how much furniture I have at the shop that I need to restore. I can't even begin to tell you how many small tables and chairs I have waiting to be worked on. How 'bout we refinish them together and you can use them and also sell them?"

"But aren't those for your grandmother?"

"She has so much, she won't mind. Her shop can only hold so many pieces of furniture. Plus, I get new items all the time."

"Well, as long as your grandmother will be all right with me using them, then yes, I would love to help you restore them."

"That's one thing that we can do as you work more on your business plan. Next, I love that you are planning to use different plates and utensils as well, but one thing you must keep in mind is lead. Many of the older dishes and teapots have lead in the glaze, so we'd need to test them before use. Also, they can't have any grazing in the glaze because that promotes bacteria growth in the cracks."

Candice looked at him curiously. "How do you know all that?"

"I learned most of it from my grandmother. When you've been dealing in antiques as long as she has, you learn a thing or two."

"Is there anything you don't know?'

"About antiques, nope. About you, yes?"

"Well, ask away," Candice challenged.

"I guess one important thing would be, when is your birthday?"

"July 21st. When's yours?"

"January 30th."

"Okay, now I want to ask a question. Besides Taekwondo, did play any sports?"

"You name it, I probably tried it. I would have to say soccer was my favorite as a child. But now I enjoy watching a football game with an ice-cold beer. How 'bout you?"

"I loved dance class. The recitals we performed for our parents were always fun. I have one, a food you hate?"

"Liver and onions. My grandmother swears one day I'll love it, but it's never going to happen."

"I'm with you, but I'd like to add escargot. Tried it once and I just didn't care for it."

"I've never had it, nor do I want to try it."

Shane's phone started to ring. "It's Kevin." He answered it on the third ring. "Hey man, find out anything?" Shane did not speak for quite a while. "Okay, I guess that's good news. Thanks. Yeah, we'll be over probably close to three. See ya then." Shane felt a little relieved as he updated Candice. "So, in a nutshell, Brent made bail and went straight into rehab. He'll be there hopefully for thirty days. The judge set his trial date after he is done with rehab. As far as the attempted break-in at my place, they're still making a case against him. Looks like we won't have any more visits from him for a couple of weeks." Once Shane said that last sentence, he knew there was no reason for him to stay with Candice any longer.

"That's good news. I hope rehab helps him fight his demons, whatever they are," Candice softly said.

"I guess I should let you have your place back. I know it was tough having me invade your space, so I'll just go pack my things."

Candice did not comment. She wanted to tell him to stay, that she enjoyed his company and loved waking up next to him. Instead, she watched him go into her room to gather his belongings. She did not want him to feel smothered or scare him off, so she quietly sat rubbing her thumbs together.

Shane returned with his duffel bag full and placed it by the door. "Let's have some dinner before I leave." Shane walked into the kitchen and pulled out leftover lasagna. He felt leaving was the right thing to do, give her back her home, but inside he was starting to feel the emptiness.

Candice walked up behind him in the kitchen, laying her head between his shoulder blades and encircling her arms around his waist.

"Shane?"

"Yeah," he said, concentrating on slicing the lasagna.

"I don't want you to leave," her voice was meek. "Please stay."

"I'm not encroaching on your space?"

"No, I kinda like you in my space, and to be honest, I love waking up in your arms."

"Well, that's good, because I love having you in my arms. So, I guess we are both happy in the morning."

"Look, I know we're moving pretty fast in this relationship, but somehow it feels right. I can't explain it, but it just does. So, I want you to have these." She reached on top of the refrigerator for the spare keys.

Shane stood there looking at the keys. *Oh, no...this can't be happening. Shit, I'm getting way too involved. Damn, abort abort!* Candice placed the keys in his hand, and he curled his fingers around them. They were now his lifeline to her, but somehow, he felt they were more like an anchor pulling him down. Aubrey quickly materialized in his mind, as he saw the exact moment in their relationship where he had committed himself to her and then she took him for everything he was worth. He tried to reason with himself that Candice was nothing like Aubrey.

"Shane, are you okay?" Candice tried to get his attention.

"Yeah, I'm fine." However, he could not convince himself of that, so why would she believe him?

"Did I say something wrong?"

He looked at her with brooding eyes. *Be honest.* "I need to be brutally honest."

Candice felt her heart rate speed up. "Okay. I like honesty."

Careful. "When I dated Aubrey, she too handed me her keys. From that point on, we were never apart. And we both know, that did not end well. I just don't want to make the same mistake twice. So, I can't accept your keys. You understand I'm not ready to take that step yet." He handed her back the keys.

"Okay, I understand. I had my heart broken too by a man I once adored, and now he's stalking me. At least, he was as of yesterday. I get that you are scared, hell, I'm terrified, but I trust you. Since you're friends with Stella and Kevin, you must have some redeeming qualities. Anyway, I'll move on. The key situation won't happen again. I think you heading home now would be a good idea. I need some time to think about what I want and what I'm willing to do without." Candice left the kitchen and went into her room. "Oh, and Shane, lock the door when you leave." With that last statement, she went into the bathroom, shut the door, and started filling her bathtub.

Shane put the food away slowly, washed the few dishes, and left.

After she heard the door close, Candice filled a glass with wine and took it into her bathroom. She slid down into her tub, allowing the bubbles to cover her body. She replayed her conversation with Shane and their talk earlier about Brent. A small smile crossed her face knowing Brent was getting help. *That's a good thing. Let's hope it works.* Then she let herself go to the painful thought of Shane's reaction to her offering. She was only trying to make him feel welcomed into her life, but it seemed to have had the opposite effect. As hard as it was going to be, she would have to let him come to her in his own time. She took another sip of her wine. The one person she wanted to talk to was Stella. Her insight into Shane might prove helpful, but for now, she was just happy Brent was in rehab, and she didn't have to worry about him showing up. As for Shane, she was going to miss his warm body, but she has slept alone for a year. She would manage just fine, once again.

Shane turned into his driveway and sulked into the house. He had ended the evening in the worst way possible, by hurting Candice. He absolutely could not take her keys. Shane was trying so hard not to rush the relationship, but clearly, by the way he felt leaving her house, it proved he did need to slow down.

"Honey, I didn't expect to see you tonight. Everything with Candice's ex-boyfriend under control now?" Beatrice asked.

"Well, he's was arrested for DUI and drug possession. Right now, he's in rehab. So, she's safe for a while."

"That's good to know."

"Yes, it is."

"Something else bothering you, dear?"

"Nothing I can't handle."

"Okay, I'm going to head into my sewing room, but before I do, I just want you to know that whatever it is, it will work itself out."

"I know it will. I just really hurt Candice's feeling tonight, and I feel horrible. But honestly, I'm terrified of the feelings I have for her. You out of everyone must know I can't go through losing everything again. Hell, I just finished paying off the damn lawyer."

"I think she probably understands. I'm sure she feels the same way. Trust is a very fragile thing. Once it's lost, it's hard to ever find it again with anyone. You two both need some time to get a good foundation under your feet."

"I don't want to lose her in the process."

"If you two are meant to be together, you will be. Just lLet it all happen naturally and try not to over think things. Just enjoy the lovely woman she is."

"Thanks, Grandma." Shane kissed her on the forehead before heading to his room.

His cell phone alerted him to a text.

Candice—Goodnight.

Shane—I'll see you in the morning. Sorry bout 2nite.

Candice—It's okay. And about tomorrow, I'll take the bus.

Shane quickly dialed Candice.

"Hello."

"Hey, I need to talk to you," he said with a shaky voice.

"Yeah." Candice could not think of a polite way to respond.

"Look, I know I hurt you, and I'm really sorry."

"Apology accepted. Now I want to get some sleep."

"I still want to pick you up tomorrow and drive you to work."

"That won't be necessary. I got myself to work every morning just fine without you. I think I remember how to get on the bus." She was very curt.

"Please let me drive you."

"No, and also I don't want to see you this week. I want time to decide if I can deal with a one-sided relationship. Seems I was willing to put my heart on the line, but yours is off limits."

Shane went silent. "Shane, you still there?"

"Yeah, just thinking about what you said. You're right, I'm not being fair to you. I'll give you the distance you need."

"Well, maybe I'll see you Saturday at your Grandmother's store."

"I'll drive you there."

"Nah, I can make it on my own, but thanks for offering. Also, I'm going to cancel meeting the realtor and football on Sunday."

"I want to go look at the house with you, and we told Stella and Kevin that we'd go to watch football."

"Shane, the house is just a pipe dream. I have enough stress in my life right now, so I really don't need to worry about some stupid dream. I need to find a good paying job. And as for football, you go enjoy your day with Kevin. I have things I need to do that I've been putting off."

Shane was once again speechless.

"Shane...good night."

"Night." Shane tossed his phone aside and laid on his bed fully clothed in the dark. *I'm better off ending this before I get too emotionally involved.* But the problem was, he left his heart at Candice's condo.

Candice sat on her couch with the bottle of wine and poured herself another glass. Looking back at what transpired, there was nothing she would have done differently. If opening her heart and home to him chased him away, then so be it. Better it happened now then later when it would take a long time for her heart to heal. She took one last sip of her wine, then crawled into her bed and cried herself to sleep.

Twelve

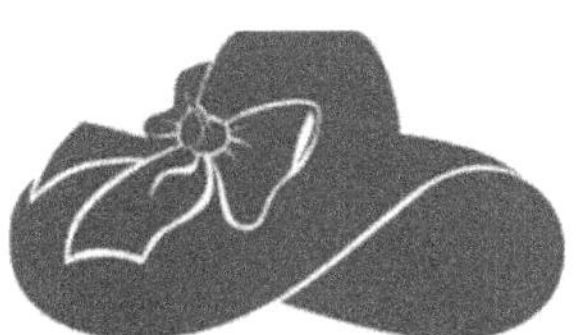

The sound of the alarm jolted Candice out of a dream that was so disturbing the shrieking sound was welcomed. She peeled her swollen eyes open.

Getting ready for work was taking her longer than usual. She was so tired from crying and lack of sleep that she walked through her room like a zombie.

Candice leaned against the wall while waiting for the elevator. *This is going to be one long day.* The thought of crawling back into bed crept into her mind, but she knew Jazzlene needed her, so she trudged on.

Once Candice stepped into the crisp morning air, she felt a little better. The bus stop was on the next corner. A few people were already waiting, some with coffee in their hands. Candice approached, thinking she should have stopped and bought herself a latte. That undoubtedly would have perked her up. The bench was empty, so she sat down, feeling too tired to stand for even five minutes.

A car pulled up to the bus stop. "Hey beautiful, let me give you a ride."

Candice looked up to see Shane standing next to his car looking directly at her with worried eyes.

"Thanks, but I'll take the bus." She was going to be stubborn and stick to what she said last night.

Shane approached Candice. "Come on, we'll go get a coffee. Looks like neither of us slept last night." He offered his hand to her. Reluctantly, she took it and followed him to his car without as much as a peep.

Once they were driving, Shane spoke, "Babe, I'm really sorry I hurt you last night. That was not my intention." Shane paused to see if Candice would say anything, but she remained silent. "When you handed me the keys, I had a moment of panic. I just want everything to work with us, and well, honestly, I'm having a real hard time taking this relationship slow." Shane pulled up in front of a coffee shop and turned to look at her.

Candice was peering out her side window. "Babe, can you please look at me?" Candice turned her head upon his request but refused to make eye contact. Shane reached his hand under her chin and tilted her head in an attempt to meet her eyes.

"I'm not sure what you want from me. I've tried to give you the space you need, while still showing you that you are part of my life and welcome anytime you want. The key was my way of letting you know my heart belonged to you, and that I trusted you," Candace explained.

"I told you yesterday that I'm not sure what you are doing to me, but it's scaring the hell out of me. I've never felt this way, not even with my wife. I thought I loved her, but this...this thing I feel for you...is so much more. Last night I did not sleep at all because you weren't next to me. I thought about everything we said to each other. Our hopes and dreams, what we want out of life and our relationship, and I came to one conclusion, I can't live without you, not for one minute."

Candice sat stunned as her eyes started to water. "I'm scared as hell too, but you know what? I was willing to take the leap and trust you."

"I know, and I let you down. I can't begin to apologize enough for that."

"I told you last night, I accepted your apology. What really hurts me is that you compare me to her. I'm not her. I know more about your ex than I should. From what I've heard, she was a cold-hearted bitch that dragged you through the wringer. I'm not that kind of person. What is yours is yours. I'll never take anything from you. I'll never cheat on you or lie." She looked away from him with her last statement.

"You're right, I was unfair. I've kept every woman I've dated at arm's length, until you. You're the first and only woman since my divorce I've taken to my home and formally introduced to my grandmother." That made Candice smile.

"And I'm so glad you did. I love your grandmother. I never knew mine."

"Well, I'm happy to share mine with you. So, can we call a truce? I'll wave the white flag and surrender myself to you, every part of me."

"Yes, I would like that, because honestly last night, being alone felt so wrong," Candice whispered, trying to hold back more tears.

"I want to accept your key, as long as you understand I will not just pop in without letting you know I'm on my way. It's still your home. I'm not going to move in with you unless we are married."

Candice lifted her eyebrows at that statement, so Shane continued. "I think the mistake I made with Aubrey is I confused lust for love. After we started living together, it seemed marriage was the obvious next step. The problem is, a marriage can't survive without love, and I don't think we were ever truly in love."

"Well, Shane I do believe we've officially ended our first disagreement. Hopefully next time we have an issue we can work it out without retreating to our separate quarters. I know I told you to leave, but as we both can see now, that was probably not the best solution. You and I look like something the cat drug in."

"Agreed. No leaving upset or mad. Now come here and let me kiss you." Candice was more than happy to comply as she leaned over and let Shane devour her with his mouth.

"Oh, and one last thing," Shane said as he pulled away from the kiss.

"Yes."

"We're still going to look at the house on Sunday. It's not a pipe dream. All hopes and dreams are important to explore. So, we'll go with an open mind." Shane kissed her forehead and then stepped out of the car. "Let's go get that coffee now."

Jazzlene walked into her studio and found Candice sitting on the couch with her feet on the table. "Hey, you look tired."

"Yeah, I didn't sleep at all last night." Candice stood to go get another cup of strong coffee.

"You know you should take a break from sex and try to sleep every once in a while."

"I wish that was my reason for being tired."

"Well, are you going to make me beg for details?"

"Shane had a bit of a meltdown when I offered him the keys to the condo."

"I would think that would have made him a happy man."

"You'd think, but oh hell no, he freaked out. Needless to say, I was alone in my bed last night, unable to fall asleep."

"He left you alone? I thought he was protecting you from Brent."

"About Brent, he's in rehab. He was arrested for DUI and drugs. He'll be gone for at least thirty days."

"Well, that's good that he's getting help, and you'll have some peace for a month."

"That's what I'm thinking. Maybe his irrational behavior is due to the drugs."

"I'm sure you're right. I never trusted him, but the stalking, now that took him to a new level."

"You're telling me. Hey, here's another bit of interesting news. Shane's best friend is a cop named Kevin," Candice paused to let that piece of information sink in.

Jazzlene thought for a second. "Kevin, as in Stella's husband, Kevin?"

"One and the same."

"So, Shane is the man Stella has been trying to introduce you to for over a year now?"

"That would be him. Guess fate always has a way of working things out." Candice mischievously grinned.

"What's with that look?"

"I'm just wondering what went on in that darkroom yesterday. Seemed you and Steve got a little cozy in there. Or at least that was my observation when I saw how disheveled you two were when you came out."

Jazzlene blushed. "Speaking of Steve, when did he transform into the hunk of a man who walked in here yesterday? I mean, damn, I had a hard time keeping my hands off him."

"Well, from what I suspect, he felt the same way. You know he's always had a thing for you."

"Yes, but let's just say I was a stupid, naive teenager. Although, now I see the errors of my ways when it comes to Steve. He called me last night, supposedly, to ask questions about the website. And we ended up talking for two hours. We're going out Thursday for dinner since my Friday and Saturday are booked."

"You have Sunday afternoon off," Candice informed Jazzlene as she reviewed the calendar.

"Yes, thank goodness."

"Well, maybe you can invite Steve to watch football on Sunday. Shane and I are going to Stella's so the men can watch football. I'm sure two more in the mix would be welcome."

"I'll ask him. I bet he would enjoy that. It seems universal. All men bond over football."

"Guess it's like women bonding over shopping." Candice tossed in.

"And gossip, can't leave that out," Jazzlene added.

"Can I presume you are officially moving on from my brother?"

"I love your brother. He's great for a romp in the sack, but he has serious commitment issues. I can't wait forever for him to grow up."

"I don't think he'll ever grow up, and I love him too, but Steve was mature even as a teenager. He always had his shit together."

"Just don't say anything to your brother yet. We're on a break, and I'm free to date who I want. But you know, there's no sense rubbing his nose in it."

"Don't worry, I won't say anything except if he asks. I won't lie, either. I'll say you're dating and leave it at that."

"Thanks. I'll talk to Steve about Sunday. Now it's time for me to get some work done."

Candice sat at her desk, willing five o'clock to arrive. The moment the long hand hit the twelve, she set the answering machine and turned the sign on the door to *closed*.

Jazzlene came out of the darkroom just as Candice's phone began to ring. She looked at the caller id and saw it was Shane.

"Hi, how was your day?" she asked.

"Good, I got my second wind around four, so I'm going to be about fifteen minutes late. I'm on my way now. I just had to make a quick detour."

"Okay, see ya soon." Candice turned to Jazzlene. "So, what are your plans tonight?"

"Steve's stopping by in a few minutes to show me what he's done so far on the website. Then who knows what the night has in store. I'll keep my options open." Jazzlene smiled.

"Wow, he's working fast on the site. Guess when that's what you do for a living, you become pretty proficient at it."

"How 'bout you? What are you doing?"

"I think I'm going to curl up next to Shane and go to sleep."

"Really? You have that gorgeous man, and you're going to sleep?"

"Well, maybe not at first, but I bet I'll be out like a light soon after."

"Oh, there's Steve." Jazzlene went to unlock the door. "Hi."

"Hi," Steve said to both women. "Hope you don't mind me keeping you here, but I want to see if I'm taking your site in the right direction before I put too many hours into it."

"You're not keeping me at all. This is quite exciting."

Candice powered up the computer and moved to sit on the couch. Steve went and found a chair in the break room and placed it next to Candice's desk. He sat in the chair vacated by Candice and started tapping on the computer keys.

"Jazz, sit next to me so you can see the screen." She sat, leaning over to view the monitor. Her long dark tresses fell onto Steve's arm and tickled his skin, but he did not move.

"That looks great."

"I made a few different pages so you could choose the look you like." Steve flipped to another page.

"Oh, I think I like this one even better, if that's possible."

"Well, how 'bout this one." He opened another page.

"Each page looks better than the last," Jazzlene praised.

After looking at six more pages, Jazzlene asked him to go back to page four. "I think that's it. It's exactly what I see in my mind when I hear the name Jazz Photography."

"Okay, so that's the design I will use throughout the site."

"Candice, come and take a look at this and tell me if you agree."

Candice did not respond. Jazzlene peered over the top of the screen. "She's asleep," Jazzlene whispered.

"Rough night?" Steve murmured back.

"Yeah. She didn't get much sleep, yet she shows up here and puts in a full day."

Shane walked through the door, noticing Candice asleep on the couch. He caught four eyes looking at him over the top of the computer screen. Jazzlene motioned for him to come over.

"Tell me your opinion of this page Steve designed," Jazzlene softly spoke.

"It's perfect. I love the logo, too," Shane quietly said.

"Shane, I think you and Steve met the other night."

Steve put out his hand to shake Shane's. "Yes, we did."

Feeling the sexual tension between Steve and Jazzlene put Shane's mind at ease. Friday, he felt Steve was a threat, but now he knew that was not the case. Steve plainly only had eyes for Jazzlene.

"I guess I'd better get Candice home. Neither one of us got much sleep last night." Shane did not offer any further explanation.

"Yeah, she said she was tired, but she stayed and worked the entire day. I told her to go home, but she refused."

Shane knelt in front of the couch. "Candice honey, time to go home." He brushed the hair from her eyes.

She rolled over with her back to him. He rubbed it in an attempt to rouse her from sleep. "Babe, time to wake up," he whispered.

"Good luck with that. You may need to just throw her over your shoulder and carry her out." Jazzlene laughed, thinking of caveman Shane hauling Candice over his shoulder.

He scooped her up into his arms and kissed her. Her eyes fluttered open, and she smiled. "I thought I was dreaming. Did you rub my back?"

"Yes, but that still didn't wake you."

Suddenly, she noticed she was in the studio and not at home. She scanned the office and saw Jazzlene and Steve at the computer.

"Hey, sleepy head, your man has come to take you home," Jazzlene said. "I'll see you tomorrow."

Shane set Candice down so she could walk to the car. "Yeah, see ya in the morning."

Shane opened the car door, leaning in to reach for something. "Accept these with my deepest apology for my behavior last night." He handed her a dozen long-stemmed red roses.

"Thank you, but let's not make a habit of disagreeing. Although I do love the make-up roses, they are so fragrant."

"I also stopped and got some Chinese food for dinner." Shane did not want to waste time making dinner. He needed to get home, eat dinner, make love to Candice, and then hold her the entire night.

"Thank you for dinner. That was very good."

"You're welcome. It's from my favorite Chinese restaurant."

Candice rinsed her plate and put it in the dishwasher. "I'm going to take a quick shower."

"Okay, I'll put the food away."

Shane whistled as he cleared the table and put the leftovers in the refrigerator. He found some matches in the drawer, entered Candice's room, and lit some candles while she was in the bathroom.

She walked into the room with her hair wrapped in a towel. However, that was the only part of her covered. With a sultry look, Candice walked over to Shane and hugged him. He slowly pulled the towel off her head, letting the damp hair fall around her shoulders.

"Go dry your hair while I take a quick shower." He kissed her and then spun back in the direction of the bathroom.

"Maybe I can't wait for you to take a shower. What if I want you right here, right now?"

"You have to wait. I've been working in the shop all day. Believe me, it will be the fastest shower humanly possible." Shane stripped naked and was at full staff. "See this?" He gave Candice a full-frontal view of his extraordinary body. "This, my love, is what you do to me."

"Get your ass in the shower, so I can have some of that." Candice picked up the blow dryer and started to dry her hair.

In Shane's effort to make up for last night's debacle, he did everything possible to take Candice to a place of ecstasy over the next hour. Making sure he met all her needs before allowing himself to fill her with him. Soon they were lying face to face and wrapped tightly in each other's arms.

"Babe?" Shane broke the silence.

"Yeah."

"I love you. It's a love I've never felt and don't understand, but I know I can't be without you next to me after last night.

"I love you, too. But the difference is I do understand how I feel and what this all means to me. So, I will let you set the pace in this relationship and follow your lead. I'll be here when you're ready for me with my heart for you to take."

Shane smiled. "I think I'm on my way to being ready. You're helping me see the possibilities of our mutual attraction and love. This thing we've got is more than just sex. Every time I come in you, a piece of my past is replaced with a piece of my future. I'm starting to feel whole again."

Candice nuzzled her head onto his shoulder and tenderly kissed him. "I'm glad I'm the woman who can do that for you. And since we're on the subject of love, please make love to me again."

Thirteen

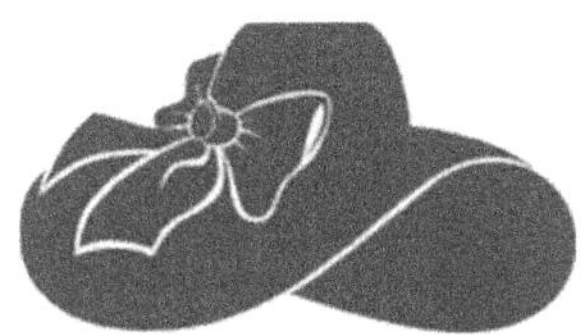

"Honey, are you almost ready?" Shane called from the living room.

"Yes," Candice responded, coming into view. She was wearing a sleeveless summer dress with a pastel floral print. It hugged her body nicely, accentuating her curves. She complimented the dress with a pair of wedge sandals.

"Wow, the perfect choice for today. You are too cute in that dress." This was the first time Shane had the pleasure of seeing Candice wearing a dress.

"Well, I'm sure what I have on under this dress does not qualify as cute. Should I show you?"

"If you show me, I guarantee we'll be late." Shane stood up, and Candice saw he meant what he was saying. "I'll unwrap my special gift later tonight."

Candice carefully stacked the containers housing the goodies she was transporting to the antique store. "I think I've made enough variety for a good taste test."

"More than enough. Did you put some aside for tomorrow?"

"Yes." Candice looked back at the table. "I think this will take three trips to get everything to the car. Can you grab those dishes? I thought I'd plate the treats on those."

Shane picked up the serving plates and escorted Candice to the elevator.

"This is going to be an interesting day. If the *yes* replies to the email invitation I sent are any indication, it will be a great turnout."

Candice started feeling apprehensive. "Are you sure I made enough? I'd hate to run out."

"Look at it this way, if you do run out, that means everyone loved them, and they will want to know where to purchase them."

"Yeah, you're right. Leave them begging for more."

"And that's something you seem to be very good at." Shane leaned over and kissed her. "I just can't get enough of you."

"That goes both ways," Candice purred, exaggeratedly batting her eyelashes.

"Okay, cute dress and flirtatious eyes will win every time. I say we head back upstairs."

"I seem to remember a saying, 'good things come to those that wait.' So, you'll just have to wait," Candice jokingly responded.

Beatrice was holding the back door open when they arrived. "Good morning," she welcomed brightly. She was definitely a morning person.

Shane kissed her cheek. "Mornin'. Where are we setting up?"

"I have a dining table in the middle of the store ready," Beatrice responded.

Candice followed Shane's lead and gave Beatrice a kiss. "Thank you for letting me do this here."

"It's my pleasure. Now, I have fresh coffee, tea, milk, and water. I think those pair well with sweets."

"Oh yes, you're way ahead of me. I didn't even think about the refreshments," Candice confessed, dismayed that she overlooked the drinks.

When they entered the store, Candice realized how much time Beatrice put into making this day perfect. On the large dining table was an exquisite tablecloth with hand-embroidered flowers accenting the crisp linen. A fresh floral arrangement was in the center of the table with Candice's new favorite flowers, red roses. There were several empty antique serving dishes.

"I thought you might like to use those dishes to arrange the treats."

"Yes, they are beautiful." Candice removed the lid from the container with the truffles. "I think this smaller plate would be perfect for the truffles."

"May I try a truffle?" Beatrice asked. The scent of the chocolate was hard to resist.

"Of course, you may." Candice smiled, turning to Shane. "Babe, do you know where I put those display cards I made?"

"I think you put them in your purse," Shane replied.

"Oh no. I left my purse at home. I had my arms full and didn't even realize I wasn't carrying it."

"I'll run back and get it," Shane offered, heading toward the back door.

"So dear, I hear that Brent is in rehab. I guess that eases your mind a bit?" Beatrice questioned without prying.

"Yes, I was pretty shocked, but it explains his irrational behavior."

"Drugs can ruin a person's life if they don't get the help they need. Seems this is a blessing in disguise for him."

"I would have to agree."

"And how are you doing? I know Shane was having some difficulty a few days ago. I spoke to him briefly when he came home."

Candice stopped plating the cookies and looked at Beatrice. "I'm trying to understand and give him space. I've never gone through the betrayal he's experienced. Of course, I've had a broken heart. But no one has ever taken me for everything I had. So, I understand why he's being very cautious."

"Yes, that has been very hard for me to watch him deal with, but in the end, it really is better he got out of that marriage. We'll leave that in the past and move forward."

"Well, I just want to say one thing on that subject; I don't understand how anyone could be so cruel to another person."

"I don't either." Beatrice walked over to Candice and took her hands. "He loves you very much." Candice looked into Beatrice's comforting eyes. "The first time he brought you to the house, I could see it in his eyes. You only see that look in a man when he's truly in love. It's the first time I've seen Shane have that passion." Candice continued to listen to Beatrice, desperately wanting to hear her insight into Shane. "When he came home on Sunday night, he looked sick. At first, I thought that was what was wrong, but then he told me he was scared. You were making him question everything about himself and love. I know he thought he could just turn and walk away, but I knew better. You see, my dear, you can't turn off true love even when you try to protect your wounded heart."

"I don't want to lose him. I'm trying so hard to understand what he needs."

"That is very wise. He'll figure it out. It didn't take long for him to go out and find you the next morning." Candice raised her questioning eyebrows. "I heard him leave. In fact, I'm pretty sure he was up all night. I kept hearing him pace the hallway. I don't think he got one wink of sleep."

"How can you know after only a few weeks that a person is the right one?" Candice asked Beatrice, looking to her for wisdom.

"You just do. The heart knows what it knows. Take my late husband and me. I met him when I was fifteen and knew we'd be married one day. From the moment I met him, he had my heart. I can't explain it. It just is." Beatrice smiled at the memory of her husband. "There will always be good times with bad times sprinkled in, but only remember the good times and let the bad slip away."

"Thank you. You've really helped me."

"No reason to thank me. I just know my grandson, and I love his choice of the woman he will marry. This time for the right reasons." Candice choked on hearing that last statement. "Don't be so surprised. You must feel it too. It's hard not to notice how you two look at each other. I can see you two can't keep your hands off each other. The chemistry is undeniable."

Candice blushed and turned away. *Were they that obvious?*

Shane walked in, holding Candice's purse. "Here, babe." He handed her the small paper placards that he found inside her purse. He also took note of

Candice's flushed face. *What had Candice and his grandmother been talking about?* "You okay?"

"Yes, fine. Your grandmother was telling me about—oh, never mind." She stopped mid-sentence, trying to decide how much to divulge.

"What did she say?' Shane needed to know because Candice was obviously embarrassed.

"How we can't keep our hands off each other." Candice felt coy.

"I'd say she's right on the money. Like now, I want to take you in the back and tear that dress off," Shane whispered in her ear.

"Stop, or I'll never get through the day," she ordered with an alluring smile.

Beatrice walked into the back room to turn on the music.

"Now that is nice," Candice acknowledged, listening to the soft melody playing.

Shane wrapped his arms around her waist, pulling her close as they swayed to the music.

"Okay, you two, back to work." Beatrice let them know their private moment was over. "Candice, Shane made these questionnaires based on the treats you were bringing. I think it would be great to have each person rate the treats and give comments."

"What a wonderful idea. You made these?" Candice turned to Shane.

"Don't look so surprised. I'm a man of many talents."

"I'm just wondering how you found the time."

"I had Stacy make them for you."

"Oh," Candice sounded disappointed.

Shane could sense her jealousy. "She's studying graphic design and trying to build a portfolio, so she was excited to help."

Candice took a closer look at the questionnaire. The artfully crafted form gave the impression that Candice cared about her future customers. "They are nice, but isn't it a little over the top for marketing research?"

"First impressions, babe, they matter."

"I'll look at Stacy's portfolio if I need a graphic designer. If she can make a questionnaire pop like this, I can only imagine what she can do for a logo or menu."

"Wise business decision. She's very good at what she does. She won't let you down."

"Well, I think it's time to unlock the doors," Beatrice told them, keys jingling as she headed for the front door.

Candice paced around the table for the tenth time, checking to make sure everything was in place.

"I'm gonna head out. I need to go to the dojang and get in a workout."

"Dojang?"

"Where I practice taekwondo. I've skipped a couple workouts."

"Oh. Well, you go have fun. I'll talk to you tonight."

Just as Shane left, the first customers entered the store.

"Welcome," Beatrice warmly greeted. "I didn't expect to see you." She gave the woman a heartfelt hug.

"I just got back into town, and this seemed like a great way to start my day. Visit a dear friend and sample something sweet."

"Candice, this is my friend Maxine. We go way back to our youth."

"Hello," Candice spoke, a little reserved.

"Candice is dating our Shane."

"Really?' The sound of surprise in Maxine's voice caught Candice off-guard.

"Well, we've only been dating a few weeks." Candice clarified, feeling slightly defensive.

"I seem to remember him smitten with Stacy," Maxine claimed with an unbecoming and sheepish grin.

Candice's heart about stopped. *No, no, no. She had to have misheard Maxine.*

Beatrice jumped in. "Maxine, why don't you try one of these truffles. Here's a questionnaire for you to fill out about the treats you try today."

"Can you excuse me a minute?" Candice asked, fleeing the room without waiting for a response. She stood in the stock room, trying to slow her breathing. *How could this be? He said total honesty, but he boldfaced lied.*

Candice calmed down, knowing she had to stay focused for Beatrice, she put a lot of faith in Candice. She returned to the storefront to find about twenty people all nibbling on her treats.

Beatrice saw Candice and motioned for her to come over. Then, putting her arm around Candice's waist, she held her tight. "Things are going great. I believe their taste buds are dancing."

Candice looked around and listened to the compliments. She had yet to hear one negative remark.

"Excuse me, everyone, I would love to introduce you to Candice. This lovely woman baked these wonderful sweets for you. Your comments are most welcome. She wants your honest feedback."

Candice tried to find her voice. "I am very happy you all took time out of your day to help me. I'm working on a plan to introduce these wonderful desserts to the public, and any input is greatly appreciated."

"Well miss, I for one have never tasted anything as mouthwatering as these truffles," a woman spoke from across the room.

"Oh, then you must try these kumquat cookies! They're out of this world," another woman proclaimed.

In a matter of one minute, the entire room of tasters was comparing notes and trying another morsel of sweetness. The bells above the front door kept jingling as more people arrived.

Candice stood back and watched as each plate slowly emptied. She prayed she made enough but had clearly underestimated the vast outpouring of support Beatrice's customers would bestow upon her. Beatrice had formed a loyal customer base because she was a trusted, caring woman that everyone knew, loved, and respected.

As the day wound down, Candice felt both blessed for all the compliments and overwhelmed at the responsibility the recipes were asking of her.

"Well dear, I think you have your answer. Now the question is what are you going to do?"

Candice looked bewildered. "Honestly, I don't know."

"You've been working on that business plan, right?"

"Yes, I have some ideas jotted down."

"Then we start there. I'll help in any way I can. We need to see this endeavor come to fruition. For some reason, those recipes were entrusted to you. One cannot turn its back on fate."

"You have done so much to push me forward."

"It seems *Grandma Pela* wanted those recipes to live on, and I can't think of a better person for her to have chosen."

Candice gave Beatrice a hug that spoke volumes. "I never knew my grandparents, but I dream they would be just like you."

"I would love for you to call me Grandma."

Candice gave her another squeeze before letting go. "I guess we should get this table cleared." Candice started removing the empty dishes.

"I'm going to head home now. I'll have Shane pick up my dishes later this week."

"Candice, don't overanalyze what you heard today. Maxine doesn't always know what she's talking about."

"I'll try." Candice's eyes gave her sorrow away.

"Honesty and talking always work. Just be true and honest." Beatrice advised.

"I don't think I'm the one that's not being honest."

"I mean honest with yourself about what you are feeling." Beatrice clarified.

Candice exited through the front door, deciding to walk home instead of taking the bus. Her cell phone played the familiar ring tone she assigned to Shane. Ignoring it, she entered a store and started to walk around looking at anything to divert her thoughts. She heard the ping that she had voicemail, so she decided to listen to it.

"Hey babe, I'm at my grandmother's store. She said you already left. So, call me back when you get this."

Candice was not ready to talk to Shane, so she put the phone away. She had no idea what to say to him when she confronted him about lying to her.

She left the store and continued to walk towards her home. Approaching a bar that a friend owned, she decided to step inside. Everyone turned as she walked up to the bar and took a seat.

"Hey, Candice, what brings you here?" Her friend Rafe, and owner of the bar asked.

"I was walking home and decided to stop in, say hi, and have a drink."

"What's your pleasure?"

"I'll have a Cosmopolitan."

Rafe started mixing her drink, placing it in front of her.

"How much do I owe you?"

"It's on the house."

"Thanks. So how are your wife and kids?"

"Great, growing up too fast if you want the truth. I'm missin' out on a lot being here every weekend. But it's the payoff for owning your own business."

"I would think that would be hard on you."

"Well, I have finally found a trustworthy manager, so I can take a lot more time off. I know my wife loves having me around more."

Candice downed her drink. "I'll have another."

"You okay?"

"Yeah, just a long day and I'm not ready to go home," Candice sighed.

"You know, Brent's been coming in here a lot. I think he's looking for you."

"Yeah, he's been showing up at my place too. I can't get it through his thick skull that we're over, and there will never be a 'Brent and Candice' again."

Candice's cell rang again. She knew it was Shane, so she did not even take it out of her purse. That did not escape Rafe's watchful eyes.

"So, I suspect boyfriend trouble?"

"You got it. Give me a shot of tequila."

Rafe hesitated. "You should pace yourself."

"Yeah, I know, but just give me the shot."

Reluctantly, Rafe poured her a half shot of tequila.

She downed it, followed by her second Cosmopolitan.

"So...oh yes, you were asking me about guy trouble. Yes, I have a trust problem, but I'll get over it or him, whichever comes first."

"I'll be back in a sec," Rafe said as he went to fill some other drink orders.

Three hours later, the bar was starting to fill up as the sunset. The music pulsed through the bar, encouraging people onto the dance floor. Several of the customers were friends that Brent and Candice used to hang out with on weekends at Rafe's.

"Hey, Candice, what brings you here?" Noah, a friend of Brent, asked.

Candice turned around. "Hey, it's been a long time since I've seen you." She stood up to give him a hug.

"Want to dance?"

"Sure. Rafe, can you stow this behind the bar?" Candice handed him her purse.

Noah took her hand and led her to the dance floor. "I heard Brent is in rehab."

"Yes, that's what I've heard too." She did not elaborate on the other more disconcerting details.

"He's been quite the mess since you two broke up."

"Well, what can I say, he screwed up, and I can't forgive him for what he did." Candice shrugged her shoulders.

"I get it. He has a problem with monogamy. I don't blame you, he told me what happened."

"Yeah, well it's over and done. I've moved on."

"You were too good for him anyway."

The song ended, and Candice wanted to go sit back down. "Thanks for the dance Noah."

"Anytime," he smiled walking her back to the bar. "What are you drinking?"

"Cosmo, but I think I should stop for the night." Candice was one drink away from losing all her inhibitions.

"Rafe, a Cosmo for Candice and a shot of whiskey for me."

Rafe looked at Candice. "I think she's had enough for one night."

"I can have one more then I have to get home. I have a busy day tomorrow."

Rafe watered down the drink as much as he could without being obvious.

"One more dance before you leave?" Noah asked after emptying his shot glass.

"Sure, why not." Candice stood, trying to keep her legs steady. It was a slow song, so Noah was able to hold her upright. She laid her head on his shoulder and closed her eyes. *What the hell was she doing letting some guy that was not Shane hold her so intimately?*

When the song ended, she stood back looking up at Noah. The longing in his eyes was unmistakable, but she pretended not to notice.

"Rafe, can you hand me my purse?" She pulled out her cell phone and saw three more missed calls from Shane. Covering her ear, she tried to listen to them, but the music was too loud.

I'll just text him back.

Candice—I s u 2maro—She hit send.

Her cell phone pinged.

Shane—Where are you?

Candice—At bar

Shane—Which one?

Candice—Se ya 2mro

Shane—Damn it, which fuckin' bar?

Candice—Nite

"I'm gonna head out. See you soon." Candice stood up and held onto the back of the chair as she tried to get her bearings. Then, she quickly sat back down. "Rafe, toss me some of those pretzels."

Rafe placed the bowl in front of her. He noticed her cell phone was now lying on the bar and saw her text light up. "Maybe you should respond to that text."

"Nah, I told him I'd see him later." She rested her head on her hand.

Her phone rang. "You going to answer that?" Rafe asked.

"Nope."

Rafe saw that it said, *Shane*. "Is Shane the guy you're pissed off at?"

"Yep."

"Mind if I answer it?" Rafe asked.

"No, be my guest." She felt pleased with herself. Let Shane deal with hearing a man's voice answering her phone.

"Hello," Rafe said.

Shane could hear the music in the background. "Who's this?"

Rafe started walking toward the backroom so he could hear Shane. "Rafe. I take it you're looking for Candice?"

"Yes, is she there?"

"Sitting at my bar. She was pretty pissed when she dropped in earlier tonight."

"Which bar is she at?"

"Rafe's All Nighter. You know where it is?"

"Yeah, keep her there, I'm on my way."

"I'll try, but she's pretty determined to leave."

Rafe went back behind the bar, but Candice was gone, and so was Noah. "Shit."

Noah had his arm around Candice, trying to keep her from falling over. Finally, they made it to her building and entered the elevator. Once inside, she leaned against the wall and slowly slid to the floor.

"Come on Candice, you need to stand up." Noah picked her up off the floor.

Shane stormed into Rafe's, making a beeline for the bar. "Where is she?" he asked with a sharp tone of panic when he did not see her.

"She left with a guy named Noah. Here's her cell phone." Rafe handed the phone to Shane.

"Do you know where they went?"

"No, but I assume she went back to her place. For what it's worth, she's known Noah for years."

"Thanks." Shane pocketed her phone heading back to his car.

Candice held onto Noah as they walked down the hallway to her door. She fiddled with the keys, trying to get them into the lock with no success.

Noah took the keys. "Let me." He inserted the key and unlocked the door.

Candice made it to the couch with his assistance then heavily landed on the cushions.

"Thank you," she said, before closing her eyes.

Noah sat there a minute, deciding if he should put her to bed or leave her on the couch. He pulled the blanket lying over the back of the sofa and covered her with it. *Damn, even plastered to the hilt, she was beautiful.* He sat just staring at her.

Shane pulled into the parking garage and ran to the elevator. He knew she was alone, drunk, and with some guy who could take advantage of her.

The door opened, and Noah looked over to see Shane coming into the condo.

"She's passed out," he said, standing up getting ready to leave. "Not sure what had her upset tonight, but I've only seen her like this once before."

Shane tried to register that last comment Noah made. "Why would you think she was upset?"

"Because Candice never gets wasted. Last time I remember her like this, was when—never mind, that does not matter," Noah stopped himself.

"How do you know her?" Shane needed to find out if Noah was once more than just a friend.

"She dated my friend for a few years. We used to all hang out together."

"Oh, I see. So Rafe's is the old stompin' ground?"

"Well, you could say that. Her old stompin' grounds, the rest of us still hang out there on the weekends."

This was not good. She was trying to reconnect with her past. Find some sort of support from people she used to be close too. *What the hell happened today that sent her seeking comfort?*

"Thanks for making sure she got home safe. I'll take it from here."

"You're welcome." Noah made his way out the door.

Shane sat on the couch confused and scared out of his mind. When Candice refused to answer his calls, he was upset, but once the garbled text came in, he went into a full-blown panic mode. If it were not for Rafe answering her phone, he would still be looking all over San Francisco for her.

He walked into the bedroom and turned down the bedding. When Shane picked her up from the couch, she lay limp in his arms like a sack of potatoes. He carried her to her bedroom and gently placed her on the bed. He unbuckled her shoes and tossed them into the corner. Taking her dress off was not going to be easy. He rolled her onto her side to unzip the back and then flipped her onto her back to pull her arms out of the armholes. While he was doing this, she did not move at all. She just kept on sleeping. He realized if Noah wanted to, he could have had his way with Candice, and she may never have remembered. Once he removed her dress, her lacy lingerie greeted him. He gazed at her for a few seconds before pulling the blankets up to cover her beautiful body.

Shane went into the kitchen and got a big glass of water and some aspirin. She was going to need those in the morning. He climbed into bed, snuggling next to her. Candice squirmed away from him.

"Stacy," she mumbled.

Shane was not sure he heard her right. "What?"

"All lies," she said barely auditable.

Shane knew he was not going to get answers tonight, but he sure as heck would find out what was going on in the morning.

Fourteen

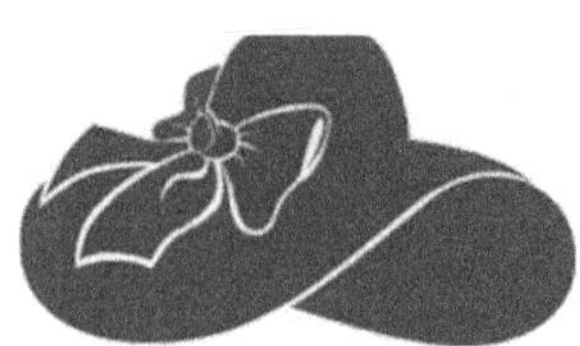

Candice rolled over and saw Shane watching her. "What are you doing here?" Candice questioned, feeling groggy. "The agreement was you don't come over without letting me know. Your rules, not mine."

"How's your head?" He tried to remain calm.

"Sore."

He reached for the water and aspirins. "Here, take these."

"Thank you."

"Now what the hell happened yesterday? I heard everything went great and you got only positive compliments. So, between great and drunk, what happened?"

"Let's just say I found out some information you were keeping from me."

"Like what?" Shane was dumbfounded as to what it could be.

"Does Stacy ring a bell?"

"I told you nothing is going on between us. She's just an employee."

"Really, so you didn't date her? Because Maxine said, you did. You can't have someone as an employee if you dated. I saw the way Stacy looked at you."

Shane smiled.

"Oh, you think this is funny?" Candice spat out.

"No, but didn't we make a promise to talk to each other if something was bothering us?"

"Yeah, I planned on talking to you, but—how did I get home?"

"You don't remember?"

"No, this is not good." Candice shook her head.

"Seems your friend Noah walked you home. He was sitting on the couch with you when I arrived here last night."

Candice was horrified. "Oh, god no. I'm sorry."

Shane did not respond.

"How did you find me?" Candice finally asked, somewhat confused.

"Some guy named Rafe answered your phone and told me you were sitting at his bar. So when I got there, you were already gone."

"And that is why I don't normally drink, but I was so confused and hurt by what Maxine told me."

"Again, we need to talk if something is bothering us. Maxine has a granddaughter named Stacy. I dated her for a few months, but it never went anywhere. That is the Stacy she was referring to, not the young Stacy working for me. So, you see love, you must not jump to conclusions. This all could have been cleared up with one phone call."

"I'm so sorry."

"Just don't scare the hell out of me like that again. If you want to hang out at a bar, just let me know where you are, and I'll come get you when you're ready to come home. Any guy last night could have taken you home and done whatever he wanted. You would never have remembered who he was or what happened. You were passed out when I got here."

Candice got up slowly to use the restroom. "Oh, god my head is pounding."

"Yeah, you're going to feel pretty crappy today."

Candice noticed she was only in her bra and panties. "Did you take my clothes off or did I?"

"I did. See what I mean about you not remembering what happened last night?"

When she returned, Shane lifted the blankets so Candice could climb back in bed. "Now what I want to do is rip those lacy panties off of you. Ever since I undressed you last night, that's all I can think of."

"Not now, I have a headache."

"I believe you, but that doesn't stop me from wanting you." Shane ran his hand along her inner thigh, inching up to the spot he was aiming to reach. Candice opened her legs for him, welcoming his warm hands.

"Take me," she said softly into his ear.

Shane removed her bra so he could feel her warm breasts on his chest. He pulled down her panties, and she slid them the rest of the way off. Then, crawling on top of her, he rested his hands on either side of her on the bed. Candice took her hand and guided him into her so there would be no mistake that she wanted him. No headache was going to stop her body from taking in his pleasures.

She moaned quietly as he kissed her neck. Opening her legs wider, she relaxed into the rhythm of his thrust, allowing him to sink deeper into her.

He looked into her eyes, connecting on a deep level of trust. They locked gazes as Shane continued a slow, steady thrust, hitting the spot inside her that caused her to tighten her muscles around him. He knew she was close if he could only hold out a few more minutes. When he felt her tighten around him again, he heard the undeniable sound of her pleasure, he let himself release inside her. He wanted to restrain himself, but he could hold back no longer. They continued to watch each other until they both hit their last shudder and Shane collapsed on top of her.

"Is your headache gone?"

"No, but who cares," she hugged him.

"Where is this house?" Shane asked as he backed out of the parking space.

"Noe and 24th." Candice put on her sunglasses.

"Still got that headache?"

"Yes, but it's starting to subside a bit. Remind me not to drink like that again."

"Well, I wasn't there to stop you or I would have." Shane rested his hand on Candice's leg.

"I hope I didn't make a fool out of myself. No telling what I did. Although I think I slowed danced with Noah," she confessed, not sure if it had been real or a dream.

"Did you now?" He turned and looked at her.

"I think so. I can't remember if I slowed dance with him, or if it was you holding me last night. I just remember laying my head on someone's shoulder and them holding me."

"Well, I did hold you all night, so let's just assume that's what you remember, okay?"

"Okay." The guilt was setting in. Candice probably did let Noah hold her a little too intimately, but there was nothing to change that now.

Shane continued until he reached Noe and 24th. "Where to now?"

"Just park anywhere, and we'll walk."

Shane found a parking spot. "It's right over here," Candice said, pointing toward the tri-level Victorian. She stopped in front of it, as captivated by its beauty as she was the first time she saw the house.

"Is this the house? This one right here?" Shane pointed, wanting to make sure there was no mistake.

"Yes. What do you think, location wise?"

"Noe Valley is very trendy, so I think it's a great location. Look at all the foot traffic."

"That's what I thought. Of course, the outside needs some paint, and the tree should be pruned way back, but it's so charming, right?"

"It's very cute. A sweets café would be perfect in the commercial space." Shane turned and looked across the street.

"Wait until you see the inside of the apartments." Candice was growing excited at the prospect of walking through the house again.

Shane got very quiet as he looked at the house. *This is going to be interesting.* He hoped that the business plan they worked on would be enough to persuade the owner.

Trevor arrived right on time with the elderly owner of the property. All eyes collided and Candice's mouth dropped open.

"Hey dad," Shane said, addressing Trevor. He did not seem surprised to see his father.

Dad? How did she not know? Oh yeah, she only knew Trevor by his first name, Candice tried to piece it together.

The two men hugged. "What are you doing here?" Trevor asked.

Beatrice looked as shocked as Candice did. "Would you mind telling me what is going on?"

"Yes, mother. This is Candice, the woman that fell in love with this house."

"Shane, did you know about this?" Beatrice turned to Shane.

"Nope can't say that I did. I'm as surprised as you are."

"Let's go inside and discuss this." Trevor unlocked and opened the door to the commercial unit.

The four of them stepped inside and then Trevor closed the door.

"What is going on?" Candice was still confused, and her headache was not helping her think clearly.

Shane turned to Candice. "Babe, this is my grandmother's house. The house I lived in until I was seven."

Beatrice spoke up, "Candice is this the place you've had in your mind for the sweets café?"

"Yes, I think it's perfect and adorable. And I have to admit, the apartments are incredibly special. I fell in love with this home."

"So, what would you change?"

"Nothing, except fresh paint and yard clean-up. I love everything about this house."

"I see. So, would you rent out the apartments or convert it back into the original single-family home?"

"Oh, I guess I would rent out the top floor and live on the second. Maybe someday when I have a family, I'd find the need to convert it back to a single-family home."

"And that business plan we've talked about, do you have that done for me to review?"

"Shane and I have been working on it, but it's not complete yet." Candice was starting to shake. She wanted to have all the correct answers for Beatrice.

"Okay, I'd like to see what you have so far. I believe my dear, we can work something out that will make you and I both very happy."

Trevor and Shane remained quiet. They knew not to interrupt Mrs. Beatrice Anders when she was talking business.

Beatrice turned to Shane. "I expect you to help Candice get this commercial unit up to code and with a kitchen that will meet her baking needs?"

"Yes, of course, part of her plan was to use some of the furniture in my shop for the business. Then she can sell it on consignment. Would that work for you?"

"Fabulous idea. There's no room to display everything in my store."

Trevor finally spoke. "Mother, so as far as I can tell, you're interested in selling this place to Candice?"

"No, I'm interested in partnering with her, and mentoring her until her business is profitable."

Candice swallowed. "I don't understand. I thought you wanted to sell this place?"

"If I sell it to you, you won't be able to afford the startup cost to open the café. So, as I see it, we can work as partners. I'll be a silent partner. The commercial space will be rent-free. You will pay me a percentage of your profits should there be any. I suspect from my experience, the first year or two you will be building your business. After that, more money will go out before you start to see a profit. Then, once your business can stand independently without my help, we'll renegotiate a deal to buy it. I suspect somewhere around the five-year mark, maybe sooner."

"You believe in me that much?"

"I certainly do. I know you have a mind for business and a passion for those recipes. I also believe that fate has brought us together to help one another. I have one request."

"Yes."

"You must live in one of the units, as well as managing the other one."

"How much do you want for the rents?"

"Well, Shane told me you have a condo you own. Is that correct?"

"Yes."

"Then why don't you rent out your condo. What you receive in rent for your condo, is what the rent will be here."

"You're serious about all this? It's such a shock. I'm having a hard time comprehending the situation."

"What is going on, my dear is that I have faith in you and I am going to help you fulfill your dream."

Trevor stepped forward. "I will help you rent the other apartment and screen the applicants."

"So, we'll sit down and discuss everything when you bring me your business plan. Now Shane and Trevor, please go take a look at this space and then find me the best people to help us get this unit up to code."

"I'll make some calls tomorrow," Trevor told her.

"I'd liked to go upstairs so I can see how the apartments look," Beatrice requested with authority.

As they walked up the stairs, Shane reached for Candice's hand. He needed to draw on her strength before entering the apartment.

"So, do you remember which room was yours?" Trevor turned to Shane to see the eyes of the little boy he once was.

"Yes, I remember. It was this one here." Shane walked into the bedroom and looked around. It was exactly as he remembered.

"This was your room?" Candice held tight to his shaking hand.

Suddenly, Candice remembered the story of the family that once lived in this house. Shane was the little boy who lost his mother to cancer. His MOM tattoo must be his way of keeping her close to his heart. Now she understood the reason he kissed her fingers after she traced the letters of his tattoo. She had to fight back the tears as she looked at Trevor. She empathized with the sad reality that his wife died in this house.

Beatrice looked around. "I think everything looks good. But, Trevor, I want you to have someone come out and check all utilities before Candice moves in. Hire one of those home inspectors."

"I'll get on that tomorrow, as well."

"I'd like to see the smaller apartment," Beatrice informed Trevor. Once she completed her assessment of the third story, she was satisfied.

"Dad, I guess I should introduce you to my girlfriend now." Shane had not let go of Candice's hand since leaving the commercial unit.

"Well, since I've already met her, I think no introductions are necessary. Although, I would like to say officially 'nice to meet you' as Shane's girlfriend and not just the beautiful woman who loves our home."

Candice smiled. "You know Mr. Anders, I hadn't even met Shane the day I came to see this place. Earlier that day, I had met your mother before calling about this house. And I guess the stars aligned to make all this possible."

"You have to trust in fate," Beatrice paused, "there's always a reason for everything."

Trevor turned to Shane. "Have you visited your sister lately?"

"Yes, last week, but maybe I'll stop by today and introduce Candice to her."

"I think that is a great idea," Trevor stated. "Is there one night this week we can all get together for a family dinner?"

"I have all week open, how 'bout you Candice?" Shane squeezed her hand.

"I'm free too."

"Fine, let's meet for dinner Wednesday around seven at that little Italian place on the corner," Trevor suggested.

"We'll be there," Shane replied.

"Okay mother, I think I shall drive you home, and we'll discuss how you want to handle the specifics of this transaction."

Beatrice gave Candice a hug. "Believe in yourself. We will make this happen."

"Thank you." Candice kissed her cheek, still a bit in shock.

Shane watched as his father and grandmother strolled off.

He took both Candice's hands lifting them to his lips and kissed them. "Now, I will take you to meet my sister."

Candice's head was spinning from the overload of emotions, and her hangover wasn't helping the situation. "I would like that. You've only mentioned her once if I recall."

Shane once again grabbed Candice's hand, entwining his fingers with hers. He watched as traffic whizzed by. Once it was safe, he pulled Candice across the street, making his way to a little house. He knocked loudly on the door.

The door opened. "Good day Mr. Anders. Come in." The man stepped aside to let Shane and Candice enter.

"Hi Carlos, is she in the backyard?" Shane questioned.

"Yes, enjoying the birds," Carlos responded.

They walked past the kitchen. Candice saw a woman preparing a meal. "Hello, Angie." Shane waved to her.

"Good afternoon," Angie replied as she continued to cut vegetables.

"Marni," Shane called out, stepping into the backyard.

Marni quickly turned her head in the direction of his voice. Her few sounds let him know she was happy to see him. He walked over to her and knelt to make eye contact with her.

"Marni, this is my friend Candice," he introduced, speaking clearly.

Marni reached her hand toward Candice. "Be careful. She has a death grip."

"Yes, I know," Candice acknowledged, reaching for Marni's little hand. "Do you mind if I sit with you?"

Marni looked at the empty spot beside her, a nonverbal invitation for Candice to sit. Marni reached up and felt Candice's long hair.

"How do you know about her death grip?" Shane asked, slightly confused.

"I met your sister the first day I found your grandmother's house. A van pulled up in front, I guess they were coming home from an excursion. As they headed toward the house, I had the honor of meeting your sister. Marni held my hand, and I could not get her to let go." Candice smiled at Marni. "Right? You remember meeting me?"

Marni frantically shook Candice's hand to let her know she remembered.

"See, she remembers," Candice said to Shane.

Hector came into the backyard. "Hi, want to see my flowers?" He pointed to a garden of wildflowers.

"Those are beautiful," Candice said, turning to see a colorful garden.

"Hey, I know you. You broke your shoe. I made a rhyme." Hector laughed.

"Yes, I remember you too." Candice smiled.

"Marni, do you want to show me what you made at school?" Shane asked, taking her hand to help her stand up. "Marni here is a great artist," he proudly informed Candice.

"I'd love to see your artwork too," Candice said, following them into the house. "Are you coming, Hector?"

"No, I must water my flowers," he replied as he turned the hose on.

Colorful watercolor paintings hung along one wall of the dining room. Marni went and pulled one off the wall, then handed it to Candice.

"For me? Thank you." It was the prettiest mix of colors, blending to form a kaleidoscope effect. "I will frame this when I get home." Candice took the picture with delight.

Tom was sitting on the couch listening to music.

"Hi Tom," Shane said, walking over to shake Tom's hand.

"Tom, Tom Morgan. Nice to meet you."

"Tom makes those incredible sculptures." Shane pointed to a bookshelf lined with glazed clay pieces.

"Wow, they're very detailed and beautiful." Candice picked one up and could feel the rough texture of the piece. Tom was blind and relied on his sense of touch to enjoy his world. Candice closed her eyes to enjoy the tactile sculpture.

Candice walked over to Tom. "Tom, I love your sculptures, they feel beautiful."

"Tom, Tom Morgan. Thank you."

"You're welcome." Candice took his hand and gave a gentle pat.

Shane looked at his watch. "We really have to get going, Stella and Kevin are expecting us soon."

"Okay. Nice seeing everyone and Marni, thank you for my picture." Marni grabbed Candice's hand and shook it wildly.

"Marni, you need to let go," Shane instructed a moment later, kissing her forehead. She quickly let go of Candice's hand and grabbed his hand. "I love you too. See you next week."

Shane and Candice sat in his car. "Well, I'd say this was a day of surprises," Shane remarked, stating the obvious.

"Yes, I need a few days to let it all sink in. But do you know what the best surprise of the day was for me?" Candice asked.

"There are too many to choose from, so tell me."

"Finding out that Marni is your sister. When I met her a few weeks back, I fell in love with her warm spirit. I can see the love she has in her eyes. I just feel so blessed."

"Yeah, she is sweet." Shane wiped his eyes. "Not many people see her as the special person she is. They just see her outer appearance and her limitations. She understands everything we say, she just can't verbalize. She has her own unique ways of communicating what she needs and how she feels. Like her handshake tells you she is happy to see you. When she doesn't let your hand go, that means she doesn't want you to leave."

"Why does she live in that house and not with family?"

"It's too hard for just one person to tend to her needs. My grandmother is too old, and my father has to work. My grandmother owns the house Marni lives in. When she couldn't find a suitable group home that could meet Marni's needs, she applied for a license to run her own group home. Carlos and Angie are married and live in the house with their son Hector. Grandmother also has part-time help so Carlos and Angie can have some quality time together. Each resident attends school to build their skills and gain experience in a social setting with other special needs adults."

"Wow, your grandmother really is a smart, caring businesswoman."

"When my mother died, Marni was only five. She lived at home with us until my mom got too sick to care for her. Then grandma hired some nannies that could take care of her special needs, but once Marni was around seventeen, grandma thought she should be in a home that could give her the attention she needed."

"Will she be joining us for the family dinner?"

"Sure, we can pick her up on our way there," Shane replied.

"I'd like that. Then, if I do happen to move in across the street, I could check on Marni at least once a day."

"You'd do that?"

"Of course. She's family, and as far as I know, I'm sorta family too. Your grandmother told me to call her grandma yesterday. So, the way I see it, I'm an honorary member of the Anders family."

"I don't know what to say. You're the first person I introduced Marni to that accepted her like their own. Aubrey was uncomfortable around her and would never visit her."

"Really, I don't get that, then again, from what I hear she was not a very caring person."

"No, she was not," Shane agreed.

"How would you feel with me living in your childhood home?"

"It felt good to be in there today. It brought back some very sentimental memories. However, I do have one request."

"Which is?"

"Don't change my room."

"Tell you what, since you'll be there a lot anyway, why don't we make that your space. You do what you want with it."

"No, it's going to be your home, just leave the wallpaper up. I remember picking that out with my mother."

"Nope, if I agree to this business proposition your grandmother discussed today, then I must insist that the room be yours or I don't enter into this agreement."

"We'll cross that bridge when we get there. We have a lot to do to get this idea off the ground."

"Fair enough. Now let's go celebrate with our friends. Without any alcoholic beverages," Candice added, rubbing her head.

"Sorry we're late," Shane announced as he stepped into Kevin's house.

"I brought some goodies," Candice said, holding up the plate.

"We can have them for dessert," Kevin suggested.

"How much of the game did I miss?" Shane asked, trying to catch the score.

"You only missed the first five minutes. Go grab a beer," Kevin said, not taking his eyes off the game.

"Glad you could make it, Steve," Shane said as Steve walked out of the kitchen with a beer.

"Hey, I'm not gonna turn down Jazzlene's invitation. I'd be a fool." Steve smiled.

"Are the girls out back?" Candice asked.

"Yeah, I think Stella's showing Jazzlene her garden or something," Kevin answered with a shrug.

The guys got comfortable on the couch in front of the enormous flat screen TV. "Now this is the way to watch football," Steve commented.

Candice made her way out to the backyard. "Glad to see you finally got here," Jazzlene said. "I got a frantic call last night from Shane. What the hell happened?"

"Oh, just me overreacting to something I misinterpreted. The usual nonsense that is courtesy of my overactive imagination."

"So, you're fine now?" Stella asked.

"Yeah, I just have a killer headache, but serves me right for not trusting Shane."

"Shane is a really great man. So, now you can see why I was trying to introduce you two for so long." Stella smiled.

"You are right about him. I don't know why I didn't listen to you. Where are the kids?" Candice asked.

"Taking a nap. They should be awake as soon as the guys start yelling at the TV."

"Well, let me see if I can tell you about my interesting day. You might want to freshen up your wine, this may take a while."

Candice gave the girls the entire story from the day she saw the house to what transpired over the past few weeks.

"So, are you telling me you're not going to work for me anymore?" Jazzlene asked with a tinge of sadness in her voice.

"Well, I'll work there for a little longer and then find you a great assistant."

"I'm gonna miss you being there when I arrive every morning. Everything runs smoothly when you handle the details."

"Maybe I can work a few hours a day for you," Stella offered.

"I would love your help, but I'm gonna need someone full time," Jazzlene explained.

"Well, if you ever need me to step in for a day or two, just let me know."

Candice turned to Jazzlene. "I need to talk to Steve about seeing my condo because if he's really interested in renting it, I need to know,"

"I believe he's serious," Jazzlene replied.

"Okay, I'll talk to him at halftime."

"What is going on with you and Steve anyway?" Stella asked, tilting her head. "And may I just comment on how incredible he looks. Bet you wish you didn't ignore him in high school."

"Well, he's always been a super nice guy. In high school, I was dating that idiot John, and by the time we broke up, Steve was dating what's her name."

"So, the burning question is, what does he look like under those clothes?" Candice probed.

"Probably better than you can imagine," Jazzlene replied, fanning herself.

"I don't know Jazz, I have a vivid imagination, and I can picture him bare ass naked."

Shane slid the glass door open, holding Kara in his arms. "Stella, the kids woke up. Kevin changed Kara and told me to bring her to you." Shane gave Kara a little kiss before handing her off to Stella.

"Thanks." Stella lifted her blouse discreetly so she could feed Kara.

Little Wesley came barreling out the door and ran straight into Candice's leg, giving it a bear hug. "Canny, up," he said, lifting his arms in the air.

"Hey sweetie, how's my little man?" Candice picked him up and settled him on her lap.

Shane watched as Candice bounced Wesley on her leg.

Kevin walked over to Stella and covered her with a receiving blanket. He was uncomfortable with his wife displaying any part of her breast in front of other men.

"Anyone want another beer or a refill on their wine?" Steve asked, poking his head out the door.

"You can pour me some more wine, please." Jazzlene held up her empty glass.

The men retreated into the house while the girls caught up, sharing their sordid details about their men, that would remain between the three of them.

"Seems like you and Candice are getting along pretty good," Kevin stated.

"She's the one," Shane declared.

"But you've only known her a few weeks," Kevin remarked.

"Well, all I can tell you is, this is so different than how I felt about Aubrey. I thought I was in love with her, but it was nothing like the way I feel about Candice."

"I always knew you two would be good together," Kevin replied with the confident smirk of a man who knew he was right.

"I should have listened to you, my all-knowing friend." Shane chuckled.

"How 'bout you Steve, things with Jazzlene feel right?" Kevin questioned.

"I'm actually surprised by how well things are going. I thought we'd go out once, and that would be where it ended, but so far she seems to be open to our dating exclusively," Steve answered.

"Oh Steve, if you're interested in possibly renting Candice's condo, I think you two could work something out. She's going to need to rent it pretty soon," Shane informed him.

"Sounds good. I know I should have stopped by during the week, but I got busy at work. I'll stop by this week and check it out. What's a good day for you two?"

"Thursday, say around six?"

"I'll be there. I'll ask Jazz to go with me."

The evening ended with everyone planning to get together the following Sunday for another day of friendship, laughter, and of course football.

Fifteen

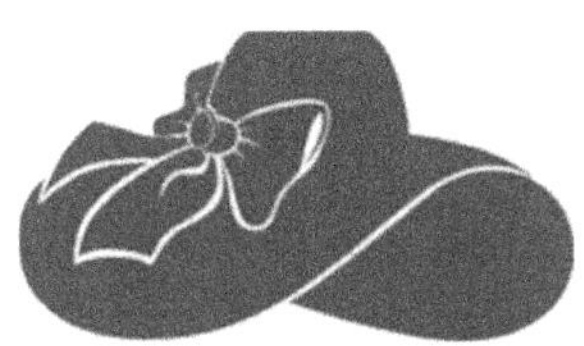

"Marni, are you ready to go to dinner?" Shane asked, helping her put her sweater on.

Marni's big, expressive brown eyes and enthusiastic hand gestures conveyed a definite yes.

Candice reached for Marni's hand before walking her to the car. Shane followed behind, watching as Candice began to sing a song while gently swinging their clasped hands.

The little Italian restaurant was buzzing with happy diners. "It sure is busy in here for a Wednesday night," Candice said, as they entered the crowded foyer.

"Yes, this place is always packed, but once you taste the food, you'll know why," Shane told her, looking to see if he could spot his father.

"I see your dad and grandma." Candice held on tightly to Marni's hand as they squeezed through the crowd milling around by the entrance.

"Hello," Trevor greeted as he stood up. He pulled a chair out for Marni.

Shane pulled a chair out for Candice. *Like father, like son*. "I'd like to sit next to your sister." Candice requested, stepping to the next chair.

"I'm so happy my four favorite people could make it." Beatrice smiled while tucking a napkin into Marni's top.

Before Shane took his seat, he leaned over to give his grandmother a kiss on the cheek. "This truly is a family dinner." He smiled, grateful for his family and incredibly thankful they were *all* together.

The waiter brought over a large loaf of hot San Francisco sourdough bread and set it in the middle of the table. Trevor sliced into it, allowing the steam to swirl from the soft center. Marni's eyes locked onto the dancing vapor, following it up until it slowly dissipated.

"Well, it's so nice to see the entire family here tonight. I'll bring Marni her favorite drink, Shirley Temple with extra maraschino cherries," the waiter stated warmly. "I'll give you a few moments and then be right back to take your order."

Beatrice turned toward Candice. "I have the contract in the car. I would like you to carefully review it. Then next week we'll get together to discuss any changes that may be required to meet both of our needs. I strive to have a happy and prosperous partnership."

"Thank you," Candice responded. "I'll go over it with my father." Candice relied on her father for all her financial advice. He helped to grow her savings into a nice nest egg.

"You know, I'd be delighted to meet your father if he would be willing. I think keeping him involved is important."

"Sure, I'll ask him. I know he'll want to meet everyone." Candice liked that Beatrice suggested including her father, even though she was going to discuss the contract with him anyway.

"I've made an appointment at eleven on Monday for the home inspection," Trevor advised Candice.

"That was fast. I'll try to be there with you," Candice offered.

"Babe, it's okay if you can't be there because I will be there. I want to make sure the inspector doesn't overlook anything."

Beatrice spoke up. "If you agree with the contract and the house passes inspection, you can move in at any time. In fact, I'd like you to be living there while the renovation is being done in the café."

Marni made a few noises to let them know she was listening. Candice reached over and laid her hand on Marni's leg as an acknowledgment.

Shane noticed that Candice was filling a void that the Anders' family had been unable to fill for years. Her bonding with his family, especially Marni, seemed to right his world. "So, grandmother, Candice and I have come up with some other ideas for the business, but she is doing a little research to see if it's feasible. I think you will find her additions to the business plan to be positive ones."

Candice gave him a look that told him not to say too much. "Yes, I just have some phone calls to make to see how to properly proceed."

"I'm intrigued. So far, you have a great business model, so I can't wait to hear what other wonderful ideas you've come up with," Beatrice said, glancing between Shane and Candice to see if she could figure out what they were putting together.

"Ciao," a very handsome older gentleman said as he greeted Beatrice with a kiss on both cheeks.

"Aldo, I'd like you to meet Shane's girlfriend, Candice," Beatrice introduced. "Candice, this is Shane's uncle. The one I said might be able to give you some advice."

"Oh." Candice finally made the connection that Shane's family owned this popular restaurant. *No wonder we got a table so fast.*

"Sì, I would love to help in any way I can. I could stop by the space you want to use and give you some pointers. I have a great supplier of commercial restaurant equipment. You certainly need a top of the line oven that will be dependable for years."

"I would love that. Do you think I could see your kitchen? Of course not tonight, but when the restaurant is closed."

"I would be honored to show you around the kitchen," Aldo said with pride.

"Now, how's my sweet Marni tonight? For you, I made a very special Torte di Ricotta," Aldo waved over their waiter. "Can you get Marni her special dessert?"

"Yes sir, my pleasure," the waiter said, picking up the empty dinner plates.

"Miss Candice, Monday's we are only open for lunch. So, if you'd like to stop by between five and six, I would be happy to give you a tour of the kitchen," Aldo said, with his hand resting lightly on her shoulder.

"Yes, I can make it here on Monday, after work," Candice replied.

"I must get back into the kitchen," Aldo said, giving Marni a kiss on the top of her head before returning to his chef duties.

"Well babe, you're one step closer to your dream becoming a reality. I know my uncle will steer you in the right direction." Shane was proud of his family's keen and clearly successful business sense.

"I have all of you to thank for giving me the confidence to move forward with this idea. I think if I listen to all your advice, I should avoid some of the costly mistakes most first-time business owners make," Candice said.

As the evening of family and laughter ended, they planned to make every Wednesday family night.

Shane and Candice entered her condo after a pleasurable evening.

"Well, I guess you have some reading to do?" Shane smiled.

"Yes, your grandmother put together a very detailed contract. I'll fax it to my dad, not that I need his approval, but he has some great advice and has put my money toward some profitable investments," Candice said, sitting down on the couch with a notepad and the contract.

"I'm pretty sure my grandmother covered everything in a fair way. She helped me out when I started my business, and of course, she helped me get through my financial loss by allowing me to stay with her."

"She really has a head for business. I bet my father and her will get along beautifully. Two minds thinking alike."

"You know," Shane said, taking the contract out of Candice's hand and laying it on the coffee table, "this can wait." He pulled her toward him, laying her head on his chest. "I've needed to feel you all night."

Candice listened to his heartbeat as it sped up. "It really was such a special evening. I think your sister enjoyed being with everyone too."

"That's what made the evening complete," Shane said, running his hands through Candice's hair.

"I know I'm going to be so happy living across the street from her. I can keep an eye on her. It's always good to make sure people know they are cherished and loved."

Shane's heart was opening to the possibility of love, and the person unlocking it was Candice. Her unconditional acceptance of his sister was almost more than he could comprehend. Every minute he spent with Candice, she seeped further into his heart. He was so afraid that it was too good to be true, but here she was, laying her head on his chest. He closed his eyes to feel the intensity of her closeness. Next, Candice reached under his shirt and traced the hard muscles rippling under his skin. Suddenly, she stopped, laid her hand over his tattoo, and let it warm his skin as she absorbed the beating of his heart in her palm. Her gentle, loving touch was close to sending him into emotional overload. The intensity of this relationship bordered on insanity. He never knew how important it was to find a woman who accepted him and his family, but he now understood that was the missing piece.

Shane leaned forward and kissed Candice as if she was the breath he needed to survive. Before either of them knew it, clothes were being ripped off and discarded without hesitation.

There were no words spoken, just the meeting of their eyes and an unspoken love their bodies shared.

Candice never felt this type of genuine connection with any man she had sex with. It had always been just sex and not the deep, intense relationship she was feeling.

They laid wrapped in each other arms, still joined and basking in the afterglow, not wanting to move or lose the connection holding them together. It was pure adoration binding them as one.

Shane finally broke the silence and whispered into Candice's ear, "I've fallen in love with you. More than I ever knew possible. I've never felt this way before."

"I love you beyond all reason," Candice said, lightly kissing his neck in the spot that drove him crazy.

Shane could hear Candice's breathing change as she dozed off into a blissful slumber. He wrapped his protective arms around her and smiled, looking forward to their romantic Napa weekend only two days away. He closed his eyes and listened to Candice's steady breathing as it lulled him to sleep.

"You got everything, bathing suit, clothes you don't mind getting dirty? Oh, and that cute dress you bought. I can't wait to see you in it," Shane said, picking up Candice's suitcase.

"Yep, got it all, and if I forgot anything, I'll buy it there." Candice smiled as she grabbed her purse.

"Well, let's get a move on," Shane said, giving Candice a playful swat on her rear. "We have an eight o'clock appointment."

"Oh?" Candice said, looking surprised. Shane just smiled. "So, you're not going to tell me?"

"Nope."

Of course, Candice knew Napa had so many fun and romantic things to do. She allowed her mind to imagine all the scenarios of what Shane might have up his sleeve. She also had a surprise for Shane and the excitement of this weekend was making her giggle.

"What's so funny?" Shane asked, merging onto the interstate.

"Nothing, just happy," she said, reaching over to hold his hand.

They headed across the Golden Gate Bridge. Candice remembered the little fawn.

"Oh, this reminds me, have you looked at the rescue website? They've posted some updates on our little friend. He's gotten so big."

"No, I'll have to check it out. Guess they'll be releasing him back into the wild soon."

"Yeah, that's what they told me. He's so strong now. It will only be a few more weeks before they let him go. Oh, and I decided to become a member of the rescue. I thought it was the least I could do for all the help they provide the wildlife."

"Maybe we can swing by on our way home if we have time."

"Yes, that would be great," Candice responded smiling.

Traffic was unusually light as they made it to Napa earlier than Shane expected, so he pulled into a Starbucks. "Want a coffee?" he asked.

"Yes, that sounds good. I could certainly use a jolt of caffeine."

Shane handed Candice a steaming latte and watched her sprinkle cocoa powder over the top of the foam. "Coffee and chocolate? Someone wants a lift this morning."

"Well, we didn't get much sleep last night." She winked before giving the chocolate dispenser another vigorous shake.

Smiling, Shane took a sip of his coffee. "If I'm not mistaken, you woke me up at three...not that I'm complaining."

"Well, what can I say, you were there for the taking," Candice told him.

"Baby, you can wake me up anytime you want." Shane gave her a hug.

"You know what's not fair? You can run on three hours of sleep. You're ready to take on the world, and I'm barely keeping my eyes open." Candice yawned.

"We can check into the hotel later. You can take a nap before our two o'clock appointment."

"What are we doing at two?" Candice's curiosity was starting to get the best of her.

"I'm not gonna tell you. You just have to wait and see."

They climbed back into the truck, and Shane drove another ten minutes before pulling into a parking lot. Candice's eyes went from half asleep to wide-awake.

"Shane?" she nervously said, looking out the window.

"Yes."

"Don't tell me this is what you have planned?" There was an edge of terror in her voice.

"It will be fun." He smiled at her. "And you can hold me the entire time." That was his plan all along.

"I can't." She started to panic.

"Yes, you can. It's going to be beautiful. Look, there's not a cloud in the sky, so we'll be able to see for miles." Shane exited the truck and went around opening Candice's door.

"Honey, I'm sorry but I can't." Candice continued, looking at the colorful balloon waiting to take flight.

Shane took her hand and guided her to the field where the pilot was waiting for his passengers.

"Good morning," the pilot greeted as they approached.

Candice's legs were about to give out. She felt an incredible urge to turn and run. Shane sensed her body pulling away, so he wrapped his arm around her and held her secure to his body. Candice abruptly stopped walking, planting her feet firmly on the ground. Shane nudged her, but she would not budge.

"First-time jitters?" the pilot asked, looking at Shane.

"Yes, for both of us." Shane smiled when he realized that Candice had shut her eyes.

"Well, you picked a perfect day. This is going to be a wonderful flight," the pilot voice was confident and soothing.

Candice opened her eyes and released a deep breath she had been holding while trying to remain calm. "How long have you piloted those things?" she asked, pointing to the balloon.

"Thirty plus years," he answered her with a smile.

"Is that champagne I see?" she asked, spying people with flutes in their hands.

"Yes, part of the experience," the pilot replied.

"Good, I need a glass," Candice said, her voice barely audible.

The pilot motioned for the woman handing out champagne to bring a glass over. Shane released his grip around Candice's waist and reached for her hand, lacing his fingers in hers.

"Thank you," Candice said, taking the glass of champagne and downing it. Now was not the time to enjoy the bubbling flavor. She reached for another drink but clutched it instead of pouring it down her throat.

"Babe, you're going to be okay."

"One of my biggest fears is heights. I don't want to let you down, but I really don't think I can get in that basket." Candice could not even look at Shane, so she stared at the ground instead.

"It's okay. We don't have to. We'll go do something else. Come on." He started to walk with her back to the truck.

Candice suddenly stopped and turned around, peering at the balloon. She did not want to ruin Shane's plans. He had arranged the entire weekend for them. She felt horrible that she was allowing her fear to stop her from trying something new.

"Okay, I'll do it, but you'd better hold me the entire time. Don't you dare let go of me."

"I don't think that will be a problem." Shane smiled, pulling her into a hug.

"We'd better get over there fast before I chicken out." She squeezed his hand in a death grip.

The pilot greeted each passenger entering the gondola with a firm handshake. He gave a welcoming speech and then quickly ran through their upcoming flight. "Now we'll be on our way," he said, increasing the flame, causing the balloon to slowly rising.

Candice's body started to shake uncontrollably as the balloon climbed higher and higher. Her legs could no longer hold her up, and she slowly slid out of Shane's grasp, sinking down until she was sitting on the floor of the basket.

"Honey, you need to stand to see this beautiful landscape." Shane knelt to coax her back up.

"I'm fine down here," she squeaked, wrapping her arms around her legs.

Shane kissed her forehead, then reached under her arms and pulled her back up. He stood behind her and enveloped his arms tightly around her, ensuring that she did not collapse again.

Candice leaned her head back into his chest but kept her eyes closed. She took herself to a happy spot in her mind. The walk on the beach with Shane was a great memory.

"Babe," Shane whispered in her ear.

"Yeah?"

"Open your eyes and look out at the beautiful scenery."

Candice did not want to, she liked her happy place on the beach.

The pilot informed them of Napa Valley's history and pointed out the many vineyards.

Candice listened and tried to envision what the pilot was describing, but it was just not the same as seeing it for herself. She gradually opened her eyes and scanned the scenery. It was beautiful. She looked up into Shane's eyes with a grateful smile. He kissed the top of her head but did not let his grip slacken around her again.

They landed and disembarked. A lovely woman directed the passengers to a restaurant where they would have a romantic breakfast overlooking a vineyard.

Once Candice's feet touch the grassy earth, she turned and gave Shane a hug. "Thank you for putting up with me."

"You do realize we will be riding back in the balloon, right?"

"Yes, but I'm not afraid anymore. It was actually not bad at all, once I opened my eyes. And of course, if I did not look down, I didn't get dizzy."

They entered the restaurant, and the hostess quickly escorted them to their table.

"So, why do you think you're afraid of heights?" Shane reached across the table to hold her hands.

"Well, let's see. I fell out of a tree and broke my arm. Oh, and then there was the time I tumbled down the stairs, resulting in a concussion. I fell off the top of a slide once, but luckily my dad caught me. Not too long ago, I slipped off a ladder and hit the ground pretty hard. I think that might cover it."

Shane looked concerned. "So, we'll keep the ladder climbing to me, but if we have children, you're gonna have to get back on a slide."

Children? Where the hell did that come from? Candice wondered. *He can't possibly be thinking long-term commitment already.* "I'll remember that. No ladders, I'll go on a slide, but can I skip the tree climbing and leave that up to you?"

"Sure, but what if I build a tree house? Then would you climb a tree?"

"Okay, if you go through the trouble of building a tree house, I'll climb a tree with you."

"I'm sorry I forgot how scared you were about heights. Now I remember how I had to help you down the barn ladder. I should have remembered," Shane apologized.

"It's fine. What fears do you have? I mean we're all afraid of something."

"I'm not a fan of snakes, and I see them more than I care to."

"Really? Well, if you stand behind me and hold me, so I don't fall off any ladders, or out of trees, then I'll catch the snakes for you as long as they're not venomous."

"You don't mind snakes?" Shane shivered at the thought of them.

"No, I actually like them. I used to catch garter snakes with my cousin. Let them wrap around my arm like bracelets and carry them around like they were my pets."

"Well, that's a deal, because I'd prefer not to have to catch and remove one."

It was time to head back to the balloon, but this time Candice had no fear at all. She stepped into the gondola and right up to the edge for the best view possible.

Shane made a promise to hold her the entire flight, so that was precisely what he did.

They drove a few miles toward their hotel, passing several vineyards. "We'll go wine tasting tomorrow after we meet with Maggie."

"That will be fun. Maybe I can find a few wines I really like," Candice said.

Shane pulled into the opulent hotel. Candice gasped. "This is where we're staying?"

"Yes, nothing but the best for you." He got out of the truck and went around, opening Candice's door as the valet and bellhop approached.

"Sir, let me get those for you," the bellhop offered, reaching for the bags Shane had in his hands.

Walking into the hotel lobby was like walking into a dream. Everything was perfect, from the fresh cut flower arrangements to the comfortable furniture perfect for relaxing with a cup of coffee, reading the paper, or just old-fashioned people watching.

"Mr. Anders, your room is ready. The bellhop will bring your things up shortly," a smiling, petite woman said, handing him the card key.

"Thank you." Shane put his hand on the small of Candice's back and guided her to the elevator.

Candice was speechless as her eyes darted around, taking in the Mediterranean architecture. This was by far the most beautiful hotel she had been in, and she felt like a princess being a guest here.

Shane opened the door to their suite and held it for Candice. She stepped into the room. The first things she saw were fresh flowers everywhere. Then she noticed the bottle of champagne chilling on ice with a box of Godiva chocolates propped next to it.

She tried not to cry, but no man had ever treated her with such adoration. A few happy tears welled up. "I can't believe you did all this on such short notice." She spun around and hugged him.

Shane wiped away the lone tear that made its way down her cheek. "You deserve to be pampered and loved."

Candice went into the bathroom to grab a Kleenex. There was a large bathtub and sitting next to it was a basket with bath salts, candles, a bottle of wine, and two wine glasses. "Did you do this too?" she asked, smelling the bath salts.

Shane just smiled in response.

"What time did you say our appointment was?" she questioned.

"Two. Why? You have something on your mind?"

She strolled over to him, backing him out of the bathroom and into the bedroom while unbuttoning his shirt.

A knock on the door interrupted her advances. "Hold that thought," Shane said, going quickly to open the door for the bellhop.

"Where would you like these?" the bellhop questioned.

"Over there would be fine." Shane pointed toward the closet and reached into his wallet for a tip.

"Is there anything else I can get for you, sir?"

"No, thank you," Shane said, as the bellhop retreated through the door.

Shane held the door open and put the *Do Not Disturb* sign on the knob.

"Now, where was I? Oh yes, stripping my man of his clothes." Candice continued removing Shane's shirt. She undressed Shane, but would not allow him to remove a stitch of her clothing.

"You know this is not quite what I had in mind," he said curiously.

"Well, why don't you lie down and enjoy the show," she said provocatively, as she slipped off her shoes.

Shane knew how to follow orders, especially when a beautiful woman was about to make him a very happy and relaxed man.

Slowly, Candice removed each article of her clothing and tossed them onto a chair. She walked toward Shane wearing only her jewel-adorned thong and lusty eyes. He grabbed her as soon as she was within reach and pulled her on top of him, kissing her soft parted lips. He took control, flipped her onto her back, quickly removed her panties and fit himself between her legs.

Candice softly moaned, and Shane opened his eyes to look at her. She was licking her lips in anticipation of his next move, which happened in one swift motion. The pressure of him satisfied her craving as she melded into him for a deeper connection.

Rolling onto her side, Candice rested her head on Shane's chest and listened to his heart. He rubbed his thumb gently on her temple, relaxing her more until she fell asleep against him.

"Babe, time to wake up." Shane kissed her shoulder.

Candice opened her eyes, forgetting for a moment where she was. "I guess I needed that nap." She sat up and stretched. "I feel much better with that extra sleep." She sprung out of bed and made her way into the bathroom. "Do I have time for a quick shower?"

"Our appointment is in a half hour."

"Okay, I'll be ready in twenty minutes." She turned the shower on and hopped in before it was even warm.

Candice stepped out of the bathroom wearing a cute sleeveless sundress with her hair pulled up into a ponytail. "Not sure where we're going, so am I dressed okay?"

"Yes, perfect, but don't plan on keeping that dress on too long," Shane suggestively said.

"Oh, now I am intrigued." Aside from making love out in a vineyard, Candice could not think of where Shane would be taking her.

The elevator descended to the lobby floor. The doors opened, and they stepped out. Candice held Shane's hand as they walked through glass doors leading to the spa.

"Hello," a very soft-spoken woman said. "You must be Mr. Anders. I have you down for a couple's massage."

"Yes."

"Right this way." She directed them to follow her, escorting them into a room with two massage tables.

Candice once again found herself speechless. She had never had a professional massage before because she could never squeeze this luxury into her busy day. Although she was sure on more than one occasion, a good massage would have really relaxed her.

"Once you are undressed, lie on the table on your stomach, and your masseuse will be in shortly." The woman handed them each a towel and departed.

"Have you ever had a massage before?" Candice asked Shane.

"Once," he responded, keeping his answer short.

They both stripped and climbed onto the tables. "I'm not sure if this was a good idea," Shane said.

"Why?"

"Well, it's hard to see you naked and remain unaffected. No pun intended."

"Sorry, don't think I can help you in that area right now."

Two women walked in and introduced themselves. Shortly after they entered, Candice could hear soft ocean waves coming through speakers, setting the mood for tranquility.

After an hour of deep tissue massage, their masseuses vacated the room, giving them privacy to get dressed.

"Wow, I never would have thought a massage could hurt so much and feel so good at the same time. I had sore muscles I didn't even know existed," Candice said, putting her dress on.

"I can't argue with that." Shane pulled his pants up. "Are you ready for an early dinner? We can eat in our room if you like."

"Yes, I would love to go back to the room." Candice reached for the doorknob excited to get back upstairs, open the bottle of champagne, and snuggle with Shane.

Sixteen

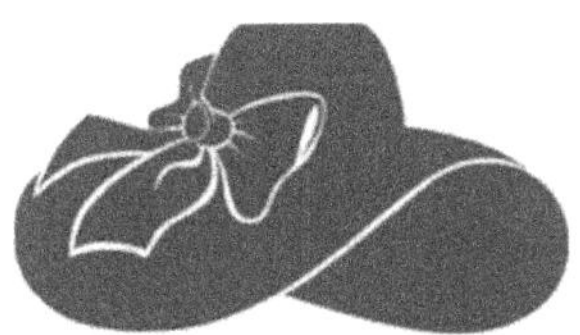

Shane pulled back the curtains to let the sunshine filter into the room. Candice stirred as the light reached her eyes. "Morning," she whispered.

"Hey babe, I'm gonna run downstairs and get us some coffee." Shane had already showered and was dressed in his well-worn blue jeans, black t-shirt, and work boots. His attire reminded Candice that they were heading out to meet Maggie and take her to the mansion.

"Okay, can you see if they have a sweet roll or Danish?" Candice pushed the blankets aside, exposing her sensual curves as she stood up.

"You better get dressed before I decide to forget about the coffee," Shane warned her as he watched her stretch.

Candice looked at the clock. "We're meeting Maggie in an hour, right?"

"Yes, I told her we'd meet her at her hotel so she can follow us over."

Shane did not want to leave the room, but he realized one more minute watching Candice may result in them being late to meet Maggie. He had to muster up an ounce of restraint. He always had trouble suppressing his desire for Candice; she sent him into overdrive.

When the door closed behind Shane, Candice decided she would check her cell phone for messages. Scrolling through her missed calls, she saw one from her dad, one from Jazzlene, and one from Brent's mom. *Oh, for crying in the mud. What the hell does she want?* Candice listened to her father's voicemail letting her know he got the contract and was reviewing it. Jazzlene informed her Steve was very interested in renting her condo. Brent's mom, however, sounded frantic, begging Candice to return the call, but did not give any specifics. Candice took a deep breath, shaking her head, and turned her phone off, leaving it on the nightstand. She stepped into the hot steaming shower, trying to clear her mind.

She would not allow her romantic weekend with Shane be tainted by the voice of her ex-fiancé's mother.

Shane walked back into the room with two large coffees and two apple fritters. "Sorry babe, no Danishes or sweet rolls, so I hope this fritter will do."

"Oh, thank you," Candice said over the hum of the blow dryer. "I'm almost ready." She tried to take the edge of worry off her voice, but Shane could see it in her eyes.

"What's wrong?"

"Nothing. I'm just trying to hurry so we're not late."

Shane noticed her cell phone was off and resting on the nightstand. "Anything to do with why you turned your phone off?"

"Look, I really don't want to talk about it or ruin our weekend. Can we discuss it on Monday?" Candice looked away, not wanting to see the hurt in Shane's eyes.

"Sure, but you'll feel better if we talk about it now. I can tell it has you upset."

"Fine. Good news, Steve wants to rent my condo, dad is looking over the contract, and Brent's mom left me a message to immediately call her," Candice said, all in one breath.

"Well, I'm glad Steve wants to rent your place. We should go visit your dad this week after work to talk to him in person. I think I should meet him too since our relationship seems to be on the fast track."

Candice lifted her eyebrows. "I agree. You and my father should meet. You're the two most important men in my life." Shane smiled at that sentiment.

"As far as Brent goes, I'm not sure what you can do. Maybe you should call her and see what she wants." Shane could not believe he just suggested Candice call Brent's mom and get involved with his insanity.

"I will call her, but not until Monday. This is our weekend, and no one is going to take it away from us." Candice wrapped her warm arms around Shane's neck and kissed him.

He rested her head on his chest and held her as if he might lose her any minute.

"Guess we should get on the road," he said, before reluctantly letting go of her.

They drove in silence to the hotel where Maggie was staying. Shane pulled into a parking space and turned toward Candice.

"You know I love you. I will do anything for you, but I need to ask you to step away." Shane's clipped tone caught Candice off guard.

The horror on Candice's face sent Shane's heart spiraling. "You're giving up on us, just because of some guy that is out of his mind?" Candice questioned in shock.

"No, you misunderstood me. What I meant was, you need to step away from him, not us. Candice, you can't help him. He has to help himself."

Relief washed over Candice's face. "I get what you are saying, but how do I turn my back on someone?"

"It's going to be hard. It's not in your nature, but you have to, for yourself and for him. He has to find his own way."

"I'll try, but I can't make any guarantees that I won't help if the opportunity presents itself."

"Do you still love him?" Shane had to know, even if her answer killed him.

"Yes, in some ways," Candice swallowed before she continued, "I don't love him as a boyfriend or a fiancée. I just love him for the person he used to be. He's not the one for me, you are. And I'm madly in love with you. But don't you see, I can't just let him destroy himself. I would forever feel responsible if I turn my back on him completely."

Shane sat quietly for a minute, thinking about how much love Candice showed his sister and how she had opened her heart to his family. He knew asking her to walk away was the wrong tactic. "Okay, I understand your concern, and I will back your decision, but please promise me you will never go see him alone."

Candice looked down at her hands that were twisting in her lap. "Don't you trust me?"

"Of course I do. I don't, however, trust him." Shane had good reason to worry about Brent's emotional and violent tendencies.

"So, if I want to go see him, you'll come with me?"

"Absolutely. You don't go without me or at least take Jazzlene with you. I just don't want him alone with you. Now let's try to enjoy the rest of the weekend." Shane stepped out of the truck. *Damn, that asshole.*

Maggie was waiting in the lobby. She was wearing straight leg blue jeans pushed into cowboy boots with a plaid long sleeve blouse tied in front, revealing a dark brown leather belt with a rose shaped belt buckle. All she needed was a cowboy hat to complete the western look.

"Hi, I'm Shane, this is Candice." He reached out and shook Maggie's hand.

"Nice to finally meet you. I can't wait to see this piece of land," Maggie said, picking up her leather purse.

"Well, it's not just land, as you could see in the photos I sent you."

"And I must thank you for sending them. I thought it was a run-down house that was not worth saving, but those pictures show it to be a beautiful home that needs a little TLC."

"Wait until you see the inside," Candice added, excited to get back into the house.

"Why don't you ride with us?" Shane offered, opening the truck's door for both women.

They arrived at the property and drove through the entry gate. "There's a long dirt drive before we get to a clearing. Then we have to walk to the house. Once all this growth is trimmed, it will be a beautiful drive up to the house. You'll probably want to put down gravel or pave it."

Maggie watched the encompassing foliage as it started to engulf the truck. "Shouldn't we stop here and walk the rest of the way?"

"We're almost to the clearing." Shane proceeded to drive through the overgrowth, letting the branches hit the truck as they inched along. They finally broke through the canopy of plants into the open field.

"Wow, this must have been where they had a horse corral. In the picture, you just couldn't see how large this area actually is," Maggie said, opening the truck door and jumping out.

"Yes, I believe you're right. The barn is just beyond those bushes." He lifted Candice out of the truck. "I made a path to the barn the last time we were up here."

Maggie was already heading to the path toward the barn before Shane could grab the flashlights.

"I think if you clean up this overgrowth, there will be a nice area over there where the stables appear to have been," Shane called out, catching up with Maggie.

"Yes, I can see that being a perfect spot for stables," Maggie agreed.

Candice was not far behind them and could hear the excitement in Maggie's voice as she talked to Shane about the possibilities of renting out horse stalls in a large stable.

"I think that would be a great idea. The barn is large enough to house hay and all the equipment you would need," Shane said, catching Maggie by the elbow as she stumbled over a tree root.

Maggie caught Shane's eyes. "Thank you," she said, with a glimmer of something that seemed like more than just gratitude.

Candice picked up her stride to catch up. Once she reached Shane, she latched onto his hand, giving it a possessive squeeze. He turned and shrugged his shoulders, knowing Candice saw the same look he noticed in Maggie's eyes.

They reached the barn, and Shane swung the doors open. "Here," he said, handing Maggie a flashlight.

Maggie walked in and shined the light around the empty barn. "This is perfect." She moved deeper into the barn.

Shane stood with his arm around Candice's waist, pulling her closer. "So, are you ready to go see the house?" he asked as Maggie started to walk toward him.

"Yes," she answered, brushing against him lightly as she passed.

Candice rolled her eyes at Shane as they followed Maggie out of the barn.

"There's the path to the house." Shane pointed toward it while closing the barn door.

Maggie took off in the direction of the path.

"Next time she does that, I'm gonna stick my foot out and trip her," Candice said, annoyed. "And you better not catch her this time." Candice swatted his butt.

"Got it," he said, knowing she was kidding.

Candice was not surprised women were attracted to Shane. He was solid muscle with gorgeous shoulder-length black hair and mesmerizing bedroom eyes the color of dark chocolate with golden highlights. If a woman did not take a second look, Candice would be surprised. Maggie, however, was shamelessly flirting and did not care that Candice was watching her. In fact, Maggie appeared to be enjoying the little game she was playing.

"We'll catch up with you in a minute," Shane yelled as Maggie disappeared into the foliage.

He hauled Candice behind the truck out of view and devoured her mouth with a kiss so intense it left Candice weakened. "I don't see anyone but you. She can flirt and throw herself at me, but there's only you."

"I love you," Candice whispered breathlessly before she reached up and ran her hands through his silky hair.

"Let's get this over with fast so we can head to the wine tasting," Shane suggested, stepping away to retrieve the screwdriver from the truck.

They caught up with Maggie at the house. She was already on the porch, walking around to the back. "This place is huge," she commented, looking around.

"Well, the inside is just as impressive," Shane informed her as he began to remove the screws from the plywood covering the back door.

"So, do you know people that can help me do the cleanup and renovation?" Maggie asked, moving closer to Shane.

"Yeah, I know landscapers and a few construction people," he answered, pocketing the screws. "But I don't do that type of work myself. I just dismantle and salvage what can be reused."

"Well, I guess I'll hire you to remove some stuff I don't want." She smiled at him.

Shane set the plywood against the wall and motioned for Maggie to enter. She looked around the kitchen. "This kitchen is big enough to run a catering company."

"Yes, it would be perfect for that. This house would make a beautiful bed and breakfast. There are so many rooms, each could have a different theme." Shane directed her through to the large ballroom. "You could possibly rent this room out for small receptions, special occasions, or maybe have Sunday brunches here. It would be very intimate, and the guests would love it."

"I can see where you are going. That's a great idea," Maggie concurred.

"And you could have the check-in area here by the front door." Shane offered as a suggestion on how to plan for a bed and breakfast inn.

They proceeded to the top floor. "I believe this was your father's room. It feels like he's still here," Shane said as a chill went through the air.

"This is surreal. I can't believe all this belonged to a man unknown to me, yet I feel so close to him in this room." Maggie looked around, taking in the remnants of her father's possessions.

"And through this door is the copula." Shane opened it so Maggie could step in and see the expansive view of the property.

"This is so cool." Maggie turned in a circle so she could appreciate the expansive property.

Once they finished viewing the spacious house, Shane offered his opinion and advice on the easiest way to turn the house into a bed and breakfast. Candice remained quiet, listening to Shane's overview of how to make the home a profitable business. His insights always intrigued her.

"There's a pool and that small house I told you about. You'll need a pool guy to inspect the pool and do any repairs. That will be a perfect spot for guests of the inn to relax."

"My granddaughters will love having a pool," Maggie said.

"Yes, I'm sure they will," Shane agreed. "How old are they?"

"Annie's three, and Janice is five." Maggie smiled as she thought about her two darling grandbabies.

"You'll want to put a locked enclosure around the pool," Shane advised, always thinking about safety. Something he did not take for granted because of Marni's need for constant supervision.

"I will have to call my husband and have him fly out. He's going to be so thrilled to have all this land. Maybe he'll even learn to make wine. I did see grapevines on this property, right?"

"Yes, but I know nothing about winemaking, so you'll have to research that."

"The last thing to show you is the cottage. It's full of boxes and furniture. It might make a great home for your family." Shane led the way to the small home.

"This is too cute. I'll have to go through all those boxes and see if I can piece my father's life together. It appears some are important, judging by the labels. My father and his mysteries," Maggie said, trying to wedge herself through the narrow pathway between boxes to the back of the house.

"Did you know she was married?" Candice whispered to Shane.

"Nope." Shane looked as surprised as Candice did.

Maggie came back toward the front of the house. "I think this place will be a great home for us. My husband has been out of work for a month, so I know this will be a wonderful way for us to start fresh. If I can make this house livable, I can slowly get the other part of this land ready."

"When I get back to my office, I'll email you the names of some people that can get the roads cleared for you," Shane offered.

"That would be great. Thank you." Maggie lifted the lid of a box marked photos. She grabbed a few albums and then replaced the cover.

"So, that pretty much does it for the tour of this property," Shane said, closing the door to the house.

"This is going to be interesting. I was shocked to find out my dad had been alive all these years. Mom had no idea what had happened to him. I can tell you, he broke her heart. She was so in love with him. She said he was different from anyone she'd ever met. I guess that is an understatement. He lived a very secretive life." Maggie smiled as she looked at the mansion. "I can't wait to bring my mom here. I bet she'll want to run the bed and breakfast if we decide to convert the main house."

Weaving through the pathway back to the car, Maggie once again led the way. She was full of energy and seemed to be running on adrenaline.

Sitting in the truck returning to her hotel, Maggie looked through the photo album. She slowly turned the pages, soaking in each face that smiled back at her. "This must be my father when he was young." She showed Candice the picture. "He has the same eyes I do."

"Yes, I can see the resemblance," Candice responded after viewing the picture.

"Oh, and this is a picture of him holding me." Maggie stared at the picture while running her fingers over it.

Candice remembered from the story that he had never met his daughter, which was untrue. The pictures revealed he was proud and in awe of his little girl.

Shane pulled into the hotel parking lot, went to the passenger side of the truck, and opened the door for Maggie. "So, I'll email you the contacts that I think will be able to help you with the overall revitalization of the property."

"Thank you." Maggie gave him a hug. "I really appreciate everything you have done and are doing for my family." Then she turned to Candice. "It was so nice meeting you. If I do decide to open a bed and breakfast, you two will have to be my first guests," she said, smiling.

"That would be nice," Candice said, realizing that perhaps Maggie was not flirting before. She was just a warm spirited person.

"Now I think I'll get in my rental car and head back there to start looking through those boxes," Maggie said as she turned toward her car.

"Well, here." Shane handed her a flashlight and his screwdriver. "You might need these."

"Thank you. I'll be in touch."

Shane got back in the truck. "Well, that was interesting." He rested his arm on the back seat.

"Yes, it was." Candice scooted closer to Shane, leaning her head on his shoulder. "I was surprised she is a grandmother. I mean, did you think she looked old enough to have grandchildren?"

Shane chuckled. "Nope. Children that age, yes, but not grandchildren."

"Maybe they're step-grandchildren or something. I want to know what she's drinkin' to stay so young."

"Guess it's all in the attitude. Think young, stay young. Look at my grandmother. She's the energizer bunny."

Candice could feel Shane's cell phone vibrate in his pocket. "Do you need to answer that?"

"No. This weekend is about spending my time with you. Now, I have a restaurant I want to take you to for lunch before we go wine tasting."

"Yes, sounds good 'cuz I'm starved." Candice placed her hand on Shane's thigh, tenderly squeezing it.

"I wouldn't do that if I were you, or we may need to head back to the hotel and skip lunch," Shane warned, placing his hand on her.

"Well, I can't think of a better way to spend the afternoon."

"Really? Because we're almost to the restaurant, so tell me now if you want to skip it."

"Oh, well, I wouldn't want to ruin your plans." Candice tried to move her hand up Shane's leg, but he held it in place.

"I want your hand there, just don't...you know—" He tried to focus on his driving, but Candice was not playing fair.

"You mean, don't move it like this?" She inched her hand toward his inner thigh.

"Exactly." Shane turned into a parking lot.

"Or this?" Candice kissed his neck.

"We can always come back for dinner." Shane left the parking lot without stopping and headed toward the hotel. "Seems your appetite is for something other than food."

"Yeah, I guess I just want my dessert first."

Four hours later, Shane was pulling back into the restaurant's parking lot.

"By now, you must be starving." Shane could hear Candice's stomach rumble.

"Yeah, but I'd skip a meal anytime to be alone with you."

"Come on." Shane held the door for her.

"Ah, Mr. Anders, I expected to see you at lunch," an older gentleman commented.

"Yes, I had some unexpected business to take care of." Shane squeezed Candice's hand.

"Well, I have your table ready." The man led them to a dark corner far from the main dining room.

"Thank you, Giorgio," Shane said as Giorgio placed the menus in front of them.

Candice looked up at Shane, puzzled. "How come you have your own table here? Do you bring all your girlfriends here?" A tinge of jealousy appeared in Candice's voice.

Shane gave her a devious smile before answering. "Actually, I did a job for Giorgio. I removed some old woodsheds on his property. Then I used the wood and made him some furniture pieces. This table is one of them. And the reason he calls it my table."

Candice looked down, admiring the table, and ran her hand over the lacquered top. She noticed a set of letters carved in it. GP + NC. "You picked a piece of wood with initials carved into it to create this table?"

"Yeah, the story is, Giorgio, carved those into the shed when he was dating his wife in high school. I thought using that piece of wood for the tabletop would be special."

"If I move into your grandma's place, will you make me a table?"

"Sure, I'd love to."

Giorgio arrived with a bottle of wine. "Special for you, Mr. Anders, from my personal collection." He poured two glasses of wine.

"Excuse me, I'll be right back." Candice got up and made her way toward the restroom. This gave Shane the few minutes he needed to check his cell phone. He checked his texts first and saw the one he was waiting for from Kevin.

Kevin—Brent had left rehab but voluntarily returned, so everything is fine.

That was the logical explanation for his mother's frantic call to Candice. He saw a voice message from his father, so he started to listen to it. When he noticed Candice returning, he ended the call and put his phone back in his pocket.

"That was a message from my dad. The inspections were completed early, and the written report should be on his desk by Tuesday. I'm updating the commercial space alarm system and adding it to the rental units. That job should be done by Friday. So, if you want, you can move in next weekend."

Candice looked dismayed.

"What's wrong?" Shane questioned.

"How come I didn't know about the security system?"

"Well, I honestly forgot to tell you."

"How much is this going to cost? And what's wrong with the system already installed?"

"The system in the commercial space is so outdated. I want some cameras installed like I have at my place."

"Well, you still didn't tell me the cost, and I really don't think it's necessary."

"Yes, it is necessary. You don't need to worry about the cost. I'll sleep better knowing that you are safe."

"I can always just get a big dog."

"Really? And when will you have time to take care of a dog? Anyway, this is not open for discussion."

"What? I don't have a say?" Candice snapped. "Maybe I should just stay in my condo and look for a real job."

"Like Brent can't get in there if he wants to. And that building is supposed to be secure."

"I get your point, but I think once he's out of rehab, he'll leave me alone."

"Babe, you realize his drug use has nothing to do with his obsession with you."

"I think it's adding to his delusion that I want to be with him. And I understand your concerns, so if it makes you feel better, I'll install the security system. But you have to let me pay for it."

"My grandmother will not allow that. She wants to write it off as a business expense."

"Fine, I'll discuss it with her then."

"Good luck with that." Shane smiled, knowing he had just won this battle for her safety. "Now, let's order our dinner."

Seventeen

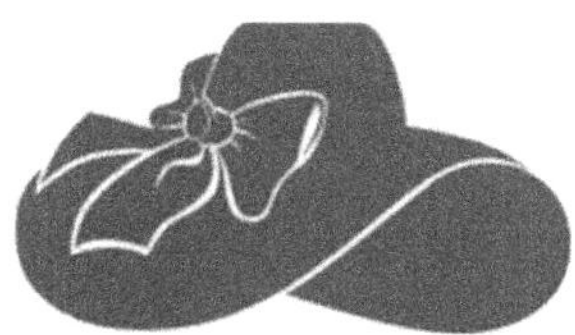

The first thing Candice did before she made the coffee for Jazz was to turn on the heat, then the lights. After a few romantic days away with Shane, Monday was not welcome. She got very little sleep over the weekend and already missed his warm arms protectively encasing her.

As Candice waited for the computer to boot up, she retrieved her cell phone, debating whether to turn it on. She was not ready for any more messages from the Gallager family.

Four voicemails and fifteen missed calls awaited her. The first message was from her father regarding the contract Candice had faxed him, and after careful review, he wanted to meet with Mrs. Anders. Wednesday night, he would drive into San Francisco. *Okay, his voice sounded positive.* Next was a message from her mother, just wanting to check on her and see how things were going. Mrs. Gallager's frantic message was still in the voicemail box, and Candice skipped it immediately, not wanting to hear her worried voice again. The last one was from Brent, as were the fifteen missed calls.

"Candice honey, where are you? I stopped by your place and waited, but you never came home. I need to talk to you. Call me. I love you." The message ended. Candice stared at the phone.

Shit, shit, shit. Candice dialed Mrs. Gallager's number, feeling nauseated.

"Hello," a soft voice answered.

"Hi, it's Candice. Sorry if I woke you. I just got your message. What's up?" The nervousness of Candice's voice did not escape Mrs. Gallager.

"Oh, Candice, everything is okay right now. Brent walked out of rehab on Friday and left a note saying he couldn't live without you. I was calling to warn you because I knew he would try to find you. He's just not thinking clearly.

Seeing you with that other man set him spiraling out of control."

"I'm sorry, truly I am, but he's been out of control for a while. I think the drugs are just magnifying it." Candice sighed. "But honestly, he's always had control issues."

The words *right now* repeated in Candice's mind. "He needs help and the support of those that love him. Sorry, but I'm not that person anymore. I care, but I won't allow him to control me like he used to. I don't know what else to say except thank you for the warning."

"I understand, and we're working with the psychologist to help him accept things as they are. I just wanted to keep you safe."

"Thank you. I appreciate that. Guess I should get back to work." Candice ended the call and laid her head in her hands, trying to keep the tears from spilling.

The computer was ready and waiting, giving Candice a reason to escape Brent and start her day. She noticed several emails with the subject: *Job*. She opened the first one to find a resume attached. Candice decided to start weeding through all the applications she received. It was paramount that she find a perfect replacement for Jazzlene. It would also help ease the guilt she felt about leaving her. The qualities the new employee would need to possess were essential. The candidate must have a happy disposition, the ability to multi-task better than most, knowledge of photography, and the availability to accompany Jazzlene on photo shoots when needed. And, most important of all, make a great cup of Joe to keep Jazzlene from getting a caffeine headache. She was a bear without her caffeine.

Jazzlene strolled through the front door. "Good morning. Is everything okay?"

"Yeah, just another incident with Brent but supposedly he's back in rehab."

"What do you mean...*back* in rehab?"

"Seems he left Friday trying to get to me. He's really lost it, and I'm worried about him. And for myself."

"Have you let Shane know what's going on?"

"No, not yet. I had a call over the weekend from Mrs. Gallager, which he knows about, but I ignored it. I just called her back a few minutes ago. Anyway, for now, he's safe or maybe I should say the same for myself."

"Well, you need to be careful and aware of your surroundings," Jazzlene suggested, her eyes showing the depth of her worry.

"Hey, to change the subject, you would not believe the responses to your ad." The last thing Candice wanted to do was dwell on Brent. "There has to be close to fifty applicants and counting. I'll sift through each one, weed out the noes, and phone interview the maybes. If they pass my interview, I'll set up a time for you to personally interview them."

"What would I do without you? Hopefully, we can find someone quick so you can train them for me, too."

"I'd love that." Candice handed a piece of paper to Jazzlene. "Here's your schedule for this week."

"Thanks. Oh, and I didn't tell you, but I'm going to New York to do a shoot for the travel magazine next month. You want to go? All expenses paid. We could have a great time paintin' the town."

"I'd love to, but let me get back to you on that. I'm pretty sure I will be too busy with the café remodel and hiring people. But maybe I can get away for a few days."

"Well, let me know soon, so I can find someone else, 'cuz I'm gonna need an assistant for this shoot."

"Will Friday be too late? My dad is coming Wednesday, and I'm sure all the details will be hashed out with Shane's grandmother by then. After that, I'll have a better idea of the timeline."

"Yeah, Friday will work. By the way, Steve's very excited about your place. Are you really going to leave him all your furniture?"

"Yeah, it just won't look right in the house. It's way too modern, so I'm going to buy a few antique pieces."

"Steve left all his stuff in storage when he moved back up here. You're really helping him out by offering to leave the furniture."

"Seems like you two are getting along. And I'm really enjoying our Sunday football get-togethers, but I'm guessing that once I open the café, I won't be able to see my friends like I'm used to. Or at least until I have employees that I trust."

"Well, maybe Stella and I can stop by the café on Sunday's while the guys watch football."

"Oh, now there's a great idea if she'll go for it," Candice said while opening Jazzlene's website to see all the changes Steve made.

"What do you think?" Jazzlene's eyes focused on the new homepage.

"This is perfect, very professional. I think I'll have to hire him to do my site."

"He already told me he would."

"Really? That would be great."

Steve fitted right in with Kevin and Shane, which was good because the women really loved being together.

"So, have you told my brother yet?" Candice asked, trying not to sound too judgmental.

"No, we haven't spoken in over a month. And until I know Steve and I are exclusive, I'm gonna keep whatever this is, Steve and I have to myself."

"I get it, but be honest with him. I know he's not marriage material, but you should let him know you've moved on."

"First of all, your brother is the one who strings me along. Isn't he seeing someone right now? I know that's why he hasn't called. He's obviously hooking up somewhere else."

"I'm not sure. I haven't talked to him either. But, even if you and Steve don't work out, you should stop running back to my brother."

"You're right. I think I'm ready to move on and Steve might be the person to break the spell. I never think about your brother when I'm with Steve. Hell, I rarely think about him when I'm not with Steve."

"It's about time," Candice said, knowing her brother was not nearly good enough for Jazzlene. "And how 'bout Steve, have you told him about my brother?"

"Yes, Steve knows I have an on-again-off-again relationship with him."

"How'd he handle that tidbit of information?"

"He didn't say much at the time, but he questioned me last night. Wants to know if I've seen your brother since he and I have been going out. Of course, I said no, and if I do decide to see your brother, I'll let Steve know."

"Well, if my opinion is worth anything, I think Steve is more long-term boyfriend material. He's the one you should be investing your time in, not my *'can't commit to anything'* stepbrother."

"Yeah, you're right." Jazzlene contemplated what Candice was saying.

The phone began to ring ending the conversation and pushing both women into work mode.

It was 9:00 a.m. and Shane pulled up in front of his childhood home in Noe Valley. He was meeting the sales rep for the alarm company. Shane was not taking any chances when it came to Candice's safety. He planned to have every window and door alarmed in all three units, along with several video cameras installed. And if that wasn't enough, he was also requesting a portable panic button for Candice to carry in her pocket. The sooner the security system was installed, the better he was going to feel.

The tree trimmer his father hired was already at work cutting back the tree in the front of the home. It was long overdue. Just the removal of a few branches breathed new life into the tree and revealed the beauty of the house.

He had so much to do, between taking Candice to look at paint chips at lunch and getting back to his shop to make sure things were running smoothly. His plate was full, but he would not have it any other way, he loved being busy. He was falling so deeply in love that there was nothing, he would not do for Candice.

The morning flew by. Shane arrived to take Candice to the paint store.

"So, do you have any idea what color you want to paint the house?" he asked as she picked out several different colors of paint chips.

"Well, the first time I saw the house I thought a very pale pink, almost white, with deep plum trim. Like these colors here," she offered, showing him the color palette in her hand.

"Oh, that would be really nice. I like it."

"Really? I could go in a different direction, like gray or something earthier."

"No, I love the colors. They are so you."

Candice smiled as she examined the colors. "How 'bout we buy a few samples and paint them on the house. See if we still like them when they dry," she suggested.

In less than ten minutes, they were walking out with several pints of paint in various shades of pink and plum.

"Let's go drop this off at the house. I want to show you something."

Candice turned quizzically looking at Shane. "You're just going to have to wait until we get there," Shane told her, turning on to 24th Street.

Candice's mouth dropped when she saw the tree perfectly trimmed and the house was no longer hidden. "Wow, it really changes the appearance of the house. Can we go paint the color samples onto the house?"

"Sure." Shane handed her the keys to the first-floor unit. "Go open the door, and we'll put the colors on the back of the house."

Candice fiddled with the lock and had the door open before Shane closed the trunk of the car. "Come on slow poke, I have to get back to work before my boss docks my pay."

Shane kicked the door shut and followed her out the back.

"So, as soon as you decided on the color, I'll have the painters get to work."

Candice lifted the lid from the first can. "Oh, look how pretty this is." She dipped the paintbrush into the can and started spreading it on the wall. "I like this."

"Paint the plum you like next to it." Shane held up the open can of plum paint.

"Yep, I think this is it, but maybe we should paint some of those other colors, just in case your grandmother doesn't care for these colors."

"Don't worry about her, she's not going to care what color you paint the house. She's just so excited for you. It's like you've breathed new life into this house."

"Can we go what changes are happening in my new home?" Candice asked, looking toward the second story.

"Sure." Shane put the lids on the cans of paint and grabbed her hand. They climbed the back stairs and entered through the back door.

Candice looked around at the empty rooms before making her way to Shane's childhood bedroom and stepped inside. She closed her eyes and thought about the little boy who once slept in this room. The little boy who lost his mother so young. Shane came up behind her, wrapping his arms around her waist and softly kissing the top of her head. She tilted her head up to look into his eyes and could see that he too was remembering his childhood.

"Are you sure you are going to be okay with me living here? I mean, I can take the top apartment."

"Yes, I'm fine. This feels just a little weird. It's flooding my mind with memories of my mom. Once when I was sick, she spent the entire night sleeping next to me rubbing my head."

Candice remained quiet. She turned around so she could embrace Shane and looked up into his glistening eyes. He took a deep breath and continued, "We are going to make new, happy memories here," Shane whispered, releasing Candice.

She sat down in the middle of his bedroom and reached her hand out to him. "Come sit with me."

He slowly dropped to the floor facing her. Candice scooted in between his legs and put her hands on each side of his face. "You know how much I love you?"

Shane brushed the hair out of her eyes. "Why don't you tell me?"

"Let me show you." She pushed him onto his back and straddled him. Shane looked up and had a devilish look in his eyes.

"I like where this is going." He laughed, enjoying her hands that were caressing him as she slowly unbuttoned his shirt.

Revealing his tattoo, she laid her head his chest so she could hear his heart speed up in anticipation of what she would do next.

Getting dressed a short while later, Candice spoke, "How's that for a new memory in your old room? You think you'll want this room back now?"

"Oh yeah. This room now holds a memory I will never forget," Shane answered, zipping his pants. "And I think that paint is probably close to dry now. Let go see if you still like it."

Candice quickly skipped down the stairs leading to the backyard. "Yes, I think this is exactly the color I want."

"Done. I'll call this afternoon and set up the paint crew."

"I can do some of the scheduling. I know you have a lot going on at the shop."

"Nah, it's a simple phone call. And don't forget we are going to see Aldo today after work."

"I won't." Candice looked across the street. "Should we go say hi to your sister?"

"She's still in school. But we'll be seeing her on Wednesday."

"I forgot to tell you, my father is driving up here on Wednesday instead of us going there. He wants to meet your grandmother."

"That's great. We'll all have dinner at her house so we can go over the contract."

Shane shut the car door and strolled around to the driver side getting in the truck. "Thank you for the new memory." He smiled, lacing his fingers through hers and giving a gentle squeeze.

"Well, I'm sure we'll be making much more in that house." Candice lifted Shane's hand to her lips.

Things were quickly falling into place, and Shane knew that between his father and himself, they could have the café ready to open in two months, three max.

Candice had interviewed several candidates over the phone and invited three of them to come in for a one-on-one interview with Jazzlene. It was looking promising that she would find a qualified, eager replacement.

Jazzlene emerged from the darkroom. "I thought you'd be gone by now."

"I'm just waiting for Shane to get here. Because unfortunately, he's stuck in traffic. Oh, and I have three applicants that sound like they just may be perfect for the job."

"Wow, that was fast."

"I've set up the interviews tomorrow afternoon because you have a two-hour break in the day."

"Great, maybe you can sit in to observe and throw in questions if you think of anything I forgot to ask. I trust your instincts."

"I'd love to."

"You were gone a long time for lunch. Did you find the paint colors you wanted?"

"Yeah, then we stopped by the house to paint a sample on the walls to make sure I liked them. I'm going with a pale pink and a dark plum for the trim."

"That sounds very nice and perfect for that house."

"And the tree has been pruned so you can see all the beautiful detailing of the house. I'm gonna look for a bench to put under the tree."

"Seems like things are moving along pretty fast."

"I know, between Shane and his father I think they pretty much have it all figured out. Or at least the house stuff, I still have to decide how to arrange the café."

Shane pulled up out in front. "Well, I'm gonna get going, we're stopping by his uncle's restaurant to look at how he set up his kitchen. He's helping me come up with the best layout for mine."

"Well, have a great night. I'll see you in the morning," Jazzlene said and locked the door behind Candice.

After their hour tour of Aldo's kitchen and of course, the meal he insisted they sit and eat, Shane walked Candice to her condo. "I'm gonna head back to the shop. I have some last-minute business to finish up." He pressed his warm lips against hers and kissed her until she could not breathe.

"So, are you coming back?" Candice sounded disappointed.

"No, I think I'll sleep at my place, but I'll be by to pick you up in the morning."

"Okay." After one last kiss, she released his hand and walked into her place.

Shane wanted to stay with Candice, but he also wanted to try to slow down the growing desire to be with her every minute of every day. It was a battle he seemed to be losing. He could barely sleep at night if she were not next to him.

He arrived at his shop and delved into completing the first of three tables he was making for Candice. The memory of her sad eyes when he said he was not coming back haunted him, but he knew once she realized he was spending his nights working on furniture for her café, she would be happy.

Candice sat on her couch going through her mail. One letter with no return address was in the pile. She recognized the handwriting and placed the envelope on the table. Having one man obsessing over her and one man leaving her to spend the night alone was more than she wanted to think about, so she turned on the TV and relaxed while watching a reality show until she fell asleep curled up on her couch.

Eighteen

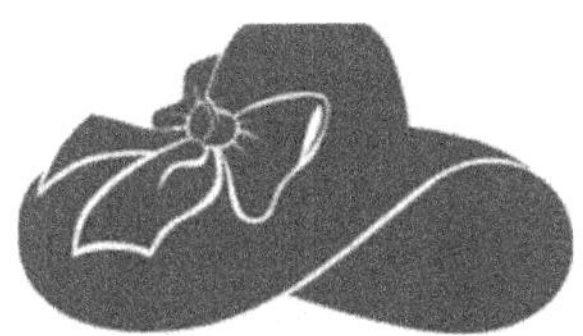

Wednesday arrived, and Candice woke up once again alone. She was not happy when she felt the cold spot next to her as she reached for Shane. That was two nights in a row that he chose not to spend the night. When they were together, everything seemed perfectly fine. Candice was miffed by the distance he appeared to be putting between them.

Panic set in as she realized going into business with his grandmother would not be a good idea if Shane were already distancing himself. How would she cope without him when she would still have to spend time with his grandmother? She would have to analyze what this would mean for her sanity. She decided to wait until after her father met Beatrice and then weigh her options.

Shane arrived at 7:30 a.m. to pick her up for work. He smiled when she stepped out of her building and wrapped her in a warm embrace.

"I've missed waking up next to you," Shane told her, placing a kiss on her forehead.

"Then why haven't you been staying with me?" Candice questioned with sadness in her voice.

"I've been staying at the shop until after midnight. So, you'd be asleep by the time I was done, and I don't want to wake you."

"I don't mind. Why are you working so late anyway? This doesn't have to do with you helping me, does it?"

"I've been working on a special order, and I need to work when I can find free time. But I'm taking tonight off." Shane met her lips and softly kissed her, then quickly patted her rear. "Now get in the car so we can go get some coffee, I need a caffeine fix."

Candice scooted into her seat and rested her hand on Shane's as he shifted into first gear. "I made a variety of treats to share with my dad. Maybe if he tastes them, he'll understand what the fuss is about."

"I'm sure you are right." Shane agreed, pulling away from the curb.

"You know, I wish you would reconsider your self-imposed, *not coming over without letting me know*, rule" Candice nibbled on his earlobe.

Shane looked down at her with longing in his eyes. "Oh, since your dad is picking you up at work today," he held out his hand, "here are the keys to your new house. Maybe you'd like to take him on a tour."

"That would be great. Thank you." Candice held the keys and ignored the fact that he did not respond to her previous plea.

11:00 o'clock and the first of three candidates for the job arrived.

"Hello, you must be Clancy." Candice stood as she greeted him.

"Yes," he replied before he extended his hand and gave her a firm handshake.

"I'll let Jazzlene know you are here. Have a seat, I'll be right back." Candice turned to summon Jazzlene.

Clancy had the look of a metrosexual man. There was not a hair on his head out of place. His eyebrows were expertly shaped to perfection. His face was clean-shaven. Although he was casually dressed, his attire still screamed designer threads.

Jazzlene rounded the corner, and Clancy stood up.

"Hello, I'm Jazzlene. This will be informal, so we'll just sit on the couch." Jazzlene stepped toward the couch and motioned for him to sit.

Candice sat at her desk to listen in while Jazzlene conducted the interview. She made notes on her computer so Clancy would think she was working and remain relaxed. However, she was really making her 'pros and cons' list to discuss with Jazzlene.

Clancy was looking for a job where he had a variety of duties. He did not like sitting still for too long and enjoyed interacting with people. His real asset or bonus was that he had studied photography in college and continued to dabble in it as a hobby. Traveling with Jazzlene on photo shoots would not be a problem for him, as he liked exploring the world. From his politeness to his confidence, not one thing ended up on the con side of the list. Neither Jazzlene nor Candice could find anything wrong with him. So far, he was number one, but he was the first person interviewed. Maybe the other two would be just as impressive.

Candidate two was Eve, a young, petite woman about twenty-four, still enrolled in college and looking for a part-time job. Her past job experience was serving as a barista, and she loved interacting with people. She had a smile that never left her face and was probably one of those people that pretended to be happy even when their heart was in turmoil. She had little experience with computers and scheduling but claimed she was a quick learner.

The final candidate of the day was Fiona, a very tall, statuesque woman with long brown hair that she had pulled back into a high ponytail. She was in her thirties and had just moved to San Francisco from a little town in Iowa. Her limited resume included being a waitress and volunteering for a non-profit that feeds the homeless. She also loved the public, but more importantly, she excelled at helping people.

After Fiona left, Jazzlene and Candice sat down for an in-depth discussion. All three candidates could work, but Clancy's knowledge of photography gave him the edge. Plus, he seemed to have people skills, a quality needed for those sometimes-stressful situations of Jazzlene's job.

"So, I guess I'll give him a call and offer him the job," Jazzlene concluded as she made her way to the phone.

"And those other two women would probably work out well for the café." Candice was starting to get into hiring mode. "After tonight, I'll know exactly what will happen with Beatrice's business offer."

"Well, then maybe I'll wait until tomorrow to call Clancy. If you change your mind, you'll still need a job."

"No, go ahead and call him. If things don't work out on my end, I'll find something. I'm confident my father will be on board, especially after he tastes the cookies I'm bringing tonight."

"This is getting exciting. I can't wait to be your first customer." Jazzlene's eyes sparkled with admiration.

"I can always count on you to boost my ego. I love you for always supporting me."

At 5:00 p.m. and Candice's father arrived to pick her up. He walked into Jazzlene's studio with a beautiful woman on his arm. Candice's mouth dropped open.

"Don't look so surprised," he said, with a glint of love when he looked at both women.

Candice was still speechless.

"Honey, we've wanted to talk to you," the woman said, not taking her eyes off Candice.

"What is going on?" Candice motioned with her hand between the two of them.

"Well, long story short, your mother has moved in with me and—"

Candice cut him off mid-sentence, "And you think you two can make this thing work? How many years has it been since your divorce?"

"We never stopped loving each other," her mother added.

"Well, I always knew you two cared for each other, but this, really...well, I'm in shock right now." Candice stood there staring.

Finally breaking the uncomfortable silence, Candice spoke, "Well, I guess we should get going. You two can tell me what is going on in the car." Candice reached into her desk drawer, grabbed the plate of cookies, and then took out her purse.

Candice climbed into the back seat of her dad's car. "I have the keys to the house and thought we could stop by for a tour."

"Sounds great. Where to?" her father asked while placing his hand on her mother's thigh and giving it a little pat.

"24th and Noe." Candice snapped out, still bothered by her parents and their newfound *lost* love. Then she remembered they always seemed to take vacations at the same time.

"So, how long has this been going on? I've already figured out you two probably took vacations together."

"It's complicated," her mother offered.

"Well, enlighten me. I have all night."

"What can I say? Your father was my high school sweetheart. I've always loved him, but there was a point in my life I thought I missed out on other things and I guess I was just lost for a while."

"Mom, you have been married to *another man* for fifteen years," Candice spat back, irritated with her mother.

"Honey, don't be mad at your mother. I wasn't the best husband back then. I drank too much and didn't give you or your mother the attention you both needed."

"I'll give you that, dad. But, oh hell, forget it. I hope you two know what you are doing." Candice sealed her lips and closed the subject.

"We are working on it, and we both want this." Her mother tried to assure her.

"Fine. Can we just go look at the house now and talk business?" That was the only thing that was going to make sense to Candice. She understood business but apparently not love. Heck, if her parents could work out their differences, then maybe Shane would eventually dump her and run back to his ex-wife. Her mind was going to an ugly place. The only thing to help it now was walking up the steps of her future business.

Candice turned the key and pushed the door open. "After you," she said, stepping aside and allowing her parents to enter the commercial space.

Her father walked through, letting out a slow whistle. "This is pretty darn nice."

"Okay, so each of you close your eyes," she instructed. "Now, I'm handing you a cookie but don't open your eyes. Just eat it and imagine you are sitting in a quaint little café enjoying this cookie with hot tea."

Both her parents obliged her and took their first bite. Candice waited for a moan, a comment, anything positive, but they both remained quiet as they took another taste.

"May I have another?" her mother asked, finishing the first cookie.

"Here," Candice handed her a chocolate cookie, "try this one."

"Okay, the suspense is killing me. What do you think of the cookies?"

"Well, I'll take another," her father responded, with his eyes still closed. "I need another taste test." He chuckled.

Candice handed him a chocolate cookie. "I'm not a fan of chocolate, but I must say this cookie is just bursting with flavor. There has to be something else in it besides chocolate." He let the cookie rest in his mouth. "Oh, just a hint of mint, right?"

"No, you're tasting a sprinkle of anise, dad. But you know I could probably substitute the anise for mint."

"Can we open our eyes now?" her mother questioned.

"Yes. So, what do you think?"

"Well, honey the cookies are fabulous, and this space is quite adorable, but you realize it will require a lot of your time. When will you have time to date?" Her mother actually whined.

"Mom, really? The first thing that comes to your mind is my dating. Not how wonderful those cookies are or that your daughter wants to open her own business," Candice snapped.

"I'm just saying you're not going to have a social life."

Candice rolled her eyes. This is why she did not tell her mother about her plans. "Why don't you let me worry about my social life, and I'll keep my nose out of your love life."

"From a business standpoint I think you have a great idea, so let's finish this tour," her father suggested, trying to avert a meltdown among the women.

"Okay, you two look around, I'm gonna call, Shane." Candice pulled her cell phone from her purse.

Shane answered on the first ring. "Hey, babe, what's up?"

"I'm at the house. I'm wondering if you want me to pick up your sister?"

"My dad picked her up earlier. But thank you."

"And...ah...do you have room for one more?"

"Yeah, why?"

"My father decided to bring a guest without checking to see if it was okay first."

"Don't worry. The more, the merrier, right?"

"I guess." Candice looked at her parents, who happened to be holding hands.

"You all right? You sound a little pissed."

"I'll explain later. We should be there within a half hour."

"I'm headin' over there now, so I'll see you soon."

"Okay, I just have to finish showing them the house, and I'll be there with my bonus guest."

"Bye." Shane hung up.

"I want to take you outside and show you the colors I've chosen for the house." Candice unlocked the back door and led her parents to the backyard.

"Oh, this yard is so cute." Her mother stared at what was once an English garden, but now the only inhabitants were weeds.

"I think I can put a vegetable garden over there." Candice pointed. "And some wildflowers sprinkled throughout the rest of the yard, maybe a trellis or two."

"That would be darling. I can see a birdbath in that corner."

"Let's head up the back stairs to the apartment I'm going to live in." Candice turned to climb the stairs.

Once they had inspected all three units, her father looked satisfied.

"I'm not sure if those cookies wore me down or if this is just a special place, but I can see your vision, and I like it." Hank followed her out the door, still holding her mother's hand.

"We should get going," Candice suggested as her father surveyed the surrounding neighborhood.

"This is a great neighborhood for your business. You might want to think of adding Wi-Fi for your customers."

"I did think about that, but it might be too small. I don't want all the tables taken up by people hanging out and not buying."

"Good point," he agreed. "I guess it wouldn't hurt people to get away from their gadgets and enjoy a peaceful afternoon."

"Honey, if you need help, I'd love to come in and work a few days a week for you. Maybe help you bake?" Irene enthusiastically offered.

"I may take you up on that if you are serious."

"Of course I am."

"Well, good 'cuz I'm gonna need help and a lot of it."

Hank pulled into the long driveway leading to Beatrice's beautiful, well-maintained house. He let out another whistle. It was something he did when he was surprised. "Well, this is someplace."

"Wait until you see the inside," Candice added proudly. "Beatrice has some of the most beautiful antiques."

Irene opened her car door and stepped out. She scanned the yard before settling her eyes on the house. Just as her focus reached the porch, the door opened, and the most handsome man she had seen in a long time walked out.

Shane approached, meeting Candice's gaze. "So, how was the tour?"

"It was great. I saw all the changes you've been making. Looks like the security company has been hard at work?"

Shane smiled. "They said they'll be done by Friday."

Hank and Irene stood there for a few moments watching their daughter interact with Shane. "Ahem." Hank cleared his throat.

Candice turned, embarrassed that when she was around Shane, nothing else mattered. "Sorry. Shane, this is my father Hank and my mother, Irene." She lifted her eyebrows and gave him a look that warned him not to ask any questions.

Hank released Irene's hand to shake Shane's outstretched hand. "Nice to meet you, son." Hank made eye contact with Shane giving him a look that said *you better treat my daughter right.*

"Nice car," Shane tossed in, looking at his car next to Hank's. They were so similar. He remembered Candice telling him about her father's car and the memories of shifting the gears for him.

"I've had my baby for years," Hank said, referring to his car while turning to look at it.

Irene quickly gave Shane a hug. "I loved the house. Candice said you lived there when you were little. She even showed us your room."

"Yes, it's been in the family for years." Shane looked at Candice, then at her mom, and once again Candice. "You two look exactly alike." Irene was a little shorter than Candice was, but their eyes and hair were the exact same color. Their smiles caught his attention; one was a lustful take me to bed smile while the other was a warm, caring smile.

"Shane, is the car locked?" Candice asked. "I left my business plan on the back seat."

"I grabbed it for you, it's in the house." He reached for her hand. "Let's go introduce your parents to my family."

They entered the foyer at the exact time Beatrice came around the corner, looking as regal as ever. She knew how to dress for success. Taking full command of the situation, Beatrice led the group into a mahogany infused study. Candice realized that this is where she conducted and held her business meetings.

Beatrice waited for everyone to take a seat before she sat. This was not the time for pleasantries; it was the time to get down to serious business. "Thank you for coming. I'm Beatrice, Shane's grandmother and also the woman who would love the opportunity to be a business partner with your daughter."

"Hi, I'm Hank, and this is Irene, Candice's mother. I've scrutinized the contract you prepared, and I like what I've read."

"Good, I'm trying to be fair because I believe in your daughter."

Everyone else remained quiet as Hank and Beatrice spoke to one another.

"If you have tried her baked goods, you know they are exceptional. Your daughter also has a great mind for business. I know she will be very successful."

"Yes. I can't agree with you more. And those cookies we sampled today were—"

"Amazing," Shane interrupted.

"Yes, amazing," Irene agreed, throwing in her two cents.

"Okay, it sounds like we are all in agreement that the sweets are wonderful. So, my next question, have you read her business plan?" Beatrice questioned, keeping constant eye contact with Hank.

"Yes, and I find it very detailed; if she follows that plan, she can't fail." Hank turned to Candice as though giving her his approval.

"So, Candice, you said you had some other ideas you wanted to add to the business plan?" Beatrice recalled.

"Yes, here's what I really would like to do. This would make the business more meaningful to me, not just tasty treats."

Everyone's eyes were now focused on Candice.

"You know how Tom makes those beautiful tactile sculptures, and Marni paints colorful, abstract art?" Beatrice nodded, while Hank and Irene seemed bemused. "Well, I've been in contact with the school Marni attends, and they gave me a list of people I can get in touch with to help with my idea." Everyone was now looking confused. "Okay, here's what I want to do. I want to put the artwork in the café for sale. Like, I can take Marni's artwork and frame it. Maybe copy some of them and create greeting cards. Tom's sculpted pieces and other wonderful artistic pieces from other disabled adults and children could also be displayed on the walls and shelves for sale." Candice paused to let that sink. "I would only take a small percentage from each sale. I'm not in it for the money. I just want to give them a place to showcase their talent. I want my café to be filled with and surrounded by love."

"That's a marvelous idea. And Shane, don't you have a few great shelf units in your warehouse?" Beatrice asked.

"Yes, I do." He did not want Candice to know he already had them stained and ready to load into the store. That was just one of the surprises he had for her.

"And I was thinking of hiring some disabled adults. I know there are a lot of capable people from that community that need a job." Candice beamed. "And I guess the other thing we really need to do is make sure a ramp is installed for wheelchair access into the café. Oh, and we need to have the bathroom handicap accessible as well."

"Well babe, you really have been thinking this through." Shane was so proud of her.

"Candice, once again you remind me of why I wanted to go into business with you." Beatrice's voice changed from all business to that of the loving grandmother she was.

"And I have one last idea, but this really has nothing to do with the business...how would you feel if we rented the upstairs unit to a disabled couple? Say, maybe someone with Down Syndrome?"

At that point, Beatrice had a hard time keeping herself from jumping up and hugging Candice. "Well, why didn't I ever think of that? That is exactly what we'll do."

Candice stood and made her way to Beatrice and leaned over to give her a kiss on the cheek.

"If we're all in agreement, then why don't we sign the contract and then we can go eat?" Beatrice handed the pen to Candice. She gladly signed the papers, knowing she was on her way to fulfilling her dream.

Shane showed them the way to the dining room. Beatrice, however, remained in the study, needing a moment to gather herself.

"Dad," Shane called out to his father. Trevor turned around after tying the bib around Marni's neck. "This is Hank and Irene, Candice's parents. This is my father Trevor and my sister Marni." Shane stood behind Marni rubbing her shoulders.

At the mention of her name, Marni went into her frantic inaudible hello, waving her hands above her head.

"Nice to finally meet you." Trevor shook Hank's hand and kissed Irene on the cheek.

Marni quickly stood up and grabbed Irene's hand, squeezing it tightly. Irene sweetly spoke to Marni, "My, my, aren't you strong?"

"Yeah sorry, but she gets excited to meet new people." Shane unlatched Marni's fingers from around Irene's hand, letting the blood flow back into her fingers.

"I like a firm handshake." Hank walked over to Marni to shake her hand. "Hi, I'm Candice's father, so happy to meet you." Marni giggled and squeezed as tight as she could. "Yep, that's one hell of a grip you have."

Shane observed the exchange between Candice's parents and his sister. They accepted her just like Candice did. There was no false tone or discomfort in their voices or actions. It was genuine caring for another human.

They sat around the table laughing and enjoying the incredible meal Aldo had prepared and sent over to them.

"You know that you can move into the house this weekend if you want," Shane informed Candice. "I can have Josh help me move your furniture, or at least the few items you're taking."

"Really, everything is done?"

"Well, not everything. But the important stuff, like the alarm system, which you know will be done by Friday."

"I'd love to come help set up your home," Irene offered. "Maybe we can go shopping for accessories once you're settled in."

"That would be fun." Candice had not spent time alone with her mother in over a year. And once she broke up with Brent, she tried to keep her distance. She really did not want to hear her mother tell her *I told you so* again.

The evening wound down with everyone enjoying a few of the cookies Candice brought. And of course, Marni only wanted the chocolate ones, so Candice made sure Marni got the last one left on the plate.

Nineteen

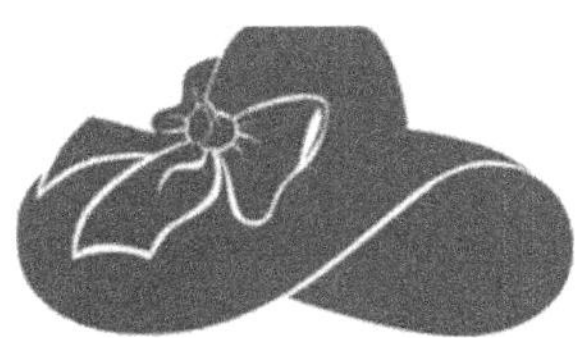

Shane drove down Mission Boulevard toward Candice's condo. "That was an interesting evening."

"Need I tell you how shocked I was? I mean, my dad just shows up without warning with my mom on his arm." Candice shook her head. "It seems like they've been divorced forever, and there they were, like two love-struck teenagers."

Shane laughed. "I thought they were cute together."

"Sure, because they're not your crazy impulsive parents. I still don't exactly know what is going on with those two. Apparently, they've decided to live together."

"Well, like you said before, it's best to stay out of their personal life."

"I sure have good advice, now all I need to do is listen to myself. This brings me to something I want to talk to you about."

"Which is?" Shane already knew what she wanted to discuss, but he humored her by asking.

"Can you please remove your stupid rule? I don't sleep well when you're not next to me. I could care less if you come in at five in the morning, just please crawl into bed with me," Candice pleaded.

"I'm trying really hard to take this slow. I don't want to screw anything up."

"Well," Candice pressed her hand between his inner thighs, "you're making me feel—" She stopped mid-sentence. "Look, I'm just worried we're going backward in this relationship. You're staying away more and more, and I really miss you."

"I know babe, but right now I can't help it. I've been working on making sure everything runs smoothly with the café and house renovation, trying to run my business, and then restore some pieces of furniture for a client. So, it's gonna be like this for a few more weeks."

"I get that, but you can still come home to me. Use your damn key and let yourself into my house because you have already taken up residence in my heart."

Shane smiled. "Damn, you make it hard to follow my self-imposed exile."

"Good, that was my goal." Candice glided her hand up Shane's thigh, massaging as she progressed.

"You better stop now, or I'll never make it into the condo. It's been too long." Shane pulled her hand from between his legs and kissed it.

"That's not my fault. Hopefully, this is a lesson you only have to learn once." She tried to pull her hand away to continue her sensual assault, but Shane would not release it.

"I did love your father's car." He quickly tried to change the direction of her thoughts.

"Of course you did, they're almost identical, although I prefer yours more?"

"Why?"

"Because yours smells like you and it's comforting." Candice deeply inhaled. "And you are intoxicating."

Shane entered the underground parking garage. He could not get the keys out of the ignition. Candice was already out of the car and opening his door. "You having trouble there, Ace?"

Shane looked up. "Sorry, someone distracted me."

"Well, I think I can help." She leaned in and removed the keys twirling them around her finger.

"You do realize I really shouldn't leave the car yet." He let his eyes drift to his lap.

Candice looked around. "No one's even here. We can be upstairs in no time."

"You know my self-imposed rule?"

"Yeah."

"Well, I agree with you. So, I think I'll just scratch that one rule off the list."

"It's about time you came to your senses." Candice stepped back so Shane could get out of the car.

"Come here," Shane pleaded, watching Candice walk away.

"You need me for something?" She smirked and allowed her eyes to travel south.

"You can see my problem, so can you at least let me walk behind you in case we run into one of your neighbors."

Candice took Shane's hand, dragging him to the elevator as fast as her legs could move. Finally, the doors opened, and an elderly couple greeted them.

Candice quickly stepped in front of Shane, obstructing their view of his current state of arousal. The gentleman nodded holding the *open door* button until his wife safely exited.

"Good evening," Candice squeaked out, trying not to giggle. "Going for your evening stroll?" she asked, knowing their nightly routine.

"Yes, the Mrs. and I love a brisk walk after dinner." He tipped his head as he followed his wife.

The door closed and Shane backed Candice up against the mirrored wall, pressing his body against her so she could not move. Not that she wanted to escape his physical bondage. Snaking her arm past his, Candice reached his back pocket and placed her hands inside them. She felt his firm butt cheeks and squeezed them. His reaction left her breathless. Shane's mouth was exploring hers with every thrust of his tongue. That tantalizing treat lasted until the elevator came to a stop and the doors opened.

Shane kicked the condo door closed while ripping open the front of Candice's blouse, sending buttons flying in all directions. He reached around to unhook her bra as he slowly walked her back toward her bedroom. Then, laying her beautiful naked body softly on the down comforter, he turned, walking away and leaving her aching for him.

"Where are you going?" she choked out between a passionate groan.

"I'll be right back, just give me a sec." Shane turned on the shower so he could take a quick rinse.

"Well, if you're taking a shower, I'm gonna enjoy the show." Candice could feel the heat of her lust causing her to lick her lips in anticipation.

"You know you could join me if you want." Shane teased her by turning his back toward her.

"Not fair." She sulked. "Turn back around. I want the full-frontal view so I can see what awaits me," she playfully ordered.

Shane stepped out of the shower and looked for his towel. "Looking for this?" Candice approached with a soft towel and began drying him attentively while not touching the one place his body begged her to stroke.

Candice looked up into Shane's smoldering eyes. "I think I've waited long enough; can you just stop teasing me already." Candice quivered as Shane began licking down her neck to her breast.

"Is that better?" he asked, walking her back toward the bed.

"Much." Candice lay on her back and wrapped her legs around his waist, ensnaring him. She had Shane right where she wanted him. This time he did relinquish control until she finally succumbed from exhaustion.

The radio started playing, and Candice slowly rolled over to turn it off. Every muscle in her body screamed at her. *I really need to start doing yoga if I'm going to try any more of those crazy positions*. Shane pulled her against his body, gliding his hand along her hip.

"Mornin' babe. Did you sleep well?" He delicately kissed the back of her neck.

"Yes, very good." She rolled over to face him. "Thank you for staying last night. This is how I want to wake up every morning."

"Me too." Shane finally conceded. "There's no turning back now. Our parents have met, and you're now my grandmother's business partner. So, we're pretty much in it for the long haul."

Candice reached up and ran her hands through his messy hair. "Yep, no turning back now. The way I figure it, if your grandmother loves me, then you have no choice but to love me too."

"She does know people, but I don't need her to tell me you're the perfect woman for me."

"Hungry?" Candice yawned, hearing Shane's stomach rumble.

"Starving." His stomach let out another loud growl. "I'll go make us some eggs and toast." He threw on his boxers and headed to the kitchen. "Babe, you want some orange juice?" Shane asked while looking in the fridge for the eggs.

"Yes." She removed two glasses from the cabinet. "I think I might have some ham in there too. We could have ham and scrambled eggs."

Shane placed the eggs and ham on the counter before retrieving the orange juice. "I thought you liked your eggs over medium?"

"I do, but scrambled is fine too." Candice poured the orange juice and handed Shane his glass. He drank it in one fast gulp. "More?" Candice held up the orange juice container.

"Yeah, thanks. I didn't realize I was so parched. We need to remember to bring water to bed if we're going to have a marathon of lovemaking."

"That's easy enough to arrange." Candice took a sip of her orange juice. "Should I put on coffee or are we gonna stop by Coffee Palace?"

"You better make it. I don't think we'll have time this morning." Shane whisked the eggs until they were frothy.

Candice pushed a shadow box aside so they could sit at the small dining room table.

"What's that for?" Shane looked over at the empty box.

I'm going to make a shadow box with Grandma Pela's mementos. I'm thinking the newspaper article, apron, her old rind grater, and some of her handwritten recipes. Then I'll hang it in the café where everyone can see it."

"What a great idea. I can make you a bigger box if you want."

"You're too busy right now. I think this one will work."

They were into a comfortable domestic mode making breakfast, eating, showering, and heading out the door to work. It made Candice feel complete.

Something she never felt before, not even when she was with Brent.

"Shane, I know I'm putting this relationship into hyperdrive, but maybe you would consider moving some of your stuff into my new home."

Shane looked at the road while fiddling with the radio. "Why don't we get you settled in first, and then we'll see what happens."

"Okay, but I'm still leaving your bedroom just for you. And that is something you can't argue about. My home, my decision."

Shane pulled up in front of Jazzlene's studio. "I'm gonna pick you up at five, but then I have to go to the Dojang and work out. After that, I have to head back to the shop and work on that special order."

"Okay. Are you going to come over after you're done?"

"Yeah, but it will be late, so don't wait up. I'll try to be quiet."

Candice waited for Shane to open her door. "See you at five." She reached up and wrapped her arms around his neck before kissing him goodbye. "I love you," she softly endeared next to his ear.

"I love you too." Shane held her longer than he usually did. He kissed the top of her head and scooted her towards the door. "I have to leave before we need to head back home."

The minute Candice heard him say *home,* she knew some of his walls were starting to crumble. She turned and waved as he drove off.

Heading inside, Candice followed her daily routine, turning on music, booting up the computer, making coffee, reading emails, listening to messages, and waiting for Jazzlene to arrive.

The door opened and in strolled a very tired but happy looking Jazzlene. "Hi, let me tell you about my night."

"Okay, then I have to tell you about mine. You better go grab some coffee first."

"Good idea, be right back." Jazzlene found an oversized mug and filled it to the brim.

"So, what's going on?" Candice took a seat next to Jazzlene on the comfy sofa.

"Well, last night I was making dinner, and someone knocked on the door. Steve went and answered it."

"I can guess who was there."

"Yep, in the flesh. Anyway, Steve invited him in and offered him a beer. Of course, your brother took it and then the two of them sat down to watch football. At some point, they got into a discussion about some bad call last week, like old buddies."

"What did you do?"

"I finished making dinner and wondered if I had entered the Twilight Zone. Anyway, once dinner was ready, Steve invited your brother to eat with us. And you know what? He did. Like he was invited to dinner by some good friends."

"That had to be weird."

"I can't even tell you how mortified I was. Then after dinner, he left saying he'd call me. No questions, nothing."

"What did Steve say?"

"Well, I asked him why he invited him in, and he said he wanted to size up his competition. Doesn't that sound like a guy thing to do?"

"So, what were his conclusions or better yet, what are yours?"

"I can honestly tell you after being apart from your brother and with Steve for the last few weeks, Steve wins hands down. There is no competition between them. I think Steve knows that now by, well, let's just say we had fun after dinner."

"So, I guess you've finally decided to move on?"

"I guess I have. Steve is just so patient and good to me."

"I'm very happy for you." Candice nodded her approval.

"Now what is it that you wanted to tell me?"

"For starters, my father showed up last night with my mother on his arm."

"Where was I? How did I miss that?"

"I think you were in the back somewhere. Anyway, apparently, my mother has moved in with my father."

Jazzlene stared at Candice in disbelief. "Wow, that is strange. They've been divorced for fifteen years."

"I know. They were like two horny teenagers hangin' all over each other. I guess this has been going on forever. Remember when I told you that I suspected they took vacations together? Well, now I know I was right."

"So, I guess your stepbrother will no longer be part of your family."

"I'll always consider him a brother, but I guess you're right."

"Okay, so the night actually went from uncomfortable to pretty darn remarkable. I signed all the papers last night. We're on track for opening in a few months. Beatrice loved my ideas, and we're going to implement them."

"It sounds like everyone got along."

"Yep, as if we have known each other for years. Anyway, Shane told me I can move into the house Saturday. So, Steve can move into my condo Sunday if he wants."

"Wow, he'll be excited. I know he's been sleeping at my place lately, but he feels bad encroaching on my space. Not that he is. I like him there."

"I'll give him the keys Saturday after I clean the condo."

"What about New York?"

"I'm pretty sure I'm in. Shane said he could handle things while I'm gone. And he actually said he thought I should go, because once I open the business, I'll have little time to myself. Do you have the actual dates we'll be gone?"

"Yeah, they're on my phone." Jazzlene scrolled through her calendar. "Here they are. We would leave on an early Sunday morning flight and come back the following Saturday evening."

Candice jotted down the dates. "Okay, let me just ask Shane one last time and make sure it won't cause any issues."

"We're going to have so much fun," Jazzlene said, standing up to start her day.

"Guess I'll give Steve a call." Candice reached for the phone.

"I can call him," Jazzlene offered. "I want to hear his voice." She smiled as she pulled her cell phone out of her pocket.

"Hey babe, can you take lunch at noon?" Shane asked. "I have something to show you."

"Sure. What is it?"

"I have to show it to you."

"Okay, I'll be ready at noon."

Shane, punctual as always, stepped into the studio at twelve sharp. "Ready?" A strange smile crossed his face.

"Yeah." Candice grabbed her purse and turned the *Be back at 1:00* sign around to face the sidewalk. "So, what has you all excited?"

"Well, you'll see it soon enough."

He drove down 24th and found a parking spot at the curb.

"Something wrong with the renovation?" Candice kept in step with him.

"Nope." Shane opened the door to the café and walked straight through, then out the back door. "Remember the termite work that needed to be done in the utility room?"

"Yeah, that wall was in pretty bad shape."

"Well," Shane turned on the light, "look."

Candice turned toward the wall that had been removed, and she stood stunned. Before her was a decorative door with an unusual design carved into the wood.

"When they took the wall down, this was behind it. It's locked, so I have to remove the doorknob, but I wanted you to be here when I did. I know that you like exploring as much as I do."

"Where do you think it leads?"

"I don't know. I called my grandmother, and she said she had no idea. That wall was always there, so we're going to find out together."

"Wait, the design on the door looks really familiar. I've seen it upstairs. Come on." Candice was running up the stairs to the 3rd-floor unit. She made her way to the large bookshelf. "Give me a boost." She placed her foot into Shane's hand, and he hoisted her up.

"What are you doing?"

She twisted the key-shaped finial, releasing it. "Doesn't this look exactly like the design carved into the door?" She held up the finial.

Shane looked at her as if she was crazy. "I suppose."

"I think I see it," Candice excitedly said.

"See what?" Shane was confused.

"The key to the door." She reached into the hole that the finial had rested in. "Look!" She showed him a key.

"Well, I'll be damned."

Candice returned the wood finial to its proper spot before Shane let her down. "How did you ever figure that out?"

"I don't know. Maybe it was my keen observation skills. Or maybe I've been reading too many mystery novels. Let's go see if it works."

Shane could not keep up with Candice. She was down two flights of stairs and back in the utility room before he could even lock the apartment door.

"Hey, hurry your ass up," she shouted from inside the utility room.

"The moment of truth." She put the key in the lock and turned the key. "It worked." Candice was both shocked and amazed.

"You're pretty clever," Shane said. He turned his flashlight on before heading down the flight of stairs.

"There has to be a light switch here somewhere." Candice felt along the side of the wall. Her fingers stopped at the telltale signs of a switch, and she flipped it up. Overhead, a single light came to life.

"I don't believe it." Shane took in the vast underground room.

Lining one wall was what appeared to be a wall to ceiling wine rack. An oversized roll top desk sat across the room facing the stairs. And the things that could not be missed were two ancient distilleries in front of the far wall.

"This had to be an underground brewery back in the prohibition days." Shane walked to the desk and rolled the top up.

"Wow, this is the best find ever." Candice was giddy. "Do you think those things still work?" She pointed to the distilleries.

"Not sure." Shane had ledgers in his hand and started flipping through them. "Seems the original grocery store sold more than just food. According to this ledger, my family was running a very profitable bootleg business."

"I wonder if your grandmother ever heard the stories."

"I'll have to bring her by to see this." Shane opened a desk drawer and found a stack of photos. "Look." He handed them to Candice after he viewed them. "I think that is my great-grandfather." Shane pointed to a handsome man surrounded by a group of people. "I'm pretty sure those are all relatives."

"We should make a photo collage with these." Candice shuffled through the photos.

"I'm gonna have to get someone out here to tell me what those distilleries are worth and if they still work. Heck, we might be able to brew our own beer."

"That would be cool, but you know what would be cooler?"

"What?"

"Seems to me that this basement is large enough to turn into a man cave for you. You could have a big screen TV, man-size recliners, and of course your own home brews."

"Or you could use it for storage for the café, maybe an art studio. Didn't you say you want to have a place to set up a sewing machine and learn to make quilts? Maybe a space for you would be better. You could paint or whatever you want."

"It's big enough for both. When I say both, I mean your man cave and storage for the café. I don't think I'm going to have time for any crafting. Between baking all day and taking care of my man, I'll be too busy for anything else."

"We'll discuss this more, later."

"I still like the theater man cave idea. Just because I'm calling it a man cave does not mean I won't be down here enjoying the man in it."

Shane smiled. "Well, in that case, I just may consider it." He hugged her. "Guess I should get you some lunch before I take you back to work."

Candice grabbed her smiling Kool-Aid pitcher and filled it with water. She set it on the nightstand with a large glass. *If Shane wants water, he shall have it.* She rolled over and drifted to sleep, dreaming about the roaring '20s.

Twenty

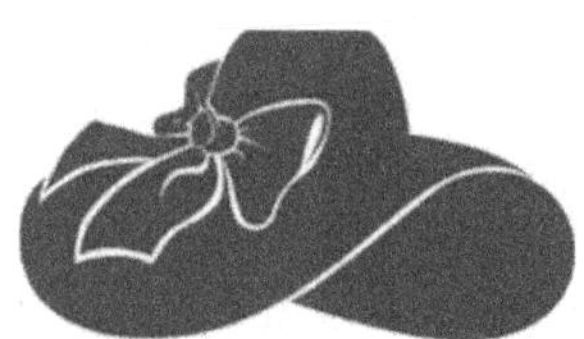

Saturday morning. Bacon sizzling, coffee brewing, and a glass of orange juice delivered by her sexy man was the perfect way to start the morning right.

"Time to get a move on, babe." Shane leaned over and kissed Candice's forehead.

"How can you be dressed and ready to go? You got less sleep than me last night?"

"We've got a busy day. I promised Steve I'd help him move his stuff after we get you settled." Shane pulled back the covers, exposing Candice to the chill of the morning. He would have to resort to another tactic if that did not get her rear in gear.

Candice fussed but rolled out of bed, tightly wrapping her bathrobe around herself and covering her voluptuous curves. "I'm gonna have to remember to sleep with old lady flannels from now on so I don't freeze in the morning."

"You have some of those?"

"Well, no, but maybe I should buy some."

"Nah, don't waste your money. I prefer you naked."

The buzzer outside the building alerted them. "Who the heck would be here already?" Candice walked to the intercom. "Yeah?"

"Hey honey, it's mom and dad. We're here and ready to help."

"Okay, I'll buzz you up." Candice turned to Shane. "I didn't know they were coming to help, did you?"

"Nope, but the more help we have, the faster we'll get done."

Hank and Irene stepped off the elevator just as Candice opened her front door. "Oh God, they're all over each other in the hallway. How embarrassing." Candice sounded mortified.

Shane laughed. "Remind you of anybody in particular?"

"I'm nothing like that. Well, at least not in public."

"I would have to argue with you on that. But I remember a little PDA at the park not too long ago. Not that I'm complaining, just pointing out."

"That was different."

"How so? We were lying on a blanket in the middle of the grass field."

"Yeah, but it was dark, and no one was there to see us." Candice tried to defend her position without even being able to convince herself.

Hank walked in and gave Shane a slap on the shoulder. "We ready to get this move rollin'? If we wait for Candice, it will be noon before we have the truck loaded."

"Dad, since when have I ever been late? Plus, I had no idea you were coming to help. Let alone being here before seven."

"Chop, chop." Hank shooed her away.

"It's okay, Hank. She has time. We'll run over to my warehouse and pick up Josh." Shane explained, grabbing his keys. "Babe, just relax and eat your breakfast. We'll be back soon."

Shane and Hank left, leaving Candice to face her mom. "So, you want to tell me what you are doing?" Her annoyance was impossible to miss.

"Well, without giving you the dirty details, let's just say your stepfather was involved in some things I just couldn't put up with anymore. And well, your father has always been there for me, even after everything I put him through. So, when I called him needing a place to sleep one night, he didn't hesitate to come and pick me up. He's always been there for me, no matter what I've done."

Candice sat quietly, absorbing what her mother had just said and trying to understand it. "I'm not gonna pry into your personal life, but please mom, don't hurt dad again. Once was enough." Candice still held resentment toward the way her mother destroyed their family.

"I can promise you I will never hurt your father again." She sounded resolute, mixed with a bit of sorrow and regret.

"Mom, when you said your wedding vows to dad and then Stan, didn't you say you promised to honor and cherish them until death do you part? Didn't you promise them both the same thing?" Candice's spite was loud and clear.

"Yes, I did." At that point, Irene shut up. She could not explain her choices because she did not even know why she made them herself.

"Fair enough." Candice took her last bite of eggs. "I'm gonna go get dressed." She headed to her bedroom and closed the door, needing some space to calm down.

Plopping down on her bed, she understood that she would have to forgive her mother at some point. But until her mom proved she was true to her word, Candice chose to be cautious.

There was a knock on her door. "Honey, the guys are back." Irene's voice was soft.

"Okay, I'll be out in a minute." Candice walked toward her bathroom and disrobed, snatching her jeans off the counter.

Shane snuck up behind her, making her jump. "You all right?"

"Yeah, just a little irritated. We'll discuss it later." Candice zipped her pants.

"Maybe we should discuss it now."

"No. We'll talk about it after my parents leave. I will stay neutral right now before I say something I'll regret."

"Okay." Shane handed Candice her t-shirt that was lying on the bed. "You might want to put this on before you head out there."

"Right." Candice almost walked out of her room shirtless.

"I'll have Josh ride with your parents so we can talk. Will that help?"

"No. And I'm sure he'll be more comfortable with us."

Once the truck was loaded, Shane secured the most important item, the bed. Finally, they were ready to head to the house. Candice sat quietly, staring out the window, until she realized she was being rude to Josh.

"Hey Josh," Candice turned to make eye contact with him, "thank you so much for helping us. I really appreciate it."

"No prob, anytime." Josh gave a slight head nod.

"Shane tells me you've been working extra hours at the shop." Candice was trying to get Josh to say more than three words.

"Yeah, he's been busy." Josh simply replied.

Great; four words, or technically, five. "Well, hopefully, once the café renovation is complete, Shane will be at the warehouse more." Candice was starting to feel guilty monopolizing Shane's time.

"I enjoy it," Josh stated with a smidgen more enthusiasm.

Great, back to three words. This was like pulling teeth.

"Babe, Josh is used to handling the warehouse on his own. I'm often not there. That's why he's my on-site manager handling the day-to-day functions at the store when he's not at school."

Shane had to double park in front of the house. Steve and Jazzlene were already sitting on the porch waiting for them.

"Do you know if there was a place around here to get a hot cup of tea?" Jazzlene asked as they got out of the truck.

"I'm workin' on it." Candice stepped past Jazzlene, bumping her with her hip. "Maybe you can stop by in another month, and I'll hook you up." Candice continued up the stairs to the second floor and unlocked the door.

Steve helped unload the truck as Josh and Hank carried the frame to Candice's bed. "Which bedroom do you want this in?" Hank asked his daughter.

"Just set it all in the living room. We have to unload the truck quickly since

Shane's double parked."

The men had the big pieces moved into the house, leaving just the boxes to unload. "I can't believe we got it all here in one trip." Candice did not have much since she left most of her furniture for Steve.

"Babe, we'll help move Steve's stuff into the condo. While you three can stay here and unpack."

"How long will you be?"

"Not more than an hour. Steve doesn't have much to move," Shane said, looking down at his watch.

"All right. Do you think we should have pizza delivered?"

"I'll stop and pick some up on the way back."

Candice finally made it beyond the living room and walked into the dining room. "Oh!" She let out a gasp that had Jazzlene running to see what was wrong.

Up against the dining room wall was her beautiful credenza. Shane had stained and varnished it for her. An antique oval dining table in the center of the room was stained to match the credenza, with six beautiful chairs circling it. The two chairs at the head of the table had armrests and cushioned seats. A tear rolled down Candice's cheek. She now understood why Shane had been spending all his nights working late.

"What's the matter?" Her mother came up and put her arm around Candice.

"Shane said he had a special order for a client. So, he's been working most nights until two in the morning. Then he'd get up at seven and drive me to work. This is what he's been doing every night just so he could surprise me."

Jazzlene sat down in one of the cushioned chairs. "This is very nice." She ran her hand over the top of the table.

Candice wiped her eyes. "Jazz, can you help me set up the bed? Mom, can you hang my dresses in the closet?"

The girls had the bed set up with fresh sheets, clothes hung in the closet, and the dishes put away in the cabinets, all before the men returned.

"You need a dresser and some nightstands." Jazzlene pushed the boxes of t-shirts, jeans, and undergarments against the wall.

"I know. I'm looking for something that will match the house."

"What are you going to do about living room furniture?" Her mother inquired, her voice echoing through the empty front room.

"I'm trying to find an antique couch I can have reupholstered and maybe a wing chair or two. Once I find the couch, I'll know what style coffee table and lamps I want."

"What's this?" Irene picked up the oversized hat that Candice placed on the credenza.

"Oh, since we have time, let me tell you." Candice started from the beginning of the story, not leaving out one detail from the time the unusual hat landed on the porch to her first laying eyes on Shane.

"It sounds like fate intervened." Irene reached up and moved the hair out of Candice's eyes, just as she did when Candice was a little girl.

"We have pizza," Shane announced, coming through the front door.

"Great, we're starved." Candice pulled out some paper plates to avoid dealing with washing dishes.

"And beer," Steve added, holding up the two six-packs.

Hank and Josh entered, carrying a dresser. "Put that in the bedroom," Shane instructed.

Candice's eyes got wide, and her mouth dropped open. She stood there speechless.

Steve and Shane headed out the front door, followed by Josh and Hank. Candice stood on the porch watching Shane and Steve carrying a beautiful couch.

"Is this what you had in mind?" Shane asked, meeting her glistening eyes. "It's almost identical to that picture you showed me."

"Where did you find it?" she choked out.

"It was in the back of my shop waiting to be reupholstered. I bartered a job with one of the best in his trade. I hope you like the fabric I chose. It's pretty close to the original fabric."

Hank and Josh both carried in a wing chair that complimented the couch. Before Candice could grasp what Shane had done for her, the men brought in a beautiful coffee table and two nightstands that matched the dresser perfectly. Finally, Shane and Steve unloaded a china cabinet. Shane converted it into a shelf unit for the TV, ensuring it retained the Victorian style.

"You refinished everything for me?" Candice tried not to cry, but his generosity overwhelmed her. A few tears escaped and slid down her cheek. From Beatrice's faith in her to Shane working day and night for her to the group of friends helping, she realized how truly blessed she was.

"We're definitely going to need that man cave." Shane decided as he twisted the beer cap off.

"I knew you would warm up to the idea." Candice took the beer from his hand and downed what was left of it.

Josh grabbed a slice of pizza. "I'm gonna head back to the shop unless you need anything else?"

"I think we're good. Thanks, man." Shane patted him on the back.

"We're gonna head out too so I can go enjoy my new home," Steve said, reaching for Jazzlene's hand.

Candice gave Steve a hug. "Thank you so much for all your help."

"I should really thank you for letting me rent your condo."

"I'm just so happy you were interested. That made the decision to move here so much easier."

Irene finished clearing off the table.

"We should get going too. Let you settle into your new home." Hank motioned to Irene with a flirtatious gesture that did not escape Candice's notice.

"Okay, you two, behave. I saw that." Candice gave her father a hug and then turned to her mom. "Thank you for your help."

"Anytime. If you need me to help set up the café or work for you, like I said earlier, just call me. I'm here for you, honey."

"I'm sure you'll get a frantic call from me begging for your help." Even though Candice felt cheated out of her childhood with her father, she knew her mother never intended to hurt her.

Shane sat on the couch with his arm thrown over the back. "Come sit and enjoy your living room with me." Candice kicked off her shoes and pulled her feet onto the couch, curling up into Shane's side and laying her arm over his stomach.

"Since you don't have cable yet, we'll have to find something else to do."

Candice rubbed her hand across his jaw. "I like the scruffy look on you."

"You tellin' me to grow a beard?"

"Not unless you want to. Just sayin' this is pretty sexy, that's all."

"Well, you probably won't like it once it's scratching your delicate skin. Then, you'll be begging me to shave it."

"Let's give it a try." Candice stood.

"Wait. I need to show how to work the security system." Shane grabbed her hand and pulled her back into his arms. "This system is linked to your computer, so you can log in and see what's going on while you're at work. There's a video screen by the front door to see who's approaching or standing there before you open it. We need to set the alarm code, which we'll do in a minute. I know you'll think I'm paranoid, but I want you to carry this panic alarm. That way, all you need to do is press it, and the alarm will sound, and a signal will be sent to alert the alarm company."

Candice looked at Shane, amused. "Really, you think I need a panic button?"

"Well, better safe than sorry. Just humor me."

"Okay, sir, I will always keep that button with me. Maybe you should just move in here, and I won't need a panic button. I'll have you and those lethal arms to protect me."

"Even if I lived here, you'd still be home alone sometimes. So maybe I should get you some pepper spray, too."

"I think you are worrying too much unless you know something I don't." Candice cocked her head to the side.

"I know exactly what you know, and that is that your ex seems to be hovering over a ledge right now."

"Yeah, you're right about that," Candice conceded. "But can I change the subject?"

"Sure. Do you want to discuss why you were so upset earlier?"

"No, I wanted to ask you if we could move the desk up from the basement so I can set up a work area. Your grandmother took all the papers out, right?"

"Yeah, she's going through them. We'll move it up tomorrow."

"Oh, speaking of tomorrow, I thought maybe we could take Marni to Delores Park for a picnic."

"She would love that. I have to finish staining some furniture for the man who reupholstered this couch and those chairs, but I should be done by one."

"So, do you want me to help you tomorrow?"

"Sure, if you want."

"Okay, I really enjoyed it when we worked on the credenza together."

Shane played with her hair. "Now, no more stalling. What had you upset today?

"I'm a little upset with my mom. I grew up raised by another man, not my father. I missed my dad so much. And now, when I'm an adult, they decide to rekindle their romance. I feel cheated. Like, those bonding years with my dad and as a family, they've passed and can never be replaced. All those lost memories. I should just let it go, but it hurts so much."

Shane could understand her hurt and frustrations. He too, felt a terrible loss when his mother died. "Sometimes I wish my father would have found someone and remarried, so I would have had a maternal figure, but then I suppose I would have always compared her to my mom. And no one can live up to a child's memory of their mother."

Shane and Candice held each other as their childhood memories swam around their heads.

"I didn't think I'd feel this way, but it's tough being in this house," Shane confessed.

Candice crawled onto his lap. "I'm so sorry. We can leave and return to your place if it's too much for you."

"It's okay. I just need to grieve a little and push past the pain. I'm not sure I really ever mourned her death. I was too little to understand that my mother was not returning."

"Well, we will just have to create some happy memories here. If I had to leave my child, I would want them to remember how much I loved them. I would want them to find happiness because I hope I can still watch from heaven when I'm gone. And just maybe give them a sign that I will always love them."

"Hmm, that's a nice thought. So, do you want to go make a happy memory?"

"I thought you'd never ask." Candice rubbed her lip along the stubble on Shane's face. "Yeah, you're right, this is pretty rough, but I still like it."

Shane picked up Candice and carried her down the hall to the bedroom.

Twenty-One

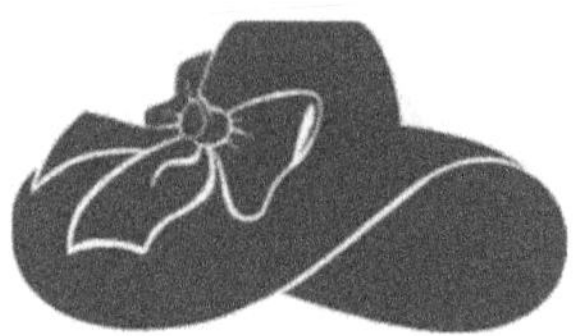

Candice stood in her historically restored kitchen watching the sunrise through the window. The house felt like home; it seemed to welcome her. There was a sense of belonging. A feeling of family she had not experienced since she was little. Maybe it came from knowing Shane started his life in the house, or perhaps it was because she woke up tangled in his arms.

Before moving, Candice purchased a percolating coffee pot. There was nothing, in her opinion, better than a cup of freshly percolated coffee, so she left Steve, her drip coffee maker, in favor of her new stovetop brewer.

"Hey, sexy." Candice turned upon hearing Shane's footsteps. "Sleep well?"

"Yeah, actually better than I've slept in a long time. Something about the creaking sounds this house makes, well, it was so familiar and soothing." Shane stretched.

"I know exactly what you're saying. It was like the house was singin' a lullaby."

"You know how last night you said you'd try to come back in a dream and send a message to your loved ones?"

"Yeah." How could Candice forget that heartbreaking discussion?

"Well, last night was the first time I've had a dream about my mother in years. I guess being in this house uncovered memories, I tried to keep buried."

"Did she say anything to you? In the dream, I mean?"

"I can't remember. I only remember her smiling and messing with my hair."

Candice reached up. "Like this?" She ran her fingers through his morning hair. "Because I must say it's hard to keep my hands out of your soft hair." Candice massaged his temples.

"Sorta, but it seemed she was trying to fix it, not really mess it up. I never realized how much that meant to me. Her touch, her perfume, I remember it all now."

"Babe, this might just be me, but I believe you must always remember those that have passed. Talk fondly about them, share their stories, and keep them close to your heart, because once you stop thinking about them and telling people how special they were, they are truly gone. Because our memories keep them alive, and we can pass their love onto our children."

"Good point. I'll remember that." Shane took the cup of coffee Candice was offering. "Now, about these children, we're having? How many are we having?" He lifted his eyebrows when she faced him.

"How many do you want? I'm open to your input on the subject," Candice joked with her off-colored sense of humor.

"Hmm, I guess we'll start with one."

"Okay, one it is. We can revisit this discussion after we have our first child."

"Great coffee, by the way. You were right about the coffee pot. I should have never doubted you."

"And you wanted to buy one of those single cup makers. Glad I could talk you out of it."

"Hey, don't knock those; I have one in my office."

"And how often do you use it?"

"Never, but Stacy swears by it."

"Oh, speaking of Stacy. Can you spare her for an hour or two to go over the design for the logo and menu? I want to double-check that I have everything done before leaving for New York."

"Sure, what day?"

"Well, I'll be training Clancy Monday, so maybe I can swing by the shop on Wednesday."

"I'll let her know." Shane rinsed his coffee cup out. "We need to get ready to leave, or we might have to skip going to Kevin and Stella's today unless we get a move on."

"Okay, I got dibs on the shower," Candice yelled, running down the hall.

"It may be smaller than the one in your condo, but I know we can both squeeze in."

Driving directly to the back of Shane's workshop, Candice reminisced and smiled.

Shane glanced at her. "I know what you're thinking."

"You do?"

"Yep, and I think of that day too, every time I work here. Just me with my memories, thinking of you in my overalls. You looked so damn cute. I wanted to tear them off."

They walked into the shop, and Candice saw all the pieces of furniture Shane was restoring at various stages of completion. "Go take a look at the furniture over there." Shane pointed to the back of the shop. "Anything you want for your café or house is yours."

Candice felt like a child allowed to try all 31 flavors of ice cream. She wandered around each piece, imagining how to use it in the café. Then she noticed two natural wood shelves. Candice immediately thought of Tom's sculptures being displayed on them.

"Hey Shane, you weren't considering staining these shelves, were you?"

"No, I decided they're pretty cool left raw. I just need to square them up. They lean to one side."

"Good, because I agree Tom's sculptures and Clara's Jams would look nice on these."

"I thought that same thing when I brought them here the other day."

"Maybe I should look into finding local authors who might want to sell signed copies of their books."

"That's a great idea. Did you see those two roundtables off to the right? I thought they would look nice in your living room."

"They're a perfect size. Just a little lemon oil to bring out the wood grain, and they'll be stunning."

"We'll take them with us when we leave."

Candice finished her sweep of the inventory. "I saw a few pieces perfect for the café. I stuck post-it notes on them."

"Good. I'm almost finished here, and then we'll pick up Marni for her day at the park."

It was a short walk to Delores Park, and Marni was excited, clapping her hands and smiling.

Candice made sandwiches for their picnic and packed Marni's favorite chocolate cookies to surprise her.

Shane unfolded the same blanket Candice and he had used on their romantic evening in the park under the stars. Marni sat as close to Candice as possible, making sure their legs touched while Shane lay back on his elbows watching the little kids run around.

"That's going to be you someday," he said to Candice.

"No, that will be you. You have more energy for running around than I do. I'll pack the picnic lunch and let you play catch with the kids." Twice in one day, they were on the subject of children.

"Okay, deal."

Marni finished her sandwich and pointed to the cookies. "Sure, they're all yours." Candice handed her the bag.

"Looks like the clouds are rollin' in. We better start headin' back before it starts to rain," Shane commented, helping Marni up.

"We'll have to do this again on a nicer day. Right, Marni?" Candice said, clasping Marni's hand as they began their walk back up 24th street.

Shane wrapped his arm around Candice's waist and pulled her closer. "How lucky am I? I got to spend the afternoon with my two favorite women."

"I'd say pretty lucky." Candice felt the first sprinkle of rain land on her face. "We better pick up the pace if we don't want to get soaked."

"Marni, hop on." Shane squatted so she could jump onto his back. "See ya at the top," he challenged, speeding up the street.

By the time Shane made it to the top of the hill, Marni was laughing as Candice leaned over holding her side, trying to catch her breath. "Looks like someone needs some exercise," Shane observed, stating the obvious since he had not even broken a sweat.

"When you're right, you're right." Candice grabbed the bottom of his t-shirt to wipe her face.

"I could take it off and hand it to you if you like."

"That's okay, I'm good."

They got Marni into her house just as the clouds decided to shed their tears.

"Well, that was a nice afternoon. We can either head over to Kevin's, or I can hook up your DVD player and watch movies by the fire. Your choice."

"Let's see, football or cuddling by a fire beside you. Do you really need to ask?"

"I'll let Kevin know we're stayin' in."

"No, we better at least go for a few hours. I know Stella looks forward to our visits."

Once Stella, Jazzlene, and Candice left the room Kevin turned to Shane. "We have a problem," he said matter of fact.

"Which is?"

"I guess I should fill him in," Steve suggested, looking toward Shane. "So, last night, a guy showed up at the condo. I, of course, had no clue who he was or how he got in. But I figured it out pretty damn fast when he asked what I was doing there with his girlfriend. Jazz was on the phone with the police, and I guess he heard her because he bolted."

Kevin spoke under his breath, "There's a warrant out for him, so keep an eye on Candice."

"I told Jazzlene not to tell Candice that Brent was back at the condo looking for her," Kevin spoke softer, hearing the women coming down the stairs.

"Okay, thanks. We'll finish this discussion later." Shane looked up as the women entered the room.

"Hey, you want to hold a little angel?" Candice had Kara bouncing on her hip.

"Sure." Shane cradled Kara like a porcelain doll, afraid he might break her.

"She's not fragile." Stella laughed. "In fact, you could toss her in the air, and she'd probably enjoy it. Although, on second thought, I shouldn't have said that. No tossing of my baby."

Shane held up his empty beer bottle. "Hey babe, can you get me another beer?"

"Sure." Candice headed to the kitchen, where she found Steve pouring chips into a bowl. "So, Steve, how was the first night in your new home?" Candice questioned.

"It was very nice to sleep in my own room. And the place is pretty soundproof. I can't even hear the traffic noise, and that's a busy street."

"And you really can't hear the neighbors either. Oh wait, there is one neighbor that really should move their bed away from the wall."

"Oh yeah, I heard them, but honestly, I was too tired to care."

"I forgot to warn you, my ex Brent might show up at the condo looking for me. He's in rehab, so you shouldn't have to worry, but if a guy about 6'2" with a pierced eyebrow and shoulder-length brown hair shows up, tell him I moved. He can get pretty mean, so be careful."

"Okay. I'll keep my eyes open for him." Candice had no idea how true that statement was, but she noticed Steve's face scowl.

"Sorry, I should have told you earlier. I try not to think about him, but he's been stalking me."

"No worries." Steve grabbed a beer from the fridge. "How was your night?"

"It felt like I've lived there my entire life. I was so at peace in that house."

"Looks like we're both pretty happy with our new living arrangements."

"Yeah, things are certainly changing for us. Who would have thought you'd start dating Jazz after the night I ran into you at the restaurant? Or that one shopping trip to an antique store would lead me to Shane."

"Well, as long as your brother stays out of the picture, I'll be happy."

"I don't think you have to worry about that. I think Jazz has finally moved on. You're number one in her eyes."

Steve's eyes lit up. "Good to know. I don't want to rush anything. I'm taking it slow."

Jazzlene walked up behind Steve and hugged him. "Halftime's over. You're missing the game."

"Guess that's my cue." Steve headed out of the kitchen.

Candice looked at the men, noticing Kara asleep, snuggled in Shane's arm while Wesley sat comfortably on his lap. "How you doing in there, Ace? Need any help?"

"Doin' good, just seeing what two children would feel like. I think I can handle it."

Stella spun her head toward Candice. "What?" Candice whispered, shrugging her shoulders.

"Just making an observation, that's all," Stella whispered.

"He said he slept really well, and he woke up happy. I think the house reminded him of family, you know, those feelings of love. So, guess he's feeling a little sentimental right now."

"Well, he's going to be a great father someday. Just sayin', in case you don't already know that."

"I have to agree." Candice watched Shane adjust the arm holding Kara, trying not to disturb her.

"Guess I should put her in her crib, but watching him hold her is cute." Stella waited for a commercial break before walking in front of the TV. "I'll take her."

"It's okay. I think she's comfortable. I really don't mind."

When Stella removed Kara from his arms, he felt a strange emptiness. "Hey babe, come sit with me for a minute."

Yep, everything was back to normal once Candice curled up against him. She was the sanctuary that held his heart, and there was nothing he would not do for her. He knew the minute he woke up; she was the woman to give him back his family. Or, more importantly, the memories of his mother's love.

Monday morning arrived too fast. The last thing Candice wanted to do was leave Shane's warm embrace. The weekend flew by and proved to be life-changing. She could actually feel positive energy surrounding her at the house. It was hard to explain, but she felt peaceful. Even Shane seemed to open up, allowing his heart to lead him in the right direction.

Clancy walked into the studio five minutes after Candice.

"Good morning," he cheerfully greeted.

"Hi, are you ready to get to work? Because the first and most important order of business is making the coffee. When Jazzlene walks in on a Monday morning, she requires an immediate caffeine fix."

Clancy let out a boisterous laugh. "That I believe I can handle."

The phone rang. "Jazz Photography, how may I help you?" Candice asked politely.

"Babe, I won't be able to make it for lunch today. My grandmother needs me."

"Is she okay?" Candice could not disguise the worry in her voice.

"Yes, she's fine. She just has some business to discuss with my father and me."

"Oh good, you had me worried. Well, give her a kiss from me and tell her I'll see her Wednesday."

"Will do. Love you."

"Love you, too."

"Is that how we end all our calls?" Clancy teased.

"Sorry about that. I'll try to be more discreet next time." Candice countered, blushing.

"Well, I'm going to go make that coffee now. Does Jazzlene like it weak or strong?"

"The darker, the better. I usually put in two large scoops."

Clancy was a quick learner. He answered the phones, scheduled clients, updated the website, fixed the copier, and anything else Candice threw his way.

"Well, it's noon, so if you want to walk to the deli, we can grab a sandwich. Jazzlene won't come out of her darkroom until around two."

"Sure, I'd love that."

They walked the two blocks to the deli and found a seat by the window. "So, why are you leaving Jazz?"

"I'm opening a café in Noe Valley in a month or two."

"That sounds exciting."

"Yeah, it sorta fell into my lap. Couldn't pass up the opportunity. How 'bout you? Why did you apply for basically an office job?"

"I love photography and thought maybe I could learn from the best. But, as I see it, Jazzlene will need all the help she can get. Did you read that article on her in Photography Today?"

"Yeah, it was pretty awesome. You're right. I've noticed an influx of calls since that article."

"So, I figure she'll need someone to really help. Go on shoots, maybe do some studio photography for her. Once I prove myself to her, of course."

"You just keep showing up on time, having the coffee made, and being ready, willing, and able to do anything she asks, and I'm sure she'll be happy to let you do some studio shoots for her."

"Thanks for your advice and help. You really are a great teacher."

"Since you have caught on so fast, I'm considering taking Wednesday off. Would that be okay with you?"

"Sure."

"Good, I have some stuff I need to take care of. Well, I guess we should start heading back. Our hour is up."

Shane pulled into his grandmother's driveway. It felt strange. It was as if he did not live there anymore, even though all his belongings were still there. Maybe he would grab a few things to keep at Candice's place.

Trevor was already there and waiting at the kitchen table.

"So, what's this about?" Shane asked his father.

"I'm not sure." He looked concerned.

"Well, boys, you might as well sit down," Beatrice instructed before sitting herself.

"What's that you got?" Trevor noticed the file she was carrying.

"Remember that paperwork I took from the desk Shane found in that hidden basement?" Trevor nodded. "I found this."

She handed Trevor a small stack of documents. He quickly reviewed them and then passed them to Shane. Both men waited for her to continue.

"As you can see, per those papers, the house does not belong to me." She met Trevor's eyes. "Your grandpa Anders had this *Will* drawn up, and it clearly states that it is to go to his eldest son upon his death; that would be your father. And upon his death, it goes to his eldest son, you. So, the house is yours, Trevor, and I will change the deed to reflect that. Therefore, my contract with Candice seems null and void since I had no legal right to enter it."

"Mom, we can just leave it in your name. It belongs to you," Trevor advised.

"No, we must abide by your grandfather's wishes. He wants the house to stay in the Anders family."

"I know you want to do the right thing, but really I don't need it or want it." The memories the house held crushed Trevor.

"Okay, so then you can pass it to your son." Beatrice turned to Shane.

"So, this means Candice can never buy it?" Shane asked.

"Right, if we are to follow your great-grandfather's Will."

"Oh, hell. What am I supposed to tell her? You want me to crush her dream?" Shane stood up and started pacing around the kitchen. "I can't do that. She trusts us to help her."

"I will still help her get her business going. And we all agree she can use the commercial unit as long as she wants. She just can't buy it. So, that's really the only thing that is changing. Oh, and the contract must be between you and her."

"I can see only one way to ensure she gets the house that she's in love with."

"What's that, dear?" Beatrice asked, already knowing the answer.

"I'm going to marry her."

"Don't you think you're rushing a bit, son?" Trevor inquired. "You haven't been dating that long."

"Well, nothing has ever felt so right. I can't sleep without her. Every minute of every day, she's in my thoughts. There's nothing I won't do for her. I love her like I've never loved any woman before. You've seen her with Marni. She's got a heart full of love."

"Yes, I understand, but I just don't want you to be hasty," Trevor explained.

"Dad, I understand where you're coming from. My first marriage ended badly, but Candice is not Aubrey."

"No, she's not. I just want you to give it more time."

"What difference does time make when you're in love? It's not like we're teenagers."

"I will support whatever decision you make." Trevor patted Shane on the back.

"What I need from both of you is not to mention any of this to Candice. Instead, I want to propose, get married, and then have you sign the house over as a wedding gift."

"Maybe you should tell her about the *Will*. Then, let her decide what she wants to do."

"If I do that, she may back out of opening the café. And that's her dream. I can't do that to her. So, I won't do it."

"It seems that you have this all figured out," Beatrice concluded.

"One more thing, just to ease both of your minds. I was planning to ask Candice to marry me anyway. So, I'm just moving it up by a few months."

"You know her better than we do. I'll trust your instincts." Trevor backed off.

The first thing Candice asked when she got in the car was, "What did your grandmother want?"

"Oh, she wanted to show us some things she found in the desk drawer. You know, pictures, ledgers, stuff like that."

"Well, basically, what we already knew."

"Sorta."

"What do you mean sorta?"

"She had some legal documents that she needed to understand. They belonged to my great-grandfather."

"Oh." Candice did not dig further. It was apparently family business.

"So, how did the new guy work out?" Shane quickly diverted the subject.

"Great. He picked up on everything and pretty much ran the show today. So, I'm going to take Wednesday off to meet with Stacy. Then after that, maybe I can help you at the shop."

"Actually, they should be done upgrading the electrical in the basement. So, on Wednesday, I'm going to meet with the contractor and get an estimate on finishing the basement."

"Oh, so you're making a space for yourself. Does that mean you're moving in?"

"I told you I won't live with you unless we're married."

"Just thought I'd ask." Candice purred into his ear. "Don't you enjoy our mornings together?"

"More than you can imagine."

Candice leaned over and kissed his cheek.

"I need to talk to you about something I discovered yesterday." Candice could not find her voice because she heard the fear in Shane's voice. "Brent showed up at your condo Saturday. Seems he skipped out of rehab again. Anyway, there is a warrant out for him, but as of a few hours ago, they have not located him. I think you're safe, but please keep the panic button on you. And make sure you always set the alarm."

"Why didn't anyone tell me this last night?" Irritation laced Candice's words.

"I told them not to. I didn't want to worry you unless the authorities didn't find him. And since he's still out there, we need to be cautious."

"This is never going to end, is it?" Tears of frustration welled in her eyes.

Shane wiped them away. "They'll find him soon. Kevin is out there looking for him. He knows some of the places Brent used to frequent, so he's asking around."

"I know you're trying to protect me, but please don't keep this kind of stuff from me."

"I'm sorry, I really thought they would have found him last night, and I figured, why worry you for nothing. Forgive me?"

"Nothing to forgive, but if it makes you feel better, I forgive you."

"It does." Shane rested his hand on her leg because that was as close as he could get with the gearshift between them.

"I think I like the truck better. At least then I can curl up next to you." Candice let her fingers softly graze along the top of Shane's hand.

Shane found parking right in front of the building.

"Let's run over and see Marni," Candice suggested. "I told you once I moved in, I'd check on her every day."

"That you did." Shane entwined his fingers with hers as they crossed the street. He was quickly getting used to this feeling of home.

Twenty-Two

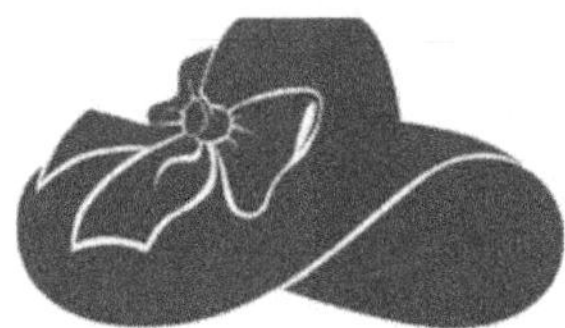

Looking out the plane's window, all Candice could see were the fluffy clouds below and blue skies around them. "I can't believe I'm on my way to New York," Candice excitedly expressed, peeling her eyes away from the window long enough to look at Jazzlene.

"I know, and this will probably be the last time you'll be able to get away for a while. So, we'll make sure to do all the touristy things."

"I haven't slept apart from Shane in a month. Ever since Brent's been missing, he's been glued to me, which, I might add, I love."

"Can't say I blame him. Brent's unstable, but I always suspected he was slightly off."

"So, let's not dwell on him. Clancy seems to be working out, right?"

"He's the best. And I've taught him some things that will really help me out."

"So, you're comfortable giving him the keys to keep things running smoothly?"

"Yeah, it's hard, but I have to trust someone. And anyway, Steve will keep an eye on the place."

"When we get back, I'm going to really buckle down and start hiring people," Candice stated. "And I already have one employee hired."

"Really? That's good."

"Yeah, she's going to assist me with baking."

"Where did you find her? I didn't realize you had started looking."

"She's the woman who rents the apartment above me. Her name is Joy, which fits her smiling face. Anyway, this will be perfect for her, and I may have her help customers, too. I think she would be great with the customers. You can't help but love her."

"How are your new tenants working out?"

"Well, they're very quiet. Her husband, Bart, works at a thrift store. Pricing stuff, I think. Anyway, I'm positive I will enjoy having them as tenants. Hopefully, they'll stay a long time."

"How did you find them?"

"Beatrice told Trevor which agency to contact. That woman is a wealth of information. Every time I have a question, she has the answer. And if she doesn't, she knows someone who does. Anyway, Trevor interviewed applicants, and this darling couple was the first to apply."

"They're both disabled, right?"

"Yeah, they both have Down syndrome and are high functioning. I check on them every few days to ensure they're okay. They like helping out. In fact, Shane barbecued the other night, and Bart wanted to help, so Shane had him flipping the burgers."

"Sounds like things are falling into place."

"They are. You should see the logo Stacy designed. It's perfect."

"So, you finally settled on the name?"

"I really like, *Sweet Treats for All.* It pretty much covers it. I will offer choices for vegans, those with gluten allergies, and nut-free versions. I'm also going to carry soymilk and other non-dairy alternatives. I mean, the more options I have, the more customers I'll get."

"That's great marketing."

"I'm also thinking of offering a breakfast quiche. Maybe soup and sandwiches at lunchtime. Something simple. But for now, I'll start with the baked goods."

"Well, the quiche fits into that. Maybe you can make pot pies. That will keep the baking theme going."

"What a great idea. That could work. I know I saw *Grandma Pela's Flaky Piecrust* recipe. I'll have to experiment and come up with something. Now we're really brainstorming."

"This makes my mouth water, just thinking about all the wonderful foods you will be baking."

"Hey, were you able to enlarge those photos I gave you of Beatrice?"

"Yes. Clancy should finish those while we're gone."

"I love the one with Beatrice in her bathing suit in the Sutro Baths."

"That's one of my favorites, too," Jazzlene agreed.

The pilot's voice crooned through the plane's cabin, "This is your captain. We are on the final descent into New York. On behalf of your flight crew, we hope you enjoyed your flight. The weather is currently in the seventies, so it will be a beautiful day for those visiting the city. We are a few minutes ahead of schedule, so those passengers with connecting flights will have plenty of time to make them."

Candice looked out the window as they approached New York City. "It's beautiful."

Jazzlene leaned over Candice's lap, trying to see out the tiny window. The plane banked sharply, giving her a spectacular view of the city below. "This is going to be a great adventure."

The women made their way to the baggage claim area. Candice pulled out her cell phone.

Candice—Just landed in New York.

Shane—Have fun. Talk to you tonight. I love you.

Candice—I love you too, and I already miss you. Not sure how I'll sleep without you.

Shane—Yeah, it will be lonely without you in my arms.

Candice—Our bags just arrived. Talk to you later.

Jazzlene grabbed her bags as they circled the carousel for the second time. She was texting Steve and had missed them sliding down the conveyor belt.

"Ready to see if we have what it takes to hail a cab?" Jazzlene chuckled. "I hear it can be quite the challenge."

"I think the real test will be on the streets of New York." Candice laughed after spotting the line of taxis waiting for their next fare.

"Where to, ladies?" the cab driver asked in a thick Brooklyn accent.

"The Waldorf Astoria," Jazzlene sang out.

Shane read the last text from Candice as he entered what was soon to be her café. "Okay, Gabe, we have five days to complete this café before Candice returns."

"I think I'll have it done in four. And once the inspector signs off, I'll move on to the final stages of the renovation. So, you should be able to load the furniture after that."

"Good. Is there anything I can do to help speed it up?"

"Nah, I've got my men on it."

"Hey, I've meant to ask, has Maggie called you about a house in Napa?"

"Yeah, as a matter of fact, she did. I'm headin' out there next weekend to look at the job."

"You're gonna love the place. It is one remarkable piece of property."

"I guess she's considering turning it into a bed and breakfast. I don't suppose you planted that idea?" Gabe questioned.

"Yeah, I suppose I did. But you'll see why when you get out there. It is perfect for a bed and breakfast." Shane felt his cell phone vibrate in his pocket.

Candice—We're staying at the Waldorf, it's beautiful.

Shane—I think you're being spoiled, and only I'm supposed to spoil you.

Candice—Well, let's add New York to our must-see list, and then you can spoil me.

Shane—Done!

Shane waved as he headed for the door. "Catch you tomorrow, Gabe." It was almost noon, and he told Kevin he would meet him for lunch.

"Hope I'm not too late. I stopped by the café to see how the work was progressing," Shane apologized, taking his seat.

"No prob, I just got here." Kevin put cream in his coffee to cool it down.

"So, is there any good news?"

"No, I've been to all the places I know he frequented and came up empty."

"Maybe we should hang out at Rafe's All Nighter and see if he turns up there. Apparently, that was where he and Candice used to hang out."

"Worth a try. But I won't get there until after the kids are in bed. Say around ten? Anyway, not much will be going on before that," Kevin concluded.

"We got to find him before she gets back." The stress on Shane's face was apparent.

"We'll find him." Kevin tried to reassure Shane, which had little impact.

"Unless he's caught, I can't stop worrying. I am so in love with Candice that I can't even think clearly. She has such hold on my heart that sometimes I think it skips a beat."

"Well, do you think I would have tried to fix you up with a woman that wasn't incredible?" Kevin raised his eyebrows.

"No, of course not, but I wasn't into the blind date thing."

"Good thing for you fate stepped in."

"She has a heart of gold. Did I tell you that every night she checks on my sister? And then, she runs upstairs to check on the tenants. She won't relax until after she's checked on them."

"Yeah, Stella told me she was like that. Evidently, in high school, she volunteered at a special needs school."

"She never told me that. You'd think that would have come up in conversation."

"Well, since it's just who she is she probably didn't think anything of it."

"Guess you're right."

"There's a lot about her you will learn, but hey, I'm not gonna tell you. She needs her mystery."

Shane sheepishly looked at Kevin. "There's something else I want to discuss." A nervous tension had built around Shane's eyes.

"You don't look too good."

"I'm fine, but here's the thing, I'm going to ask Candice to marry me." Shane paused long enough to let that statement sink in. "So, I'm going to start looking at rings while she's gone."

"Wait, you've only known her a few months. Don't you think you're rushing into this? I mean, I know better than anyone what a wonderful and perfect woman she is for you, but really, what are you thinking?" Kevin was stunned.

"I'm not thinking, I'm just following my gut, and it says I can't live without her. Look, I told her I would never live with her unless we were married, but I find myself unable to leave her at night. I love falling asleep next to her and waking up with her wrapped in my arms."

"I get it. I feel the same way about Stella. She's my piece of solace and my soft spot. However, I dated her for almost two years before I asked her to marry me. I would think after Aubrey, you'd want to be sure," Kevin countered.

"I am sure because Candice is the complete opposite of Aubrey. Being married to Aubrey was a nightmare, so being married to Candice would be my *Sweet Dreams*. They're yin and yang."

"So, what is your timeline? Getting married in a year or two?"

"I guess I'll have to discuss that with her if she says yes."

"Oh, no doubt she'll say yes. I overheard Stella and her talking the other day. I think she's as in love with you as you are with her. They were whispering, but I still caught a few words here and there."

Shane raised his eyebrows. "Like what?" he quizzed.

"Oh, well, let's see, that you are good in bed. And I heard *rock hard*, but I'm not sure what she was referring to. I can only imagine."

Kevin looked at his watch. "I've gotta get going. Stella has a hair appointment, and I'm on daddy duty."

"Thanks for listening, man."

"I'm always here for ya." Kevin stood up.

"I'll swing by and pick you up at ten?" Shane offered.

"Yeah, ten will be good, but we'll only stay an hour or two. I have work in the morning."

"Sounds good." Shane threw some money on the table and followed Kevin out.

"As I see it, we grab a purse full of film and head out," Jazzlene suggested.

"Where to?"

"Doesn't matter, let's just go explore. We'll find a street vendor and try a hot dog."

"I am starving." Candice tossed the rolls of film into her oversized bag.

"I want to take a ton of pictures for myself. Some abstract and maybe some of the locals. Then tomorrow we'll focus on the sites I need for the magazine."

The hustle and bustle of the city were much more exuberant than in San Francisco, where the people seemed more laid back.

"I think I smell coffee." Candice could smell the aroma two blocks away. "I desperately need a cup." She pushed her way through the crowd.

Jazzlene was taking pictures from all angles. "Hey," she called out to Candice. As Candice spun around, Jazzlene took a few snapshots of her. She wanted to memorialize their time in New York.

"Want a coffee?" Candice hollered from the corner.

"Sure, black." Jazzlene jogged, trying to catch up to Candice.

"Let's find a place to people-watch while we enjoy our coffee," Candice suggested, trying to escape the bustling foot traffic.

"And I thought downtown San Francisco was busy. This is something else." Jazzlene sat next to Candice on a bus stop bench.

"I say we hit up a nightclub or something. Kinda get out and let loose with the locals."

Jazzlene put her arm around Candice. "I was just thinkin' that same thing. That must be why we're best friends."

They finished their coffee and strolled down the street with their arms linked. "You think we can get that cute guy to take our picture?" Candice pointed.

Jazzlene looked at the man that had just made eye contact with her. "Worth asking." She walked over to him. "Hi, I'm Jazz, and this is Candice. We're wondering if you wouldn't mind taking our picture?"

"Sure, I'd be happy to. You, ladies, aren't from around here, are you?"

"No, we're from San Francisco," Jazz offered her cell phone to him. "Just aim and click."

"I think I got a few good ones." He handed the cell phone back to Jazzlene.

"Thanks," Jazzlene said, reviewing the pictures. "And they say New Yorkers aren't nice."

"Email those to Steve and Shane." Candice was giddy with excitement and energy now that the caffeine had kicked in.

"Let's go to Times Square. I think we might be able to walk from here." Jazzlene had her walking shoes on.

Both girls' cell phones alerted them to texts.

Shane—Babe, you two look so cute.

Candice—We're walkin' to Times Square.

Shane—Have fun.

Candice—Always

Steve—I already miss you, but I see you're having fun.

Jazzlene—Miss you too, and yes, we are. We're out and about in this crazy city, enjoying the local entertainment.

Steve—Stay out of trouble.

Jazzlene—Easier said than done

Steve—You two stick close together.

Jazzlene—We will, I promise. And you know I keep my promises. So, you make sure the bed is warm when I get home.

Steve—I'll be painfully waiting.

Candice looked up at the buildings in Times Square as Jazzlene took more pictures. "These pictures are going to be so cool."

"Should we buy tickets to a Broadway show?" Candice wanted to pack in as much culture as possible. "I mean, who comes to New York and doesn't go see a play?"

"Not us. Let's go buy those tickets." Jazz replied, thrilled to be standing in Times Square, soaking in the energy of the city.

Several hours later, the girls were ready for some nightlife. "So, I think we're almost there." Jazzlene looked at the directions she had written down. "It's supposed to be a nice club for music."

"Oh, there it is." Candice saw the neon sign.

They crossed the street and entered the club. Not too busy since it was Sunday night. "I bet you can't even get in here on a Friday or Saturday."

They slunk up to the bar to order a drink. "What can I get you, ladies?" The bartender asked, throwing a towel over his shoulder.

"We'll have two sex on the beaches," Jazzlene suggestively ordered.

"Coming up." He winked at her.

Candice leaned and whispered into Jazz's ear, "Was that a sexual innuendo? Coming up? Really?"

"Well—" Jazzlene did not even finish her sentence before she burst out laughing.

"Would you like some cream?" the bartender asked straight-faced.

"Yes, just a squirt." Jazz replied with a flutter of her lashes.

"There ya go. There's always more where that came from, just don't be afraid to ask."

"Oh my god, he's really laying it on thick." Candice chuckled. "Oops, sorry, didn't mean that to sound the way it did."

"Drink up," Jazzlene instructed, downing her drink.

"You're going to hit the floor."

"Sorry, but he got me a little hot."

"Another?" the bartender asks, removing the empty glass.

"Yes, that's about the best sex on the beach I've ever had."

"How 'bout you." He turned to Candice.

"I'm good. Sex on the beach is not all it's cracked up to be." Candice teased.

The music was pumping, and by drink three, Jazzlene was one tipsy Californian wanting to dance the night away in New York. "Come on, sweetie, let's dance." She grabbed Candice and led her to the dance floor.

"No dirty dancing with me tonight," Candice warned.

"Okay, promise."

Jazzlene and Candice danced nonstop through several songs. However, once the slow music played, Candice drew the line. "Ain't gonna happen."

They made their way back to the bar. "One more drink, then we better head back to the hotel." Candice knew they had a full day scheduled, and as it was, Jazzlene would probably have a slight hangover in the morning.

"Back for more?" the sexy bartender asked.

"Yes, I'd like a climax this time." Jazzlene boldly said.

"You want a climax too?" He shot his eyes to Candice.

"Nah, I'm done for the night."

The bartender set the drink in front of Jazzlene. "Enjoy your climax."

"I know I will." Jazzlene sipped it slowly while watching the bartender shake a drink. "Hell, look at his arms," Jazzlene leaned over and not so quietly said to Candice. He heard and just smiled.

"Think of Steve. He should tide you over," Candice told her.

"Did I ever tell you what he does with his tong—" Candice cut Jazzlene off.

"No, and I don't want to know. Let's go back to the hotel, and you can have phone sex with him while I take a shower. Seems that hunk of a man over there has you hot and bothered."

"Okay, I'm ready." Jazzlene stood on wobbly legs and quickly righted herself, and the girls left, their first day in New York topped off with whipped cream and fun.

Twenty-Three

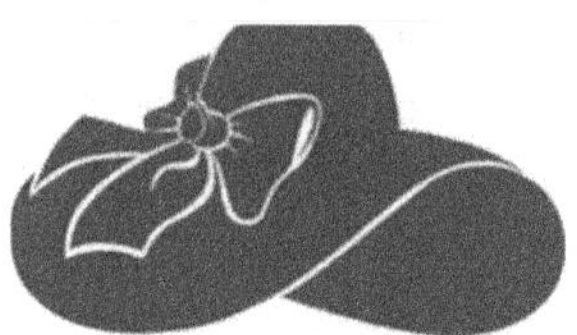

Candice was putting the finishing touches on her hair. "I say we go back to that first nightclub for a farewell drink."

"That sounds great. We'll start there before we hit the other clubs. Let's have one drink at each place." Jazzlene suggested, looking in the mirror.

"You realize we'll be plastered if we do that, right?"

"Yeah, let's go have some fun."

The friends headed out onto the streets of New York.

Candice looped her arm through Jazzlene's. "I'm gonna miss this city." Her voice had a melancholy tone.

"I feel ya. We got to see and do so much. We couldn't have squeezed more into this trip if we had tried."

They walked into the nightclub, enjoying the warmth it offered from the chill outside and took a seat at the bar. Fortunately for them, the same eye candy they met the first time was working.

"What can I do for you ladies tonight?" he asked, remembering them with a wink.

"I would like multiple orgasms," Jazzlene responded, winking back.

"And you?" He turned to Candice.

"I'll have what she's having." Candice did not make eye contact with him.

The bartender quickly made their drinks and placed them on the bar. "So..." he looked directly into Jazzlene's eyes, "what are you up to tonight?"

"Well, we're spending our last night in your beautiful city having one drink at each club we've visited on our stay here." Jazzlene took a dainty sip from her glass.

"Oh, you're not from around here?" He looked disappointed.

"No, San Francisco. We're here for work, headin' home tomorrow."

"That's too bad, if I knew last time you were just visiting, I would have shown you some great sites the tourist don't know about."

"Maybe next time. I'm sure I'll be back on another assignment someday," Jazzlene offered.

"Well, look me up. I'll be behind this bar." He placed another drink in front of the girls. "These are on me."

"Thank you," the girls said in unison.

He turned to make his way to another customer.

"What was that? You have Steve waiting for you at home." Candice smacked her arm.

"Hey, I can flirt if I don't touch. Anyway, I'll never see him again so what's the harm?"

"Well, I guess none, but how would you feel about Steve overtly flirting?"

"I get your point, but damn, he's one hot guy."

"Well, I won't argue about that." Candice turned to enjoy the view. "And he has a fine ass."

"You know, we better get out of here. We might get ourselves in trouble." Jazzlene stood up and waved goodbye to the bartender.

"We never did ask him his name," Candice mentioned.

"I know, I didn't want to. That would have seemed too personal, and then I would really get myself into trouble."

The girls trotted off to the next club.

"Okay, so let's move this against the wall," Shane said as he and Josh lifted the shelf.

Everyone was buzzing around the café hanging artwork, arranges the tables for good traffic flow, and wiping down the display case until it sparkled.

"Where should we put this?" Irene asked, holding up the unique hat.

Shane turned to see what she was holding. "I have a special spot for it. That hat apparently led Candice into my life." Shane had made a beautiful hat stand from a wavy tree branch he found on one of his job sites.

"That is beautiful," Irene complimented.

"I think she's going to like it." Shane found a spot near the front door. He placed the hat on the stand, angling the brim so the feathers would show.

The refrigerator was now cold enough to start loading and the two commercial ovens were installed and ready to use.

"Shane, do you want me to start heating the food?" Stella questioned, admiring the stainless-steel ovens.

"Yeah, put the lasagna in at 350° in about 15 minutes. By the way, where are the kids?"

"At my sister's for the evening." Stella turned the oven on to preheat it.

"Joy, would you mind putting these sculptures on that shelf?" Shane pointed to the shelf now against the wall.

"Sure, Mr. Anders," she answered smiling.

Steve arrived with a dolly stacked with boxes. "Do you want these in the storage area?"

"Yeah, just put those where the laundry is. I'll move them down to the basement later after I go through them," Shane responded as Stacy walked through the door.

"Shane, I've got the menus in my car, but I need Steve and the dolly."

Hank was helping put up the storefront sign. "That looks so nice." He stood back, admiring the signage with Kevin.

"It really is nice." Kevin crossed his arms while looking up at it.

Shane stepped outside to get a look at the incredible sign he had ordered. It was a circle painted to resemble a cookie and underneath it read, *Sweet Treats for All,* in gold raised lettering. "I think it turned out pretty nice. Thanks for hanging it."

Beatrice and Trevor arrived with a box of vases and fresh-cut flowers. "Trevor, run over and get Hector. I'm sure he'd love to help with the flowers." Beatrice instructed, looking around at the café's transformation.

Candice loved retro things, so when Shane found an old pink rotary phone, he bought it. With the wiring for the landline upgraded Shane could hook the phone into the plug. He reached into his pocket for his cell phone and dialed the new business number. The pink phone began to ring, and everyone turned around. It had been a long time since anyone heard a loud ring like that.

"Oh, that brings back some memories," Trevor remarked, walking in with Hector and Marni.

Beatrice brought Hector to the sink in the kitchen and helped him position flowers into each vase. The mere sight of the flowers filled him with glee. It did not take much to make Hector happy. Plants and water were the two ingredients that brought him joy above anything else.

The tables were set with teacups, dessert plates, champagne flutes, and soft pink cloth napkins rolled and secured with gold napkin rings. Each napkin rested on a dessert plate, adding a touch of elegance. In the middle of every table sat a vase with fresh flowers. It was the perfect and final addition to a flawless presentation.

"I just really want to thank everyone for helping me pull this off. I could not have done it alone. I know you all gave up yesterday and today to make this happen and I know Candice will be touched by everyone's support and generosity."

"Shane," Steve interrupted, "I got a text, their flight just landed, so we'd better head out."

"Hey everyone, in about thirty minutes, you can head up to our apartment and wait there. I don't want Candice to see you through the window of the café. Once you know we've entered the cafe, sneak down the back stairs to surprise her," Shane directed, sounding like the host of a house decorating show.

Pulling up curbside at SFO, Shane saw Candice and Jazzlene lugging their bags toward the car. His heart jumped, and his palms started to sweat at the mere sight of her. Six days was too long to be away from her. He wished that people were not sitting in her apartment waiting for them because right now just spending some alone time with Candice would make him a happy man.

"Hi babe," Shane hopped out of the car, "let me get those." He picked up the bags and slung them into the trunk. "What the hell is in these?"

"We did a little shopping," Candice replied coyly. "I know I shouldn't be spending money, but I bought some things for you." She rested her arms on his shoulders and kissed him.

Steve and Jazzlene were releasing each other from their embrace when airport security came up. "You need to load the vehicle and depart."

They piled into the car. Jazzlene was all over Steve in the back seat.

"Can't you at least wait until you get home?" Candice laughed at her friend.

"I could try, but what's the fun in that?" Jazzlene giggled like a schoolgirl.

"Shane, pull over and let Steve drive. I want to hop in that back seat and have what she's having," Candice joked.

Shane squeezed Candice's thigh. "I hear the back seat of a car is overrated."

Finally, after circling the block, Shane found a spot in front of the house.

"We'll grab your bags in a minute. I need to show you how much work has been completed while you were gone." Shane reached for Candice's hand and led her to the front of the café. "Look up."

Candice's eyes gravitated to the beautiful sign above the entrance. "Oh my god, it's exactly what I wanted. The gold lettering stands out against that dark background. And the cookie, just fab."

"Fab? I haven't heard you say that in years." Jazzlene teased.

Shane unlocked the door and held it open for Candice and Jazzlene. He flipped on the lights and watched Candice's reaction. She stood there like a deer caught in headlights. Her body did not move, but her eyes shifted in all directions, mesmerized by the finished dining room.

"Well, you're either in shock or disappointed by the lack of response."

"Uh," Candice tried to form a sentence.

"SURPRISE!" everyone yelled at the same time.

Candice jumped, making her falter slightly, but Shane was right there with his arms steadying her.

Irene ran up to her daughter. "What do you think?"

"Umm," Again, Candice was speechless as she stood looking at all the faces of everyone there.

"Everyone helped me get this place ready so you could open for business," Shane leaned over and whispered in her ear.

Candice looked up into his eyes. "Thank you," she mumbled, barely able to speak between the sobs she was trying to hold back.

"We all love you and believe in you. This is our gift to show you how much you mean to us," Shane said.

Marni quickly made her way to Candice, grabbing both of her hands and shaking them with excitement. "Hi, Marni. Did you help with this?"

Marni shook her head and continued tightly holding onto Candice's hand.

Candice turned to Jazzlene. "Did you know about this?"

"No, I'm as shocked as you."

"Dinner's almost ready," Beatrice announced.

That was when Candice smelled the food baking. "My ovens are in?"

"Everything is done. The refrigerator is stocked, dry goods are put away, utensils are in their spots, and dishes and cups are washed. I think the only thing left for you to do is hire your employees."

Candice turned toward the front door when she heard the bells jingle. Carlos, Angie, and Tom came bounding through with great excitement.

"Ms. Candice, welcome home," Carlos cheerfully greeted her.

"Tom, Tom Morgan," Tom said, holding Angie's arm as she led him into the dining area.

Candice gasped when she noticed the hat on the stand next to the front door. "Where did you find that stand?" Of course, she knew the answer before asking the question.

"I made it for you. I thought the hat should welcome the guests as they enter."

"I love it. I was going to hang it above the door, but that is so much nicer. People will really notice it there." Candice made her way toward the front door. "You know, people are going to want to buy that hat stand."

"Well, there's only that one. Just for you."

Candice continued to wander through the dining room, looking at each dinette. No two tables were the same. She stopped dead in her tracks. "You made this too?" She pointed to the handcrafted table.

"Yes, and those two over there, but this is our table." Shane pointed down. The initials SA + CS with a heart around them were engraved into the wood. Then he pointed to the brass engraved nameplate on the side of the table that read *Sweethearts*. "So, this is the sweetheart table, and that over there is *Romance.* Instead of numbers, I thought names would be cute."

"Boy, you pretty much thought of everything." Candice noticed the vases on the tables with the flowers. "Hector, did you put those beautiful flowers in the vases?

"Yes, Ms. Candice," he proudly answered.

"Thank you."

Stella and Beatrice were plating the food in the back.

"Okay, everyone can sit because we'll be the first to eat in Candice's new café." Shane pulled the chair out for Candice at the *Sweetheart* table. "I'll be right back." He leaned over and kissed her cheek. Candice sat there, still stunned.

"We're going toast to Candice and her new business." Shane popped open the bottle of Champagne and walked around pouring some into each glass on the tables. "Here's to Candice and her dreams coming true."

"I just really want to thank you all for helping me. I know it was a lot of work, and I truly could not have done it without your support. So, let's drink up." Candice clinked her glass with Shane's.

Shane then pulled a remote out of his pocket and pressed a button. Softly in the background, soothing music started to play.

"You put a sound system in here?" Candice lifted her eyes to meet his.

"Well, since I was having surround sound installed in the basement, adding a sound system up here was simple." Shane shrugged.

"And who is this we're listening to?" Candice did not recognize the music.

"That is a local band. You know how you were thinking of featuring local authors?"

"Yeah."

"Well, I thought you could also find local musicians and sell their CDs. So, this is one of the bands I thought you would like."

"That's a great idea. I wonder if Steve—"

"I hear my name! What are you wondering?" Steve asked from the *Romance* table.

"Well, since you're going to make my website, I thought maybe we could have a section to sell things like greeting cards, books, CDs, things I can have multiple copies of," she answered.

"Sure, that's easy enough."

Stella and Beatrice were placing the food in front of each person.

"You know, I'd be happy to handle the online orders. I could swing by twice a week, package the items ordered, and drop them off at the post office." Stella offered. “And I’m also great at accounting if you need help in that area.”

“Who’s going to take care of the kids?” Kevin turned to Stella.

“You are.” She smiled. “They need bonding time with their daddy.”

It got very quiet as everyone dug into their meal. Candice kept looking at everything. Then, she caught a glimpse of the shadow box she made with Grandma Pela’s mementos. It was hanging on the wall behind the counter.

“That looks nice there.” She pointed to the shadow box.

“I thought she’d want to be commemorated where her treats are being displayed.”

“I think you’re right.” Candice let her eyes travel to the counter. “A pink phone?”

“It goes with the pink house and other pink accents. It’s not too much, is it?”

“No, I love it.”

“I wanted to get an old cash register, but I think a new one would make your life a little easier for booking purposes.”

“Can we gut an old register and put the computer inside? That’s something to look into.”

“I hear you two over there and I pretty sure I can make that happen,” Steve informed them. “You find the register and leave the rest up to me.”

“My man loves tinkering with computers,” Jazzlene proudly added.

“And a few other things,” Steve quietly said, reaching for Jazzlene’s hand.

Stacy made her way over to Candice. “I brought the menus and had a few t-shirts and aprons made up. I thought that would be a cute, casual uniform.”

“I can’t wait to see them.” Candice had really grown to love Stacy.

“They’re in the back. If you like them, I can get you a good price for the printing.”

“Thanks. I’ll let you know tomorrow.”

Josh walked up behind Stacy. “You almost ready?” he questioned.

“Yes, in a few minutes.” She smiled back at him.

“Candice, you really outdid yourself with this,” Josh praised.

“Well, it’s really all Shane. I had ideas, he listened to them, and then he made them happen.

Everyone started to mingle as they waited for the dessert portion of the meal.

“Honey, I couldn’t be more proud of you.” Hank released Irene to give Candice a hug.

“Thanks, daddy,” she replied. “And this is for you.” He handed her an envelope.

“What’s this?”

“Just a little something I started when you were born.”

Candice peeked inside. “Saving bonds?”

"Yeah, every year I'd buy one for you. Thought now was the time you needed."

"I don't know what to say." Candice kissed his cheek.

"Just say you'll use them to follow your dream."

"I will."

It was getting late. Carlos and Angie had taken Hector, Tom, and Marni home earlier.

Candice reached for another strawberry covered in chocolate. "These are so good, Stella. Maybe you should work for me."

"I told you I'd love to help in any way I can," she replied sincerely.

Beatrice had the kitchen cleaned up and sparkling like new again. "Looks like our job here is done." She turned to Trevor. "Shall we hit the road?"

"Whenever you're ready, mom," Trevor responded.

One by one, everyone left. Candice stood in the middle of the café, soaking it all in.

"Tomorrow, we should start pricing the items for sale, organizing the storeroom, and placing an ad for help," Shane said, scheduling their day.

"Yes. Sounds like a plan. Now can we go get my bags and head upstairs? You have no idea how much I've missed you. And how I want to thank you for all this," she said, spinning around.

Shane laughed. "I can't think of anything I want to do more."

Twenty-Four

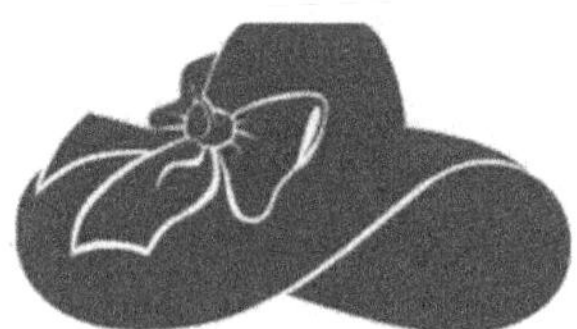

Shane could hear the shower when he entered the apartment carrying Candice's suitcases. He quickly set them down on the floor and followed her voice until he reached the bathroom. This was the first time he heard her sing in the shower.

"Are you happy to be home?" he asked after she finished the song.

"Yes, I can't even begin to tell you how homesick I got. Or maybe I should say, Shane sick."

"I know exactly what you mean. I couldn't even stay here with you gone. It's just not home without you here."

Candice turned off the water. "Can you hand me that towel?"

Shane held the towel up, slowly walking toward Candice.

"Hurry up, it's freezing."

"I can see that." He mischievously grinned while enjoying the view a moment longer, and then wrapped the soft towel around her glistening curves. "Better?"

"Much. We both had a hangover when we got on the plane this morning."

"What did you girls do last night?" Shane raised his eyebrows.

"Well, we had sex on the beach, and a few orgasms, or maybe they were climaxes."

Shane laughed. "By yourself?"

"No, Jazz was there instigating our evening of fun. We had one drink at each club we had visited during our trip or maybe two. I can't remember."

Shane kissed the top of her head. "How's your head now?"

"Well, let's just say four aspirins later...at least my eyes don't hurt anymore."

Shane walked her toward the bed. He pulled back the covers and climbed onto the bed pulling her with him. "Lay your head in my lap, and I'll massage away your headache."

Candice curled up with her head comfortably resting in his lap. "I need to remember not to mix different alcohols. I think that's where we made our error."

"That and probably the amount you drank. You need to pace yourself."

"Hey, I can't help it if Jazzlene kept getting us free drinks. I think we paid for maybe two drinks the entire night."

"Really? And how did she manage that?" Shane was curious, although he knew the answer.

"Come on, you've seen it, she's like the flame to a moth. She smiles, and the guys gravitate to her."

"I could say the same thing about you."

"Difference is, she eats it up and I don't."

"Well, what about Steve? He's pretty crazy about her."

"Oh, Steve doesn't have anything to worry about. She's falling hard for him. I mean, she completely cut the ties with my brother. She's never done that before."

Candice looked up as Shane kept rubbing her temples. "Thank you."

"My pleasure." He moved his hand to rub her neck.

"No, I mean thank you for surprising me with the café. I'm still having a hard time putting my feelings into words. I can't believe you pulled it off in five days."

"I had help. Everyone here tonight pitched in. I ran them ragged."

"Well, it means a lot to me. And everything you did was exactly how I pictured it."

"It didn't hurt that I found your rough drafts of the layout and what you wanted to include in the dining area."

"I thought with having to increase the size of the kitchen, the dining area would seem too small. But I actually think it feels cozy and welcoming," Candice said, closing her eyes.

"I agree. It turned out pretty nice if I do say so myself."

"Oh, and I spoke with Carlos to see if he would let Hector help me with the back garden. Well, I don't need to tell you how excited Hector got when his father said yes."

"I forgot to point out the bench I put under the tree in the front. I remember you wanting one there," Shane told her.

"I totally missed it. I was too intrigued by the sign."

"I think I need to put a light shining on the bench and maybe a birdbath somewhere under the tree, too."

"Let me put my robe on and go see it." Candice started to sit up.

"Not tonight. You lay right next to me. We'll see it in the morning."

"I love you so much. I can barely breathe right now." Candice closed her heavy lids, yawning.

"Yup, you've got it bad for me." Shane chuckled bending over and kissing her forehead. Within a few minutes, Candice's breathing started to slow as she drifted off to sleep. So much for reconnecting, but all that really mattered was she was home and in his arms.

A sound roused Candice from her dream. She looked through the haze of sleep, trying to remember where she was. When a warm arm found her, she scooted closer to him.

"Mornin' babe, did you sleep okay?" Shane asked, running his hand along her arm.

"Yes, it felt good to be in my own bed. Sorry, I fell asleep." She rolled over to face him.

"Well, hangover plus jet lag will do that to ya."

"Let me go make you breakfast. We have eggs, right?"

"Last time I checked. But stay here. I'm not ready to get up just yet." His hands began to roam her body.

"Mmmm," she blissfully moaned. "I should go away more often if I always get this warm welcome home."

"No, next time we go together." He continued to explore her soft curves. "Although, it gave me the perfect opportunity to surprise you."

Candice gazed into his eyes. "Any more surprises planned?"

"Maybe a few," he softly replied, flipping her onto her back. "Now, no more talking, only moaning." He covered her mouth with kisses.

"Okay, now I really need to get up and make you something to eat. I can hear your stomach growling." Candice found her robe on the floor. Shane had a satisfied grin as he watched her pick it up.

"Yeah, I am pretty hungry now," Shane commented as his stomach roared again.

"So, I guess the plan is we go downstairs and organize the storage area, then price the stuff, and what else did you have in mind?" Candice asked, flipping the eggs.

"Well, after we do those two things, maybe you should make some cookies to get a feel for the kitchen."

"Great idea." She turned off the burner once the coffee was done brewing. "Coffee?"

"Yeah, I'll get it." Shane poured two steaming cups of coffee. "You know, when I was at my grandmother's, I had a cup of coffee, and compared to perked coffee, well, let's just say you spoiled me."

"I try." Candice buttered the toast and placed it on a plate beside the eggs. "Here ya go."

"Thanks, looks good." Shane put some of Clara's jam on his toast. "Sandy said she'll have the jam ready next week. So, if you like, we can drive to Napa and pick it up. Maybe Saturday."

"Oh, that would be great." Candice dipped her toast into her egg yolk.

"Or we can pick them up during the week and go to Coit Tower on Saturday."

"I like that idea better. Once I officially open the café, our weekends will be so busy."

"I'll be right back." Shane left the room and returned with a little box in his hand. "I wanted to give this to you last night, but you fell asleep, and I don't want to wait any longer." He opened the box.

"Oh, that's beautiful." Candice watched as Shane removed the necklace with an elegant heart and fastened it around her neck.

"Beautiful, just like you. I had it custom-made, so it's one of a kind."

"Thank you." One single tear sat on Candice's cheek. "You keep doing—oh, just come here and kiss me." She jumped into his arms and wrapped her legs around his waist.

"Well, what can I say when I get reactions like that."

"I love you. I love it. I love everything."

"Now you'll always know my heart is with you." Shane touched the necklace, saying those words as if he was putting himself and his soul into the heart locket.

"I love it when you get all sentimental."

"Good, because I don't plan on stopping."

They finished their breakfast, freshened up, and headed to the café. Candice once again stood in the dining area feeling stunned.

"I still can't get over how you pulled this off."

"If the truth be known, it almost didn't happen. I had an issue with the building inspector that set us back a day or two. But with the help of our families and friends, we made it happen."

Candice noticed a woman looking in the front window. She walked to the door. "Hi, we should be open in a week, just finishing the restoration."

"The neighborhood is buzzing. Everyone is so curious. Coffee, tea, bakery?" the sweet elderly woman quizzed.

"Well, you'll be able to get all three here. It's a sweet shop, mainly cookies, pastries, and soft candies, but I'll be offering coffee and a variety of teas to complement the treats."

"Huh, that sounds interesting. I'll have to stop by when you're open. I'm always in the mood for something sweet."

"Please do," Candice replied sincerely with a shy smile.

"Well, you have a lovely day." The woman turned, pulling her little dog with her. "Oh, will my little Lady be welcome?" She looked down at her dog.

"Not in the café, but certainly on the patio." Candice pointed to the open spot where she planned to have a few tables.

"Perfect. She loves sitting in the sunshine." Lady pulled on the leash, ready to continue her walk.

"Future customer?" Shane asked from the back door.

"Hopefully." Candice followed him into the laundry area.

Shane grabbed the utility knife and started opening boxes. "Oh good, I was afraid these wouldn't get here before opening." Shane pulled out heart-shaped cookie cutters.

"What are those for?" Candice looked puzzled.

"Well, I thought maybe on the grand-opening day, you could give away a cookie cutter with a heart-shaped cookie, maybe the first hundred people."

"That's another great idea. How do you come up with these ideas?" Candice examined the cookie cutter. It was no ordinary heart shape. It appeared slightly misshapen on one side. "These are very interesting."

"Well, I found them online, on some crafty site. They're handmade."

"Did they have other designs? Because I could sell these if they wholesale them to me."

"Yeah, you'll have to look at the site. There were so many, it was hard to choose."

After opening each box, they carried the overstock to the basement before loading the shelf.

"I will call those two women I interviewed for Jazzlene and offer them a job. They would both be perfect for *Sweet Treats*."

"I remember you liked them. You probably only need two people per shift."

"I was thinking the same thing. But, of course, I also have a few disabled people I want to hire, and then I'll be set."

After emptying the boxes and pricing what was on the shelves, Candice looked satisfied. "It's all coming together, thanks to you."

"You're my muse. You just inspired me to see your vision." Shane hugged her.

"Maybe I should see if Joy wants to help me bake. Then I can gauge if she can handle that job."

"Good idea. While you do that, I'll ask Hector if he wants to help plant some flowers around the bench."

"Oh right, the bench." Candice made a beeline out through the front door. "This is so cute. Where did you find it?"

"It was actually at my shop, just sitting out back."

"You really do have everything a person can want."

"I try."

Candice and Joy worked well in the kitchen together. Joy was very methodical when measuring out the ingredients. Candice removed the first batch from the oven.

"Here," Candice handed Joy a cookie, "our first taste test."

"Hmm, these are good. Can I bring one up to my husband?" Joy asked with cookie crumbs on her lips.

"Sure, take him a few." Candice set some on a small plate for her to share with Bart.

"Thank you." Joy skipped out the back door.

If those cookies stay on the plate, I'll be surprised, Candice thought.

Stepping onto the front patio, Candice saw Marni sitting on the bench watching Shane and Hector planting impatiens.

"Those are so pretty," Candice praised, sitting beside Marni.

"Hector picked out the colors he thought matched the house best." Shane patted Hector's back.

"See Ms. Candice, pink, purple, and red." Hector's looked up at her.

"Yes, very nice choice of color. I'm glad you're here to help. I didn't even know what type of flowers I wanted, but these are perfect."

"They do good in shade," Hector informed her.

"Hector knows everything about plants, so I'm sure he will have your garden in the back bursting with color. Right, Hector?"

"Right, Mr. Shane." He nodded his head.

"Well, when you're ready for a break, I have a cookie for you hard-working men."

Candice sat on the bench, enjoying the sun and watching Shane's muscles flex every time he moved.

"What?" He noticed her staring.

"Just enjoying the view," Candice answered with a beckoning grin.

"See, I told you she would like the flowers," Hector told Shane.

"Yes, you did." Shane stood up. "I think we should go have some cookies."

"Yep, cookies." Hector copied Shane and dusted his hand off on his pants.

Candice held Marni's hand and led her inside.

"Well, that turned out to be a productive day." Candice laid her cell phone on the kitchen counter. "Both Eve and Fiona are interested in the job. So, looks like I'm well on my way to being staffed by opening day."

"What day are you thinking? Because we really should start spreading the word about the opening day celebration."

"I'd like to shoot for two Saturdays from now."

"Once you give me the okay, I'll email grandma's customers and ask them to spread the word. Possibly contact a few local magazines and food blogs."

"I'm bet since I'm going to offer vegan and allergy-free treats, I could probably reach out to those communities online, as well."

Candice stirred the spaghetti sauce she was making.

"I'm going to take a quick shower. I feel grimy after playing in the dirt with Hector." Shane pulled his t-shirt over his head.

"Dinner will be ready in about twenty minutes," Candice said. "So, make it quick."

"Okay, babe, do you mind if I stay tonight?" Shane asked.

"What kind of question is that? I've only begged you to move in, so you feel the need to ask?"

"Well, it's still your place." He winked, turning to head out of the kitchen.

"Not if I had my way." She called after him. "Now, get in the shower already. You're filthy."

"Yes, ma'am," Shane chuckled, moving quickly down the hall.

Twenty-Five

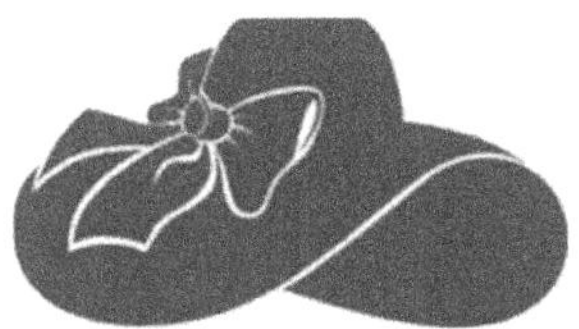

Candice stood by the window watching the sunrise. "It's going to be a beautiful day," she avowed as Shane walked up behind her.

"Yes, it is," he agreed, brushing her hair aside to kiss her neck. "We should think about getting on the road soon."

Every day over the past week was busy for both of them. Shane had several possible salvage jobs to assess while Candice was busy training her new employees and ensuring she was ready for opening day.

"Sorry we couldn't get to Napa during the week. And I promise we'll get to Coit Tower today," Shane apologized for dropping the ball on picking up the jam in Napa.

"Why are you apologizing? You've been so busy I don't even know when you have time to sleep."

"I have been busy. It's like all at once, everyone is doing spring cleaning."

"Well, the weather has been unseasonably warm, so that may have something to do with it. Like today, it's gorgeous when normally we'd be bundled up."

Shane opened the car door for her without his usual kiss on the cheek when she went to sit down.

"Can we stop by the wildlife rescue on our way back and check on the fawn?" Candice turned to see Shane's eyes. They seemed so distant.

"Sure." He meekly smiled.

Candice flipped through the radio stations to find something to brighten Shane's strange mood.

"So, have they found Brent yet?" She usually tried not to mention this subject, but she wondered if it had anything to do with Shane's subdued mood.

He gripped the steering wheel as his jaw clenched. "No, they're still looking for him. Kevin said they have no leads."

"Oh." Candice was trying to stay positive. "Well, he'll turn up. I mean, really, where can he go?"

"Well, until they find him, you keep that panic button with you. And keep your eyes open." The tone of Shane's voice implied an order, not a request.

"I will." Candice sat with her hands tightly clasped in her lap.

"Babe, I'm sorry if I sounded harsh. It's just...I can't always be there to protect you."

"I really don't think he'll do anything."

"That didn't sound convincing." Shane reached for her hand.

"Well, there's really nothing I can do. And his behavior is starting to scare me. So, I'm not sure how to handle this."

"You're doing the right thing. Live your life and be aware of your surroundings. Trust your gut. That's all you can do." Shane hated telling her that because he would hide her somewhere if he could until the police found Brent.

"Yeah, I know," Candice mumbled.

Both deep in thought, they rode in silence the rest of the way to Napa.

"Hey guys," Sandy called out from the kitchen of *Clara's Sweet Jams*.

"Hi, I'm so excited you agreed to let me sell your jams in the café." Candice finally started to relax.

"Well, this is as exciting for me as it is for you." Sandy pointed to two boxes. "They're over there. I gave you several jars of each."

Shane picked up one of the boxes and carried it to the car.

"So, it looks like you two are getting close?" Sandy looked for the answer on Candice's face.

"Yeah, we've been dating for a few months now."

"Shane's a good guy. Too old for me, but I can still enjoy the view." Sandy smiled as Shane walked back in.

"I have to agree with you on that...about the view, I mean." Both women watched Shane pick up the second box.

"You know you're both very obvious," Shane told them.

"We can't help it if we like what we see." Sandy gave him a playful wink.

"So, how much do I owe you?" Candice pulled out her checkbook.

"Each jar retails for $4.00, so wholesale will be $2.00. I gave you fifty jars to start with, so a hundred."

Candice started filling out the check. "Thanks so much." Candice gave Sandy a hug. "Come by the café, and I'll hook you up."

"I can't wait. Why don't you two sit down and let me get you something." The oven bell dinged. "Ah, the cinnamon rolls are done."

"Then we'll have two cinnamon rolls and coffee," Candice said, inhaling the pleasant smell of cinnamon.

"Coming right up."

Shane pulled into the Marin Wildlife Rescue. He hopped out and made his way to Candice's door.

"I can't wait to see how big he is." Candice grabbed her purse.

"Welcome," a young lady said as they entered.

"Hi, I'm Candice, and we brought a fawn in a few months ago. We just wanted to check on him."

"Oh, he's out in the back. Follow me." She led them outside to several large enclosures.

"He's so big," Candice commented.

"Yes, he's doing quite well. He did have a minor setback, but he's doing much better now. I believe they will be releasing him back into the wild soon."

"That's good, I guess." Candice watched as the fawn walked to the fence.

Shane pulled out his cell phone. "I think he remembers you, babe."

"I doubt that, but he does seem friendly." She touched her hand to the fence, and he nudged it with his nose.

Shane took a few pictures. "Well, we need to get going." He hated breaking up the little love fest but had a schedule to keep.

They were walking back to the car when Candice stopped. "Wait, I forgot something." She ran back inside. "I became a member but thought I would donate a little more money today."

"That is wonderful." The girl filled out a receipt. "Thank you so much." She took Candice's check. "Enjoy the rest of your afternoon."

"I will. Thank you for taking such good care of him." Candice exited the building smiling from cheek to cheek.

Shane was leaning up against the car. Arms folded across his chest, legs crossed at the ankles, and smiling. "What did you do?"

"I gave them a little more money to help." She turned to look at the building. "We need more places like this."

"And more people with your compassionate heart." He reached out and pulled her to him, embracing her.

"You ready for a hike?" Shane asked, turning off the car.

"Yes, I've got my walkin' shoes on."

Shane had to park several blocks from Coit Tower. "We have to walk up Telegraph Hill and then take the stairs to the top of the tower. No elevator for us."

"Of course not. You like seeing me sweat, don't you?" Candice tugged on his hand to slow down.

"Maybe just a little." He tugged back, dragging her up the hill.

They finally reached the base of Coit Tower. "Only a flight of stairs to go." Shane wiped the sweat from Candice's brow.

"Are you trying to kill me?" she panted.

Shane laughed. "Of course not."

"Okay, then I really need to start exercising. I know I always say that, but I just need to force myself to do it."

Shane looked behind him and then quickly turned Candice toward the entrance to the tower. They walked into the lobby area and to the counter to buy tickets.

"Looks like you're in luck." Shane pointed to the stairs.

Candice looked toward a sign, observing that the stairs were off-limits to guests. Relief and then sadness crossed her face. "I really wanted to see the murals in the stairwell."

"I think they offer guided tours for viewing the mural a few times a year. We'll have to add mural viewing to our *must-see* list."

"Yeah, I like that." Candice stepped aside and waited while he bought the tickets for the viewing area at the top of the tower.

They rode the crowded elevator in silence. It seems whenever you are in an elevator with strangers, no one talks and the silence feels strange. However, once the door opened, the riders walked out and conversed again.

"The view is spectacular," Candice expressed in amazement, spinning around 360 degrees and absorbing the magnificent San Francisco skyline.

"Not as beautiful as you are." Candice blushed at his sentiment while he lightly brushed the back of his hand across her cheek.

Shane knelt on one knee. "Remember when I told you I would not move in with you until we were married?" She nodded her head. "Candice Rayann Smythe, you have opened my heart to love again. And I love you more than I ever thought possible. I wake up every morning thinking of ways to show how much you mean to me. When you were in New York, I missed you so much. I can't imagine another day without you in it. So, will you do me the honor of being my wife and having my ten children?"

She looked down with wide eyes at the ring he was holding. "Yes. Yes, Shane Trevor Anders, I would love to be your wife and mother of your *four* children."

Shane quickly stood up and wiped the tears away from her eyes. "You make me so damn happy," he said, hugging her until she could barely breathe.

Everyone who witnessed the proposal broke out in applause, and one person whistled, earning him a sharp elbow jab to the ribs. Shane laughed upon realizing that all eyes were indeed on them.

Reaching for Candice's left hand, he gently slid the ring onto her finger.

"Fits perfectly." He lifted her hand and softly kissed the back of it.

"Yes, everything is perfect." Candice grabbed him and kissed him more passionately than she should have in public. But who cared? Certainly not her.

Shane stood behind Candice, wrapping his arms around her as they enjoyed the view of San Francisco. The entire vista was the backdrop of their story. So how appropriate they were standing high above it and gazing upon their city where their love began.

"We have a dinner reservation at Greens, so we can do some more sightseeing or go home and freshen up."

"Hmm, that's a difficult choice, but right now, I want to go home."

"Home it is."

"So, does anyone know you had this planned?" Candice asked curiously.

"Just your father, Kevin, and Jazzlene. Which means Stella and Steve probably know too."

"Your dad and grandma don't know?"

"They knew I was thinking of asking you, but I did not tell them when or show them the ring. I thought you would want to do that."

"And you told my dad but not my mom?"

"Correction. I *asked* your dad if I could have his permission to marry you."

"Did he give you a hard time?"

"No, not once. I assured him that you weren't pregnant. I think he was taken aback by the fact that we haven't been together very long. But when you know it's right, the time doesn't matter. What matters is being completely bound to you for the rest of my life."

"I agree, and it's not like we just got out of high school."

Shane pulled up near their house. "We'll discuss where, when, and what type of wedding you want over dinner, but right now, I'm aching to hold you."

"Mr. Anders, your table is ready," the hostess said, leading them to a table in front of the window.

Candice sat across from Shane with the glow of happiness surrounding her. Or maybe it was the afterglow of the entire afternoon.

"So, babe, what are your thoughts on the wedding? Small or big?"

"I definitely want a small wedding. Just our family and close friends."

"I was thinking the same thing. Now, are you thinking of a church or something else?"

"I just want an outdoor garden setting."

"Well, I might have the perfect place. Gabe went and looked at Maggie's house to give her an estimate for renovations. She decided to do the renovation and open the bed and breakfast, so—"

"Yes, that's exactly what I want. When we first saw that house, I thought it was a great place for an intimate reception. We could get married by the pool and have a dinner reception in the banquet room."

"There's only one problem."

"What?" Candice's face went pale.

"It won't be ready until late summer. Do we want to wait that long?"

"Maybe we can get married in your grandmother's backyard. It has a beautiful garden."

"She would certainly love that. Then we can have a small dinner reception there."

"Or, and this one you might really like, we could go up to Virginia City and get married in the Gold Hill Hotel."

Shane's eyes looked confused. "You want to get married in a hotel?"

"Not just any hotel, the Gold Hill Hotel is Nevada's oldest hotel just south of Virginia City. It's really quite charming. We can rent the rooms or stay in Tahoe and party the night away with our family and friends. Possibly catch a show."

"I'm intrigued."

"When we get home, I'll pull up the website and show it to you."

"So, if we decide to get married there, I guess we'd want springtime after the winter thaws a bit."

"Yeah, it won't be too hot. I'll see what they have available."

"Let's shoot for April or May," Shane suggested.

"Okay. Then we can stay at Maggie's for a weekend once she has it open for business."

"Now, how do we want to tell people? Should we stop by my grandmother's on the way home, or maybe invite everyone to the house for an engagement party to tell them then?"

"Because we're both busy right now, why don't we tell your family? I'll call my mom tonight and let everyone else know when we see them. Since we're going to Kevin and Stella's tomorrow, we can tell them then."

"You're always one step ahead of me."

Their dinner arrived just as the sun was setting. "The end of a wonderful day," Candice said, looking toward the Marina.

"I must admit I was pretty stressed about being able to pull it off without you finding out first."

"You were acting a little weird this morning. I never thought it was nerves. I thought—"

Shane cut her off before she could mention Brent. "Well, you know, I wanted it to be perfect."

Candice reached across the table with her newly adorned hand to grasp Shane's hand. "And it was. Every moment of today was special."

Twenty-Six

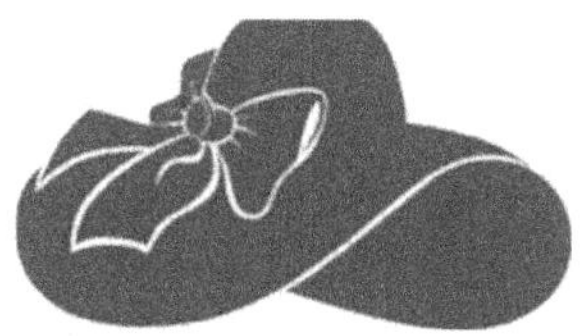

San Francisco Newspaper's Food Review
By Tammy James

Sweet Treats for All

I visited this bakery/café and met the owner, Candice Smythe. She had a clear vision for the café. One: offer the best-tasting treats that *everyone* can enjoy. Two: feature local artisans' works. Three: hire disabled adults. Well, she accomplished all three when she opened this beautiful eatery.

Ms. Smythe ensures that everyone who visits her café can enjoy her treats by offering gluten-free, nut-free, vegan choices and traditional delicacies. They are truly *sweet treats for all*.

From the moment you walk through the front door, the enticing scents of sweetness make your mouth water, and that happens before you even taste one of her sinful indulgences. I was lucky enough to sample each treat she had in her display case, and I can honestly say there was not one I did not enjoy.

Nibble after nibble, my taste buds were delighted and tantalized. I could not tell the difference between cookies made with eggs and vegan cookies created without eggs. Sweet Treats for All now offers breakfast quiches and mini potpies for lunch, so I will have to go back and try those on another occasion.

Therefore, if you are in the Noe Valley area, pop in and try one of Candice's delicious treats. I'll bet you can't eat just one.

The artwork displayed for sale is incredible. The people from the disabled community created most of the pieces. She also offers signed novels by San Francisco-based authors and CDs by local musicians. There is something for everyone.

While chatting with Candice, I learned she is a native San Franciscan. The story illustrating how she found this location is enthralling. A large hat blew off her head and rolled down the street, stopping in front of a house. That Victorian house is now the location of her café, and that extraordinary hat is on display next to the front door. Apparently, that is not all the hat led her to, as it seems it led her to the love of her life (and now fiancée), Shane Anders. I would say she followed that hat down the street toward her dreams.

Jazzlene sat across from Candice, awaiting an answer to her question about *why* Shane refused to move in with Candice.

"He said he's not living with me until we're married, but really it's a matter of semantics. The only thing of his that is *not* at my house is his bed." Candice sighed heavily.

"I know, that's what I'm saying, but I guess if it makes him feel better, then there's no harm in letting him believe his own lie."

"It has to do with his ex-wife. Anyway, he's trying hard not to make a mistake or repeat anything he did with her."

"From what we've both heard from Stella, the only thing he did wrong was date and then marry her."

"Well, I guess we do learn from our mistakes." Candice defended Shane's error in judgment.

"So, how are the wedding plans coming along?" Jazzlene knew moving the conversation out of the dark side was best.

"We've set the date for April 27th, so mark your calendar. And if you have a job scheduled that day, you'd better have Clancy cancel it because my best friend has to be there."

"Okay, done." Jazzlene marked the date on her cell phone calendar. "No way am I missing your wedding."

"Good, because I can't get married without you by my side. I may need you to hold the Kleenex box for me."

"That, I can do." Jazzlene gave her a hug. "I'd better let you get back to work. I just wanted to check in and see how you were doing."

"I miss seeing you every day. We're both so busy now," Candice whined a little.

"I miss you too." Jazzlene agreed. "My busy time of year is starting. All those spring and summer weddings. I book up fast." Jazzlene walked toward the door to leave.

Fiona was restocking the display case with fresh cookies. "You can't make these fast enough," she told Candice.

"Guess I'll have to start making triple batches in the morning."

Someone was always sitting at a table enjoying a treat with something to drink. From the day of the grand opening, the place was busy. Candice often had to make more cookies and cupcakes throughout the day. The tossing of stale treats she feared she might have, did not happen. In fact, she could barely keep up with the demand.

"The breakfast quiche and those mini pot pies don't last either," Candice remarked while wiping down a table. "I may have to hire another baker. Joy is a great help, but she needs at least two days off in a row."

"I don't mind helping you bake. I'm an early bird anyway." Fiona offered.

"Thanks, I appreciate that. I'll let you know."

The bells jingled as the door opened. Carlos brought Tom, Hector, and Marni in for their afternoon milk and cookies at two o'clock. Candice started this routine the day she opened her doors. It was one way for her to stay connected to Marni. And now that she was so busy and had little time to spare. What time she did have, she wanted to spend with Shane.

"Hi, my lovelies," she called out as the group approached their reserved table. No matter how busy the café got, they could always have a table ready for them at 2:00.

"Tom, Tom Morgan. Hi." He waved in the direction of Candice's voice.

"The flowers look pretty," Hector said proudly.

"Yes, I am always delighted with your choice," Candice praised.

Hector arranged fresh flowers in vases every morning before school and placed them on the tables. Candice took the discarded flowers and displayed them in her apartment. This little job always starts Hector's day off on the right foot.

Marni sat down in her usual chair so she could see the people entering the café. She loved to people-watch.

"Here's a chocolate cookie for you." Candice placed the cookie in front of Marni. "And a kumquat lemon drizzle cookie for you." She handed Tom his favorite cookie. "And here's a truffle for you." Hector liked the cayenne kick of the truffles. "And what can I get for you today, Carlos?"

"Hmm...surprise me," he said, tucking a napkin into Marni's collar. "I can't decide."

"Okay, one surprise creation for you." Candice retrieved a persimmons cookie from the display case. "Try this. It's new."

The table got quiet as the four of them nibbled away on their treats.

Candice went back behind the counter to put on another pot of coffee.

"Can I take my ten-minute break?" Fiona asked before heading out to the backyard to sit in the sun.

"Of course, I've got it covered." It always got slow for an hour after lunch, but once school let out, it picked up again.

The bells jingled again above the door. Candice saw a stunning woman wearing chic clothes and carrying a designer purse Candice could never afford, approaching the counter.

"Hi, what can I get for you?" Candice asked with a welcoming smile.

"You must be Candice, the owner?"

"Yes."

"What a lovely little café." The woman looked around at all the artwork and handcrafted items for sale.

"Thank you. It's been a joy opening this sweet café."

"I read the article in the newspaper and felt I had to come in and meet you."

"I'm glad you did," Candice replied sincerely. The article brought in a lot of business.

"So, you're the woman that stole Shane's heart?" She eyed Candice up and down.

Marni approached the woman, grabbed her hand, and frantically shook it.

"She's saying hi," Candice quickly explained. "Marni, you need to let go."

The woman vehemently ripped her hand out of Marni's hand, causing Marni's hand to smack hard against the table. Marni grabbed the woman's hand again. Candice stepped forward to unlatch Marni's hand.

"Marni, stop it!" the woman ordered sternly.

Carlos jumped out of his chair and reached for Marni.

"Keep her away from me," the woman hollered.

"Sorry, Ms. Aubrey. She's just so happy to see you," Carlos apologized.

Fueled by anger, Candice snarled, "Excuse me, Aubrey is it? I'm going to insist you leave now. You are not welcome in my establishment. No one treats my customers with disrespect."

"Well, you won't have any customers with that motley crew taking up space." She turned to look at the table.

Candice stepped closer to Aubrey and got in her personal space. She did everything she could to not slap her. "Get the hell out, you pretentious bitch, before I call the police and file trespassing charges."

"Candice, do you need my assistance?" Steve probed upon entering the café and witnessing the anger on Candice's face.

"No, she was just leaving." Candice glared at Aubrey. "Oh, and Aubrey, if you ever show your face in here again, I will not hesitate to call the police. This is your only warning."

Aubrey turned on her heels and left.

"Who was that?" Steve asked, shocked at how mad Candice was. He had never seen her that angry before.

"That would be Shane's pitiful ex-wife. I can't believe he was actually married to her. No wonder his head was so screwed up."

Steve turned to see the woman hailing a cab. "We all make mistakes. Thank goodness we learn from them."

Candice brought another cookie to Marni. "I'm so sorry, honey." She kissed Marni on the top of her head. "You know I love you, and you are a special woman. Unfortunately, some people don't deserve your love."

Marni grabbed Candice's hand and shook it. The simple gesture meant everything to Candice.

"Well, now that the drama is over, what are ya doing here?" Candice focused on Steve.

"Just wanted to check in to see how you're doing. And, of course, drop off the rent check."

"Oh, you could have mailed it," Candice said as she took the check.

"I know, but then I would never see you. I mean, you women don't even hang out on Sunday at the house anymore."

"Are you men missing us bringing you a beer?"

"Something like that." Steve smiled. "It's not just me. It's also Kevin and Shane. We like having you ladies with us."

"Well, Shane does have that cool man cave. So you guys can hang out here."

"Kevin said it's too much work. He'd have to bring the playpen and pack the entire house."

"Oh? If that's his only excuse, I can buy a playpen and keep it here. Playpen, diapers, formula, what else is there?"

Steve grinned. "You would do that too, wouldn't you?"

"Of course, if it keeps our men happy." She patted his back. "I'll call Kevin and tell him his problem is solved. This Sunday, football in Shane's bat cave."

"Well, I better get back to work. I took a late lunch." Steve exited with a whistle.

Fiona walked in from her break as the after-school crowd tromped through the door.

Candice was sitting on the couch reading a book when Shane finally arrived home from work.

"Busy day?" Candice looked up at his mud-splattered clothes.

"Yeah, but kinda fun too. Got out to a job site, and it just so happened they owned a few ATVs, so we went out riding."

"Well, that's one hard day at work." Candice put her book down. "Want me to heat up your dinner while you get showered?"

"Sure, what did you eat?"

"A bowl of tomato soup and grilled cheese sandwich. My comfort food."

"Bad day?" Shane looked at her, worried.

"I'll tell you about it after you get washed up."

He removed his shoes and left them by the front door. Then he started to strip out of his muddy clothes and carried them to the laundry basket on the back deck. Candice put the bin out there specifically for situations like this. She did not want him tracking dirt through the house.

"Before you head into the shower, give me a kiss." She laid her arms on his shoulders, stood on her tiptoes, and sweetly kissed him. "Now go shower so I can cuddle with you." She pinched his butt, sending him on his way.

Once Shane had finished his dinner, he pulled her against him on the couch. "So, why did you have a bad day?"

"Well, it started off really good. I'm seeing a lot of repeat customers, which is great. But then a woman came in, and I had to ask her to leave."

"What did she do to upset you?" Shane still did not understand what had Candice so upset. Hell, he could not even get her to file a restraining order against Brent.

"Marni was excited to see her and started shaking her hand."

"We both know Marni can be intense." Shane tried to make an excuse for the woman.

"I don't care! The way she spoke to Marni was unacceptable. I demanded she leave and told her that if she ever returned, I would call the police and file trespassing charges." Candice had worked herself into a frenzy.

"Babe, some people just have a hard time understanding disabled people."

"I don't give a flying rat's ass. You do not treat people like that. She pulled her hand away so hard, Marni's hand hit a table."

"Was Marni okay?" Shane was now getting a little pissed.

"Yeah, she seemed fine, but she'll probably have a nasty bruise. And do you want to know the worst part?"

"There's more?"

"Yep. Your sister knew her and was so happy to see her."

"Who was it?" Now Shane was curious about whom Marni would know and be excited to see.

"Your ex-wife." Candice spat out venom. Her blood was boiling.

"I'm so sorry. How did you even know it was her?"

"She said she wanted to see the woman, who stole your heart, which I thought was strange. But when Carlos addressed her as Ms. Aubrey as he was apologizing, I knew it was her. I almost slapped her across the face. I was so upset."

Shane chuckled with wide eyes. "I can't believe you almost hit her. My sweet Candice wouldn't hurt a fly."

"Well, she assaulted Marni, and no one hurts my family."

"I'm pretty sure you'll never see her again."

"I hope not because who knows what I'll do next time. I'm not a violent person, but she hurt Marni, and I just about went overboard."

"And now you understand why I'm divorced."

"What I don't understand is why you married her in the first place. She's an awful person."

"I was young and dumb and thought I was in love. But now I know what real love is, so that was a lesson I guess I needed to learn to know when the right woman came into my life."

"I guess we both had to go through a rough patch to find each other." Candice laid her head on his chest.

Shane ran her hair through his fingers. "Shall we go to bed?" he whispered in her ear.

"It's early."

"I didn't mean to sleep, sexy." Shane lifted her into his arms and carried her to bed.

Twenty-Seven

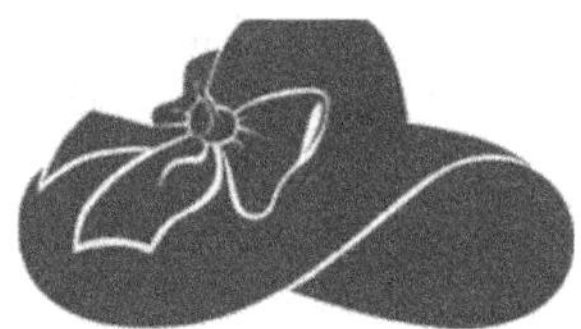

Six weeks had passed since the grand opening of *Sweet Treats for All,* and Candice was settling into a comfortable routine. Fiona helped bake, and Eve also worked the weekends to help bake. They were both friendly, hard workers, and the customers loved them.

Candice wanted to make sure they could handle running the café while she was away getting married. She hated the idea of closing for a few days, and both women assured her they could manage the café in her absence. She was training them to be part of her management team. So, having them jump in and learn everything was easing Candice's mind about leaving her café in their hands.

"I'm going to head out to the store. We are running low on milk," Candice told Fiona. "You can let Sabrina off after the tables are wiped down."

Sabrina was a young woman affected by cerebral palsy. However, her disability did not hinder her from doing a great job. She warmly greeted the guest and helped them decide which dessert to try. Her smile alone could convince them to buy more than they probably needed.

"Okay, take your time. I'll lock up if you're not back before closing," Fiona said while washing a few dishes.

"Thank you." Candice grabbed the keys to Shane's car and headed out the front door. It got dark early, but that did not mean Shane would get home anytime soon, so she had plenty of time for a store run.

She was loading the trunk of the car when she heard the footsteps. "Hi, honey," said a deep, controlled voice.

Candice slowly turned toward the voice she knew so well. "Brent, what are you doing here?" She tried to keep the alarm out of her voice.

"I came to take you home." There was a wild, scary look in his eyes.

"I can't, Brent. I found my place in this world, and it's with Shane."

Brent noticed the ring on her finger. "You can't marry him."

"But I am. I loved you once...hell, I still love you, but you're not enough. Your love only runs so deep before you will stray again. And I'm just not going there with you. Sorry, but you have to let me go," Candice stoically said, trying to pull her arms away from him.

"Honey, please, I made a huge mistake, but you're the only woman I ever loved. I don't know how to live without you. I've tried, and I just can't." Brent lowered his head in defeat as he released Candice's arms.

"I will always be your friend, but not your lover. That part is gone. But my heart will always have a spot in it for you." Tears escaped her eyes, and Brent reached up and wiped them away.

"I promise to love only you. I'll prove myself. Please," Brent begged.

"I can't. You betrayed my trust more than once. I just can't."

"Your friendship is not enough. I need all of you. I want a family with you, a home," Brent pleaded.

"I have a family now and a man that mended my heart. Please try to understand that we weren't good for each other. And quite honestly, your temper scares me. You need to move on and heal." Candice stepped back, trying to put a safe distance between them. Brent stepped forward, not allowing her to move away from him.

Candice knew she should scream or call for help, but she did not want to see him in jail. That would not help his mental state. He needed psychological help, and she would do her best to persuade him.

"Brent, you can't keep me. I don't know what you think you'll accomplish with this, but you're only pushing me away." Candice did her best to remain calm and reason with him.

Her cell phone rang, and Brent grabbed it and turned it off before tossing it in the trunk.

"Don't you see, honey, you belong to me? No one is going to have you but me." Brent's eyes darkened as he pulled his eyebrows together. "No one!" he shouted.

Candice looked around, trying to plan her escape, when Brent leaped forward, quickly spinning her around and covering her face with a rag. She kicked wildly and clawed at his hand holding the rough cloth but realized her mistake too late. I should scream, run, anything. Those were her last thoughts before she slipped into the blackness. Brent picked up her limp frame and placed her in his car. He quickly bound her hands and feet before casually driving off.

Slowly, Candice started to come out of the drug-induced sleep. She looked at Brent as he drove, trying to read his face. It was blank. "What are you going to do now, keep me captive? People will look for me," Candice asked, panicking.

"I'm going to keep you so no one can steal you from me," Brent nonchalantly answered.

"I'm not yours!" Candice yelled.

"Yes, you are. And only mine," Brent sternly responded while driving along Highway 1.

Candice sat staring out the window into the darkness. She had left her panic button on the counter at the café. Shane was going to be so upset with her. That was the one thing he made her promise to keep with her at all times.

"It's gonna be okay, honey." Brent put his hand on her leg. "I made a nice home for us."

"Where are we going?" Candice tried to push his hand off her leg, but he squeezed harder.

"You'll see." Brent turned off the highway and onto a side street.

Shane walked into the house. "Babe, I'm home," he called out when he noticed she was not in the living room as usual. He checked all the rooms, discovering that Candice was not in the house.

He quickly made his way down to the café. The door was locked, and the restaurant was dark. He checked the basement, but she was not there either. Pulling out his cell phone, he tried to call her again. It went straight to voicemail, just like the other times he called.

He unlocked the door to the café and turned on the lights as he stepped inside. On the counter, he saw the panic button, which caused him to become alarmed. He reviewed the work schedule to see who was working the closing shift. *Ah, Fiona, hopefully, she could shed some light on where Candice might be.*

"Hi Fiona, it's Shane. Do you happen to know where Candice is?"

"She left at around five to go to the grocery store. We were low on milk. So, I closed the café before she came back. Why?"

"Nothing, she's just not home, and it's not like her to not answer her cell phone."

"Well, maybe she had a few more errands to run. Or maybe she met up with Jazzlene. You know how those two are."

"Right, I'll give Jazz a call. Thanks." Shane hung up with a sinking feeling sucking him under.

He called the only person he knew could help. "Hey, what's up?" Kevin asked. Shane never called this late.

"Candice is missing. She left at around five to go to the grocery store and has not returned. She's not answering her cell." Shane could barely keep the fear out of his voice.

"Okay, I'm on my way over. Do you know what store she usually shops at?"

"Well, usually Costco, but Fiona said she was just going out to buy some milk. So, I'm thinking maybe the Safeway down the street?"

"You call Jazz and see if she knows where Candice might be. I'm on the road now."

"Jazz, it's Shane. Do you happen to know where Candice is?"

"I haven't talked to her at all today. Why?"

"I came home from work, and she's not home. And she's not answering her cell either."

"Steve and I will be right there."

"No, it's fine. Kevin is on his way over. We're going to go see if we can find her. Supposedly, she went to the grocery store. I'll call you later."

Kevin pulled up in front, and Shane hopped into the car. "She left the damn panic button in the café," Shane grunted.

"We'll find her. The battery is probably dead on her cell." Kevin tried to reassure Shane.

"I have GPS in the car, so we should be able to track where it is."

Kevin turned to Shane. "You have GPS in your car?"

"Well, I figured I could retrieve it if someone stole her."

Kevin laughed. "Yeah, it is a sweet ride. I guess it's wise to protect your investment." Kevin pulled into the Safeway parking lot and immediately saw Shane's car with the trunk still up.

"Fuck, this is not good." Shane hopped out of Kevin's car.

"Don't touch anything," Kevin ordered as they approached the car.

The trunk was full of groceries, and Candice's cell phone was beside the bags.

"That fucker took her!" Shane yelled.

"Let me call this in. We'll get the crime scene detective on this." Kevin called the station.

"Home Sweet Home," Brent announced as they pulled off the dirt road and parked in front of a house. "Do you remember this place?"

"Yes," she mumbled. No one would ever find her here. She had completely forgotten about this place.

Brent opened her car door. "Come on. Let me show you how I fixed it."

Candice remembered the time Brent, and she went on a hike and came across this abandoned house. They had climbed through a window so they could explore the place.

Brent opened the door to reveal the transformation he had made. He had managed to get a bed and couch into the ramshackle building. Lining one wall was enough dry and canned food to last months.

Candice knew she was not going anywhere unless she could figure out how to escape. The best she could hope for was to try to talk some sense into Brent.

"Remember how we made love on this floor for hours, and then we woke up the next morning to the birds singing?"

"Yeah." Candice stared at the floor. The memories were beautiful, but the man before her now was not the man she once created those memories with.

"You said you always wanted a house in the woods. Well, honey, I'm making your dream come true."

"We need to go back now." Candice was unable to think of anything else to say.

"I'm going to make love to you. Show you how much you mean to me." He reached for a pair of scissors and cut her top off. He was not going to chance by untying her hands. It was too early, and he knew she would bolt if she found the opportunity. "I've waited a long time to have you back in my arms."

"Brent, please don't. Just hold me. That's all I want right now. To be held."

Brent took his shirt off and held her against him. He ran his hands through her silky hair and caressed her face with his lips. "I always loved your long hair."

She remembered those soft hands, but the love she once felt when they touched her was gone. She tried to keep the repulsion she was feeling at bay. That last thing she wanted to do was piss him off.

"Kevin, you know that necklace Candice wears?"

"Yeah."

"Well, it has a GPS tracker in it. So, if she's wearing it, we should be able to find her."

"I've never seen one of those."

"I had it made. Something told me she'd always keep it on and that Brent wouldn't realize it was anything suspicious."

"Okay, let's get the detectives to trace it."

There was so much buzz around the car. The one thing that was determined from the investigation was that there was no blood and no evidence of a struggle. The detectives were trying to get a hold of the surveillance videos of the parking lot and the store to see if they could get a good picture of her abductor.

Brent lightly kissed Candice. "I've missed you so much." His hands were shaking. "We'll take it slow. I'll show you how much I love you. I'll be gentle."

"Brent, I'm exhausted. I had a long day. Can we just go to sleep in each other's arms?"

"If that is what you want." He laid her on the bed, removed her shoes, and then her pants. "You are even more beautiful than I remember." He stripped out of his clothes and snuggled up next to her while wrapping his arm around her waist and securing her to him. Candice tried to roll over to her side, but he held her facing him. He stared into her eyes, the darkness from before vanishing into lust and desire.

This is not going to go well if I can't stall him. "Good night," Candice softly said. "We need a good night's rest so we can go on a hike tomorrow."

"Okay, honey." Brent passionately kissed her and then rested her head on his chest.

How she got him to agree to let her go to sleep shocked her. Maybe he really was trying to prove his love. Even if he was off his rocker, he did seem to care about her.

"Brent?"

"Yeah."

"Thank you for understanding that I need time. You really hurt me, and you must build that trust again." She was saying anything to appease him.

"I know. I really fucked up, but I will make it up to you. Now go to sleep so we can get an early start on our hike."

"Okay, they got it. She's in the Santa Cruz Mountains," Kevin advised Shane.

"I'll be damned. The necklace worked?"

"Sure did. Our detectives have called the FBI since this is considered kidnapping."

"Isn't there a 24-hour policy before they will start looking?" Shane had always heard that.

"No, we know she was taken, and we now know where she is, so they'll go get her."

"So, do you want to head to Santa Cruz with me? I've got to be there when they rescue her." Shane asked.

"Of course, I'll drive you. Just let me call Stella, and we'll hit the road."

Candice lay trapped in Brent's arms. She could see the metal of the scissors reflecting in the moonlight. Yes, she could reach them, but she could not hurt Brent, so she just closed her eyes and tried to fall asleep. She was going to need all the strength she could muster to try her escape on the hike.

"Candice?" Brent whispered. She did not answer him, choosing instead to feign sleep.

Several hours seemed to pass, but Candice was not sure. She only knew her body hurt from not moving, but she did not want to wake up Brent and have to fend him off again. So, she tried to mediate and take her mind to a field of wildflowers. She pictured herself running barefoot and letting them tickle her feet. It seemed to work in yoga, so it should work now, but she was having a hard time staying focused. All she really could think about was how worried Shane must be. And that it may take weeks before she was found. She knew she could not hold off Brent's advances that long.

She could hear a deer outside rustling the leaves, or maybe it was a mountain lion. That thought scared her. The rickety house would not keep a hungry cat from getting in. She kept her eyes on the scissors just in case she needed them. She moved her leg slowly, trying to stop the cramp that was threatening her calf.

"Where ya going?" Brent pulled her tighter.

"I'm trying to stretch my leg. It's starting to cramp."

"Let me massage it for you."

"It's my left one."

Brent sat up and worked the muscle that was pulling.

"Thank you, I think that worked."

Brent did not stop. His hands gently massaged as they made their way toward her inner thigh. She began to tense the closer he got to what he really wanted.

"Relax, honey. I'm not going to hurt you."

"I know, but I'm nervous. It's been a long time."

Brent unhooked her bra that happened to clasp in the front. He stared down at her, running his tongue between his lips.

"Do you know how gorgeous you are?"

"More gorgeous than an emerald, if I remember," Candice responded.

Brent then let his tongue slide from her lips down her body, across her breast as he continued toward her belly button ring. Candice let out a gasp when he pulled down her panties.

"That's right. I knew you would enjoy this. You just allow me to make you feel good."

The happy memories of the Brent she used to know flooded her mind, and she started to cry. Not because of what he would do next but because her heart was breaking for the person he used to be. Gone forever...unless he got help.

"Brent, I need to pee first." Candice actually did need to pee.

"Okay, I set up a toilet." He helped her up.

"Thank you."

"Well, I knew we would be here for a long time."

Brent walked Candice over to the porta-potty behind the wall. He stood on the other side of the wall to give her what little privacy he could, fearing she would jump out a window.

Once he had her laid back on the mattress, he removed his boxers. There was nothing small about Brent. He stood 6'2" and weighed 230 pounds, with solid muscle from head to toe. Looking at him now, Candice was surprised that Shane could effortlessly subdue him. Even though Shane was a fourth-degree black belt in martial arts, she thought Brent would have put up more of a fight.

Brent straddled Candice, "I'm going to go slow. I don't want to hurt you."

Candice remained quiet. Sure, she could scream. Try to fight back, get up, and run. Then she remembered what the face of the man at the bar looked like after Brent pulverized him. He could really hurt her if he wanted to. She understood that, so she closed her eyes and focused on something other than what Brent would do next. She could feel him positioning himself while he held her bound hands above her head with his other arm.

Before she knew it, the door burst open, and the police had their weapons drawn.

"Freeze! Don't move."

Brent complied. Candice wrapped her arms around her naked body and cried. It was over.

"Please don't hurt him. He needs help," Candice managed between sobs.

A female officer wrapped the sheet around Candice and quickly untied her hands. "Are you okay?"

"I'm fine." Candice quivered as she rocked herself on the mattress. "I just want to go home."

Shane rushed through the door and ran straight to Candice. He knelt, trying to make eye contact, but she refused to look at him. Instead, she rested her head on her legs.

"Babe, look at me." Tears flowed down his face. "Please." he choked out, but she did not look up.

"We need to take her to the station to get her statement," the soft-spoken female officer said.

Shane looked at her, "Can you give us some time alone, please?"

"Yes, we'll be waiting outside." She turned and left.

Kevin stood at the door a moment and then retreated as well.

Once everyone was out of sight, Shane wrapped his arms around Candice and let her cry into him. "Baby, it's okay. You're safe now."

"How did you find me? I thought it would be a long time before anyone found us." Candice managed to say between gasps as her crying slowed down.

"You know this necklace?" He held it in his hands as she nodded. "It has a GPS tracker in it. I thought Brent would chuck the cell phone, and he did, but he would never suspect the necklace had a tracking device in it."

"Can I dress you now?" Shane softly asked.

"My shirt was cut off."

Shane removed his shirt and put it on Candice. He saw her pants on the floor and helped her into them. He pushed the hair away from her face. "Did he...uh...hurt you?" Shane did not know how to phrase his question.

"Physically no. But emotionally, yes. My heart is breaking."

"Hopefully, he'll get the help he really needs now." Shane tried to sound sympathetic when what he really felt like doing was knock the shit out of Brent.

"I hope so. I'm not going to press charges. I can't."

"I don't think you have to worry about that. The DA will take over the case. This is kidnapping, so you really don't have any say."

Candice stood up. "Can you take me home now?"

"I'm afraid not. First, you need to go to the station and give your statement."

"Well, I don't want to. I want to go home and take a bath."

"I'll take you home as soon as the police are done."

"Fine, let's get this over with." Candice stormed out of the dilapidated house. "Where the hell do you people want me to go? I want to go home so let's get this over with," she yelled so no one could miss her aggravation.

"Babe, calm down."

"Don't tell me to calm down. I stayed calm for—what time is it?"

"Four in the morning," Shane responded.

"Okay, I stayed calm for eleven fucking hours, so if I want to yell, I will." Candice finally unraveled and fell apart.

Shane turned to the officer in charge. "Can I take her home and bring her back tomorrow? I don't think she will be much help right now."

"Yes, I just need her name, address, and phone number." The officer had his pad open and ready to write the information down.

"Kevin, we're ready," Shane called out to his friend. "Come on babe, we're going home."

The sun was just about to rise when they got back to San Francisco. "Thanks, Kevin. I'll call you later," Shane said. Candice remained quiet and walked to her house ahead of Shane.

"No problem. I'm so happy we found her safe and unharmed."

"Yeah. Hey, you think I'll be able to get my car later today?"

"Most likely. I'll check on that for you and give you a call."

"Thanks, man." Shane shut the car door and headed up to the house.

Candice was already in the bathroom with the door locked.

"Babe, you need anything let me know?"

"Yeah, I want you to go home and leave me alone."

"Can you open the door so we can talk?"

"There's nothing to talk about. I'm not the same woman I was yesterday. Things have changed." Candice opened the door a crack. "Please leave me alone. I don't want to hurt you too."

"But you are hurting me by asking me to leave."

"Okay, you want to know, then try to understand this...I don't want to hurt you, but...Brent had his hand all over me, and I didn't even put up much of a fight. Sure, I asked him to stop with some lame excuse. But honestly, his touch felt good. I remembered what we once had, and I missed it. I can't commit to you if I can feel that way about him. So, we must call off the wedding and go our separate ways."

"You can't mean that! You just need to rest. We can deal with everything later. We'll get through this."

"Shane, I love you enough to know I have to let you go. Today proved one thing to me, I still love Brent. Not as a boyfriend but as a friend and I will not testify or say Brent kidnapped me. I won't do that to him. I'm going to say I willing went with him. I will not be the one to put him in jail when he needs the help that jail can't fix."

"I get that. You've said that ever since I met you. But you caring about him should not stop you from being with me."

"How can I be yours when I still have feelings for him?"

"You have memories of the good times. And yes, I'm sure feelings because you still love him, but are you *in love* with him?" Shane demanded. "Is he who you wake up wanting in the morning? Do you fall asleep thinking about him?"

"No, I am not in love with him. And no, I do not think of him in the morning or before I fall asleep. Instead, I think of you."

"You begged me so many times to move in here. I wanted to, but I was so afraid of getting too close. But look around. All my stuff is here. This is my home also, and if you kick me out. If you really want me to leave, I will, but think about it because if I walk out that door, there's no turning back. I can't go through this again. My heart is being torn out by the one person I trusted with it.

"Relationships have their ups and downs. I'd say this is one of our down moments, but we don't throw in the towel and give up. We fight to make it work. And this situation has nothing to do with us and our relationship. Don't you see that?"

Candice nodded. "But how can you still want me knowing I didn't stop Brent? That it felt good to have him talk to me like he used to. How?"

"Because you told me you're not in love with him. I can accept that you care about him, hell you care about everyone. That's who you are. I can accept that he brought back wonderful memories, but stop and think about all the times he cheated on you. The time he beat that man, think about who he really is, and I'm sure the few kind words he said to you really mean nothing."

Candice let Shane's remarks run through her head. "What if I had sex with him? Would you still want me then?"

"Did you?" Shane knew they were alone the entire night and Brent did have the house set up to spend time with her.

"No, but just when the police busted in, we were about to." Candice cast her eyes to the floor not wanting to see the sorrow in Shane's face.

"Did you say no?" Shane tried to remain even keel.

"I didn't say anything; I just closed my eyes and tried to think of something happy, so I wouldn't have a memory of it."

"So, doesn't that tell you you didn't want him? Damn it, Candice, look at me." Shane lifted her chin.

"I feel so confused."

"Well, why don't we go climb into bed together and get some rest, I'm sure you'll think clearer once you've had some sleep."

"I can't go to bed. I have to open the café."

Shane was surprised at how quickly she turned. "Okay, we'll go down and bake together. Get everything done so that when the morning crew arrives, they can take over. Then we'll get some sleep."

"You don't have to help me. I can handle it."

"But I want to help you."

Shane faced Candice and held both of her hands. "We're in this together. We laugh together, cry together, feel each other's pain, we always have to be there for each other no matter what. Do you understand you can't walk away from this? What we have is special."

"I don't know how I ever found you. You make everything seem so simple."

Shane lifted her hands to his lips. "Where's your ring?"

"I forgot about that with everything else going on. Brent made me take it off and tossed it in the woods." Candice started crying again. "I'm so sorry." Shame crossed her face again.

"Well, we'll go look for it later. We're supposed to go to the station to make a statement tomorrow, but we'll look for the ring first. The Brent situation can wait."

They started gathering the ingredients to make all the treats for the day when Fiona walked in. "Good morning."

"Hi," Candice said, pulling out the measuring cups.

"Morning Ms. Candice," Joy said skipping into the café.

Shane turned to Fiona. "Do you think you and Joy can handle making the treats? Candice has been up all night. She needs some sleep."

"Sure, this will be a great way to prove I can handle the café while you two are gone on your honeymoon."

Candice turned to Shane with a sad look.

"Thank you. If you need anything, I'll be upstairs. Come on, babe, you need some sleep." Shane laced his finger in hers and took her upstairs.

Once they were up in the apartment, Candice started to cry again. "I think we should postpone the wedding. I don't think I'm ready."

"Okay, if that's what you want. But for the record, I don't agree. If I had my way, we would not postpone it. I'm so ready to be your husband. But if you're not ready, we'll wait."

"I'm gonna take a shower." Candice waited for the water to get hot and stepped under it. She thought about the last fourteen hours and how much had changed. The illusion of Brent's love made her crazy. Was she willing to give up Shane and his family for the memories of a man that continually hurt her? Or should she let Shane go and just focus on taking care of herself? Her head was spinning so fast that she got a migraine.

"Do you feel better?" Shane asked as Candice stepped into the bedroom.

"No, I have a headache now."

"Lay down, and I'll go get you an aspirin."

Candice crawled under her down comforter and curled up on her side.

"Here, babe." He handed her a glass of water and something he found in the cabinet for headaches.

"Thank you." She laid her head back down.

"Do you mind if I lie next to you? Or would you rather be alone?"

"Lay with me."

Shane climbed in next to Candice, and she moved into his arms. He rubbed her head until she fell asleep, while he lay there trying to figure how to reassure her that he was not upset with her.

Twenty-Eight

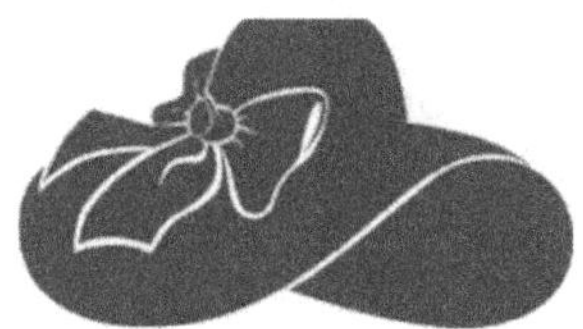

Shane snuck downstairs to check on Fiona in case she needed help. "Hey, I just wanted to see how things are going?"

"We have everything under control. Right, Joy?" Fiona responded.

"Yep, we're good." Joy giggled.

"Okay, let me know if you need help." Shane retreated out the back door. He quickly called Josh to make sure things at the warehouse were running smoothly. Once he was assured he was not needed at his business, he returned upstairs. Candice was still peacefully sleeping. He crawled into bed next to her and felt the warmth of her body. There was no way he could let her go without a fight.

Candice woke up and felt Shane holding her. She placed her hand on his. She thought about everything Shane had said earlier. How she was breaking his heart. The devotion he gave her. She wanted to feel the same way, but instead, she felt like she had betrayed him. She rolled over and laid her head on his chest. She saw him looking at her.

"Did you sleep at all?" she quietly asked.

"No, not really. I've been trying to figure out how to make this right again."

"I think it will take time, as you said. I just need a few days. The whole ordeal kinda did a number on my head. And I don't want you to be mad that I didn't try to stop him...that I didn't fight back."

"I'm not mad, babe. I don't know how many times I will need to tell you that. Nothing that happened was your fault. But let's say you did fight back. What do you think he would have done?"

"I don't know, but that guy's face at the bar kept running through my head. I knew he could really hurt me if he wanted to."

"So, you tried to keep him calm so he wouldn't beat you, right?"

"Yeah."

"And somehow, you think I'd be mad at you for trying to protect yourself. I mean, you know what makes him tick and gets him agitated. I actually think you handled the situation pretty damn good."

"Really?"

"Of course. You kept him calm and let him think he was winning you over, right?"

"I guess."

"Well, I'm proud of how you handled everything. You remained focused on staying unharmed any way you could."

"I suppose." Candice was trying hard not to let the victim role take over. "Can you kiss me now and turn off the negative thoughts in my head?"

"Like this?" Shane softly kissed her. "Or like this?" He put a little more passion into the kiss, stealing her breath.

"The second one," she purred in his ear.

"How 'bout I kiss you here?" He kissed her neck. "And here?" He moved down to her shoulder.

"Yes, keep going," she moaned.

Shane lavished her with kisses over her body but did not kiss the most sensitive parts of her skin. It was not about turning her on but showing her affection while making her feel safe again.

"I'm sorry about earlier. I don't really want to postpone the wedding. I just thought I betrayed you, and you deserve so much better than I can give."

"First of all, you did not betray me. So that discussion is done. And there is no one better for me than you. So, the way I see it, I'm a very lucky man."

"And the wedding, should we hold off on that?"

"If I'm the one making the decision, we get married as planned."

"You sure you want to marry a crazy, unstable woman?"

"You're neither. You just had a traumatic experience, but you know what? You'll come out a stronger person." Candice rolled on top of Shane. "You always want control," he noted as she leaned over to kiss him.

"Not true, only sometimes. But right now, get naked," Candice jokingly ordered.

"I'd be happy to. Any other requests you have for me?"

"Hmm, can't think of any right now, can you?"

He flipped her over, so she was now on the bottom. "Yeah, I can, and this is something I have to be in control of."

Candice licked her lips in anticipation. "I'm all yours."

"I'm gonna run down to the café. I feel so bad for not being there today."

Candice ran a brush through her hair.

"I went down while you were sleeping. Fiona and Joy were doing great. That's one thing you won't have to worry when we're on our honeymoon."

"That's good to know. I may need to give Fiona and Eve a raise if they keep this up."

"Yeah, good help is hard to find. Always keep those employees happy."

"I'll be back in a while." Candice went out the back door and met Joy heading up the stairs.

"Hi Ms. Candice, how are you feeling?"

"Much better, thank you. And also, thank you for working so hard today."

"You're welcome. I'll see you in the morning." Joy smiled bigger than usual.

"Fiona, I'm so sorry about today. If it weren't for you taking over, I would have had to close for the day."

"Oh, it was really fun. Joy and I turned on some hip-hop music and started dancing around while baking. She's so much fun to work with. Nothing seems to upset her. She just keeps smiling."

"I know, I love her disposition. Anyway, I will be here in the morning, but I have to leave at around eleven. Think you can handle another day on your own?"

"Sure, I believe Sabrina will be working with me in the afternoon."

"Yes, you're right, she is scheduled. You may have to close up because I'm not sure how long it will take tomorrow."

"Okay."

"You can go now, and I'll clean up." Candice shooed Fiona, knowing she put in a long day.

Candice turned up the CD that was playing and started to clean up the kitchen. Shane came through the back door and stood there unnoticed, just watching her. She shook her hips as she washed each dish and then started to sing along with the song. When she turned and caught a glimpse of Shane, she jumped back and dropped the plate.

"You scared the hell out of me. How long have you been standing there?'

"Not long, but I was enjoying watching you. I came down to let you know Kevin called, and I can go pick up my car. You want to tag along or stay here?"

"I'll stay here and finish cleaning up. Why don't you pick up some Chinese food on the way home? Or maybe Indian, but not the hot stuff."

"Okay, There's Kevin now. I'll be back in about an hour." Shane gave her a quick kiss.

"I love you," Candice called out before Shane closed the door.

"Love you, too." He blew her a kiss.

"So, how's Candice holding up?" Kevin inquired with concern.

"Not well. After you dropped us off, she told me to leave and said she couldn't marry me." Shane stopped talking to pull himself together.

"I'm pretty sure she didn't mean it. She's just in shock." Kevin tried to reassure Shane.

"She feels like she betrayed me by not fighting Brent and allowing him to touch her."

"Maybe she should speak to a therapist to work through what happened to her."

"Yeah, that's not a bad idea. We talked for a long time, and I finally got her to take a nap. She woke up in a better mood. But I know it might not last long."

"You're right, she's gonna run through a lot of emotions for a while, but you have to understand it's not you and support her. Let her be angry, cry, whatever she needs to move past this."

"She said she's going to say she went willingly with Brent. She won't say he kidnapped her. She feels like he needs psychiatric help, not jail."

"Well, I'm sure the psychiatric part is true, but they found her bound."

"She said she'll tell them it was part of their game playing."

"This has got to be eating you up. How are you feeling?"

"I'm so pissed right now, but I'm trying to understand why she feels like she needs to protect him."

"I don't think she protecting him, she's trying to get him help. There's a difference. Your woman has a big heart." Kevin explained.

"Your right. That is one of the things that I love about her."

"Let her do what she needs to. Because if she feels she helped him and didn't hurt Brent, she'll heal faster. If she feels guilty, it will destroy her and your relationship with her."

"You're right again. That may be the only way for her to accept her guilt for not fighting back," Shane agreed.

"The other thing that might really help her is talking with Jazzlene and Stella. Candice will be able to divulge her feelings and what happened that she won't tell you. I'll let Stella know the girls need to sit down with her."

"Thanks, because if I lose her, well I don't think I'll ever be the same. Aubrey ruined me financially, but Candice holds my heart and everything I am."

"Well, with the support of you, her family, and her friends, I think everything will work out," Kevin offered his encouragement.

"I guess." Shane looked a little glum. "Thanks for the ride."

"You're welcome, talk to you tomorrow."

Shane walked into the house with Indian food. "Babe, dinner's here."

"I'm in the bathroom," she yelled loud enough for him to hear her.

Walking into the bathroom, he could see a pile of long blond hair in the sink. "Why did you cut your hair?" He tried not to sound as shocked as he felt.

"Because he liked my hair long, and he was running his hands through it." She sounded matter of fact as if Shane should have known that.

"Oh." Shane was at a loss for words. "It's cute."

"I'm gonna dye it dark brown tomorrow. I don't want to be the woman he's attracted to anymore."

"Okay." If he told her he liked the color of her hair, loved it long, so it covered his body when she lay on top of him, she would probably start to think he was just like Brent.

"I'm starved. Let's go eat." She made her way into the kitchen and started dishing up the food.

Shane's heart was breaking. He did not know what to say or do. But he was going to have to try something. "Babe, you know by changing your looks, you're letting him still have control over you."

"All I'm doing is trying to be the opposite of what he likes."

"I understand that, but what do you like?"

"I don't know anymore. I liked not being afraid every time I stepped out the door. In fact, I'm beginning to think I should close the café. I'm thinking of moving away so he can't find me. I know I told you I'd marry you, but I have to leave. I can't stay here. If I do, he'll never leave me alone."

"Candice, stop it. You're not moving away, you're not closing the café something you love, you're not allowing him to destroy your life. Listen to yourself." Shane barely controlled the volume of his voice.

"He's already destroyed my life. I'm just taking it back."

"No, you're not. You're running away and leaving me behind. Don't you understand how much I love you? We can get through this together, but you will be alone if you leave. I can't go with you."

"I know that, and I'm not asking you to." Candice left the kitchen, went to sit on the couch, and picked up her book.

"Don't shut me out, damn it." Shane grabbed the book.

Candice sat speechless, looking at the book in his hand. "Can I have my book back?"

"Not until you promise me you won't leave."

"I can't promise that, but I can promise to let you stay here and keep my stuff."

"You know how you keep saying Brent needs help?"

"Yeah."

"Well, you need help. You're coming undone, and you aren't thinking clearly. You've cut all your hair off, you're leaving me and going god knows where, you're giving up a dream to own your own business that in six short weeks is doing great, and you're leaving your family and friends, because of one man, one fucking asshole of a man. So right now, we need to get you some help."

"I don't need help, I just need to start a fresh life where no one knows me, and I'll be safe."

"Here's your book. I'm gonna go out for a drink. I'll be back later." Shane looked at her eyes, but they were empty.

"Bye, have a good time." She opened the book and began to read.

Shane leaned over and kissed the top of her head. "I'll be back soon."

He sat in his car and called Hank and Irene. He had nowhere else to turn. He explained to them everything that had happened. They were on their way before they even hung up the phone. Then he called Jazzlene and left a message. He hoped someone could get through to her since he seemed to be making matters worse.

Shane walked back into the house, but Candice was gone. *Not again.* He noticed her purse still on the table, and the back door ajar, so he headed down the stairs. The café was dark, but he could see a light coming from the laundry room, so he went inside and walked down the stairs to the basement. Shane found Candice curled up on the couch, watching a movie. He quietly went back upstairs to call Hank and let him know to text him when they arrived.

"I wondered where you went." He sat down next to her on the couch. "Come here, and I'll hold you."

"That's okay. I'm fine where I am."

The rejection was killing Shane. "Okay, then I'll just go back upstairs and put the dinner away."

Candice just stared at the TV in a trance.

"Thank god you're here. I don't know what to do. She needs help. She's completely pulled into herself and says she's moving away from everyone. She cut all her hair off because she said he liked it long. I can't lose her," Shane rattled in clipped sentences before completely falling apart.

"Where is she?" Irene asked in a soothing voice putting her arms around Shane.

"The basement watching a movie," Shane muttered.

"Hank, maybe you should go. She isn't happy with me right now."

"Hey, puddin', can I sit with you?" Hank looked to Candice for acknowledgment.

"Sure." She did not turn to look at him.

"You want to talk to your old man? Maybe I can help."

"Oh sure, you couldn't even keep your own wife happy, and you think you can help me? Well, I don't need your help. I have it figured out, so you can go home now."

Hank was shocked. He had never heard Candice ever speak with such disrespect. "We all love you and want to be there for you."

"Like how you were there for me when I was a little girl?"

"I deserve that. I thought I was doing the right thing, but I was so wrong in how I handled everything. And right now, you're making some mistakes you might end up regretting. That man upstairs loves you more than his own life, and you are ripping his beating heart out. Why?"

"Because I don't deserve him. He's too good to me, and you know what they say when it's too good to be true...well, Brent treated me good at one time too. He professed his undying love, and then he hurt me. Shane's going to do the same thing."

"Shane is nothing like Brent. Why can't you see that?"

"All you men are the same."

"Not all men are that way. Don't lump every man in the same category. Sure, your mother and I had problems, but people grow up and mature. I'm a different man now than when I married your mother. I just had to grow up."

"Dad, save your speech."

"You know Shane is falling apart upstairs."

"Yeah, just like Brent did when I told him to leave."

"Candice, you need help."

"What I need is for everyone to leave me alone. That's what I need. Now please go home." Candice shut the TV off and left the basement, with Hank following closely behind her.

Candice walked into the apartment. "Hi, mom. You and dad were just leaving. And I'm going to bed." She exited the front room and marched down the hallway.

Irene's mouth dropped open. "I've never seen her like that."

"What am I going to do?" Shane looked defeated.

There was a knock at the front door. Hank opened it. "Sorry I took so long." Jazzlene stepped into the house.

Irene turned to Jazzlene. "This is really bad. I don't think any of us can get through to her. She's like a completely different person."

"Where is she?"

"In our bedroom," Shane answered.

Jazzlene knocked on the door. "Leave me alone. I'm trying to sleep."

"Candice, it's Jazz. Can I come in?"

"No, I told you, I'm going to sleep."

Jazzlene pushed the door open. "Sorry, but we need to talk. What happened today?"

"You're kidding, right?" Candice sat up but left the light off.

"No, I'm not kidding." Jazzlene sat on the edge of the bed.

"I'm not going to go into the gory details. Ask Shane to tell you. He pretty much knows everything. Now would you please leave so I can get some rest? I have a plane to catch in the morning."

"Okay, do you want me to take you to the airport?"

"No, I'll take a taxi. But thanks."

Jazzlene solemnly walked into the front room. "She said she had a plane to catch tomorrow morning and told me she needed to rest. After that, she wouldn't tell me anything else except to ask Shane if I wanted the gory details. And did she cut her hair off herself?"

"Yes," Shane said.

Hank answered Jazzlene, "She thinks that Shane will hurt her like Brent did."

"Shane, call a rape hotline. Maybe they can help us find someone to come to the house tonight. We can't let this get any further out of hand. If we can't stop her from leaving, we may lose her forever." Jazzlene started pacing the living room.

Shane found a number on the computer. "Okay, they gave me the number of a local therapist. I called her, and she's on her way. I'm going to go talk to Candice and see if she's calmed down at all."

"Candice?" Shane sat on the bed. "I know you think...well, really, I don't know what you're thinking. But I'm not Brent. I won't be nice to you one day and then hurt you the next."

Candice turned away from him. "Please leave me alone. I have nothing more to give."

"Okay, but understand I love you more than life and want you to be happy. So, if I can't do that for you, then I guess you're right, and you should move on. But know that I will never stop loving you."

"I won't be your concern much longer; I'm leaving in the morning."

"Are you at least going to say goodbye to Marni? What did she do to you? And what about those disabled people you are helping? What did they do? You're going to be leaving behind many people who care about you. And the people you are helping that no one else would give a chance to. Every day my sister gets up and faces a world that doesn't accept her, that shuns her, but you make her feel special.

"Joy and Bart, you make sure they're okay every night. Sabrina, you treat with respect. Hector gets to work in your garden. Tom can sell his sculptures. Not one person walks into that café and doesn't feel the love.

"I get it, you don't want *me*...but are you really going to give up and leave those that depend on you? You have shown them that their lives matter.

"If you're going to give up, then maybe you aren't the woman I thought you were. That doesn't mean I won't love you, but it does mean you're not the woman I thought I fell in love with. The woman I love is kind, compassionate, and caring. She healed my heart, and now she is destroying it. That's not the Candice I know."

Candice could not suppress her crying. "What's happening to me?"

"I don't know how to help you, but a woman is coming over that may be able to help us. I can't let you give up. You may not want me anymore, but please do this for yourself."

Reaching up, Candice turned on the light. "Look at what I did to myself. First, I looked in the mirror and hated the woman looking back at me. And then I cut all my hair off."

"It will grow back, and you can get extensions if it matters to you."

"How can you even want me? I'm broken beyond repair."

"No, you're not. You had a horrible experience that left you feeling vulnerable. And I do love you, but like I said, I'm not Brent, so if you want me to leave, I will. I will not stalk or bother you if you want out of this relationship. But something tells me you don't. I see it in your eyes. They still light up when you look at me."

There was a knock at the door. "Shane, can you come out here?" Jazzlene requested.

"I'll be right back." He stepped out of the room.

"Hi, I'm Julie." She took Shane's hand. "Can you take me to see her?'

"Candice, this is Julie. Can she come in and talk with you?" Shane asked.

Candice nodded her head. Julie approached the bed and sat down as Shane left the room, closing the door behind him.

Several anxious hours passed before Julie walked into the living room.

"Shane, can we talk in private?" Julie asked.

He stood up and led her into the kitchen. "Were you able to get through to her?"

"She has so much guilt. People like her who help others sometimes forget that they need help too. I got her to agree not to leave tomorrow. She's going to have emotional mood swings. You just have to understand it has nothing to do with you. She may say that it does, but it does not."

"How are we going to get through this? She wants me to leave?"

"She doesn't want you to leave. What she really wants is for the pain to go away. It seems Brent has been tormenting her psyche for years. From what I could figure out, he had total control over her and every aspect of her life when they were together. And although she left him, the scars remain. The incident that happened reopened those wounds. So, what you are hearing is the woman she was with him. She believes the tape running through her head that she is not worthy of you. That no other man would want her."

"I've never loved anyone more than her. How do I get her to understand that? I can't lose her."

"I'm going to talk to her every day until I feel she's emerged out the other side. I did encourage her to tell the police exactly what happened. She needs to be honest with them and herself. If she covers for him, he truly did win."

"Should I stay here tonight or give her space?"

"You should stay, especially now. If you leave even at her request, she'll think you've abandoned her. I realize she told you to go, but she doesn't mean it.

"The next few days are going to be really hard on you. Here's my card so you can call me any time of day." Julie wrote her cell phone number on the card.

"Thank you." Shane reached for the card.

"Oh, and she mentioned someone named Marni. She seems particularly concerned about hurting her."

"Marni's my sister. She's disabled, and Candice has taken a special interest in her."

"Well, maybe tomorrow you could bring Marni over so Candice can spend the morning with her."

"Okay, I know when I mentioned all the disabled people she was helping and that needed her, something seemed to register. She actually looked at me for a second."

"That's good because helping people makes her feel alive and happy."

"Thank you again for coming over." Shane walked her to the front door.

"You're welcome. You know, it always helps a victim to talk with someone who has been through a similar situation. We just understand." Shane stared at her, taking in what she had just said. "Don't look so surprised. Why do you think I'm so passionate about my job?"

"Sorry. I just was thinking that there is hope, since, well, you seem to be happy. So, maybe she'll be happy again."

"Yes, she will. You can count on that. It's just going to take time and patience."

Hank and Irene said goodbye to Candice. Her early outburst and anger towards her father seemed to have dissipated. But she was running hot and cold.

"I'll call you tomorrow," Hank said, kissing the top of her head. Irene gave her a hug.

"Okay, bye."

Jazzlene stepped into the room. "I'm gonna head out too unless you want me to stay with you."

"No, go home to Steve. I'll be fine."

"I'll call you tomorrow." Jazzlene hugged her friend and would not let go.

Candice pulled back and looked into her eyes. "Thank you for everything."

"I'm always here for you, you know that, right? I love you so much. I can't lose my best friend. We've both been through some rough times, and we've always pulled through. You'll make it through this, and I'll be there to help."

"I love you too." Candice let a few tears fall and quickly wiped them away. "Can you find a good beautician to do hair extensions for me?"

"Sure, but I think it's cute the way it is."

"When Brent held me, hostage, there was a pair of scissors within my reach. I could have grabbed them and used them to try to get away. But I didn't want to harm him. So, when I looked in the mirror, saw what he saw, the scissors were vivid in my mind, so I grabbed mine. I frantically started cutting my hair off. I couldn't stop. It was my only way to hurt him."

"I understand. It was symbolic."

"Yeah, I guess so."

Jazzlene sat on the bed and scooted next to Candice. "Can we just sit together? Because I'm afraid I'm losing you and I can't. I can't lose the only person that gets me," Jazzlene said quietly.

Shane crept down the hall and peeked into the room. He saw the two friends tightly hugging each other and crying. He stepped back so they could not see him.

"What am I going to do? I'm not the woman Shane thinks I am. Or the person he fell in love with," Candice choked out.

"Yes, you are. You're the same loving, caring person. And you know what? This is going to make you a stronger woman and mother. Think about it. If you can overcome the years of emotional abuse that man put you through, you will win your freedom from his hold on you. And Shane, well, that man loves you. So, you'd be a fool to push him away."

"But I said horrible things to him."

"And he understands. Hell, he got the cavalry over here to help you. You can push him away, tell him to leave and he will. He'll do that for you, but he'll never be the same without you."

"But I let Brent touch me. How can Shane forgive me for letting another man touch me?"

"You didn't *let* Brent do anything. Don't you see he had total control over the situation?"

"Well, I let him throw my ring away."

"Did you hand it to him or did he remove it from your finger?"

"He took it off, but I didn't say anything, I just let him."

"Honey, whether you said anything or not, he took it. Can I ask you something?"

"Of course."

"You told me, Brent, never physically hurt you. Is that the truth?"

Candice closed her eyes briefly before looking into Jazzlene's. Her eyes told

Jazzlene the answer. "I knew it. I always knew it, but you were so adamant that he never hurt you. I wanted to believe you."

"Sorry I lied. I am so ashamed."

"And now I understand why you didn't fight back. You knew exactly what he would do if you had."

"Yeah, I guess. But that doesn't make my compliance right."

"It explains everything. Why you didn't fight back. Why you're pushing Shane away. Do you think he will hurt you too?"

"I know how wonderful and loving Brent was when we first started dating. Then little by little, a side of him appeared until he was so ugly and beating me. By then, I was deeply in love with him, so I stayed. What's that say about me?"

"If I recall, when you caught him with those two women, you kicked him to the curb. You didn't seem afraid but empowered at that time."

"I guess I was so hurt I didn't care if he killed me. And honestly, at times, I thought he would."

"But you stood up to him, knowing he might attack you."

"Yeah, the anger and hurt wouldn't allow me to back down."

"See, you are strong. And you can make it through some of the worst things imaginable."

"What if Shane becomes that same type of man? I'm so in love with him. But if he changes? I can't go through that again."

"First of all, he's friends with Kevin. If Shane hurt you, Kevin would...honestly, I hate to think about what Kevin would do."

Candice looked over at Jazzlene with a slight grin. "Yeah, that wouldn't be pretty."

"No, it wouldn't. But the second thing is, Kevin would never be friends with anyone like that. He hated Brent. Even though they never met, Kevin knew what Brent was doing to you, but he didn't have the evidence he needed to do anything about it. You were good at keeping us all out of the loop."

"You don't think Shane is going to change on me?"

"God no! We are talking about the man that helped in every way possible to get your café open. The man that had your entire house alarmed trying to keep you safe. The man that was one-step ahead of Brent, and bought you a necklace so if something happened, he'd be able to find you. He has done nothing but try to protect you and love you. Can't you look deep into his soul and see what a good man he is?"

Candice reached up and held her heart necklace in her hand. "He told me I had his heart when he gave me this."

"You'll always have his heart. You've pretty much ruined him for any other woman. They would only get a shell of a man if you let him go. And you, what would happen to you without him?"

"I'd go on existing, but not living," Candice answered.

"And is that any kind of life to live, when you have a man out in the other room waiting for you to let him back into your life?"

"No, it would be lonely."

"Exactly. Some people never find what you two have. Don't throw this gift away. Right now you're broken and need time to heal. Let him be there to help you."

"You don't think he'll reject me like I'm damaged goods."

"None of us are perfect. We all have some sort of baggage."

"True."

"And anyway, we have a wedding to plan and look forward to."

"I can't marry him." Shame crossed Candice's face.

"Why not?"

"Because I'm not the same woman he asked to marry him."

"What makes you think that?" Jazzlene gently questioned.

"Look at me. I'm a mess. My head is screwed up. I'm not sure if I'll ever be the same again," Candice said, feeling annoyed.

"You *are* the same person. You know how when someone dies, we go through different stages of grief? And when you finally emerge out the other side, you can remember the person without falling apart. You have all those wonderful, happy memories of them and the pain you felt is there but not consuming your every thought? You don't push away the people that love you...you embrace them through the grief. You band together and help each other. Well, you will go through a similar process with this situation. But you also have to let those of us that love you hold you up and help you. Isn't that what true friendship is all about?"

"Yes."

"And if the roles were reversed, what would you do to help me? Would you let me push you away? Or what if it was Shane going through something; would you turn your back on him?"

"No, I'd be there no matter what."

"That's what I thought. So, we're all going to be there for you."

Jazzlene rubbed Candice's head. "Now, do you want me to stay with you tonight? Or would you rather be wrapped in your man's arms? Again, your choice, but if I were you, I'd pick option number two."

"Option two does sound nice. Plus isn't there a man waiting for you, too?"

"He doesn't mind sharing me with you." Jazzlene tightened her hug before standing up. "I'll let Shane know you want to talk to him."

"Jazz?" Jazzlene stopped at the doorway. "Thank you for everything."

"Anytime."

Jazzlene saw Shane standing in the hallway as she exited the room. She knew he heard everything.

"Thank you," he silently mouthed to her and then followed her to the front room.

"Okay, your turn to try and ease her mind. However, I think we got her going in the right direction." Jazzlene hugged Shane.

"And I heard her confession, so I think I understand a little more about what is really going on in her head."

"Yeah, I always suspected, but she denied it."

"I can't thank you enough. I'll call you tomorrow."

Shane walked into the bedroom to find Candice in the bathroom throwing water on her face.

"Do you want to talk?" Shane asked.

Candice turned to look at him. "Yeah, I think I need to tell you some things."

"Should we talk lying on the bed or sitting on the couch?"

"I think I need to lie down, I'm exhausted."

"Okay." Shane propped the pillows against the headboard and climbed under the blankets to get comfortable. He knew it was going to be a long night.

Candice went to the dresser and pulled out one of Shane's oversized t-shirts. Well, all his t-shirts were big on her.

"So, do you want to curl up in my arms and talk? Or would you rather I didn't hold you."

"I want you to hold me." She climbed into bed and rested her head on him.

"I was hoping you'd say that." Shane felt at home with her in his arms. "What you are going through is hard, I understand that. And I want you to know that I'm not going to leave you. We'll get the help we need, and we'll fight through this together. Can you please accept my love for what it is? I'm not trying to hurt you or control you, I'm trying to support you and help you."

"But I've lied to you. I told you Brent never hit me, but he did, repeatedly. Part of me loved him so much that I allowed it to go on. Then there was another part of me that feared what he would do if I left him. And then, there was the part that thought I deserved it. That if I could just make him happy, he'd stop."

Shane remained silent as he laced his finger between hers. "So, when he took me, I knew he could kill me if I provoked him. I played along with him, trying to keep him calm, but at some point, it all seemed so much like it once was. That he loved me and somehow, I needed to please him. It was who we were together. Part of me enjoyed his sweet words. I'm so confused as to why I would have those loving feelings for him. It doesn't make sense.

"I do love you, but I'm trying to spare you. You shouldn't be with me until my head is on straight." Candice rubbed her fingers through his chest hair.

"Thank you for telling me and being honest. But not because it makes a difference in how I feel about you but because it will make a difference in how you feel about yourself. The mother of my children needs to love herself as much as she will love her children." Shane kissed her forehead. "And you, my fiancée, will be the mother of my children. You told me you'd have four kids with me. So, I'm holding you to that."

"But I've changed. I feel like half the person I use to be."

"No, you haven't changed, you are growing and letting go of the past. And sometimes letting go hurts, but it needs to be done to move on. Don't you see that this had to happen so you could be honest with yourself and forgive yourself? You lied to everyone for years, even yourself, but now you're free to move on."

"So, you're not mad I lied. Or that I felt a connection to Brent yesterday?"

"No. You lied to protect yourself from pain. Something you thought you buried. And that connection, that was based on old memories, and remember I said sometimes we only remember the good parts of our past? Our minds won't let us hold onto the bad stuff. We force it into the background and keep it tucked away. But it's always there, ready to bare its ugly teeth if we don't deal with it. Well, this is your time to deal with the ugly truth and finally kill it."

"Julie said I can do sessions with her." Candice kept rubbing Shane's chest.

"That's a good idea. She seems to know something about what you're going through."

"Yeah, she is a domestic abuse survivor. So, she brought up some good points for me to think about."

"Maybe we can go to a few meetings together. I think that will help us both understand how to move forward and strengthen our relationship."

"I'd like that." Candice kissed the area on his chest she had been caressing.

"And I think for now we should leave all the plans we've made for the wedding in place. Let's give ourselves a few weeks to see if we really should wait. I'm hoping that Julie will help us deal with this so we can start our life together."

"Are you sure we shouldn't wait?" Candice asked.

"For now, yes. We have a few months to work through this. And, of course, we can always postpone it for later if you want. But I highly recommend you allow me to be your loving, doting husband."

"And this hair," Shane ran his hands through it, "is quite sexy."

"Really? I guess I need to go have a professional fix it. I really just started hacking at it without watching what I was doing." Candice blushed.

"Can I kiss you?" Shane did not want to push Candice, but he needed to feel her.

She did not answer him with words, she let her lips give him the answer he was looking for.

Twenty-Nine

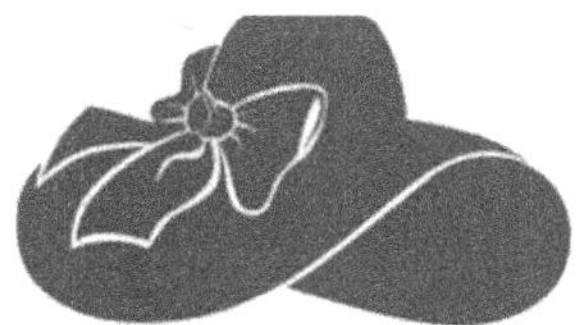

Shane woke up a little before five and watched Candice sleep. He was apprehensive about what the day had in store for them. Last night, Candice seemed to be in a better place, but her moods were so erratic that she could wake up mad, sad, or happy as a clam. Therefore, he watched her calmly sleep before the storm he expected to erupt as the day progressed.

Once the alarm started buzzing, Candice reached over and turned it off.

"Morning Ace." That was music to Shane's ears. When she called him Ace that meant she was happy.

"Morning. How did you sleep?"

"Pretty good." She rolled into his arms.

"We have a long day ahead of us. I'll go start the coffee." Shane reluctantly released her from his arms.

"Okay, I'll hop in the shower." Candice stretched as she walked toward the bathroom.

Okay, that was better than I expected, Shane thought as he filled the coffee pot.

Shane was pouring the coffee into two mugs when Candice strolled into the kitchen.

"Just in time." Shane handed her the mug.

"Thanks." She blew on it before taking her first sip.

"You want a bowl of cereal?" Shane asked, removing two bowls.

"Yeah." She sat down at the little drop leaf table in the corner. "So, I'm gonna go bake, get the goodies ready for the day. Then I guess we can head to Santa Cruz. Or I can just drive myself."

"I've already made plans to take you. Josh is covering for me, and Fiona is covering for you."

"Sounds good." Candice took another sip from her mug.

Shane sat down with Candice at the table. "While you're baking, I'm gonna run out to the shop and check on things. I'll be back around ten to pick you up."

"I'll be ready." Candice put her mug in the sink. "Better get downstairs and start baking." She leaned over and kissed Shane.

The bells jingled above the door, and Candice looked up. Shane was escorting Marni into the café.

"I brought Marni over for a cookie before she leaves for school."

Marni briskly walked over to Candice and grabbed her hand. "Hey, does this mean you're not coming at two for your treat?" Candice asked giving her a hug.

Smiling up at Candice, Marni shook her head. "Well, I might not be here, but Fiona will make sure you get your chocolate cookie." Candice handed Marni a kumquat lemon drizzle cookie. "We have to save the chocolate ones for after school."

Marni took a bite out of the cookie, making a funny sound. Not a moan but close. "Ah, so you like the lemon drizzle on top. See, trying something new is good."

"Marni, we need to get you back home. It's time for Carlos to take you to school."

Joy was placing cookies on a tray. "Hi, Mr. Shane," she called out with a wave.

"Good morning Joy. How are you today?"

"Great. I missed Candice yesterday, but now she's back, and that makes me happy."

"I'm sure it does." He smiled and hoped Candice heard the sincerity in Joy's voice.

"Babe, you almost done?"

"Yeah, just one more batch and once Fiona gets here, we can go."

"Okay. I'll be right back." Shane exited the café with Marni in tow.

Soon they were cruising down Highway 1 with the windows rolled down to let in the sea breeze.

"Are you okay with us going back to that house and trying to find your ring? I can go by myself if you're not comfortable being there."

"I think I can handle it." Candice reached over for his hand.

"If I remember correctly, it's down this road." Shane turned off onto a dirt road.

"Yeah, this looks like it," Candice agreed, glancing at her surroundings.

Shane parked the car. "You can stay in here if you want."

"I'll come with you. I know the general direction he tossed it."

Candice waited for him to come around and open her door.

"I brought my metal detector just in case we need it." He opened the trunk of the car to retrieve it.

"It should be over here." Candice walked toward a densely wooded area.

He couldn't just throw it in the dirt, Shane thought. *That would be too easy.* So, of course, he refrained from saying it aloud.

"This is going to be like finding a needle in a haystack," Candice remarked as she let her eyes survey the ground.

"It may take a while, but we'll find it," Shane reassured her or more likely trying to convince himself.

Shane turned on the metal detector and started slowly moving it above the ground. When it alerted him to metal, he bent down. "Just a bottle cap."

He kept walking in methodical lines, scouring the area for over an hour.

"Babe, are you sure he threw it in this direction?"

"Yes. Maybe it went further into the woods."

Candice lifted her face toward the sliver of sunrays that managed to squeeze through dense tree branches. The sun danced on her skin as the tree swayed in the breeze.

Shane saw her standing with her eyes closed facing the heavens, and he took her picture with his cell phone.

"Oh my god, here it is!" Candice shouted.

"I combed that area; how did I miss it."

"Look." She smiled and pointed to a straggly bush.

Caught on one of the bare branches, just like the ring toss game at the country fair, was the sparkling ring. Pulling the ring from its resting place, Shane briefly examined it.

He knelt on one knee. "Candice Rayann Smythe, no matter what has happened in the past, there is no other person for me but you. There's nothing we can't work through if we stick together. So, would you once again please make me the happiest man in the world and agree to be my wife?"

Candice looked down at him as he looked up into her eyes. "If you can accept me with my flaws and still love me then yes, I will still marry you. I will work really hard to move forward and not keep reliving my past. We still agree only four kids, right?"

"Can that point be negotiated?"

"Okay, we'll leave the number of kids up for discussion."

Shane stood up and slid the ring back onto her finger. "There, now I feel better."

"I'm curious why you propose again?"

"Because once that ring was removed from your finger the bond and vow to marry me was broken. I needed to know you were and are committed to us."

They stood in the middle of a place that caused so much uncertainty a day before and renewed their promise to one another.

"Babe, even though we're not married, we're still family. My family thinks of you as a daughter, and I believe your parents like me. So, we have a great foundation to build upon."

Candice laughed. "Oh yeah, my dad loves you. You're the son he wishes he had. I think I was pretty cruel to him last night. I'd better call and apologize."

"I'm sure he understands but letting him know you didn't mean the things you said would be nice."

"I meant them. I just never should have said those words. They were feelings I kept hidden inside and eventually they had to come out. I just didn't need to be so vicious about it."

"I guess it's time to head over and give your statement. Are you ready for that?"

"No, I'd rather let it go, but I guess letting things go is what got me into this mess in the first place."

A police officer led Candice to an area where she could fill out her statement. Shane sat next to her as she wrote what happened. Once she was done, the officer took her written statement.

"I'm going to give this to the officer on the case. He'll probably have a few questions for you."

"Okay." Candice sat bouncing her leg up and down.

Shane rested his hand on her thigh. "It's going to be all right."

"I know, I just feel like I'm throwing him under the bus."

"Ms. Smythe, I'm Officer Daniels. We met yesterday." He took a seat and nodded to Shane.

Candice looked at him, puzzled. "Sorry. I don't remember meeting you."

"That's okay. Anyway, reading over your statement, it pretty much states exactly what Mr. Gallager told us yesterday. So, he is being charged with probation violation, trespassing, kidnapping, attempted rape, and stalking. The district attorney will be contacting you. But for now, you can relax knowing he's behind bars."

"You know he needs psychiatric help, not prison."

"That's for the court to decide."

"So, I can go now?" Candice started to stand.

"Yes. Thank you for coming in." Officer Daniels stood and shook both their hands.

Driving back to San Francisco, Candice sat staring at her ring. "You know I thought I'd feel better knowing he confessed, but really I just feel so bad for him. What happened in his life to screw him up so bad?"

"I don't know. But I would guess at some point he was treated the same way he treated you."

"Well, hopefully, his attorney will be able to plead insanity or something. But, by the way, the house was set up, and the provisions means he had planned this for quite some time."

Candice phone rang. "It's Julie." Shane raised his eyebrows. *Perfect timing.* He thought.

"Hello." Candice sounded much better than last night. "Yes, we went to give my statement, and Brent had confessed everything." Candice intently listened. "Yes, tomorrow at six would work." Candice paused. "Let me ask him, hold on." Candice turned to Shane. "Can you go with me tomorrow to have a session with Julie, at six?"

"Of course," Shane responded.

"Yes, he'll be there. Okay bye."

"This will be good for you and for us." Shane smiled now that things appeared to be moving in a positive direction.

They pulled up in front of their house. "I'm gonna run back to the warehouse and do some work. Will you be okay?"

"Yeah, I think I'm good now." She leaned over and kissed him.

"I'll stop by the store on the way home and pick up dinner. I should be home around six."

"Okay."

Shane got out and opened her door. "I love you, babe."

"I love you too. And thank you for taking me today."

He lifted her hand and kissed the ring. "There's nothing I won't do for you. Thank you for wearing this again. It means more to me than you'll ever understand."

The jingling of the bells as she entered the café reminded her of what she almost gave up. Sure, she was trying to run away from her past, but by leaving everything behind, she was abandoning her future in the process. If it were not for Julie, she would be in New York, trying to blend in with all the other people.

The pink phone rang. "Sweet Treats for All, how may I help you?" Candice sang into the phone.

"Hello honey, it's Beatrice. I was wondering if I might be able to stop by, say around five?"

"Of course. I'll see you then."

"Lovely, dear. See you soon."

"Hey boss, today was so busy. Look, we're almost sold out of everything. And the artwork is flying out of here."

"Wow." Candice looked around and saw the empty spots on the walls. "Guess I better get some more framed."

"You could also sell them unframed," Fiona suggested.

"Yeah, I may have to do that."

Sabrina came out of the kitchen. "Hi, how did your day go? Because we were swamped, I'm not complaining, I just love it when it's busy." Sabrina sounded excited, not overwhelmed.

"It went pretty good. Glad to be back. So tomorrow we'll get back to our normal routine, and I won't abandon ship."

"Well, at least not for a few months, then it's honeymoon time." Fiona batted her lashes suggestively.

"Yeah, I have a lot to do before then." And no one knew how true that statement was. Because not only did Candice need to get her head clear, but she still needed to shop for a dress, a cake, order the invitations, and a special gift for Shane.

Beatrice walked into the café a little after five.

"Hello dear," Beatrice called out.

"Hi," Candice came out from behind the counter. "Let me lock up and we can either have a cup of tea here or go upstairs."

"Here would be lovely." Beatrice sat down at the *Sweetheart* table.

"I'll be right back with our tea." Candice plated some cookies and brought them to the table along with the tea.

"I know this is none of my business, but you are like a granddaughter to me, so I need to make sure you're all right after your ordeal."

"Yes, I'm fine. Thank you."

"Well, Shane was beside himself yesterday. He's terribly worried about you and was asking me how to help you."

"How much did he tell you?"

"He only told me that you wanted to leave, but wouldn't give me any details. He wanted to make sure he didn't lose you."

"So, he didn't tell you what happened yesterday that sent me over the edge?"

"No. He was completely broken though. So, I assume it was pretty bad."

"Yeah, it was bad. But he found a therapist for me to talk to. So, I think I'll be okay."

"Do you want me to help you with anything? Or if you want to talk, I'm always available."

"I don't think you want to hear about my sordid past."

"I can handle just about anything. I may be old, but I still can offer good advice and help."

"Okay, if you're up for it." Candice started from the beginning but tried to give the shortened version. Beatrice sat listening without interrupting. Once Candice was through with her tale of woe, her eyes pleaded for Beatrice's wisdom.

Beatrice reached across the table to hold Candice's hands.

"Honey, I'm so sorry that happened to you. And I certainly can understand why you felt like running away. But you must know and feel how much Shane loves you. He would never hurt you like that. Surely you two will fight, all couples do. But I know for a fact that ever since the day he met you, everything, and I mean everything he does is because he loves you and wants to give you the world."

"I think I understand that now. But I've felt so guilty for lying to him."

"I don't belive you lied intentionally. You had buried the truth so deep in order to cope. But now it's out in the open, and you can move on with a wonderful life."

"You know, everything was going so good between us, and I was waiting for something to change that. When Brent took me, it was like, now Shane will see I'm damaged goods."

"Shane doesn't see you that way. He sees the beautiful, caring, loving woman that you are. The woman he wants to be with for the rest of his life.

"Just accept that you found a man who would lay his life down for you. Who will love you until he takes his last breath. Believe me, the journey will be rough at times but so worth it." Beatrice imparted her wisdom.

"Thank you." Candice took a bite of a cookie.

"Plus, if you leave, I'd have to track you down. You're my partner and part of my family." Beatrice smiled.

"And what a wonderful family it is."

"I guess I should get going. Let you reconnect with Shane when he gets home." Beatrice gave Candice a kiss on the cheek and left.

Thirty

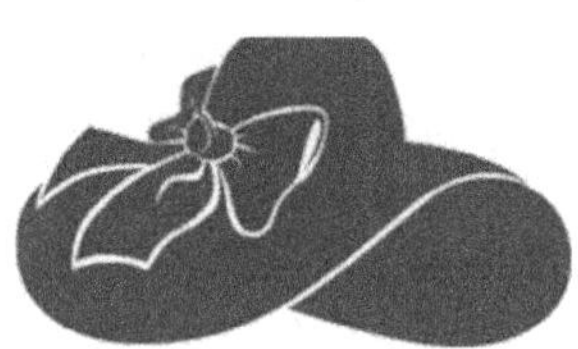

One month had passed. Candice made great strides in dealing with Brent and his abuse. The fog in her head had lifted, and she could focus once again on her life with Shane.

"Strange as this sounds, I really enjoy these couple sessions we've been going to," Shane said while changing out of his work clothes.

"They really are helping me understand what marriage will be like. And also, how lucky I am to have you. You stuck by me when I was really pushing you hard to leave," Candice said.

"Babe, I understood what was going on. Of course, I didn't like it, and it was killing me to think I might lose you, but I still knew where it was coming from."

"Any other man would have walked away. That was a lot of bullshit to walk through with me." Guilt was evident in Candice's voice.

"And that is the reason I have those rubber boots, for bullshit walking." He laughed at his lame joke.

Candice changed into a dress. "I got the invitations mailed today."

"Oh, good. You also blocked some rooms in Tahoe, right?"

"Yeah, everything is done. All you have to do is show up."

"You don't have to worry about that. Nothing would keep me from marrying you."

"We need to get going, everyone is going to be waiting for us." Shane grabbed his keys off the dresser.

"Ready." Candice fluffed her hair. "Now that my hair has grown out a bit, I kinda like it."

"Like I said before, it's pretty sexy. I like it long and covering my body, but I can look into your eyes and watch you when it's short. It's a win, win, for me."

They pulled up in front of Aldo's for their family dinner night, but tonight it was more like a friends and family pre-marriage celebration. Shane and Candice decided against the crazy bachelor or bachelorette parties, opting instead for a more subdued evening. Plus, they just wanted to have fun together.

"Looks like we're the last to arrive," Shane remarked as he noticed all the cars and people inside.

"Oh, well it's planned this way so we can make our grand entrance."

Aldo had closed the restaurant to host the private party. Everyone was invited, from Shane's employees to Candice's.

Kevin walked up to Shane and handed him a beer. "Here, drink up."

"Thanks. I really need this." Shane downed his beer.

"Nervous?"

"No, it's just been a long week. And between work and stuff, well, once in a while, a beer is exactly what is needed."

"How is Candice doing?" Stella asked. "She is getting better, right?"

"Yeah, I think she's made some major breakthroughs."

"That's good. I know it's hard for her. But she's one strong woman. And I heard they worked out a plea bargain of sorts for Brent. So that's good. Candice won't have to relive that night by testifying at a trial."

"Yeah, that was good news. Although I'd like to see him put away for longer, she's happy. So, what's the saying, happy wife, happy life?"

"And it's so true. Well, guess you better make your rounds." Kevin patted his shoulder.

Aldo had the food set out buffet style so everyone could mingle, eat, drink, and dance.

"Shall we." Shane put his hand out to Candice and led her to the makeshift dance floor in the middle of the dining room. Aldo had pushed all the tables to the outer walls of the room.

"Yes, Mr. Anders, we shall."

It was a slow song, and he held her tighter. "Did I tell you today how much I love you?"

"Yes, but I would love to hear it again." Candice looked up into his brown eyes.

"I love you more than anything else in this world." He leaned over to kiss her.

Candice pulled back. "Babe, all eyes are on us?" She giggled.

"Well then," he nibbled on her bottom lip as he pulled her closer to him, "let's give them something worth watching."

Shane licked along the opening of her lips, gently nudging them apart, he quickly slipped his tongue into her mouth. Once their tongues met, Candice began running her hands through his hair, sending a shiver through his body. He held her tight around her waist and lifted her up so he could deepen the kiss. They were lost in the moment until Steve whistled.

"We'll continue this at home," Shane whispered in her ear as they moved to the music.

"I look forward to it." Candice rested her hands in his back pockets and gave a squeeze.

Everyone ate and danced well into the night, but by midnight, the party was over. People still had to get up for work.

Shane turned to Steve and Kevin. "You want to go have a drink with Candice and me?"

Both men looked to their women and got the approving nod.

"Good, 'cuz it is karaoke night," Shane advised them.

They reached the bar in full karaoke mode. Shane went and put his name on the list. "You guys are singing with me."

"Well, that calls for a few shots first," Steve said before ordering two shots of whiskey."

"Nervous, are you?" Kevin laughed while ordering two shots for himself.

"Looks like the ladies are driving us home," Shane said, turning to the women.

"You boys knock yourselves out," Stella said. "I want to see if Kevin will get up there with you."

"Oh, he will if I have to drag him," Shane threatened.

Two shot of whiskey and two beers later, the guys were heading up onto the stage. Once the music started, there was no telling what the boys were going to do. Rod Stewarts, *Da Ya think I'm sexy* started playing, and the three amigos were in full character, strutting their stuff around the stage. Of course, none of them could carry a tune, but they were entertaining nonetheless.

Candice saw Jazzlene putting her video camera back in her purse.

"You got all that?"

"Yep, sure did."

The men stepped off the stage when the DJ read the next names.

"What the hell!" Candice turned to Shane. "You did not just do that?"

"Yes, I did. Now you girls get up there and show us what you got."

"That's not fair, you're drunk, and we're not," Stella argued.

"And what song did you pick?" Candice asked, fearing the answer.

"You'll see." Shane stepped back so the girls could pass by.

The music started, and to Candice's surprise, Shane picked a romantic song. She recognized it when the first note played, *Let's Stay Together* by Tina Turner.

Candice took the lead singing Tina's part, locking her eyes with Shane's eyes. He picked this song because it had a special meaning to him. It told the story of their love.

Once the girls finished their song Steve whistled so loud, Shane had to cover his ears.

"Thanks, babe." He hugged her. "Want that drink now?"

"No, I'm good, someone has to drive us home."

"So, are you saying I can have another shot?"

"Sure." Candice got the bartenders attention.

"Hey man, we got to head out. We told the babysitter we'd be home by one," Kevin said apologetically.

"Thanks for coming out. We'll do this again." Shane gave him the handshake followed by the back pat.

"Guess we should all be headin' out," Candice suggested.

Shane gave Candice the keys to his car. "Buckle up. This might be a wild ride."

"You were so cute up on that stage." Shane was just a little too happy about embarrassing her.

"Well, next time let me have a few shots first."

"Babe, are you going to really ban me from seeing you for two weeks before we get married?"

"Yep. You have to stay with your grandmother."

"But what if I don't want to?" Shane whined like a three-year-old.

"Sorry, but you won't see me until I walk down the stairs. Now come on, we're home. Let's head upstairs and go to bed."

"Ah, now you're talking my language because your kiss is still fresh on my lips."

April 27th and Candice was with Jazzlene in one of the bedrooms at the Gold Rush Hotel.

"You look amazing." Jazzlene adjusted the flowers in her hair.

"So, do you." There was a knock on the door. "Come in."

Stella came in with the bouquet. "They're almost ready for you."

"Did Shane arrive yet?" Candice looked out the window.

"Yeah, he's been here a while. The first thing he asked was if you were here. Like he thought you might not show up," Stella informed her.

"I know, I really scared him with my dramatic meltdown a while back, but Julie really helped me. I'm going to be fine."

"We were all so worried about you." Stella gave Candice a hug.

"Sorry about that."

"Well, I better get back downstairs. Love you."

Hank stood at the door. "It's showtime, princess."

"Okay." One last look in the mirror, then Candice followed Jazzlene onto the landing and waited for the music to start.

Jazzlene started down the stairs, and Kevin escorted her to the fireplace where the ceremony took place. Shane stared toward the stairs as he anxiously awaited Candice's appearance. His heart sped up when he saw the bottom of white satin and chiffon dress descending the stairs.

Candice came into full view, captivating Shane. His eyes traveled from her face slowly down her body.

Her hair was in a loose updo, with ringlets flowing down her back. Instead of a veil, she had baby's breath and pearls accentuating her hair. The pearls in her hair matched the *something old* pearl necklace she was wearing. It was a gift from her mother which she was told was a family heirloom.

She wore a 1920s inspired gown with chiffon overlay on the bodice. The square neckline and delicate lace cap sleeves accentuated her beautiful shoulders. The bodice was accented with exquisite hand embroidery and beading, which cascaded down one side of the skirt like a trail of flowers. The little bit of ruching on the bodice and at the empire waist gave the dress a soft touch of elegance.

Shane had to hold back his emotions and stop himself from running up and hugging her. Two weeks was too long to be away from her.

Hank held out his arm for Candice to hold. Then, he walked his daughter the rest of the way and stood with her in front of the fireplace.

"Who gives this woman to be married to this man?" the minister asked.

"Her mother and I," Hank proudly answered. He kissed his daughter and placed her hand in Shane's before stepping away.

Shane and Candice smiled at each other for a moment before turning their attention to the minister.

They wanted traditional wedding vows but also wanted to say something they each wrote.

Candice recited her special vows. "Shane, you protected and stood by me when I fell apart. Your unfaltering love brought me back to myself. I promise never to take your love for granted. I know your love is unconditional and that you will never give up on me, even when I give up on myself. I can never express how much I love you with words alone, but I will show you every day. I vow to make you happy. Without you believing in me and saving me, I might have been lost forever. I thank you for that and for asking me to be your wife."

Shane paused a moment to gather himself. "Candice, you are the most beautiful woman I've ever met. Your heart and your compassion know no bounds. You give freely of yourself to everyone. I would move heaven and earth for you and will always be the rock you need. My heart only beats for you. I promise to make your dreams come true and to help you through the dark days. With you by my side, there is nothing I can't do. Thank you for agreeing to let me into your life and for loving me. Thank you for saving me and showing me that there is someone perfect for me. I'll love you forever."

Candice dabbed her teary eyes with the embroidered hankie Beatrice let her *borrow*.

"May I have the rings?" the minister asked.

Kevin handed the rings to the minister. The minister handed Shane Candice's ring. "Shane, place the ring on her finger and repeat after me. With this ring, I thee wed."

Looking into Candice's eyes, Shane clearly spoke those words, then slid the ring onto her finger.

"Now Candice," he handed her Shane's ring, "place the ring on Shane's finger and repeat after me. With this ring, I thee wed."

Candice's hands shook as she repeated those words.

By the power vested in me by the state of Nevada, I now pronounce you husband and wife. You may kiss your bride.

Shane delicately kissed Candice, but not being allowed to see her for two weeks made it difficult not to consume her.

"Ladies and Gentlemen, I'd like to introduce you to Mr. and Mrs. Shane Trevor Anders."

"We did it." Shane grabbed Candice and spun her around.

"Yes, we did." She was smiling from ear to ear.

Champagne bottles were popped, and the bubbly was flowing.

They decided to head back to their hotel suite, where they would have cake and then go to the casino and party in one of the nightclubs.

"Mrs. Anders, you know you have to wear this dress all night, right?"

"I brought something else to wear."

"No, I want people to know we just got married. So, you're going to roll the dice in this dress, play roulette, and blackjack wearing this dress. And I'm gonna stand behind you, holding you close to me all night."

"Okay, but I don't think *to obey* was in our wedding vows."

"No, but I remember you saying you vowed to make me happy. And wearing this dress, so everyone knows you're mine, will make me a proud, happy husband. And then, when I take it off you later, I will remain a happy man."

"Well, I did vow to make you happy, so I will wear the dress all night."

Kevin and Steve decorated Shane's car but were careful they didn't damage the paint. The last thing they wanted was to ruin his *baby*.

Everyone got into their cars and drove back to Tahoe, blasting their horns on the highway and through town.

Around three in the morning, when Candice was feeling no pain and making indecent gestures toward Shane, he knew it was time to call it a night.

"Okay, sexy, let's head up to our room." Once they entered the room, Shane unbuttoned Candice's gown. What he found under it was as beautiful as the dress itself. She wore a pale *blue* garter belt and white lacy underwear that matched her bra. He removed her bra and stared at her beautiful breast. Then he removed her panties but left on the garter belt and nylons.

"This is very sexy, so I'm leaving them on, along with your pearl necklace."

"Oh, but there's so much you can do with that necklace," Candice purred into his ears.

"I'm sure there is, but it looks beautiful right where it is."

"If you say so. Now come here so I can undress you. It's been two weeks, and I can't wait any longer." She tried to unbutton his shirt but was struggling with the buttons.

"Let me help you." He had his shirt and pants off in record time. "Fast enough for you, babe?"

"Yes, now get over here and consummate this marriage."

"You know you should never make me go that long again without sex because this may take all night," Shane warned her.

"Well, I'm ready, willing, and able."

Shane enjoyed every curve of her body, sending her into ecstasy multiple times, with him following her into the depth of their love.

They spent the entire weekend with family and close friends. They all went to a show, ate, and laughed together. Nothing was better than family. When Sunday morning arrived, everyone was heading home.

"You know what, babe? That was one of the most enjoyable weddings I've ever attended," Shane commented.

"It should be. It was ours."

"Yeah, I know, but we did everything with the family. It wasn't like we got married and took off on our honeymoon leaving the celebration. We spent our time with them. It was the best."

"And we still get to go on our honeymoon."

"It's like we are having two honeymoons. Do you think you can wear the garter again?" Shane was close to begging.

"Maybe I have something else to surprise you with."

"You can't put those thoughts in my mind when we have to check out."

"Sorry. I could take care of you before we leave. Make the drive home a little more relaxing."

"I'd be a fool to turn that offer down." Shane stuck the *Do Not Disturb* sign on the door. "I'm all yours."

They arrived back in San Francisco a little after seven.

Candice grabbed one of the suitcases. "There's just no place like home."

"You're right. It feels good to know that I can officially call this place my home." Shane put the suitcase down. "Put your bag down," he instructed while unlocking the door.

He picked up Candice and carried her over the threshold. "Now, Mrs. Anders, our first home together," he said, setting her down.

"Let's go get comfortable. I have something to give you." Candice instructed.

"Oh, isn't giving me yourself enough?" Shane was happy with her as his gift.

"No, I found something I think you'll like."

She handed Shane a box wrapped in wedding paper with a gold bow. He carefully opened it, trying to save the wrapping paper and bow. Finally, he removed an envelope.

"What is this?" He looked confused.

"I bought you a piece of land where we can go on the weekends. You know, when we want to get away from the city. I thought maybe we could build a little cabin, and then the kids would have a place to run and play. I mean, the city is great, but they need to experience the outdoors too. It's not much, but it's a start."

"Thank you. When can we go see it?" Shane was excited.

"Next weekend. We can head out Saturday around ten. It's only a few hours from here."

"How did you manage to find it?"

"Well, it helps that my father-in-law is a real estate agent. I was able to pull some strings."

"Where did you get the money? It's all tied up in the business."

"Remember those bonds my dad gave me? I used a few of them."

"God, just when I thought I couldn't love you more."

"And remember when you told me about taking down Maggie's barn and being able to put it back together somewhere else and convert it into a house?"

"You recall that conversation when all I can remember of that day was holding your ass as you climbed down that ladder."

"Of course, I remember. It was an unforgettable day. Anyway, maybe we can do something like that."

"I like that idea," Shane said.

Shane paused a minute before he continued. "Now I have something to tell you. This might make you mad, but here's another memory for you. Remember when my grandmother went through the paperwork we found inside the desk in the basement?" Candice nodded. "Well, she found my great-grandfather's *will*. The house was supposed to go to my grandfather when he died to my dad, and then to me. My grandmother wanted to do the right thing, so she told my dad it was his. My father said he didn't want it, so it was offered to me. So technically, you are not my grandmother's business partner, as she felt she had no legal rights to the house. This house and everything in it belongs to us now. So, you don't owe my grandmother anything."

Candice sat there stunned, trying to understand what he had just told her. "So, you've known this for a while?"

"Yeah. I didn't want to tell you because I knew you wouldn't open the business. So, I told my grandmother to leave everything in her name until we were married. And tomorrow, she will be transferring the title to us."

"I can't believe this."

"All the money she spent to fix the house, she'll write off on her taxes."

"What if I had really left? Then what would have happened?"

"First, I would have tried to find you, and then if I couldn't, I suppose I would have rented out this apartment and closed the café. This wouldn't be home without you here. No way could I have lived here without you. That would have been two awful memories in one house."

"I can't believe this is really our house."

"Well, there is one thing. We have to work on having a son because the *will* states the house is to be left to the firstborn Anders boy." Shane smiled. "So, should we start practicing?"

"What if we only have girls?"

"Well, then I might get my ten children because we have to have one son." Shane playfully grinned as he teased Candice.

"What?"

"Well, we can do whatever we want with the house. If something happens to me, it will belong to you."

"Don't talk like that."

"I'm just sayin' it's ours. Yours and mine. Now let me thank you properly for my gift."

Wednesday's mail arrived with several congratulatory cards and one large envelope: return address: *Jazz Photography.*

"Shane, we got something from Jazz." Candice opened the envelope. Inside was a DVD. "Let's go watch it."

"Right behind you."

They popped it into the DVD player. It started with a beautiful scene of the sun rising at Ocean Beach, and then it went to Candice dancing around in her kitchen. "Oh my god, I didn't know she caught that. That was the day the hat led me to this house."

The next thing that appeared was Candice showing Jazzlene what the hat looked like on her head.

"Don't you look cute?" Shane adoringly commented.

"That's one magical hat."

Then Jazz included videos of the inside of this house. "Oh, I remember sitting in the tub imagining what it would be like to own this house."

There on the video of Shane holding Wesley and Kara on a Sunday afternoon.

Steve took a video of everyone helping with the café renovation and getting it ready for the big reveal.

When the picture of Candice and Shane standing before Coit Tower appeared, Candice turned to Shane. "She knew where you were going to propose?" Shane just smiled as the video showed him looking at Jazzlene. She caught the entire proposal at the top of Coit Tower. Then you could hear a whistle and Jazzlene telling Steve to be quiet. "Steve was there too?"

"Yep." Shane smiled.

"I remember that whistle and thinking it sounded familiar."

The video continued to the karaoke night. "Look at you three goofballs."

"Hey, we're sexy, and I think you wanted my body if I remember correctly."

Then Candice was singing karaoke with her backup girls. Steve managed to capture that performance and Shane's face while watching her.

The last part of the video was their wedding. From the night the girls spent together laughing to Candice getting ready and descending the stairs. There was not one moment missed.

At the end, it read, *To Be Continued, awaiting the birth of the first Anders baby.*

"I think that's our queue." Shane turned off the TV and carried Candice to bed.

Epilogue

A Year Later

The aroma of delectable sweetness was filling the café as the coffee brewed. Joy transferred the warm cookies onto a tray while Candice whipped up a batch of truffles.

Business was brisk in the little sweet café. Candice decided to add soup and sandwiches to the menu and extend the hours. With the longer hours, she hired some more employees. Fiona and Eve were promoted to managers, each given keys to the café. Joy still worked weekday mornings, while Sabrina worked afternoons and some weekends. The other two employees floated around to the best shifts for them, usually weekends and late afternoons.

Once Steve finished Candice's website and it went live, orders for the artwork began coming in. In addition, the online site offered a few sweets that would hold up during shipping.

Shane and Candice headed up to their little piece of land as often as possible so Shane could work on the barn house he was reassembling on the property.

Brent was no longer a parasite in Candice's head. And with Julie's help, she could forgive herself for hurting the people she loved most. She accepted and understood the past and released the power it once had over her.

Her parents were still going strong and happier than she ever saw them. They have no plans of remarrying anytime soon, but as Candice discovered, things can quickly change.

Jazzlene and Steve moved in together, and there is a rumor that Steve is going to propose. And sometimes gossip is true because Candice helped him pick out the ring.

Sure, there have been bumps in the road. Beatrice had been in the hospital with pneumonia for a few days, but she is a strong woman and got back to work as soon as it was safe.

Even the confirmed bachelor, Trevor was dating someone special. Although Shane never saw his father with any women growing up, Candice knew from her conversations with him, he did secretly date. He just did not feel it was right to introduce his children to different women until he was sure she was the right one. Plus, he did not expect another woman to raise his children. Now that they are grown up, dating is uncomplicated, and he was finding great pleasure in his new girlfriend. She also fell in love with Marni, who opened his heart to possibilities.

"Follow me," Candice said, leading the deliveryman down the hall. "Over there will be perfect. Thank you."

Candice looked at the room and was happy with the way she decorated it. It was Shane's room when he was a boy, and sad memories of his mother haunted him when he was in that room. Therefore, the door always remained closed. Candice was hoping that decorating the room would replace Shane's sadness with happy memories.

"Honey, I'm home," Shane called out.

Candice snuck out of the room, quietly closing the door.

"Down here," she replied.

"So, I got a job removing another old barn. This one will give us some more wonderful wood to work with for our mountain retreat."

"Things are moving pretty quickly with that project."

"Yeah, the guys are going with me next weekend to work on it. Kinda a guy's weekend."

"Oh, that will be fun," Candice said, although she did not find camping under the stars very enjoyable. "So, I wanted to show you something." She took his hand and led to the unused bedroom door. "Ready?"

"No, not really, but I can't say *no* to you."

Candice opened the door, revealing the new bedroom décor.

"So, what do you think?" She watched his face as it sunk in. "Why don't you go have a seat in that chair." She pointed to the new rocking chair.

He sat down and looked around the room, stunned.

"Happy Father's Day!" Candice climbed onto his lap, and they rocked together.

"Really?" Shane was still in shock.

"Yep, see this stick?" She held up the confirmation. "It says I'm pregnant."

Candice had everything a baby could need in the room. She left Shane's childhood wallpaper up and decorated with the colors in the paper. "As you can see, this room will work for a boy or a girl."

Shane held Candice and rocked her while reminiscing about the house and the memories of his mother. The room he was so happy in as a little boy would now again have a special place in his heart.

"Thank you for making me the happiest man on earth." He softly kissed her.

"Who would have thought stopping in the antique store would have led me to you?"

"It was fate, babe." Shane rested his hand on her belly. "Hey, little one, welcome to the family."

Candice unbuttoned Shane's shirt. She kissed her index finger before tracing his MOM tattoo, warming his skin and heart.

MY INSPIRATION

When I sat down to write this story, I thought of one person, my sister-in-law. She was a petite sweet girl and could express herself through her eyes. So, when you read about Marni, you were experiencing my sister-in-law. The bond between Shane and Marni was what I witnessed between my husband and his sister. We were truly blessed to have her in our life.

Behind Her Eyes

Will we ever really know what is behind her eyes? I am here to say yes if you allow yourself to see through them. That is when you will find someone with so much love to give.

We all walk through our daily routines, sharing a smile with the clerk at the store and leaving a piece of us behind. Do we make a difference with that smile? I tend to believe we do. In some small way, we touch someone's life every day.

Let us not forget the people that are easy to pass by and not make eye contact with, for they are the ones that need our smile and kind words.

I know this from watching my sister-in-law. A lovely happy woman trapped in the confines of her own body. Born with Cerebral Palsy and retardation, she never learned to speak. She walked differently than most, causing people to turn and stare.

Her only form of communication was a groan with a finger point. That could have meant she was hungry, needed to use the restroom, or a multitude of other things. However, it was effective and did get your attention that she needed something.

Remember, no one is perfect. Some imperfections are not visible, while others cannot be missed. Just smile, and speak kindly. You never know who you just made feel good; even if they cannot tell you, you can see it in their eyes.

ABOUT THE AUTHOR

Rebecca Thein grew up in the suburbs of San Francisco and has always called the Bay Area home. She and her husband have three adult children.

Rebecca has penned several poems for children. She also wrote her first book at twelve during summer vacation. That one story began her love of writing.

This is her second novel published. For more information, please visit:

For more information, please visit:
www.RebeccaThein.com
www.pinterest.com/RebeccaThein
www.instagram.com/rebecca_thein_author
www.Facebook.com/RebeccaTheinAuthor
www.bookbub.com/authors/rebecca-thein
www.goodreads.com/rebecca_thein

If you enjoyed the story, please consider leaving a review on Amazon and/or Goodreads.

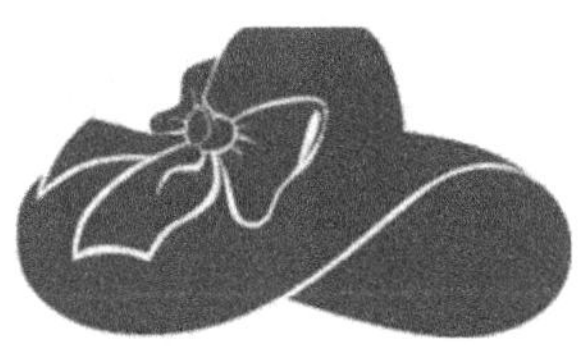

www.ingramcontent.com/pod-product-compliance
Lightning Source LLC
LaVergne TN
LVHW020535100826
845148LV00010B/1472

9780615845371